Beauty in the Details

McNally Men #1

MOLLY McCARTHY

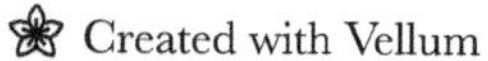 Created with Vellum

CONTENT NOTE

This book contains strong language, sexual content, and touches on some tough topics like loss of a friend and loss of a parent.

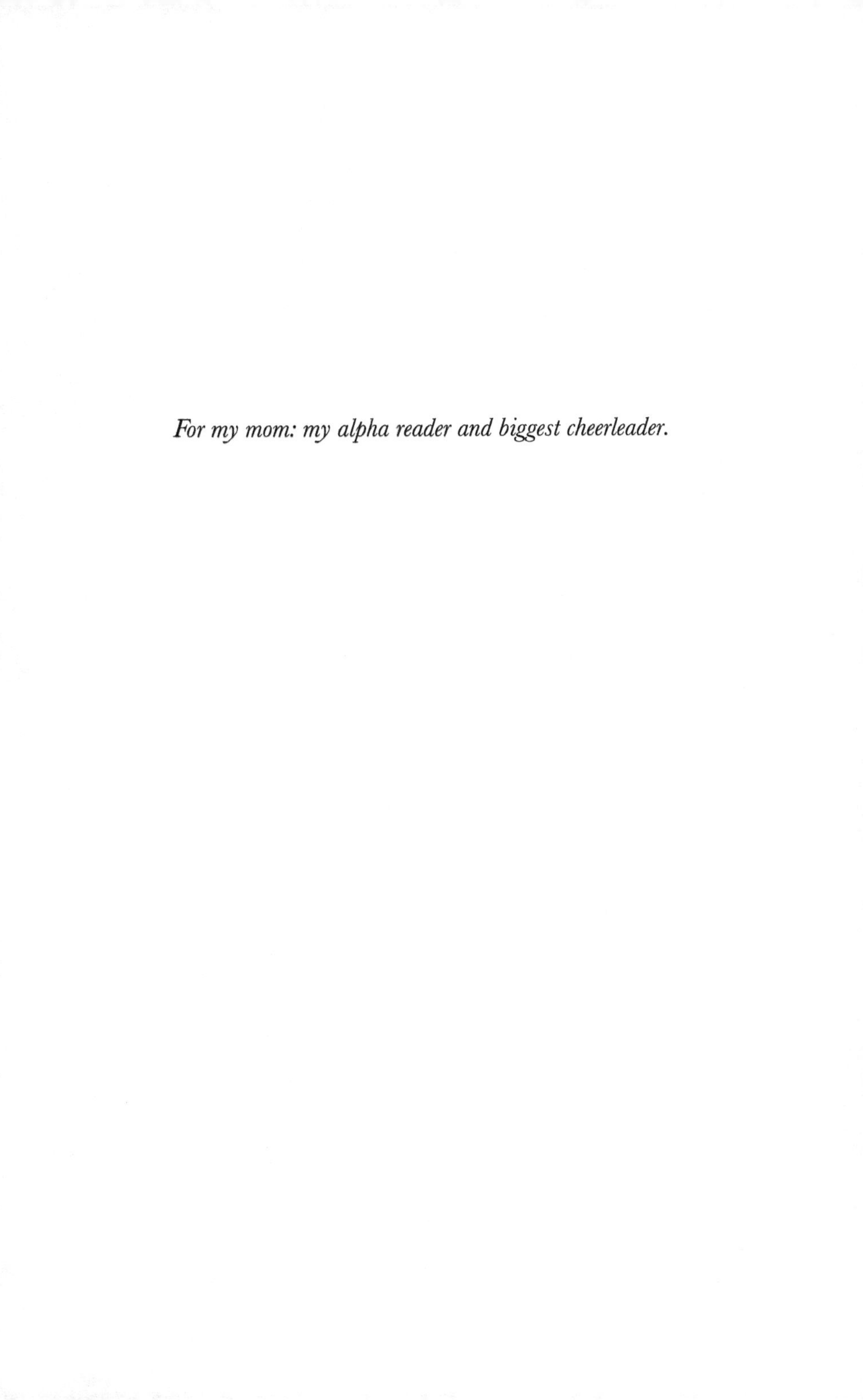

For my mom: my alpha reader and biggest cheerleader.

1

———————

The wind whipped Natalie's hair across her face as she took a deep inhale of the salty ocean air, allowing its crisp freshness to tickle her nostrils. The scent of the sea was fairly universal along every coast she'd traveled, but she swore it smelled just a little more magical around the island.

The ferry chugged around Brant Point lighthouse—the short, stubby landmark that signaled the journey to Nantucket was almost complete. A young child nearby on the outer deck whooped with excitement. A similar emotion churned in Natalie's chest, like carbonation threatening to burst. Thrilled to be returning to the island that had become a refuge during her formative years, she lamented the fact that she had ever stopped visiting.

The annual Nantucket trips with her father, Griff, held the only happy memories Natalie could recall from her childhood, as Griff spent most of his time otherwise working, worrying about making ends meet, or voicing his disapproval of her. That last point was exactly why the trips eventually ceased, but they were lovely while they had lasted. After years away from the island, Natalie hoped returning would be exactly what she needed to get her inspiration back.

The ferry churned to a stop when it reached the dock. Passengers began disembarking immediately, eager to get their vacations started. Natalie walked a little slower, adding a reverence to her steps as she made her way onto Nantucket ground. She couldn't help but smile as her feet hit that same wooden dock it had traversed so many times in years prior. Here, in her favorite place in the world, she was determined to get her groove back. If she didn't, the consequences would be…well, she didn't even want to consider the possibilities.

While waiting for the attendants to pull out the luggage carts, Natalie watched several other passengers reunite with loved ones already on the island. To one side was an old man surrounded by what she presumed to be grandchildren, and to the other, a young couple sharing an excessively passionate kiss. Multiple generations of people, each of whom had someone that cared deeply enough about them to greet them at their destination.

Natalie sighed out a pent-up breath. She saw reunions like these every time she traveled, but a pang of jealousy still jolted her each time she witnessed one. Sometimes she wished someone would be there to meet her at her destination, but she always found herself alone, plagued by that same subtle twinge of loneliness. She rubbed her chest absently, but it did little to mollify the dull ache.

The luggage carts arrived, snapping her out of her melancholy. Grabbing her battered duffel and single-wheeled suitcase off the cart, Natalie relished the familiar sensation of the luggage in her hands. She never collected more than could fit in those two bags, which wasn't much, but it was all she needed.

The wheeled suitcase bumped over the cobblestones as Natalie made her way to the visitor's center, hopeful they would be able to help her find an affordable place to stay or a lead on a job. It may have been foolish to come to the island without a plan for where she would live or how she would make money, but Natalie tried not to concern herself with such matters. She always managed to find a way to make things work.

The familiar green door of the visitor's center came into view, and a small bell at the top tinkled as she entered.

"Hi there," the woman behind the desk said cheerfully. Hot-pink lenses framed her kind eyes, and her gray curls sprang out from beneath a pink paisley bandana. Her obvious flair for color had Natalie instantly enamored.

The woman nodded toward her suitcases. "It looks like you're fresh off the boat. Welcome! Or should I say welcome back?"

"Either works," Natalie replied, dropping her duffel on the floor. "I've been here before, but it's been a few years."

"Well, we're certainly happy to have you back. What can I help you with today?"

"I'm looking for a place to stay. Preferably somewhere budget-friendly."

"Hmm, OK." The woman turned toward her computer, her hot-pink nails flying across the keyboard with a *clack, clack, clack*. "Do you know what area you're looking to stay in? Downtown is always the most expensive, but we could check out Surfside? Or mid-island?"

"Doesn't matter to me." Natalie shrugged. "I'll stay anywhere I can afford."

"What exactly is your price range?" The woman frowned when supplied with a rather small number. "How long are you looking to be here for? Just a vacation, or are you looking to live here for the summer?"

"I'm not sure, honestly. I'm hoping to stay for the summer if I can find a decent job," Natalie said. She could paint anywhere, but she relied on side jobs to financially support herself. If she could make enough to pay for food and shelter on Nantucket, why not stay for the summer season?

"Oh, there are lots of great jobs here in the summer," the woman assured her. "We have so many restaurants, and the visitors tip very generously. You'll have no trouble finding something."

The steady clicking of computer keys filled the room for a few more moments before the woman let out a disgruntled, "Hhmph." Swiveling the screen so Natalie could see the list of vacancies, the woman shot her an apologetic grin. There were some inns listed, as well as a few apartments and condos, but none fell within Natalie's limited budget. Though doubtful any of them would budge on their prices, she decided to call each one just to make sure. Thanking the woman, she hefted her bag back over her shoulder and stepped outside to make her calls.

One listing after another proved to be far too expensive. A couple of in-home apartments were possibilities, but both required a month's payment up front, which Natalie certainly didn't have. She couldn't even pay for a return ticket home if she wanted to. It was clear that the job hunt would have to come first.

A few months back, she had hit a dry spell selling her art and was forced to tap into all of her resources to avoid her worst nightmare: getting a traditional job. The nine-to-five life wasn't just unappealing to her—it was downright horrifying. She couldn't imagine being stifled in a cubicle all day. Hell, she couldn't even handle being confined to a single state.

Instead, Natalie had made some calls, groveled a bit, and managed to get one of her former art professors, Ned Brinkley, to take pity on her and give her an advance payment of five thousand dollars in exchange for ten paintings that he could show in his gallery in Boston. There was a huge exhibition coming in September, and he wanted to display the work of some of his former students. Natalie happily accepted the advance, using the money to rent a yurt in Colorado for most of the winter and the beginning of spring.

She'd expected to finish the paintings Ned needed during that time, but her inspiration was sorely lacking, and she'd created nothing worthy of his gallery. When the money was almost out and her inspiration still hadn't returned, Natalie did the only thing she could think to do. It was the only thing that had ever helped spark her creativity before. She bought a plane ticket.

The last bit of her advance got her a flight to Boston then the ferry to Nantucket. If the island couldn't get her inspiration back, she didn't know what could. All she knew was that if she didn't manage to produce ten profitable paintings by September first, she would owe Ned five grand to pay back the advance.

With barely a penny to her name, the only way she would be able to come up with that amount of money in that amount of time would be to borrow it from her father. And as far as Natalie was concerned, that wasn't an option. She would rather die than admit she needed Griff's help.

Shoving her phone into her pocket with a sigh, she silently vowed to start looking for jobs right away. But first she desperately needed coffee and something to eat. She poked her head back into the visitor's center to ask for a recommendation.

"Find a place to stay?" the woman asked hopefully.

"Yep!" Natalie lied. No need to make the friendly woman feel sorry for her. That was one caveat of her transient lifestyle —she could never blame anyone else for her woes. Every sticky situation she got herself into was strictly her own fault. Luckily, she was usually able to come up with a creative solution for just about every obstacle she faced. "I'm just hoping to grab a coffee somewhere, and I wondered if you had any suggestions?"

"Ah, I know just the spot! Danny's Place. It's not too far, just a few blocks away. It backs right up to the beach, so you can't miss it. I promise you it's the best cup of coffee on the island"—the woman hesitated—"even if it isn't much to look at."

Natalie thanked her and followed her directions to Danny's Place, nostalgia leaving a bittersweet taste in her mouth as she passed many familiar sights along the way. There was the old-fashioned soda fountain where Griff used to buy her milkshakes. The Atheneum, where she would go read books on the summer days that got too hot to be outside. The Dreamland movie theater where Griff traditionally treated her to a movie on the last night of their stays. And finally, of course, there was the illustrious Whaling Museum, which Griff always dragged her to against her will. The only part she enjoyed was the wall of paintings, which she would study while her father marveled over the whaling tools mounted on the walls and the huge whale skeleton hanging from the ceiling.

Each landmark she passed resurfaced a memory that made her smile. Natalie wondered if Griff would feel similarly sentimental, or if he was so disgruntled with her life choices that the memories they'd made when she was a child would be rendered meaningless. Probably the latter.

As she approached Danny's Place, Natalie began to understand the woman's warning about its appearance. The gray shingles that coated the two-story structure were faded and worn. The ancient wooden sign that had once proudly displayed the name of the café was horribly weathered. The windows were grimy and frosted with salt, making it tough to see through to the inside. Tall grass and weeds had taken over the garden beds in front of the building.

Despite the dreadful presentation, Natalie decided to give it a try. She knew things weren't always as they seemed and firmly believed in giving things a chance.

Silence greeted her as she stepped into Danny's. There was only one other customer in the whole café, munching on what looked to be a very healthy serving of cherry pie. Every other table was empty, and it looked like a ghost town just missing a lone, dry tumbleweed rolling on by.

At second glance, it *was* quite a charming little place, despite its initial dilapidated appearance. Small, circular, white cast iron tables were strewn throughout the space, but they needed a fresh coat of paint. Small chips had turned into large, ugly brown spots marring each and every one. Petite glass vases stood at the center of each table, which would have added a nice charm had they not been filled with wilted, rotting flowers.

Natalie's need for caffeine outweighed her desire for an aesthetically pleasing space, so she chose a spot at the counter, dropped her bags at her feet, and perused the chalkboard menu. Several items were haphazardly crossed out. It seemed to be many of the fancier drinks—a caramel macchiatto, a hazelnut mocha, and a lavender cold brew were three that she could make out behind the chalk slashes covering their names. Frowning, she decided to go with something simple that left little room for error: a black coffee.

There was no one behind the counter to order from, so Natalie twiddled her thumbs for a moment, trying to decide whether to wait it out or give up and find a different place. Just as she was about to collect her bags, a deep voice came booming from the back room.

"Carter, just stay there for one second. *Please*. I'm begging you," the masculine voice said. Despite an obvious tinge of irritation, it sounded like velvet—smooth and silky. *And sexy.*

Seconds later, the man behind the voice emerged. He looked about thirty, give or take a few years. Thick, slightly curly brown hair stuck out in many different directions, giving him a messy yet charming look. He sported stubble along his square jawline, but not the kind that was carefully planned out and trimmed—more like he had rolled out of bed too late to shave. His nose was just slightly crooked, as if it had been broken a time or two. His jeans and light-gray t-shirt with a small stain on the chest fit well over what Natalie imagined to be contoured muscles.

He stopped short when he saw her sitting at the counter and ran long fingers through his hair, disheveling it even further. "Oh, hey," he said. "I'm sorry. I didn't hear anyone come in. It's been pretty slow today. What can I get you?"

"Just a black coffee and a blueberry muffin, please." Natalie rustled through her bag for her wallet and pulled out three measly, crumpled one-dollar bills. "Scratch that, just the coffee."

The man slid over a blueberry muffin with a smile. "It's on me. I have a feeling we won't be selling out of them today, and I wouldn't want it to go to waste."

"Oh, thanks!" Natalie's cheeks warmed at his kindness. Though she was typically fairly shameless, not having the money to afford a simple pastry was rather embarrassing.

The man turned around to get her coffee, and she studied him again. He was tall—at least six feet—and lean, but clearly fit. The muscles in his arm flexed ever so slightly as he lifted the pot of coffee from its stand and began pouring some into a mug. *Yum.* And she wasn't talking about the drink.

"So, what brings you to Nantucket?" he asked, handing her the piping hot mug.

"I just needed a change of scenery, and it didn't seem like a bad place to spend the summer," she said, holding the mug between both hands and savoring the rich scent of the coffee.

"Definitely not," he agreed as he wiped his hands on a dish rag. "Where are you from?"

Natalie cocked her head to the side as she explained, "Well, I'm originally from Boston, but I spent the past few months in Colorado. Before that, I was in Arizona. Before that, New Mexico. Before *that*, California. I could go on…"

The man's eyebrows shot up. "Wow, so you travel a lot then." He braced two big hands on the counter in front of her and leaned slightly forward, the movement making the muscles in his arms jump again.

"Mhmm," Natalie mumbled, sipping her coffee to hide her wandering train of thought.

"What do you do that lets you travel so much?" he asked.

Natalie blinked, his question snapping her back to the conversation at hand. "I paint. Landscapes, mostly. I do lots of other gigs too because the art isn't that lucrative yet, but that's the reason I travel. I keep moving so I'm constantly inspired and have plenty of different landscapes to paint."

The man nodded. "Very cool. I think you'll find we have some great sights for you to paint here."

"That's what I'm hoping. My well of inspiration seems to have run dry. I needed a change of scenery."

"All those other places didn't do it for you?"

Natalie shrugged. "They were great. I enjoyed them all, and I made some nice pieces, but not many have sold. It's been a tough year. No one's bought any of my work since my last gallery showing in Phoenix six months ago."

It had easily been her worst year since beginning her career as an artist. Of course, things had started off slow after art school, while she was still establishing herself, but eventually she'd gotten into a groove and sold at least enough paintings to keep her afloat. For the past few months, though, her paintings had lacked that *je ne sais quoi* that made her earlier pieces so popular. Thankfully, Ned didn't know that, and he'd still wanted her to be a part of his show and offered her the advance.

"That sucks," the man said. "Hopefully it will change soon, though. We have the best beaches in the world here. You can't go wrong painting them."

"That's the plan. I owe a gallery owner ten paintings by September, and I figured if any place had plenty of fodder for my art, it was Nantucket. The beaches, the flowers, and this cute downtown area… There's so much variety. I definitely want to paint a portrait of Main Street."

"Just don't paint this place." The man looked around and grimaced. "That's one way to ruin a painting."

"What are you talking about? This place is very quaint. Sure, it could use a new paint job and a little work, but it has a lot of character."

"That's one way to put it." He smirked and reached a hand over the counter in introduction. "I'm Jack, by the way. Jack McNally."

"Natalie Walker." She shook his hand, fascinated by the contrast of his long, tan fingers against her slender, pale ones. Spending the winter in the Colorado mountains hadn't offered much in the way of sunbathing, so she would definitely have to work on her tan over the summer. She hoped to do that here on Nantucket, but that would depend on her job search.

Jack waved to the sea of empty tables. "I own this crummy joint."

"It is not crummy!" Natalie insisted, unsure why she defended the place. Maybe it was because she believed in fair chances, or maybe she just wanted to erase the frown on the face of the man in front of her. She much preferred that sexy smile. "It's just…worn down."

"Yeah," he agreed. "I've got *so* much going on, and I can barely keep the business side of things running, let alone do anything to make it look better. I'm just—"

A squawking little boy toddled out of the back room, interrupting Jack's downward spiral. The toddler's stiff-kneed gait made him look like a little baby Frankenstein, and the shock of blond hair that sat upon his head, as well as his bright-blue eyes, reminded Natalie of her own.

"Ack!" the boy yelled, chubby arms raised toward Jack. "Ack!"

"Carter! C'mere, buddy." Jack swung the boy into his

arms. "How'd you get all the way out here, you little rascal? Jenny!" Jack called toward the back room.

A young girl, who couldn't have been more than sixteen, walked out wearing a chocolate-stained apron and a sheepish smile. "Sorry, Jack. I know I'm supposed to be watching him. I turned my head for one minute, and he just shot off. You know how he is. He always wants you."

"I know." Jack sighed. "It's fine, Jenny. I'll keep him out here with me for a while so you can get back to work."

Jenny saluted Jack military-style and walked back to where she'd come from. Shaking his head, Jack ruffled the boy's baby-fine hair.

"And who's this precious little guy?" Natalie cooed.

"This is Carter." Jack held up Carter's hand as if he was waving. "Carter, this is Natalie."

"Nalee!" Carter repeated, his eyes gleaming with enthusiasm.

"He's such a cutie pie!" Natalie squealed. "Those big, blue eyes are stunning. He must get them from his mom." She glanced at Jack's rich brown eyes, which were gorgeous in their own right, but Carter's baby blues were utterly dazzling.

"Actually, those are from his dad," Jack said, his gaze locked on Carter, though his eyes seemed far away. He bounced the boy up and down on autopilot.

"Really?" Natalie asked, confusion clear in her tone.

Jack looked toward her and seemed to refocus on their conversation. "Oh, sorry." He slapped his forehead. "I'm not his dad. Well, I mean, I'm his guardian now. He's my best friend Danny's son. Danny and his wife, Carrie, died in a car accident six months ago." Jack frowned down at the baby in his arms, as if just now remembering he was responsible for him.

"Oh my God, Jack. I'm so sorry. I had no idea...obviously," Natalie mumbled. "That must have been such a shock." She couldn't imagine the difficulty of losing a best friend and having to take over the care of his baby all in one day.

"Thanks. We're getting through it, though, aren't we, buddy?" Jack said, a smile finally reappearing on his sculpted lips as he tickled Carter's belly. The boy giggled and twisted in his arms until Jack put him down. A moment later he was wobbling into the back room toward where Jenny worked.

"It's definitely been an adjustment," Jack added. "Not only taking care of Carter but running this business too. We had to close for a couple of months after Danny died so I could learn what the hell I was doing, but then I had to open back up in preparation for the season. The population here triples in the summer, and we couldn't lose out on that business."

"That makes sense," Natalie said. "You're still figuring things out."

"This place was Danny's dream, but I have no idea how to manage it. And I sure as hell don't know how to raise a child." Jack ran a hand through his hair again, mussing the curls. "Sorry, I don't mean to dump this all on you. I'm just overwhelmed."

"It's OK," Natalie assured him. "It sounds like you've had a tough go of it. Running a business and raising a child are things that take practice. You're new at both. You've got to give yourself a break."

She had worked at enough small businesses in her lifetime to know that there were many facets of running one. Finances, staffing, keeping stock up, marketing—there were endless jobs to be done. And though she hadn't raised a child of her own, Natalie had nannied for a family in college and understood how much work it was to care for young children.

It was at that moment that a lightbulb went off in her head. Jack desperately needed help, and she desperately needed a job. She had plenty of skills and was positive she could be of use to him. She wouldn't mind being around him all day either. Jack was eye candy, and he seemed just as sweet on the inside.

He continued his rant, periodically glancing toward the back room and raking his fingers distractedly through his hair. Each time his warm brown eyes returned to Natalie's, a rush of warmth flowed to her belly.

"I mean, there's this never-ending list of things I have to remember to buy and things I have to do, and it's just not all getting done. Buy diapers, buy groceries, clean the house, clean the café, feed Carter, feed myself…it never ends!" Jack said.

Though he was awfully cute when he was stressed, Natalie decided to put him out of his misery. "Jack," she tried to interrupt, but words continued tumbling out of his mouth. It was as if a dam had burst, allowing the contents of his troubled mind to spill out unimpeded.

"Carter wakes up at, like, six every morning, and I'm barely getting any sleep because I stay up so late getting things in order. There's no time to get ahead. I just—"

"Jack!" Natalie said loudly, and he stopped talking abruptly, startled by her raised voice. "Look," she continued. "I just got to the island today, but I really need a job to support myself while I paint. I'd like to stay at least for the summer while I fulfill my obligation to this gallery, and I have no responsibilities elsewhere. I have experience in lots of different things. I can help you with whatever you need— watching Carter, working behind the counter here at the café, or maybe replacing those sorry-looking flowers you have on every table." She shot a sideways glance toward one particularly unappealing bouquet.

Jack grimaced. "Yeah, those are pretty bad. But if you noticed from the garden out front, there aren't exactly fresh flowers to put in their places. Things have just spiraled out of control."

"Well, I happen to know a thing or two about gardening.

So, what do you say?" Natalie pushed, excitement coursing through her at the prospect of finding a job so quickly. "I'll be like your handywoman. Whatever you can't get to, I'll be there to pick up the slack. I'm a hard worker. I've got lots of skills. I've nannied before, and I love kids, so I'd be happy to help with Carter."

Jack ran a hand over his weary face. "It sounds like a great idea, Natalie. It really does. But I don't know if I can afford to hire someone else. Danny would have known our budget off the top of his head, but I have no clue what it will cover."

"I don't live extravagantly," Natalie said in her most persuasive tone. "Mostly I just need to be able to pay rent."

"Hmm." Jack's gaze turned toward the ceiling as he mulled it over. "It really would help me out. Why don't I crunch some numbers tonight and see what I can work out, then I'll get back to you tomorrow. Can you meet me here around noon?"

"Isn't that going to be a busy time for you?"

"Look around." Jack gestured toward all the empty tables. "I wouldn't be too worried."

2

————

Natalie walked out of Danny's with a renewed sense of purpose. All the place really needed was a little TLC, and she loved working on projects like that. Plus, Carter was adorable, and Jack seemed really sweet. She crossed her fingers he'd find some wiggle room in the budget for her.

Satisfaction that she had a solid lead on a job overshadowed her worry about not having a place to stay. At least she had one thing almost figured out. Once she had a solid living arrangement, she could get painting and send ten quality pieces over to Ned.

The back door of Danny's opened up onto the beach, and Natalie relished the feel of the sand between her toes as she walked down the shore. Her suitcase wasn't as pleased with the resistance the soft terrain created for its wheels, and after struggling with it for a few minutes, she finally gave up and decided to rest a few hundred feet down the beach. It was actually an ideal spot with the dunes creating a nice little cove for her to sit in. Plopping down, Natalie set her bags beside her and removed her sandals.

It was late afternoon, and the sky was clear as could be.

The temperature rested at a comfortable seventy-two degrees, and a quick check of the weather app on her phone told Natalie it would only get down to sixty-five overnight. Not bad weather to sleep out under the stars. It wouldn't be the first time she'd slept outdoors, and she guessed it wouldn't be the last. Sometimes, homelessness was the price to pay for being a vagabond, as was a pervasive sense of isolation.

Natalie had friends all over the country, but her constant state of motion, bopping from one state to another, one shore to the next, made it difficult to keep in close touch with any of them. Her ever-elusive inspiration required her to change things up often, and besides, if she ever got too comfortable and let herself get too close to anyone, she ran the risk of hurting them, and that was her worst nightmare—followed closely by working a nine-to-five office job. When she started to get too comfortable, the same thoughts looped through her mind: *Never stop moving. Never settle. Never do what she did.*

As for family, there was only Griff. Despite the chasm that separated them, he was Natalie's only remaining family, and she felt obliged to keep him updated on her whereabouts. With a deep breath to steel herself, she clicked his contact button and held the phone up to her ear.

After a couple of rings, his gruff voice rattled through the phone's speaker. "Hello?"

Natalie imagined that she'd caught him at work and hoped that would keep the conversation short. Griff was nothing if not dedicated to his job.

"Hi, Dad, it's me," she said, trying to keep her voice cheerful in the hopes that he would reciprocate her tone. *Fat chance.*

"Natalie?"

Griff's surprise irked her.

"Yes, Dad. Your only child, remember?"

"Of course," he answered flatly.

"I'm calling to check in. I just landed on Nantucket."

There was a long pause on the other end of the line. "Nantucket?" he grumbled. "What the hell are you doing there?"

Natalie sighed. Of course Griff disapproved of her choice. Nothing new there. "I love Nantucket, Dad. I've always loved Nantucket."

He should know. Griff was the one who had introduced her to the place. She would never forget when he'd first told her they were going on an island vacation. Natalie's eight-year-old mind had conjured up images of the Bahamas, Aruba, Jamaica, and the like. She'd pictured palm trees, water as clear as glass, and exotic creatures roaming around. She'd thought perhaps she would return to school with tanned skin and intricately woven braids in her hair like all the other girls did when they returned from their island vacations.

Natalie smiled to herself as she recalled her naïve expectations. Thirty miles off the coast of Cape Cod, Massachusetts, Nantucket was far from the tropical paradise she had envisioned. As it turned out, though, she'd been far less worried about palm trees, lizards, and cornrows than she was about enjoying her time with Griff. She so rarely got his undivided attention and had spent that trip, and the ones over the next ten years, basking in it. Too bad her decision to go to art school had ruined that streak.

"Yeah, well…" Griff trailed off. It looked like it would be a short conversation after all. His silence echoed through her ears until he finally asked, "Got a job yet?"

Natalie rolled her eyes, grateful he couldn't see her through the phone. "Not yet, but I do have a lead on one. I just got here today," she reminded him.

Unlike Natalie, who believed in adventure and following one's dreams, Griff valued hard work and money most of all. It was one of the greatest challenges they'd faced in their tenuous relationship and the reason that her decision to go to art school had rankled him so much. At least, she assumed that was the reason.

"Well, that's something, I guess. Where are you living?" he asked.

Natalie winced, knowing she should have seen the pragmatic question coming. "That's another thing I'm still figuring out," she answered carefully.

"Mhmm." Griff's unimpressed timbre struck her in the chest, landing there like a brick. "You sell any of those mountain landscapes yet?" he asked.

Natalie's heart thawed slightly at his recollection of her latest project—he really *had* been listening when she'd called him from Colorado—but it froze back over as soon as she anticipated his response to her answer.

"No…" She hesitated. "They weren't too popular. I'm hopeful that I'll do better here, where there's a thriving art community."

Griff grunted, and Natalie thought she heard him repeat "thriving art community" under his breath in a condescending tone. He took every opportunity to remind her how impractical, unrealistic, and foolish she was for choosing such an unconventional career. Despite his obvious pragmatism, it remained a mystery to Natalie just why Griff was quite so opposed to her decision to pursue her art. It wasn't like it was hurting him in any way. She had never asked him for anything, and hopefully, she would never need to.

"Don't you think it's time to find a real job?" Griff asked.

His question grated on her. It had been five years since she graduated from art school. Half a decade of traveling, painting, and trying to make it as an artist. She'd endured some precarious circumstances (like living in Big Sur with a woman who rarely bathed) and done some downright odd things to make money (like selling pictures of her feet online) when the interest in her art was low. Despite the occasional oddity, Natalie had done well for herself—though, not well enough, as evidenced by her current state of affairs. She knew she should have found more success by now, and Griff's reminder of that only aggravated her further.

"I have a real job, Dad. I'm an artist. You know this," she snapped.

He grunted. "I think you have to be making money at something in order to call it a real job."

Natalie inhaled deeply and pinched the bridge of her nose. Knowing she was on the verge of lashing out at him, she moved to end the conversation.

"Well, I'd better go now," she said, doing her best to keep her voice calm and even. "That job's not going to find itself."

"Let me know when you find something," Griff said, the request once again softening Natalie's hardened heart. In his own way, Griff really *did* care about her. His affection was just misplaced as judgment.

"Will do. Bye, Dad." She hastily pressed the *End Call* button and let out a pent-up breath. Talking to Griff was never a pleasant experience, but at least she'd fulfilled her daughterly duty.

Deciding the dunes would be her bed for the night, she spent the next few hours walking a slow loop up the beach and back through town to scope out the best scenes to paint. There were lines of charming storefronts, the compass rose mural on Washington Street, and the famous fountain at the intersection of Washington and Main that was always filled with seasonal flowers. A few streets over, she strolled past Easy Street harbor, which doubled as a spectacular view and the perfect place to sit and eat an ice cream while your feet dangled over the Atlantic.

Being on the island again felt both heartwarmingly familiar and exhilaratingly fresh. After years of venturing to new and unknown places, it felt good to be returning to a place that held such sentimental memories. In a way, it was like coming home.

When the sun sank low over the horizon, Natalie returned to her little cove and set up camp in the dunes. Laying out her colorfully striped Mexican blanket that had accompanied her on many a trip, she gazed out over the water to watch the sunset. Bold pinks and reds stained the sky while a couple of rogue fluffy clouds floated across the center of the sinking sun, sending bands of light cascading in every direction. Letting out a blissful sigh, Natalie took comfort in the fact that no matter where she was, the sun always rose in the east and set in the west.

When the sun dipped below the horizon and the chill of night whispered over her skin, Natalie rustled through her suitcase and pulled out a couple of cozy cardigans. The layers would keep her warm, and she'd wrap herself up in the blanket before going to sleep. First, though, she needed some semblance of dinner.

Digging through her backpack to find the leftover muffin half she'd saved from Danny's, her hand hit a crumpled piece of paper. She fished it out of the bag and smoothed it out over her thigh. It was a photo of her as a child, wearing a bikini and sitting atop a large pile of sand. She resembled a queen on her throne and was sure that was exactly how she'd felt as she enjoyed Griff's attention on one of their annual Nantucket trips. In fact, the photo could have even been taken on the very beach she now sat upon.

Natalie looked to be about twelve—not quite a woman, but not quite a girl. Right on the cusp of those teenage years, notorious for their rebellious acts and resentment of parental figures. Natalie surely didn't disappoint in that department, but it wouldn't be for a few years yet that her relationship with Griff would really take a nosedive.

Of course, he was right about one thing: it was hard to make money as an artist. She needed to find her inspiration—and fast—so she could fulfill her commitment to Ned and hopefully start selling paintings again, too. She had spent too long traveling, living frugally, and working odd jobs at odd hours just to barely get by. Five years was a long time to give something that wasn't working a chance.

Chewing on her nail, Natalie leaned her head back on her suitcase. Maybe it *was* time for her to look for a steady, more traditional job. The mere thought of it sent a shiver of dread shooting down her spine. Locked up in a cubicle in some corporate office was no better than being locked in a jail cell in her mind.

Natalie had no problem working odd jobs here and there, but committing to a career job meant giving up the freedom to travel on a whim, and it meant less flexible hours for painting. She wasn't ready to give all that up just yet. This summer on Nantucket was her last chance to turn her luck around.

With a long sigh, she carefully folded up the photo and placed it in a small, zippered pocket on the front of her backpack. Then she reached into the main pocket to locate her initial target. The muffin half was good—really good, actually—and she vaguely wondered if Jenny had baked it. Natalie's mind flashed back to the young woman's chocolate-covered clothes and wondered what Jenny had been making and if she'd get a chance to try it. She was sure that if Jack was able to offer her a job, she'd get plenty of access to delicious baked goods.

A light breeze wafted the scent of seafood toward Natalie's camp, and she wished she had more to eat. Inhaling the appetizing aroma, she reminded herself that she had a lead on a good job, and it was only a matter of time before she would be living comfortably on her favorite island.

With that reassuring thought in her head, she burrowed under her mound of cardigans, swaddled herself in her blanket, and rested her head on her backpack. The excitement of the day had worn her out, from arriving in a new place to finding what could be the perfect gig for her. With the sound of crashing waves as her lullaby, she fell asleep in minutes.

3

"Natalie? Hey, Natalie?" Jack's velvety voice summoned her in her dream. Natalie sighed and pressed her cheek into the pillow, hoping she wouldn't wake up before her mind presented her with a visual of his tall, tan body.

"Natalie?" Jack said again, but this time, his voice was accompanied by a very real tap on her shoulder. Startled, Natalie bolted upright, swaying slightly at the abrupt motion. Her shoulders sank as the reality set in that she hadn't been dreaming and that wasn't a pillow, but her duffel bag covered with a sweater. Rogue grains of sand clung to her bare legs, and she could feel the imprint of her sweater on one cheek.

Shielding her eyes against the morning sun, Natalie looked up at Jack as he stood before her in the flesh. Speaking of flesh, he was showing quite a bit of it. In just athletic shorts and sneakers, his torso was deliciously bare. His chest and stomach glistened with sweat, and her eyes zeroed in on his abdomen and the faint outline of a six-pack that graced it. Though Jack wasn't shredded, he was clearly in shape and looked as if he'd been out on a morning run.

Framing his hips with his large hands, Jack cocked his head to one side.

"Oh, uh… hi, Jack," Natalie said, avoiding his gaze as she attempted to fix her bedhead and straighten out her horribly wrinkled dress. Her position on the ground below him and the fact that she'd obviously slept outside made her feel about two feet tall.

Jack furrowed his brow as he looked down upon her. "What are you doing out here?"

"I, well… I slept here last night," Natalie admitted.

"You slept out here? On the beach?"

Wincing at Jack's incredulous tone, she gave him a silent affirmative nod.

"But why?" he asked.

Natalie let out a long sigh and worked up the nerve to look him in the eye. "I know this looks bad, but I couldn't afford a room last night, and this was my last resort. I won't be doing things like this once I have a job, I swear!" Batting her eyelashes innocently, she hoped Jack would take pity on her and offer her the job. Perhaps discovering she was homeless would persuade him.

Jack blew out a breath and sat down beside her, leaning his forearms on his knees. "You really don't have anywhere you can stay?"

Natalie would have chuckled at that if she hadn't been attempting to appear somber and destitute. "Remember how I couldn't afford that muffin yesterday? And how I said I really needed a job? Yeah, I wasn't kidding. I'm broke." Time and time again, she proved that the term "starving artist" was more than just a cliché.

Jack's big hands made their way into his hair as his gaze wandered over Natalie's rumpled, slept-in clothes and the two lonesome bags sitting beside her.

Under his scrutiny, she began babbling nervously. "Maybe

I shouldn't have come here in the first place. I knew it was expensive. I just had this idyllic vision of working in some artsy little shop and living in an apartment above it—like in all the movies, you know? I guess I'm just a dreamer, like my dad always said." She shook her head wistfully, really playing up the mournful act.

Jack sighed. "That's a wonderful dream, Natalie, and I wish I could make it come true, but I don't know if I can pay you enough to afford rent at any of the places in town."

"I'd settle for just a room in someone's house. I really don't need much," Natalie said. "I just couldn't find a place that wouldn't require a deposit to move in."

Jack scratched his chin. "You know, you bring up an interesting point about living above the place you work. I live above Danny's Place. I moved in right after Danny and Carrie died so Carter could stay in his home. It's pretty big, as far as apartments go, and they were planning to expand their family, so they added on an extra bedroom after Carter was born."

Natalie perked up at the words *extra bedroom*, the phrase like music to her ears.

"I have no use for the extra room," Jack went on. "I couldn't pay you what you're worth, but maybe I could offer you room and board in exchange for your services? You'd have full access to our fridge and the café. We could share my Jeep. If you think of anything else you'd need, we can figure out a plan for that, too."

Natalie blinked. Though he'd only had seconds to think it through, Jack already had an answer for any possible issue she could come up with. While she loved the sound of the plan, she couldn't help but feel like she'd guilted him into offering her the room.

Natalie bit her lip, wishing she could take advantage of Jack's generosity but wanting to do it with a clear conscience. "That sounds amazing, Jack. It really does. But you hardly know me. How can you just open up your home to me like that?" While she was used to unusual living situations, she knew most people weren't, and Jack had a little one to worry about too.

His gaze bore into hers, and his tone remained even and serious as he asked, "Have you ever killed anyone?"

"What? No!" Natalie cried.

The corner of Jack's mouth tugged up mischievously. "Robbed a bank?"

Her own lips began to slide into a smirk. "Nope."

"If I let you live in my house, will you steal all my money and kidnap my baby?"

"Of course not!" She laughed.

Jack's playful smile softened into a serious one. "Natalie, I'm desperate too. I need some help around here, and you seem like the perfect person for the job. It's like hiring a live-in nanny, right? People do that kind of thing all the time. I think this could work out really well for both of us."

Actually, Natalie did too. She liked Jack and Carter and everything the job entailed. Sleeping down the hall from an extremely attractive man would just be icing on the cake. *Not* that she would be indulging in that particular icing, since sleeping with your boss is never a good idea. But she could still appreciate being around it, right? It would be like someone who goes on a diet but still sniffs the indulgent foods, just to get a whiff of the pleasure they would surely bring.

"I like it," she said. "Ok, let's try it out. I promise it will be like I'm not even there, except when you want me to be—if that makes sense." Natalie frowned, realizing she was babbling again. "I won't be in your hair all the time, but I'll help out as much as I can."

Jack chuckled at her job description. "Trust me, I want you to be there. It's going to be such a relief."

Natalie jumped to her feet and clapped. "Oh, this is great! Thank you, Jack. I really appreciate this. I promise you won't regret it."

Jack grinned at her. "I never thought I would."

After discussing a few more logistical details, he led Natalie up the beach toward Danny's Place and his home, which would be hers for a while too. Despite her arguments, Jack insisted on carrying her bags. Though Natalie preferred to do things herself, she did appreciate watching his arm muscles bob up and down with the weight of the duffel. The veins on his forearm popped out ever so slightly, and she caught herself staring as he spoke.

"There's an entrance to the apartment through the café, but there's also a door in the back that leads to a staircase that goes right up there. We'll use that one."

As they walked around to the back of the building, Jack plucked a t-shirt off a fence post and pulled it on.

"*Damn*," Natalie cursed silently. She'd really been enjoying the view.

After leading her up the stairs, Jack opened the baby gate at the top and gestured for her to go through first. He followed close behind and dropped her bags in the foyer. "Come on in and look around."

The apartment had the same quaint feeling as the café, but Natalie was delighted to find that it was much less run down. Jack *had* mentioned renovations before Carter's birth. The staircase opened up into an airy living room with light-blue walls and an open layout. A large picture window domi-nated the far wall, providing a spectacular view of the ocean, particularly from the window seat in front of it. A functional couch and television rounded out the room without overpow-ering its charm.

Behind the couch was a small pirate chest that Natalie guessed was filled with Carter's toys—or, at least, it was supposed to be. Most of them appeared to be scattered around the floor at the moment. The wooden train set and chunky puzzles set up behind the couch also led her to believe it was Carter's play area.

Beyond the living room was a small but well-equipped kitchen decorated in a beach theme. Sand-colored curtains printed with blue seahorses framed the large windows. Each white cabinet featured a unique knob, from a silver anchor to a little starfish. Whoever had designed the room obviously put a lot of time and care into the details. The little touches made the apartment feel homey and comfortable.

Jack quickly showed Natalie his and Carter's rooms before guiding her to her own. "It's a little on the smaller side," he apologized, "but it's got a great view."

Glancing toward the two windows, Natalie found that they did indeed offer a fantastic view of the beach. They also let in ample light, and she could already see the exact spot where she'd set up her easel in front of them. Walls the color of sunshine made the room feel bright and warm, and the simple, white, wooden furniture and small closet would easily hold all of her things.

"It's perfect!" Natalie blurted. "Thank you, Jack! Thank you, thank you!"

Overcome with gratitude, she impulsively flung her arms around him. He didn't react at first, but after a beat, he wrapped her in his arms for a quick squeeze. With her face right by his neck, Natalie caught a whiff of his musk—salty from sweat mixed with ocean air—and had to keep herself from sighing. There was something about a sweaty man that held a primal allure.

Forcing herself to pull away, she said, "This is incredible, Jack. I can't thank you enough."

"It's my pleasure." His small smile showed a hint of vulnerability that he quickly covered with humor. "I just hope you won't change your tune when you find out there's only one bathroom we'll all share."

"Of course not." Natalie brushed off his concern with a wave of her hand. "Heck, I'd settle for no bathroom as long as I have a place to sleep. Actually, scratch that. I've taken 'sponge baths' in public bathroom sinks before, and it is not a fun experience." She grimaced and shuddered at the memories of wiping down her body in rest stop bathrooms.

"You have?" The shock in Jack's voice wasn't surprising. Most people were stunned by Natalie's tales of her days on the road. She never really considered herself homeless because she always managed to find a place to stay. She just didn't have a *permanent* home.

"Jack, you found me sleeping outside on the beach this morning. Did you think that was the first time I'd done something like that?" she asked.

"Well… yeah," he sputtered. "I assumed you were just down on your luck and it was a one-time thing."

Natalie smiled to herself. "Not even close. That's just the way I live. I move around; I make friends; I find places to stay and jobs to work. Nothing is permanent, and if that means I spend a few nights here and there sleeping outside or cleaning myself up in a public bathroom, then so be it."

Jack shook his head. "I just can't believe—"

"Ack!" Carter cried, interrupting their conversation once again as he bolted across the living room and down the hallway to the man's side.

"Hey, buddy!" Jack swooped the little boy up into his arms. "Remember Natalie? From yesterday?"

"Nalee!" Carter squealed and reached out for Natalie to hold him. She smiled as she took him into her arms.

"Natalie's going to be staying with us. Won't that be fun?" Jack cooed.

Carter beamed, a torrent of drool cascading from his wide smile.

"He's teething." Jack grimaced, and Natalie bit her lip to hide a laugh.

Jenny, the baker-slash-babysitter, was a few steps behind Carter, and she latched the baby gate before walking over to the the group. Natalie frowned as she took in the young woman's apron, which was covered in splotches of a gruesome red substance ranging from wide, uneven spots to tiny polka dots, as if something—or someone—had exploded all over her.

Jenny must have caught her staring, because she explained, "Strawberry jam. I'm a bit of a messy baker."

Natalie let out a sigh of relief that there'd been no bloodshed. "Oh, I'm sure it will be delicious."

"I'm trying something new today: strawberry-infused cupcakes," Jenny explained. "I just can't seem to get the perfect ratio of sugar to lemon juice in the filling. I thought about using pectin because it gels so much faster, but it's more expensive, so I decided against it."

Natalie nodded along, though she'd lost track of the conversation around *strawberry-infused cupcakes*. "I'm sure it will all work out," she said politely.

Jack jumped in to introduce them. "Jenny, I'd like you to officially meet Natalie. She's going to be helping out with Carter and the café."

"Wonderful!" The young woman vigorously shook Natalie's hand. "We could certainly use the help."

"You'll be seeing a lot of her because she'll be staying in the extra bedroom up here too," Jack added. Jenny glanced skeptically between the two of them but remained silent.

"Thanks for bringing him back up." Jack motioned to Carter. "You can get back to your strawberry-infused adventure now."

Jenny saluted him, waved goodbye to Natalie and Carter, and left without another word.

"Weird kid." Jack scratched his chin as Jenny retreated down the stairs. "I don't know what she's talking about half the time, but she's a damn good baker."

Natalie grinned. "I like her. She's… eccentric." It was the same quality that had drawn her to the woman at the visitor's center. Natalie liked people who weren't entirely ordinary. They kept life interesting.

"That's one word for it." Jack glanced down at his sweaty running clothes. "I've really got to get in the shower, but why don't you get yourself settled in? We can make breakfast when I'm done."

"Sounds great," Natalie hesitated for a moment. "What do you normally do with Carter when you shower?"

"I, er… well, I usually let him play in the living room and leave the bathroom door open so I can poke my head out and check on him…"

Jack's face flushed, and Natalie raised her eyebrows as she imagined the eyeful she'd get if he did that now. Though tempting, it would be far from appropriate.

"Why don't I take him into my room with me while I unpack," she suggested.

"Sure." Jack's shoulders sagged with obvious relief, and Natalie thought she detected a slight blush on his cheeks.

"Take your time. We'll be just fine," she assured him, hauling Carter into her new bedroom while Jack headed for the shower. Plucking a toy rocket ship off the floor, Natalie handed it to Carter to keep him entertained while she settled in.

It didn't take long to put away her meager belongings, and she hummed joyfully to herself as she emptied her duffel bag of clothes into the dresser drawers, leaving her small cosmetic bag on top of it so she'd remember to bring it to the bathroom. Unfolding her easel by one of the windows, Natalie placed her palette and a few tubes of paint beside it. Finally, she pulled out the two photos that she took with her everywhere.

Her humming ceased as she gazed down at the photos. The first was the one she'd come across the previous night— her on the beach as a child. The second was an even younger version of herself along with her parents. It was the last photo she had of the three of them together. Only a bit older than Carter was now, Natalie was wedged in between her mother and father at her second birthday party, wearing a princess party hat and a face-splitting grin. Though she couldn't specifically remember that day, every time Natalie looked at the picture, she could imagine how happy she must have felt. Two parents, a birthday party, and not a care in the world.

Unlike the crumpled photo she'd found in her backpack, this one was nicely framed. She couldn't risk destroying the only photo that existed of her family before it had been torn apart. Placing it on her nightstand, she turned to Carter with a sigh. "That's it. All done."

"Aww done. Aww done," Carter chanted as he flew his rocket ship through the air.

"What do you say we get some breakfast going and surprise Jack when he gets out of the shower?" Natalie asked, infusing the question with enthusiasm.

Carter nodded his head up and down, likely responding more to her tone than her actual question. She brought him into the kitchen and plopped him into his highchair.

"Let's see what we've got here," she murmured as she searched for the ingredients for pancakes. Carter watched her from his perch as she scurried around the kitchen. She was pleased to find flour, sugar, baking powder, salt, milk, eggs, and butter, but disturbed to find almost nothing else beyond those basics. There was no fruit, no vegetables, no yogurt, no sliced deli meat or cheese—nothing else that made up a balanced diet. She did discover a few packages of chicken in the freezer and some pasta in the cupboard, but that was it.

Shaking her head, Natalie wondered what the boys had been eating and when Jack had last gone grocery shopping. It was one thing for Jack to eat like a bachelor, but Carter needed proper nutrition. She put shopping on her mental to-do list.

Carter seemed to be getting bored and was desperately

struggling to escape his highchair, so Natalie quickly heated the griddle and measured out the ingredients. To occupy him, she gave Carter the task of mixing the batter. Placing him on the ground, she waited a moment for him to balance himself on his chunky little legs, then she held the bowl steady for him. He began stirring, struggling against the resistance at first but eventually getting the hang of it. Natalie made the sound effects of an accelerating car as Carter stirred faster. He howled with laughter.

They were both giggling when Jack entered the kitchen wearing a light-blue collared shirt with the sleeves rolled up, dark jeans, and bare feet. His hair was still damp, and he'd shaved, taming the stubble that framed his jaw. Natalie fleetingly wondered if he'd cleaned himself up for her.

He smiled at their infectious laughter. "What are you two hooligans up to?"

"What are we making, Carter?" Natalie prompted, pointing to the batter in the bowl and temporarily ignoring the bit that had ended up on the floor from Carter's exuberant stirring.

The boy threw his arms up in the air. "Pancay!"

"No way! My favorite!" Jack bent over to give Carter a peck on the head then turned toward Natalie. "You didn't have to cook. I would have done it when I got out of the shower."

"It's no trouble," she said, spooning batter onto the griddle. "You've had a lot on your plate lately, and you deserve for someone to do something for you."

Jack paused a moment before responding. "Wow, thank you. I can't remember the last time someone looked out for me."

"This is what I'm here for," Natalie reminded him gently then scrunched her nose in distaste. "And maybe to get some food in the house. Your fridge is practically empty."

Jack ran a hand over his recently trimmed scruff. "Yeah,

I've been meaning to go shopping. I'll make a list if you don't mind running out later."

"Not at all," she said softly. "You make that list, and then don't worry about it anymore. I'll take care of it."

"Thanks, Natalie," Jack said. "I feel more relaxed with you around already."

4

After breakfast, Natalie showered and changed into fresh clothes. It was a little cooler than the day before, when a simple sundress had sufficed, so she chose flared jeans and a navy peasant blouse with three-quarter-length sleeves. Her chunky rings clanked together as she braided her long, dirty-blonde hair. A little bit of tinted SPF gave her skin a healthy glow, and a swipe of mascara made her blue eyes pop.

Emerging from the bathroom, Natalie found Jack tossing Carter up in the air and tickling his belly as he caught him. The boy's infectious giggle had Jack cracking up, and Natalie's heart melted as she watched them play. Jack, who had been a bachelor without any real responsibilities up until a few months ago, looked beyond natural with the baby. Granted, he was stressed and—the day before, at least—kind of a mess, but she gave him a lot of credit.

"Hey, boys." Natalie waved to get their attention.

"Hey!" Jack grinned over at her then did a double take, his eyes darting over her body before landing on her face. He cleared his throat before adding, "Wow, you look nice today."

Natalie's cheeks warmed at the unexpected compliment. "Thanks." Shaking off her modesty, she struck a pose that showed off her strappy sandals. "Yesterday, you saw me after being crammed onto a ferry for an hour, and this morning, you saw me after spending the night sleeping on the beach. I should hope I look a little better now."

"I thought you looked great yesterday too," Jack clarified. "Today, you just look… really nice."

His shy smile made Natalie's heart flutter, and she knew then that he *had* cleaned up for her. "You look nice today, too," she said.

Jack's answering grin had her heart full on flip-flopping. To her disappointment, those luscious lips fell into a frown as he looked down at his watch. "It's almost ten, and my employees will be switching shifts. I'd better get down there. Are you sure you're ready to take this little dude for the day?" He gave Carter a gentle noogie.

"Totally," Natalie answered. "I think I'll take him into town to pick up those groceries, and I'd like to stop at the library and pick up some books too."

"Sounds good," Jack said. "I wish I could come. It sounds a heck of a lot more fun than standing around a dead café all day."

"Who knows," Natalie mused. "Maybe today's the day your luck will change."

"Here's hoping." Jack crossed his fingers dramatically. "I left cash and a grocery list on the table. Pick up anything else you want. Oh, and there's a playground near the library that Carter loves. Once he sees it, he probably won't let you leave."

"Well, then I guess we'll have to stop there too," Natalie said, excited to have a chance to get out and about on the island.

Jack turned to Carter, and Natalie wasn't sure her quivering heart could take any more as he began speaking softly to the boy. "I'm going to go to work, ok, buddy? You stay with Natalie, and I'll see you in a little bit. I love you."

He kissed Carter on the head and handed him over to Natalie, who took the baby's hand and directed it into a wave. "We'll see you later!"

"Have a good day," Jack said. "Stop by downstairs when you get back, and let me know how everything's going."

"You got it." Natalie saluted Jack as she had seen Jenny do the day before.

Heading to the kitchen counter, she looked over the list he had left, grunting as she scanned the pitiful items he'd requested: marshmallow sandwich cookies, ice cream, pudding, chocolate cereal, pasta, jar sauce, and bread. Seven items, and not one of them a piece of produce or anything remotely healthy.

"We'll see about this," Natalie muttered to herself as she ripped up the list into tiny pieces and threw them in the recycling bin. Strapping Carter into his stroller, she took off in the direction of the grocery store and located it with ease, delighted and comforted by the fact that she was able to navigate the island from memory.

Upon arrival, she transferred Carter from the stroller to a shopping cart and gave him a stuffed rabbit and bag of goldfish she'd stowed away to keep him occupied while she shopped. Carter, however, was more than happy to spend his time waving at each and every shopper that passed them by. Almost everyone waved back, and Natalie received copious compliments about how cute the baby was. She thanked them all and made a bit of small talk but remained steadfast on her mission. Walking past the junk food aisle without a second glance, she veered toward the produce section.

Grabbing a bunch of bananas, she considered how disgracefully Jack had been eating. Cookies, pudding, and cereal? Really? Although, his diet couldn't have been *that* bad.

An image of Jack's runner's body formed in her mind, with its long, lean muscles and that V-shaped cut in his torso that junk food *definitely* didn't get you. And those biceps she loved so much… She decided he must have been doing something right.

"Ahem," someone behind her muttered. Only then did Natalie realize she'd been standing in front of a fruit display, staring blankly at a pyramid of peaches for who knows how long.

"Sorry," she apologized quickly and bit her lip, perilously close to giggling at herself over the absurdity of drooling over her new boss in the middle of the grocery store.

Forcing herself to push the cart along, Natalie grabbed a variety of fresh produce along the way. Blueberries would make the perfect snack for Carter, and broccoli would go well with dinner. Meandering through the rest of the aisles, she found healthy alternatives for each item on Jack's list. Instead of pasta, she got a few boxes of quinoa, and instead of sugary cereal, she chose muesli.

Pleased with her purchases, Natalie transferred Carter back into his stroller and stored the grocery bags in the compartment at the bottom. Everything she had purchased would keep well, especially on this cooler day, so they walked the short distance to the library. Natalie had wanted to grab a few books for herself and some books to read to Carter, but she never got the chance. Jack was right. Carter wouldn't let her walk by the playground without letting him out to play, so she scratched her plans and spent the next hour pushing him on the swings, catching him at the bottom of the slide, and holding him up while he attempted to swing across the monkey bars.

By noon, Natalie's stomach was growling, so she figured Carter was getting hungry too. Plus, Jack was probably getting worried about them. It was her first day on the job, and she had already been gone a few hours. Not wanting Jack to think she'd kidnapped the baby after all, the pair headed back to Danny's for lunch.

"There they are," Jack said, looking up from behind the counter. "Hey, guys!"

"Hi," Natalie greeted him, excited to see a couple of people sitting at the counter, eating sandwiches. The place wasn't busy, by any means, but it was better than it had been the day before.

"Ack!" Carter wiggled around in Natalie's arms until she put him down on the floor, then he ran behind the counter and over to Jack.

"Did you have fun?" Jack asked as he picked Carter up.

"It was a blast," Natalie answered. "He wanted to try every single thing on the playground, but I think the swings were his favorite. I pushed him on them for at least twenty minutes."

Jack smiled broadly at Carter. "Sounds like a lot of fun, bud. You guys must be getting hungry."

"That's why we came back," Natalie said, "and because it was getting warm and we had produce with us."

"Oh, right. Let's put the groceries away, then we can grab some lunch." Jack turned to the young man cleaning tables on the other side of the café. "Derek, I'm going upstairs for just a second. You can handle this, right?"

The young man saluted Jack. "You got it, captain."

"What's up with the saluting?" Natalie asked, curiosity getting the best of her.

"Oh," Jack chuckled, "it's kind of an inside joke. Danny was in the Navy for a while right out of college. He started this place after he left, and some of his original workers called him 'the captain of the ship.' So, whenever he would give orders to one of his employees, they saluted him. When I took over here, I guess that kind of transferred onto me," he finished with a shrug.

"Cool." Natalie nodded. "It makes you seem very powerful."

Jack wagged his head back and forth. "Oh, I don't know about that. I don't quite have the authoritative tone Danny did." Bending over, he grabbed the bulk of the grocery bags.

"Well, they seem to respect you just fine," Natalie said as she grabbed the rest. They headed upstairs to the apartment where Carter ran off to the living room to play. Jack and Natalie went to the kitchen to put the groceries away.

After unpacking a few bags, he paused. "Wait a second. Did you get anything that was on my list?"

"About that…" Natalie pursed her lips and scratched her head. "Your list was… pretty pathetic."

A frown tugged at Jack's lips. "What do you mean?"

Deciding to take a more blunt approach, she said, "That list was full of crap. It only had sugary, preservative-happy foods on it. I decided to go with some healthier options."

Jack's eyebrows inched closer together. "So, you decided to unilaterally overhaul the grocery list and buy only the stuff you wanted."

Natalie grew defensive at his irritated tone. "I didn't just get food for myself. I got things with all of us in mind—just not the exact items you requested."

"When I gave you a list of items, I intended for you to get those specific items, not some wacky, healthified version of them. I mean," he reached over and picked up the box of muesli, "I asked for chocolate puffs. I don't even know what this stuff is."

"It's called muesli," Natalie said, carefully enunciating the word. "It's like granola, and unlike chocolate puffs, it won't clog your arteries."

"I'm pretty sure my arteries are just fine," Jack shot back, flexing a bicep to show just how in shape he was.

Natalie rolled her eyes. "Then how about Carter? Do you really think he should be eating food that's full of ingredients you can't even pronounce? He's not even two yet. His body is just developing, and you're feeding him junk."

"Oh." Jack's scowl deflated as he ran a hand through his hair. "Shit."

Natalie softened her tone. "I'm not trying to accuse you of doing anything to harm Carter. I know you're doing the best you can, but babies need good nutrition. The fun snacks are fine in moderation, but you needed to get some better food in the house."

Jack glanced down at the rest of the bags full of food he hadn't asked for. "Now I feel like an irresponsible bastard."

Natalie sighed. "You're not irresponsible, Jack. You're busy, and you're still learning how to raise a baby. You're doing your best, but you need help, and that's exactly why I'm here."

Jack's sheepish grin tugged at her heart strings. "Thanks for keeping it real with me."

"I never said I'd go easy on you." Natalie smirked.

"Please don't." Jack looked over at the couple of bags they had left to unpack and pouted. "You didn't even get the marshmallow sandwich cookies?"

Natalie groaned. "I *especially* didn't get the marshmallow sandwich cookies. Are you aware of how much sugar is in a single one?"

"No, but I'm well aware of how much deliciousness is in a single one. And I was really looking forward to having them as my midnight snack."

"I'll get you them next time I shop if you promise to eat all of the vegetables I bought today," Natalie vowed, feeling as if she were negotiating with a little boy instead of a grown man.

"Deal." Jack flashed her a killer smile, and she rolled her eyes again.

"Who am I babysitting again?" she muttered under her breath.

He shot her a glare. "I heard that."

☼ ☼ ☼

The three of them ate a lunch consisting of BLTs—courtesy of Derek—and potato chips. Carter ate a deconstructed plate of bacon, lettuce, and tomato with baby puffs on the side. As they all cleared their plates, Natalie decided that everything Derek made was delicious, and everything Jenny had baked so far was equally appetizing. The problem with Danny's certainly wasn't the food. People were just afraid to come in the door, given the building's appearance. She couldn't wait to tackle that part of her job.

After lunch, Jack retreated to his office, and Natalie took Carter to the beach to play. The baby ran around wildly for almost an hour, and when he started to slow down, she brought him upstairs and put him down for a nap. By the time she emerged from the boy's room, Jack was back in the apartment.

"Hey," Natalie greeted him, pointing toward Carter's closed door. "I think I tired him out. Playground in the morning and beach in the afternoon is a lethal combination."

"Ah." Jack nodded then sighed. "I'm sure it's the most fun day he's had in a while. I don't usually have that much time to take him places. For the most part, he either hangs out in the back room with Jenny or plays in the apartment while I do all the business stuff for Danny's." He rubbed the back of his neck bashfully.

"That's not your fault," Natalie said gently. "You're doing your best to run a business and raise a baby that you just got six months ago. You're busy, but I see how you are with him. Carter loves you. He doesn't seem to be missing anything."

Jack nodded as he considered Natalie's words, though he didn't seem ready to accept that he was doing a good job. "He does get to go to some fun places on Fridays when my mom takes him," he acknowledged.

"Oh, that's nice. She lives on the island too?" Natalie asked.

"Yeah. You'd like her, actually. She's an artist, like you. She makes pottery and sells it at a little shop close by. I'll take you there sometime."

"Cool," Natalie said. "I know Nantucket tends to attract us artistic types. I'd love to meet her." Connecting with another artist could go a long way toward renewing her inspiration. She was also admittedly curious to learn more about Jack, including his family.

"I'm sure you'll get a chance to on Friday when she takes Carter. I think you guys will get along great."

Natalie warmed at the thought of her and Jack's mom hitting it off. "So, she takes him every Friday?"

Jack nodded. "Yeah, he loves his days with *Gigi*. She likes to keep him overnight too, so I usually pick him up on Saturdays."

"Great. What do you need me to do on those days?" Natalie asked. "Will I be working at the café?"

"That's what I was thinking," Jack answered. "Working at the café but also *on* the café." He rubbed the back of his neck again. "There are a lot of touch-ups that need to be done, and I haven't had time to get around to them."

The projects that probably seemed stressful to Jack were exciting to Natalie. "Perfect!" she exclaimed. "What's up first? Gardening? Painting? Organizing?"

Jack's eyebrows shot up at her enthusiasm, and she saw him try to contain his amused grin. "I'm glad you're excited about those things, because I'm certainly not."

"I can't wait to whip this place into shape," she said, rubbing her hands together maniacally.

Despite any attempts to quell it, Jack's wide grin broke free. "Good. My number one priority is making the building look better from the road. It badly needs a new paint job. I think I found the name of the current color written down somewhere in Danny's papers."

Natalie pictured the drab, faded, gray-shingled façade. "What if we tried a new color?" she suggested.

Jack glanced over at her, eyebrows up. "I really want to use the same one," he said. "The gray shingles are a pretty famous symbol of Nantucket. People want to see them when they come here."

Natalie bobbed her head to the side as she considered that. "Yes, but that also means that almost every place has them. Wouldn't it be more eye-catching if we painted them a different color?"

The line of Jack's mouth indicated that he wasn't budging. "Maybe, but do we want to be eye-catching, or do we want to be classic Nantucket?"

If he was going to be stubborn, then so was she. "I don't know, do you want more business, or do you want Danny's to go under?" Natalie challenged. "Because if there's nothing setting you apart from other restaurants on the island, that's exactly what's going to happen."

Jack huffed out a sigh. "It was doing just fine when Danny was running it."

Natalie's heart softened as she realized that the paint color wasn't really the problem. It was Jack's grief over losing his friend. She knew better than most how grief could rear its ugly head in all sorts of unexpected ways, and though she could tell that Jack was just trying to do right by Danny's legacy, she wasn't convinced that he hadn't been handed kind of a cruddy deal.

"Was it, though?" she asked gently. "Because the damage to the building and the garden and all of that isn't something that happens overnight. Danny has only been gone a few months, right? The problems began before you took over the café."

Jack scowled, but the lines in his forehead smoothed as he considered her words.

"I guess… maybe things started going downhill after Carter was born," he admitted. "Danny and Carrie were a lot busier, and the business may have suffered a bit. Now it feels like it's all crashing down on me."

Natalie placed her hand over Jack's where it rested on the counter, doing her best to ignore the jolt of electricity that traveled up her forearm at the casual touch.

"Is your aversion to a new paint color about you wanting to be 'classic Nantucket' or you wanting to do everything the same way Danny did?" she asked softly.

Jack looked up, his eyes a little lost. "What?"

"It feels like maybe you're afraid to change anything because it would be different from how Danny did things."

Jack shifted uncomfortably and tapped the counter with his free hand. "I guess maybe I'm trying to do things the way Danny would have done them. He chose the original Nantucket gray for the exterior, and it feels like kind of a betrayal to him to change everything so soon after he's gone."

Natalie squeezed Jack's hand. "I get it," she said, "but Danny's is yours now, and the best way to honor him is by doing whatever will bring in more business. That might entail making some changes, which is scary, but it will be the best thing in the long run."

Jack took a deep breath and sighed it out, removing his hand from beneath hers. She bit back a frown, knowing he was just being professional.

"Do what you think needs to be done," he muttered reluctantly.

"Will you please trust me?" Natalie asked. "And might I remind you that I'm an artist? I tend to be pretty good with the aesthetic stuff."

"I know." Jack scrubbed a hand over his face and relaxed

his shoulders. "I'm going to try to trust you on this one, but I get veto power. You have to run your color choice by me first."

Natalie clapped her hands together, already conspiring about what paint color she would pick out. A nice sage green or a muted robin's egg blue might look nice. The job may not be as exciting as painting a picture on canvas, but anytime she had a brush in her hand, she was content.

"This is going to be great," she assured him. "You'll see."

5

For dinner that night, Natalie used some of the frozen chicken she'd found in the freezer and the broccoli she'd bought to make a stir-fry that she served over quinoa. Jack was surprised that he liked the quinoa, although it took him a few tries to learn how to pronounce the word. Carter even ate a few pieces of the broccoli. Despite her worry that the boys might be too skittish to try the new foods, Natalie was satisfied that they ended up enjoying them.

Afterward, Jack showed her Carter's nighttime routine, including a bath, a story, and a lullaby. It seemed pretty typical and totally doable for her on nights when Jack may not be available. When he knelt down beside Carter's crib and began singing softly to him, Natalie was sure her heart had melted into a puddle. Surely it wasn't healthy for one's organs to feel so incredibly gooey.

Even in the dim lighting, she could make out Jack's strong, square jawline and his sculpted lips as he crooned the words to "Twinkle, Twinkle, Little Star." The love in Carter's eyes as he gazed sleepily up at the man somehow made him even more attractive. Perhaps it was her own lack of a supportive father figure, or perhaps it was just a natural female instinct, but every time Jack made Carter laugh or gave him a kiss on the head, Natalie's heart skipped a beat.

Once the boy was fully asleep, Jack eased his door shut so as not to wake him and blew out a relieved breath.

"I guess I'll just head to my room now," Natalie whispered. "I don't want to take up your space."

"No, no. Stay out in the living room for a while. Have a beer with me," Jack invited her with a hopeful smile.

Hardly able to turn down that offer, she whispered, "Ok," and followed him out to the living room, where she perched herself on the window seat. Jack handed her a bottle before sitting on the couch nearby.

"Carter is so precious, and you're so good with him, Jack," Natalie praised, taking a sip of her beer. It was delicious— tangy with a subtle spice. She studied the label and recognized the local Cisco Brewers logo.

"I do my best," Jack said with an unconvincing shrug. "I guess I *have* learned a lot in the past few months, mostly by trial and error. Like one of the first times I changed Carter's diaper, I didn't know that whole trick about covering up his junk so he wouldn't pee all over me, and let's just say I learned my lesson after that one."

Natalie snickered. Seeing that he'd hit her funny bone, Jack went on. "Oh, and learning what foods he did and didn't like was a fun one too. One day, I gave him a bite of a mango to try, and he ended up spitting it all over my brand-new shirt —first time I'd worn it."

Natalie laughed out loud at Jack's dejected expression, and he continued to regale her with tales of his early days with Carter. As he shared story after story, she realized just how far he'd come in such a short period of time.

"How did you deal with being thrown into all of this so quickly?" she asked. "I mean, had you ever thought about having a family before this?"

"Not at all," Jack admitted, sipping his beer. "I had never

even considered getting married or having children. I wasn't at that place in my life. Before all this, I lived alone in a tiny apartment and bartended down the street at The Gazebo. I was busy living up to my title as 'the screw-up' of my family."

Natalie reared her head back in shock. "Why were you the screw-up?"

"I was that guy who peaked in high school," Jack explained matter-of-factly. "I didn't go to college. Never left the island. I didn't pursue some great career or marriage. Not like my brothers did. They both got their lives figured out while I was still here, floundering."

"You have brothers?" Natalie asked, curiosity piqued, as she believed that a person's family could affect a big portion of who he or she was. That rang true for her, at least.

"Yeah, Fletcher and Beau. My mother's prized offspring," Jack spat, waving his beer in the air as if the notion was repulsive.

"What are they like?" she asked, despite his obvious distaste.

"Fletcher is twelve years older than me. He's an elementary school teacher." Jack rolled his eyes. "I mean, come on, a guy who teaches little kids for a living? People eat that shit up. And he's got this longtime girlfriend, Christa, and they're just bound to get married. My mother's thrilled."

"He sounds just awful," Natalie said with mock disgust, managing to tease a slight smile out of Jack.

"I don't mean to sound like that," he relented. "Fletcher's a really good guy, and I love him. He practically raised me. But does he really have to be *so* perfect? In my mother's eyes, Fletcher can do no wrong, and it's been that way ever since my father died."

"Oh, Jack. I'm so sorry," Natalie said. While her mother hadn't died, she knew how hard it was to lose a parent.

"It's ok." Jack waved his hand to dismiss her pity. "It was a long time ago. He was a police officer—died on duty. I was four when it happened, and Beau was only two, but Fletcher was a teenager, so he got hit the hardest. My mom was left with a lot on her plate, and Fletch had to pick up the slack. He helped raise us, so he's Mom's golden boy."

"That must have been an awful lot of responsibility to take on, especially since he was grieving the loss of his father," Natalie commented, thinking how similar Fletcher's situation had been to Jack's current one.

"For sure," Jack agreed. "But honestly, he was really good at taking care of us. I guess that's why he became a teacher— because he was so good with kids."

"He sounds like a nice guy," she said gently.

"He is, he is," Jack conceded. "Just a little *too* good some-times, it seems. And then there's Beau, my younger brother, just by two years. He's a police officer, like my dad was. One of Boston's finest."

"Scum of the Earth," Natalie declared sarcastically, coaxing a full-on chuckle out of Jack.

"My mom was so damn mad when he told her he wanted to be a cop." He smiled, no doubt remembering his mother's ire at his baby brother. "She was terrified after what happened to my dad, you know? But eventually, she came around to be proud of him for choosing such an honorable job. I'll never forget the look on her face at his graduation from the acad-emy. She had tears in her eyes but couldn't stop beaming at him up onstage."

"I'm sure she was pleased that he was following in his father's footsteps," Natalie said.

"Yeah, she always loved when he wore his dress blues. Said he looked just like my old man." Jack's eyes glazed over, and for a moment, he looked very far away. It was the same look he got when he talked about Danny.

"Do they still live locally?" Natalie asked, wondering if she'd ever get the chance to meet his brothers.

Jack's eyes cleared as he shook his head. "They both

moved off the island after high school. Fletcher went to college in Boston, and by the time Beau went to the police academy, Fletch was already settled in an apartment and had a respectable career, so Beau went to live with him. They stayed really close. And then there's me. Right in the middle of the perfect brothers. I never had the motivation to do anything with my life, so I got stuck back here. The screw-up of the family," he huffed, waving his beer around in conclusion.

Natalie hated the surrender in his tone. "Come on, Jack. You're not a screw-up. So what if you didn't follow the same path as your brothers? Who cares? It may have taken you a bit longer to catch your stride, but you're running your own business now. You're raising a little boy."

"Well, trying to raise him," Jack clarified.

"You're doing a great job," Natalie insisted. "Raising a child alone is hard. You've only been doing it for a little while now. You're already better at it than my dad, and he did it for most of my life," she said, hoping that changing the subject to her messed-up childhood might make Jack feel better about his own family issues.

"Really?" he asked. "Single father?"

Natalie took a large, exaggerated swig of her beer. "Yep. My mom took off when I was little, probably not much older than Carter. No warning, no explanation. I guess she just couldn't handle having a kid."

"Geez, that sucks," Jack said. "Your dad didn't take it well, I imagine?"

"Oh, no," Natalie confirmed, "and he had no idea how to care for a child. Sure, he kept me clean and well fed, but I never got that warm-and-cozy feeling—not like Carter gets from you."

"You think I'm warm and cozy?" Jack asked, sipping his beer to hide a wry smile. "I thought I was a little manlier than that."

Natalie chuckled over the rim of her bottle. "I didn't mean to emasculate you. Trust me, you're all man," she assured him, thinking back to the sight of him shirtless on the beach, his sculpted muscles veiled by a sheen of perspiration. "I just meant that you love Carter, and he can obviously feel it. He'll never question whether you support him or whether you'll back him up in his decisions."

"And you had to worry about those things with your father." The way Jack phrased it as a statement, rather than a question, showed that he understood completely.

"Unfortunately, yes. Ever since I can remember, Griff's been grumpy. I don't know if he was always that way or if it's just been since my mom left, but he's always criticizing me. Every chance he gets, he reminds me that I make bad choices, that I'm unrealistic, blah blah blah. We can barely hold a conversation because he turns *everything* into a fight.

"Thank God I moved away for school," Natalie continued, "because when I told him I was going to major in fine arts, he probably would have banished me from the house forever anyway. He couldn't get past his opinion that art school was a waste of money," she said sourly, finishing off the last of her beverage.

"Man, he sounds like an ass," Jack said. "No offense," he added quickly.

"None taken. He is pretty much an ass. I try to give him some credit for raising a daughter alone while grieving the loss of his wife, but it's hard when he fights my lifestyle at every turn."

"What doesn't he like about your lifestyle?" Jack asked.

"Oh, my whole lifestyle is horrifying to him," Natalie said. "He believes in hard work, money, and comfortable living. He's not a 'do what you love' type of guy. He's more the 'do something practical even if it makes you miserable' type. I don't think he *hates* his construction job, but it certainly was never his dream. The fact that I chase my dreams of being an artist and do some unusual things to support myself along the way is baffling to him. If he knew that I was living in a house with a man and a baby that I had just met, relying entirely on them for food and shelter, he would probably have a heart attack."

"Well then, let's not let him find out." Jack raised a conspiratorial eyebrow. "And in the meantime, let's get out another round of beers. I want to hear about art school."

Natalie put her hands out in front of her. "Oh, no. I don't think it's a good idea to go past one beer with my boss."

Jack waved away her concern. "Don't think of me as your boss. Think of us as partners. There's nothing conventional about this business arrangement, so there doesn't need to be anything conventional about our relationship either. We're going to be two of the main influences in Carter's life, so I think we should at least be friends."

Noting his use of the words *at least*, Natalie answered, "I'd like for us to be friends too."

"Good." Jack flashed Natalie his sexy smile. "So how about that second beer?"

"No way," she said adamantly. "If I told you some of the stuff I did while I was in school, you would regret hiring me in a second."

She shuddered as she thought back to some of the ways she'd sought inspiration back in those days—raves, magic mushrooms, LSD. At least that part of her life had been tamed quite a bit. Partying had evolved into traveling, which proved to be a much more productive and rewarding source of inspiration.

"I don't see how I could ever regret that, but if you insist," Jack conceded. "You'd better get to sleep anyway. You're gonna have an early morning. Carter wakes up around six thirty."

Natalie groaned at the early wake up time but was grateful that at least she had a bed to sleep in.

6

───────

On her second official day as Jack's employee—no, partner—Natalie checked all the outlets in the apartment to make sure they had covers over them, tested the child locks on the cabinets, and added rubber bumpers on the corners of the coffee table and kitchen island.

The next day, she brought Carter down to the café to visit with Jenny and spent some time tidying up the place—namely, throwing out the dead flowers, organizing the counter space, and redoing the chalkboard menus.

On Friday, Jack dropped Carter off with his mom, and Natalie spent the day measuring every window and wall in Danny's and planning out what size art they could fit where. She even sketched out a plan to show Jack, fervently hoping that he'd let her pick out the pieces.

The next morning, she finally got a chance to tackle the poor excuse for a garden that decorated the front of Danny's Place. Donning denim shorts, a simple gray ribbed tank top, and a Red Sox hat to shield her eyes from the afternoon sun, Natalie surveyed the landscape full of weeds and decaying flora and wondered how long it had been since someone had tended to it. Jack definitely wasn't to blame for the overgrowth of unwanted vegetation.

Unable to locate gardening gloves, she embraced the messy project of pulling weeds with her bare hands. Careful not to remove anything that resembled an actual plant, she spent the next hour or so pulling out dead vegetation. It was somewhat cathartic to rip things out from their roots, and it was definitely fulfilling to see the pile of weeds grow larger and larger.

Stepping back, Natalie placed her hands on her hips and surveyed her handiwork. A few perennial plants remained that she was confident would bloom again with a little effort. Carter would probably have a blast helping her water them, and she made a mental note to pick up a little watering can when she stopped by Bartlett Farm to get new plants. Visions of the colorful wildflowers she would plant danced in her head. Coneflowers, black-eyed susans, bee balm, phlox, marigolds, goldenrod…

"Nalee! Nalee!" Carter interrupted her plotting as he barreled toward her crouching figure.

"Hey, cutie!" Natalie pulled him in for a hug and a smooch on his chubby cheek. Though they'd only been apart for twenty-four hours, it felt as if it'd been much longer after being together non-stop all week. She had grown so used to having him stuck to her side like glue.

Carter spotted the large patch of dirt Natalie had uncovered in the garden and wiggled out of her arms, plopping himself down and grabbing two handfuls of mud. He giggled maniacally as he smeared it everywhere, happy as a pig in mud.

Just as Natalie was about to extricate him from the messy situation, she noticed an older woman ambling toward Danny's with warm, soulful brown eyes that seemed far too familiar. Natalie realized that she'd seen them before, albeit on someone much younger and manlier.

"You must be Natalie." The woman held out a friendly hand, and Natalie wiped her own on her shorts before introducing herself.

"That's me," she confirmed, shaking the woman's hand.

"I'm June, Jack's mom and Carter's *Gigi*," the woman said. She looked the part of the quintessential grandmother, with her curly, gray locks and kindhearted smile.

"So nice to meet you," Natalie replied.

"You too. I've heard great things. Jack told me he hired you, and I, for one, think it's a fabulous idea. He really needs some help around here. And Carter loves you too. He talked about 'Nalee' all day long." June smiled warmly.

"Oh, that is so cute," Natalie said. "He's such a little sweetheart."

"He really is," June agreed.

"I've heard great things about you, too," Natalie added. "Jack told me you're an artist. I'd love to see your work sometime."

"Yes, that's right. I make pottery. You'll have to drop by my studio sometime."

Natalie jumped right on the idea. "I would love that!"

"I hear you're quite the artist yourself," June said, her lips twisting into a shrewd smile.

"Well, trying to be, at least," Natalie clarified, a blush creeping into her cheeks as she attempted to humbly explain herself to someone who *was* successfully making a living with her art. "But don't listen to anything Jack says—he hasn't even seen my work yet."

The corners of June's eyes crinkled as she responded, "Well, maybe not, but he seems to think very highly of you."

"Hey now, don't give away all my secrets." Jack's smooth voice floated toward them as he approached. "If she knows how valuable she is, she might want me to pay her more." All three laughed at the wisecrack.

"Hey, Mom." Jack greeted her with a peck on the cheek.

"How was the little bugger today?" he asked, plucking Carter out of the dirt. The baby squealed and put his chubby little hands on Jack's chest to steady himself, leaving Jack with two tiny, muddy handprints on his shirt.

"He was great," June replied. "It's always a pleasure to spend time with him, especially since he's the only grandchild I've got." She shot Jack a pointed look, and he rolled his eyes.

"Ok then, Mom," he said dismissively. "It was great to see you, but you'd better be going, right? Don't you have a mug or a bowl or something to make?"

"Alright, alright." June laughed, brushing her fingertips over Jack's shoulder, just above the mud stains. "I'll leave you alone. Have a good night." She gave Jack a kiss on the cheek and Carter a peck on the head. "Natalie, I hope to see you soon. My studio door is always open."

Natalie thanked June and promised she would stop by soon.

Jack huffed out a sigh as his mother retreated to her car. "She's dying for grandkids," he explained, "and she thinks I'm far too old to be a bachelor. A respectable thirty-year-old man would be married with two kids by now." His voice took on an incredulous tone as he said the last part, as if the thought was unimaginable.

"Well, you may not be married, but you're halfway there with the kids," Natalie pointed out.

"I guess." A look of confusion crossed Jack's face, like a storm cloud scarring a perfect blue sky. "It's hard for me to think of Carter as mine. I know I'm his legal guardian, but Danny will always be his dad. I keep feeling like any second he'll bust through the door and say, 'Just kidding, give me my son back!'"

Natalie sighed and placed her hand on Jack's shoulder, refraining from the urge to stroke it over his muscular arm. "Oh, Jack, that is so tough. I know what it's like to wish someone would come back, even though you know they never will."

Jack gave her a sad smile then shook his head as if to clear it. "What do you say we all head down to the beach? This guy could use a quick dip in the ocean to clean him up." Jack gestured to Carter's soiled hands. "When we come back up, I can grill some burgers for us and a hot dog for Carter."

"Sounds perfect. I could use a dip in the ocean too," Natalie said, looking down at her muddy legs and sweaty tank. "I'll just get ready and meet you guys down there."

Racing up to the apartment, she changed into her only bikini—a navy-blue number printed with a white paisley design—and threw on a cover-up, leaving her feet bare. Then she barreled down the stairs and out the door, stopping short as she spied Jack in the distance, standing waist deep in the water. His tan, sinewy upper body remained exposed, and his shoulder and bicep muscles bulged as he held Carter high up in the air.

Natalie watched as Jack dropped the baby down to dip his toes in the water, then his legs, then his stomach, gradually submerging him deeper and deeper as the boy shrieked with laughter. The scene was so adorable that she pulled out her cell phone and snapped a quick picture. Tucking her phone safely back in her beach bag, Natalie dropped it in the sand and continued on toward the ocean.

When she was halfway to the water, Jack caught sight of her and stared longer than was probably appropriate for "partners," so she decided to give him a little show. Walking toward the water, she shrugged off her cover-up and let it fall nonchalantly to the sandy floor beneath her, then she tugged her hair out of its ponytail and shook her head to free the wild mane that had developed due to a day out in the humidity. At the water's edge, she waded in until her stomach was submerged then dove under the surface, swimming the rest of the way to Jack and Carter.

Jack blinked as Natalie emerged from the surface of the water. "That was quite an entrance," he drawled.

Natalie smirked. "I couldn't wait to get in the water. I really worked up a sweat with all that gardening." She wiped her forehead with the back of her hand.

"Maybe this will help." Jack's mouth quirked up in a smirk of its own as he splashed some of the cool water at her. Carter squealed with delight when Natalie jumped back, sticking his tiny hand in the water and giving his best attempt at splashing her too.

Natalie gasped playfully. "I should have expected it from him, but you, Carter? You little traitor." She reached for the boy, and he came easily into her arms, giggling the whole time. Splashing water back at Jack, Natalie used Carter as a shield when he tried to reciprocate.

"Oh, it's on now," Jack declared, sweeping his arms into the water and sending a deluge toward Natalie and the baby. They both shrieked and fought back.

"Two on one," Natalie challenged with a cock of her brow. "I'll take those odds."

The predatory glint in Jack's eyes sent a burst of heat through her, scorching her insides. Her heart rate picked up as his mouth curved into a mischievous smile. The look on his face made her think of other activities that got one's heart rate up—things that couldn't be done in the middle of a busy beach—but the internal blaze was quickly drowned by another large splash.

Natalie recovered from her momentary distraction as Jack's latest assault soaked her. "Get him, Carter!" she shrieked.

Winding up his arm, the boy heaved a small amount of water toward Jack with all his might. Jack clutched his chest and fell dramatically back into the ocean as Natalie giggled and high-fived Carter. "Nice one."

Jack popped up out of the water with his arms in the air.

"Don't think you're getting off that easy," he warned as he stalked over to them like a lion hunting his prey. Plucking Carter out of Natalie's arms, he tucked the boy into his chest and grabbed Natalie around the waist, spinning her around while she squealed.

"What are you doing?" she yelped, painfully aware of Jack's hand on her hip, just above the skimpy string that made up her bikini.

"This is much more effective than splashing, don't you think?" he asked as he dragged her through the water for one more swift spin then abruptly let go. The rapid change in velocity had Natalie sinking like a stone. After a moment, she broke through the surface of the water, sputtering and blinking the salt out of her eyes.

Jack's low chuckle brought her back to the present moment. "See, Carter? That's how you do it," he was saying.

"Oh, you fight dirty." Natalie shook her head in dismay. Jack's gaze swung to hers then lowered. Her bikini top had gotten jostled in the fray, revealing more skin than it should but nothing indecent. She didn't adjust it. If Jack was fighting dirty, so would she.

While he stared at her chest, Natalie scooped her hands through the water and sent a torrent toward him, distracting him so she could sneak around and jump onto his back.

"Ah!" he called out as she mounted him, wrapping her arms around his chest and securing Carter with her hands, just in case she threw Jack off balance. He momentarily dipped lower in the water under her weight but quickly righted himself, keeping the baby above the surface.

"Oh, so that's how it's going to be?" he asked, his voice low and menacing. That inner warmth spread through Natalie like wildfire.

"You stole my shield," she reminded him, her mouth right next to his ear. "So now I'm using you as one."

"Let's see how that works out for you." Jack tightened his

grip on Carter and flopped onto his back, sending Natalie under the water again. She closed her eyes and mouth before the salt could infiltrate them, quickly letting go of Jack so she could stand up again.

"Ok, ok, I give up," she giggled, squeezing the excess water out of her hair. "You win this time."

Jack wiped Carter's eyes, though he didn't seem to mind the moisture, water baby that he was. "You're giving up that easily?"

The challenge in his tone tickled Natalie's competitive instincts. "Oh, trust me, if there wasn't a baby involved, you'd be toast," she promised.

Jack's eyebrows rose up in playful disbelief. "Is that so?"

"It most certainly is," Natalie said, reaching down to adjust her bikini back into its proper position. When Jack's eyes followed her every move, she knew that, despite forfeiting the splash fight, she was the real winner.

7

———————

The next day marked one week on Nantucket as well as Natalie's first day off. She'd been so caught up in learning the ropes at Danny's and caring for Carter that she'd barely had time to worry about her deal with Ned. Now, as she stood in front of an empty canvas, her stomach sunk under the realization that she had three months to get her groove back, or she'd be slinking to Griff with her tail between her legs to ask for money.

Stretching her neck to each side, she cracked her knuckles until they produced a satisfying *pop*. Standing before her easel should have elicited all sorts of feelings—possibility, motivation, vision. Instead, Natalie only felt dread. What if she couldn't come up with a good concept, let alone ten good concepts? What if she never made a decent painting again?

Tapping the end of her paintbrush against her lip, she glanced out the window of her bedroom. There was a long stretch of golden sand bisected by a rock jetty, a lifeguard's chair standing tall and proud, and ocean waves lapping lazily at the shoreline. The view was breathtaking and the perfect landscape for her first painting on Nantucket.

With a sigh, Natalie squeezed a few colors of paint onto her palette, hoping to do the sight justice. The cloudless sky seemed like a good place to start, so she slowly tinted a dollop of white paint with some cerulean, a bit of ultramarine, and just a touch of yellow ochre to warm up the color. With a bit of experimentation, she created the exact shade of blue she saw out her window.

The first stroke of her brush on the canvas finally brought a satisfied smile to Natalie's face. No matter how many hours she had spent painting in her lifetime, the fulfillment of creating something from nothing never faded. The smooth glide of a saturated brush over canvas was a meditative act.

Natalie blocked out the rest of the world as she recreated the beach scene outside her window. It could have been a few minutes or a few hours before the slamming of a door broke her focus. Stepping back to observe her work, she realized she must have been at it for hours, because she'd laid down the base colors of the sky, sand, ocean, and jetty and added most of the details to the waves and rocks. The ocean in the picture looked so much like the one outside the window, with its bands of different shades of blue and green topped with sparkling white foam.

The colors were right and the proportions correct. It looked realistic, and it was technically sound, but it also looked like every other painting of a beach ever made. There was nothing unique about it. It still lacked that originality that she desperately wanted back.

Ned's words from back when he was Natalie's professor echoed in her brain. *It's good, but not good enough. Keep working.* Those words had never been aimed toward her, of course, but toward her peers. Back in art school, as a bright-eyed coed with a whole lot of fresh ideas, Natalie had been a star student, always coming up with original ideas and finding fresh new ways to make her work unique.

Ned and her other professors had expected a lot of her,

and she'd always delivered. Five years later, it seemed that Natalie had lost that streak. She desperately wanted to deliver ten spectacular paintings to Ned, not only so she wouldn't have to repay the five thousand dollars, but also to prove to herself that being an artist was her true calling, and she did deserve to pursue it as a career.

Groaning, Natalie put her brushes down on the easel's ledge. On a deep breath, she rubbed her eyes, hoping that when she opened them again, the painting would magically look more special. To her dismay, it did not.

Maybe a long walk on the beach would spark something inside of her. She decided to dedicate her afternoon to studying every inch of the beach. Once she got to know her subject on an intimate level, it would be much easier to paint it.

Jack's brisk footsteps reverberated throughout the apartment, coming to an abrupt stop in the doorway to her room. Natalie turned to see him standing there, his gaze fixed on her painting. "Wow, Nat. That's incredible. It looks just like our beach."

She shrugged doubtfully. "It's a decent start."

"A damn good start," he argued, stepping farther into the room to examine her artwork.

"Just nine more to go once this one is finished," Natalie said with a sigh, looking over Jack's shoulder to analyze her work. All she saw was generic, unoriginal predictability. Yet, as Jack's gaze flicked between the window and the canvas, his eyebrows drew together, and he asked, "How are you not rich and famous by now?"

Natalie let out a nervous chuckle and began gathering up her used brushes. "You'll have to ask all the gallery owners who have turned me down for showings. Apparently, they don't think my paintings are worth the big bucks."

"Then they're fools," Jack said. When Natalie glanced

over at him, his gaze bore intently into hers. "Your work is amazing."

She picked at a speck of dried paint that clung to the handle of a paint brush. "Thanks, Jack." In her head, Natalie downplayed his appreciation because she knew this wasn't her best work, but secretly, she was quite pleased that he liked her painting. Lately, it had seemed as if Griff was right about her career as an artist being ridiculous. Jack's words reminded her that not everyone felt that way.

He scratched his head, eyeing the handful of dirty paint brushes she held. "I'm sorry to ask you this on your first day off, but I could really use your help," he said. "Derek called out, so I'm working behind the counter, and Carter is tearing my office apart down there. Apparently, two coloring books and three different snacks isn't enough to keep a toddler occupied for even a single hour. Would you mind watching him for a bit?"

Jack glanced down at his watch and combed his fingers through his hair, a clear indication of his rising stress level.

Natalie pulled her bottom lip between her teeth. "I was planning to go to the beach today to gather inspiration for the rest of this painting."

She didn't get many days off in this deal she had with Jack, and it was frustrating enough that inspiration wasn't coming easily. It would be aggravating to lose even more time by being called to work on a Sunday.

"Maybe you could just take Carter with you?" Jack suggested, his desperate tone tinged with hope that softened Natalie's resolve.

She sighed as she dumped the brushes into a bucket she'd prepared with a turpentine solution to soak. Though she hated having her plans foiled, she couldn't stand feeling like she was letting someone down. She'd done enough of that in her lifetime.

"Sure," she relented, "but for the record, I'm only doing

this because you're desperate. I take my art very seriously and plan to dedicate my weekends to it."

Jack put his hands together in thanks. "Thank you, Natalie. This won't happen again."

Though she wasn't convinced of that, Natalie supposed helping Jack out was worth witnessing the sexy smile that spread across his face at her agreement.

She followed him down the stairs to Danny's and had to press her lips together to hold back laughter at the scene she found in his office. Papers were strewn about everywhere, many of them covered in scribbles of primary-colored crayon. A heap of soggy, half-eaten crackers sat upon the desk next to a sippy cup, out of which poured a steady trickle of milk onto the floor. Carter was in the corner, watching a video on Jack's phone, happily munching away on a banana as if he wasn't in the middle of a veritable disaster zone.

Jack groaned from the doorway, and Natalie scooped the boy up, returning the phone to its rightful owner. "I can help you clean this up later," she offered as she hurried out of the room with Carter. Opening the back door, she released him onto the beach, where he took off running.

Natalie loved watching Carter explore the open expanse of sand. Every so often, he would crouch down, fascinated by something nestled in amongst the granules. Usually, it was a shell or a bug, and he would run over to her and proudly present her with a treasure squished between his chubby little fingers.

Down at the water's edge, Natalie began building a sand-castle with a bucket, inviting Carter to help her by scooping in the sand. Once full, she turned it over and showed him how to tap on the bottom to release the sand tower. He seemed to enjoy the building process, but it turned out that destroying the castle was much more fun, and Carter gleefully smashed tower after tower as Natalie built them.

In the middle of their game, a little boy with jet-black hair wandered over and began laughing at what Carter was doing. The boy looked to be about the same age and enthusiastically joined in his demolition. Natalie looked around for a parent or caregiver, but there were no other adults in sight.

"Hey, buddy," she addressed the little boy. "Are you lost?" He looked up at her and laughed, showing no signs of distress. Natalie decided to keep him busy and wait for someone to come looking for him.

The three of them continued their game with Natalie working twice as fast so both little boys would have towers to crush. Carter let out a full belly laugh every time the other boy smashed a tower, and they seemed to be competing for who could make a bigger mess. Carter really seemed to enjoy having someone his own size to play with, and it dawned on Natalie that he probably didn't get much interaction with other babies. She decided that there would have to be some play dates in their future.

"Justin? Justin!" came a distraught female voice. "Oh, baby, there you are!"

The woman ran over to them in a frenzy, her curly black hair barely restrained by a pair of sunglasses, and her tank top askew over her bathing suit. Sweeping up the little lost boy in her arms, she exhaled forcefully. "Justin, don't you ever run off like that again! You scared Mommy half to death!"

Justin laughed and struggled to get out of his mother's arms. With another heavy sigh, she plopped him back on the ground so he could continue playing with Carter.

Shaking her head wearily at Natalie, the woman said, "I am so sorry about that. I turned away for one second, and he ran off. I thought he'd gone over to the swing set up the beach, so I went right there, which sent me off track. That's why it took me so long to find him. Gosh, you must think I'm a horrible mom."

"Please," Natalie huffed, thinking of her own mother's distinct lack of interest in or concern for her whereabouts.

"It's no problem. It can be tough to keep track of these little guys."

"You've got that right. I'm Dana," the woman said, "and this little troublemaker here is my son, Justin."

"I'm Natalie, and this is Carter." Natalie shook Dana's hand and gestured to the baby playing at her feet. He looked enough like her, with his blond hair and blue eyes, to be her son. She frowned, remembering the vow she had made to herself long ago to never have kids. There was no way she would risk hurting a child like her mother had hurt her. *Never stop moving. Never settle. Never do what she did.*

"Wait, isn't that Danny Flynn's son? Such a sad story." Dana shook her head wistfully. "I thought Jack McNally had him now?"

"Yes, Jack's his guardian. I'm their new nanny," Natalie explained. "Well, nanny slash handywoman. I'm helping out with fixing up the café, working there, and watching Carter so Jack can have time to run it."

"Wow," Dana said, her eyebrows shooting up. "That's quite a job. I hope he's paying you well."

Natalie chuckled nervously. "Actually, I'm working for him in exchange for free rent. I came to the island without a place to stay, and he offered me a room if I would work for him."

Dana's forehead wrinkled. "I see. That sounds like a great deal, but I wouldn't share it too widely. Word spreads quickly among the locals. They'll consider it the next big scandal. I can see the headline now: 'Jack McNally Finds Mistress to Take Care of Dead Best Friend's Son.'"

Horrified by that thought, Natalie quickly assured her that the situation was far from scandalous. "Jack and I aren't together. We're just living together while I work for him."

"Trust me, I know how these people think," Dana replied. "I used to write a human-interest column for the local newspaper, *The Inquirer and Mirror*, before Justin was born, and people clung to the scandalous stories like rescue floats. Plus,

Jack is a good guy, but he used to have a bit of a reputation. I want people to realize that he's changed his life around."

"He really has," Natalie agreed. "He told me a bit about himself before Carter came into his life, and it seems like he's so much more responsible now."

"Well, he's obviously doing a good job if he found a nanny as wonderful as you," Dana said with a friendly smile. Turning her attention to the two boys playing side by side in the sand, she suggested, "We should get them together for a play date sometime. They seem to be getting along well."

"Absolutely," Natalie agreed. "That would be great."

"And the two of us should go on a little adult play date sometime. I'd love to show you around the island," Dana offered.

"I would love that," Natalie replied sincerely. She'd been so busy with Jack and Carter that she hadn't really had time to meet anyone else. A night on the town with Dana would be really fun.

"I could seriously use some adult company," Dana said. "I have practically every children's silly song memorized, and I can tell you the plot of every *Sesame Street* episode ever aired."

"I know what you mean, and I haven't even been taking care of Carter for very long. I can only imagine how you must feel."

"It's tough," Dana confessed. "My husband, Ryan, and I are able to get out on a date night every once in a while, but other than that, it's baby time twenty-four seven. It can really wear you down, but that's why we should get together sometime. Maybe the men can watch the boys, and us ladies can hit the town."

"That sounds awesome," Natalie said, hoping they would be able to make it happen sooner than later. She didn't know how long she would be on Nantucket for, so she wanted to embrace every opportunity.

"Here, I'll give you my number." Dana held out her hand for Natalie's phone, where she added herself as a contact.

"Let's get together soon, and we can both indulge in some actual adult conversation," Dana said before scooping up Justin.

"Sounds good," Natalie replied. "I'll see you soon!"

8

W orking behind the counter the next morning at Danny's, Natalie saw Dana once again, this time childless and clambering for caffeine.

"Coffee, coffee, coffee," Dana chanted as she sped to the register, her frizzy black hair tucked into a baseball cap. Natalie was starting to get the feeling that frazzled was Dana's natural state.

She raised an eyebrow. "In a rush?"

"Taking advantage of an hour without Justin," Dana explained as she took a seat at the bar. "Where's your little one?"

"Jack took him to get some new clothes this morning," Natalie explained as she filled a to-go cup with coffee from the carafe. "He's growing like a weed."

"They do that." Dana rustled through her purse for her wallet.

"Milk, cream, or sugar?" Natalie asked.

"No, no, and no," Dana replied as she slammed a five-dollar bill on the counter. "Don't leave room for anything non-caffeinated."

Natalie chuckled and pressed a lid onto the cup before

handing it to Dana. "There you go—one cup of pure caffeine."

Dana took a sip and let out an exaggerated groan. "You're a goddess," she said as she rose from her seat at the bar. "I'm off to enjoy the remaining"—she looked down at her watch—"forty-six baby-free minutes of my day."

"Have fun." Natalie waved to her, enjoying the novelty of having a customer that she knew. It made her feel at home, like she was a real Nantucketer now. Though she also enjoyed serving strangers and getting to meet a wide variety of people with different perspectives. It made for good conversation, even when she knew she'd probably never see them again.

The newly installed bell at the top of the door chimed as a man walked in with his daughter, who looked to be about six. The two of them got settled into stools at the bar, and Natalie gave them a moment to discuss what they wanted before going to take their orders.

"Hmm…" The father stroked his chin as if he had a long beard. "I'd like to order sixteen pieces of blueberry pie, please."

The little girl burst out laughing beside him, bringing an instant smile to Natalie's lips.

"That's way too much for us, Daddy!" the girl said between fits of giggles.

"Oh, really? But I'm pretty darn hungry," he replied with mock seriousness.

The little girl turned authoritatively toward Natalie. "We'll have two slices of pie please."

"You've got it," Natalie said, impressed by the little girl's eloquence. She grabbed the slices of pie and slid them onto two separate plates while the father-daughter duo kept chatting away. They reminded her a bit of her and Griff back in their vacationing days. She briefly wondered if she and Griff would have stopped by Danny's, had it existed all those years ago.

"Thank you," the little girl said politely as Natalie slid their plates across the counter.

"No problem. Enjoy!" she said just as Derek came over to dismiss her for her lunch break. Untying her apron, Natalie hung it on a hook in the back room and walked out the door to the beach.

The father and daughter had ignited a spark of guilt in her. She'd put off calling Griff again for far too long because their last conversation had been so draining, but she needed to at least let him know she'd officially found a job. Though Natalie knew Griff would be happy to hear that, she was sure he'd still have a few choice words for her regarding her life decisions.

Leaning her back against Danny's, Natalie gazed out toward the ocean, hoping it might inspire a sense of calm. The waves seemed to be crashing more angrily than usual, which didn't bode well.

Griff answered on the third ring with an unfriendly, "Yeah?"

"Hi, Dad," Natalie said. "How are you?"

"I'm fine," he answered, "and you?"

"I'm good," she replied, running her toes through the sand to soothe her nerves. Raking sand was supposed to be relaxing, right? Didn't some therapists have those little zen gardens on their desks? The motion didn't seem to be helping, and Natalie's stomach knotted as she said, "I found a job here."

"You're still on Nantucket?" Griff asked, the incredulity in his tone irritating her.

"Yes, I'm still on Nantucket."

"What foolish job have you found yourself this time?" he grumbled.

Natalie took a deep breath to keep from cursing him out. "Well," she answered calmly. "I'm nannying and working at a café."

"Oh yeah?" Griff asked. "And that's making you enough

money to afford a place on Nantucket?" Of course he was worried about the money.

"If you must know, the man I'm nannying for is renting me a room in his apartment in exchange for watching his baby," Natalie said.

"The *man* you're nannying for? You're living with him?" Griff asked. "What is that supposed to mean?"

Calm evaded Natalie as she felt Griff's judgment radiating through the phone. "It means that he's a single father who was struggling to raise a child alone. Sound familiar?" she snapped.

"Now, don't start in on me, Natalie. I did my best with you," Griff said loudly. "It's not my fault your mother left us. She had a mind of her own. You of all people should understand."

"Oh yeah, and why is that?" Natalie asked, her own voice beginning to rise. Her patience could only hold out for so long.

"Because you're just like her!" Griff exploded. "You left me just like she did to pursue some silly career *just like she did*. Here you are, gallivanting around Nantucket, living with some stranger! That's not real life, Natalie. You're just kidding your-self. Just like her."

Though he had always been tough on her, Griff had never come right out and blatantly likened Natalie to her mother. "Is that really what you think?" Natalie whispered as tears filled her eyes, threatening to spill over. "That I'm just like her?"

"Of course!" Griff answered. "When you left me to go to art school, it was like your mother leaving me all over again."

"Why would you say that?" Natalie wailed, tears escaping her eyes and beginning to stream down her face. "I didn't ditch an entire family like she did. I went to college, Dad. Like most kids do."

"You went to art school," he scoffed. "You can hardly call

that college. Look at you. You've got a degree, and you still have to work strange jobs to support yourself!"

Natalie put her fingers to her temple and closed her eyes. Griff wasn't wrong, but she wasn't in the mood to talk about it. "I'm not arguing with you about art school, Dad. It was eight years ago. I was eighteen. That's when most kids move out and move on. I didn't leave behind a spouse or a helpless little child. What I did was nothing like what Mom did!"

Natalie took a shaky breath as she waited for Griff to respond, but nothing could have prepared her for what came out of his mouth next.

"Your mom left our family to try and become a singer. Did you know that? She followed some girl band around like a groupie for months. Apparently, she thought they'd start letting her open for them. Fat chance of that ever working out. That's no better than trying to make a career out of painting. You silly, silly girls have no grasp on reality."

Natalie's mouth dropped open. Her mother had left their family to pursue a singing career? Griff had never told her that. He'd always just said she couldn't handle raising a child and had run away. This entire time, Natalie had been wrong. She'd been *lied* to.

Though the revelation was still fresh, it began to make sense why Griff had always compared her to her mother. Her choice of a creative career and constant travels, not unlike a music tour, were both reminiscent of her mother's choices. However, understanding where Griff was coming from didn't mean that she thought he was right.

Gathering her wits, Natalie prepared to respond. "I never knew that," she said quietly, "but it doesn't change anything. Just because we both pursued our dreams doesn't mean that my leaving you was like her leaving you. I did what most eighteen-year-olds do. Most mothers don't leave their families."

"Oh, come on, Natalie. You disgraced this family just as much as she did, if not more," Griff spat. "Look at what you're doing with your life now, moving from place to place like some kind of vagrant. It's ridiculous! You can't even settle down for more than a few months. Remind you of anyone?"

His tone was so condescending, so hurtful, and though Natalie had experienced plenty of ugly arguments with her father, this one had to be the worst. Was it the fact that she was on Nantucket that had him so up in arms?

Reining in her tears and steeling herself, Natalie turned to the phone. "I have news for you, Dad," she hissed. "I'd rather be like her than like you, because at least she's out there living her life. You're just carrying out a lonely, miserable existence because you can't even try to understand someone else's perspective for two seconds. No wonder no one can stand to be around you."

"How dare you talk to me like that, young lady!" Griff roared. "You have no right to judge me."

"I'm done talking to you," Natalie replied coldly. "I didn't call you today to fight. I called because I thought you might actually be interested in what I was up to, but I guess I was wrong. You only care about feeling bad for yourself."

She hung up without waiting to hear his reply. As soon as she hit the *End Call* button, tears began flowing again. How could she have missed that all those years? How could the truth have evaded her for so long?

Griff had never supported her. He'd always told her how he thought she was unrealistic and a failure, but Natalie had never realized that it all stemmed from his comparison of her to her mother, who she had spent her entire life trying *not* to be like. She'd never let herself settle down for long enough that leaving would cause heartbreak. She was careful not to lead guys on by letting them believe they had a future with her. She'd created a life that revolved around being the antithesis of her mother. And yet, to Griff, they were so much the same.

"Natalie?" Jack's voice, warm and silky, came from behind her. *Shit.*

Wiping her eyes with the backs of her hands, she turned around and faked a smile, though it was pointless since her eyes were red and swollen already.

"Hi, Jack," she said in a broken voice.

He hurried over to her and put a hand on her arm, rubbing it up and down comfortingly. "Hey, are you ok?"

"Um…" Natalie tried to reply, but a fresh wave of tears hit.

"Come here." Jack pulled her into his arms and held her in his warm embrace as she cried softly into his chest. Though Natalie hated showing vulnerability like this, her father had been so cold, and Jack's arms were so warm. She simply couldn't resist.

His gentle fingertips trailed up and down her back. "Shh," he whispered softly in her ear until her tears finally subsided. Pulling back, Jack cradled her cheeks in his big hands. "Do you want to talk about it?" he asked, concern clouding his handsome face.

Natalie sniffled inelegantly. "How much of that did you hear?"

"Enough to know that something's got you really upset. Is it family stuff?" he asked.

She sniffled again, desperately hoping there was no snot anywhere on her face. "Something like that. My dad basically just brought up decades worth of shit that apparently he's been holding in my whole life."

"Seriously?"

"Seriously."

Jack swiped a thumb beneath Natalie's eyes to clear away the fresh tears. "Your dad sounds like a real dick," he said, coaxing a slight chuckle out of her.

"Thanks," she said, appreciating Jack's support, even if his claims didn't remove the sting of Griff's words.

"Is there anything I can do for you?" he asked.

"No, you just being here is all I need."

Wrapping him up in another hug, Natalie relished the feeling of Jack's strong arms and wished the strength he held could be transferred into her own body. It was nice to feel both the physical and emotional support of someone else, and Jack's embrace in particular felt like a balm. She didn't want to read too much into why that was, deciding just to enjoy it instead.

"Let's get lunch," she suggested as she pulled away, ready to put her phone call with Griff behind her. No use lingering on the topic. That's what Griff had done for over twenty years, and look where that had gotten him: alone, bitter, and yelling at the only family he had left.

9

———

Still reeling from her call with Griff the day before, Natalie appreciated the peace and quiet that came along with putting Carter down for his nap. Aside from the muffled sound of crashing waves, total silence filled the room. As had become their routine, she rocked the baby until he fell asleep then idly rubbed his back for a few more minutes to make sure it stuck before gently transferring him to his crib.

Planning to try and fit in an hour or two of painting while Carter napped, Natalie exited to the kitchen and found Jack hunched over the kitchen island, frowning down at his phone and intently typing a message.

"Hey. Everything okay?" she asked, knowing he didn't usually leave the café during peak hours.

Letting out a pent-up breath, Jack looked up from his phone. "Jenny was supposed to be helping out behind the counter, but she got caught up in one of her wild baking adventures and insists she can't step away. Apparently, you need to bake cheesecake to the perfect internal temperature, and she needs to check it every few minutes." He shook his head as if the idea was ludicrous. "Anyway, I texted Derek to see if he could cover, but he's busy. Any chance you could bring the baby monitor down with you and help me behind the counter for a bit?"

Natalie's shoulders drooped. "Are you sure you need me? I was going to try and finish that painting I started over the weekend." *Not that I have any creative vision for it,* she added silently to herself.

Jack removed his Boston Strong baseball cap to scratch his head. "There's no one else."

Natalie rolled her eyes at the guilt trip but supposed it was true that there was no one else he could call. Danny's only had four employees, after all.

"Fine, but maybe you need to hire someone else if business is picking up," she said. "I can't keep dropping what I'm doing to cover your ass. Don't forget that I'm here to paint."

Jack pursed his lips as he put his hat back on. "Right. I know, and I will hire someone as soon as we can afford it," he promised.

Natalie raised her eyebrows, testing his truthfulness. Though she was happy to help him out in a pinch, it was starting to seem like there was a pinch every week. She was never going to hit ten paintings for Ned if she wasn't able to finish even one.

"I will," Jack repeated with gusto before turning back to his cell phone. "I'm going to call my mom to see if she can come take Carter when he wakes up. I'll need you until closing."

"All afternoon?" Natalie asked in disbelief. There went any chance of fitting in some painting before the sun set. "What about when Jenny finishes the cheesecake?"

Jack threw his arms up. "I don't know. She said something about macarons. I have no idea what she's talking about half the time, but she's damn good at what she does, and her baking is one of the only things bringing in customers right now, so I'm not going to question it."

"OK." Natalie put her hands up in surrender. Jack was clearly close to the edge, and she didn't want to be the one to push him over. "I'll be right down."

There were a few customers seated at the bar when she arrived, and Jack was already behind the counter, throwing sandwiches together. Natalie grabbed an apron, tied it behind her back, and got to work.

"Where do you want me?" she asked.

Jack pointed to the shiny silver commercial coffee machine on the counter. "Drinks, please. There are a couple of tickets already there."

Plucking the tickets off the machine, Natalie began preparing a couple of lattes, a cappuccino, and—bless this final customer—a plain, single shot of espresso. She was serving the drinks just as Jack was serving the sandwiches. They headed to the register at the same time and bumped into each other, colliding a bit harder than expected in their haste.

Jack grunted and wrapped an arm around Natalie's waist to steady her. She froze momentarily, the awkward embrace feeling surprisingly pleasant. Her mind flashed to when Jack had spun her around during their splash fight, and then when he'd held her after her dismal conversation with Griff. As usual, his hold was so firm, so secure. Was it wrong that she found it so comforting to be in her boss's—no, partner's —arms?

"Sorry," she mumbled, trying to step back.

"My bad." Jack dropped his hand. "I'm rushing."

"No problem," Natalie replied, rubbing her arm absent-mindedly.

Jack looked toward the customers waiting to pay. "Would you mind manning the register while I go call my mom? Carter will be up soon, and I want to make sure she's here."

Natalie nodded eagerly, hoping she didn't look as flustered as she felt. Jack reached out to squeeze her shoulder in thanks before departing for his office.

Momentarily distracted, she lifted her hand to the spot where his had been. Every time Jack touched her, no matter how casual, she felt it in her bones. Perhaps his touch affected her simply because most of her human contact lately had occurred with an eighteen-month-old, but she suspected it was more than that. The more she got to know Jack, the more she liked him. He was laid back but took his responsibilities seriously. He had a mischievous streak but was so caring that no one would ever mistake his kind heart. Not to mention that his lean build, dark hair, and smattering of stubble hit all of her hot buttons.

The only problem was that Jack was the one man she shouldn't be interested in. He controlled her access to food, shelter, and everything else on the island. If she messed things up with him by getting too involved and inevitably hurting him, she'd have to leave Nantucket. Then, she may never get her inspiration back, and she could kiss her dignity goodbye because she'd be asking Griff to pay Ned back.

With a sigh, Natalie dropped her hand and proceeded to the register. She'd just finished ringing up the awaiting customers and had served two more lattes and a pastry when Jack returned, looking as handsome as ever in dark jeans and a clean white t-shirt he must have just changed into. He'd turned his baseball cap backwards and something about that and the single curl that had escaped out the front of it stirred Natalie's insides.

"My mom's going to pick Carter up and keep him for a sleepover tonight," Jack said. "She's thrilled to have some extra time with him this week."

"That's great," Natalie replied absently, her focus on not outright ogling him.

"Yeah, he loves staying with her. She always gives him way too much dessert." Jack's sly smile told her that fact didn't upset him all that much.

"It's a grandmother's job to spoil her grandbabies,"

Natalie replied then turned back to the coffee machine, unwilling to risk the potential repercussions of looking at Jack for too long. Who knew what she might do if she did?

They worked the rest of the shift side by side, operating like a well-oiled machine. Natalie took orders and rang them up while Jack prepared food. If people only ordered drinks, whoever was available would make them. There were no more collisions, but then again, Natalie was being extra careful not to rush and risk ending up in Jack's enticing embrace again.

As the hours went on, business dwindled, and by closing time, the place was empty. They locked the doors right at six o'clock, and Jack took out two wet washcloths for them to clean the surfaces in the café. Natalie wiped down the bar in a circular motion, and when she looked over at Jack, he was doing the same thing at almost the exact same pace.

As though sensing her stare, he glanced over and smiled. "We work well together."

"We do," she agreed. "When we're not bumping into each other."

"I didn't mind," Jack said, holding her gaze and smiling at her a little too long before returning to his task. Natalie tore her eyes away from him and blinked. If he was going to blatantly flirt with her, it was going to be a lot harder to ignore her attraction.

They continued cleaning, Natalie wiping down tables while Jack wiped down machinery, until every surface shined and gleamed like it was brand new. Meeting in the back room, they threw their dirty rags and aprons into the washing machine and set it to run.

Jack yawned and cracked his knuckles. "Man, I'm hungry."

"Me too. I think I forgot to eat all afternoon," Natalie admitted.

"What do you say we go grab a burger? My mom's already got Carter for the evening."

She knew she should decline. She should go upstairs and try to continue her painting, even though the dwindling daylight would make it more difficult to color match the beach. She definitely shouldn't spend yet another night hanging out with Jack because, while being into your boss was ill-advised, getting involved with him outside of work was downright foolish—no matter what title he preferred to go by.

Despite all the thoughts that ran through her mind about why it was a bad idea, she found herself saying, "Sure. That sounds great."

☼ ☼ ☼

The Shack was a staple on Nantucket, sitting atop a huge dune at Surfside Beach and serving typical beach fare. As soon as Jack's Jeep entered the parking lot, it was encased by the tantalizing scent of fried food, and he insisted Natalie try their famous Krabby Patty, a burger made out of crab, shrimp, and scallop.

Choosing to trust the Nantucket local with her order, Natalie grabbed a picnic table with a great view while Jack waited for the food. Then, closing her eyes, she listened to the crashing waves and took a few deep breaths, allowing the salty ocean breeze to fill her lungs. There was really nothing like island air.

She vaguely registered footsteps before Jack's voice broke the tranquility of the moment. "Did you fall asleep sitting up? Did I really tire you out that much?" he teased.

Natalie opened one eye and saw that he'd returned with their food. "No," she replied, opening the other eye to give him—and the food—her full attention. "I was just enjoying the sound of the waves."

"There's nothing better." Jack handed her one of the sandwiches. "You can hear it from our place too, you know. You don't have to come all the way out here."

The term "our place" had Natalie hesitating for a moment before responding, "I know, but I haven't gotten my fill of it yet. You've lived here forever. You've always gotten to hear the ocean. I'm making up for lost time."

"Fair enough." Jack took a big bite of his burger, and she took a smaller one of her own to make sure she liked the taste.

"Mmm," she moaned as the flavors hit her taste buds. The salty shellfish nestled within the buttery bun was a potent combination. Natalie couldn't get enough of the seafood on Nantucket and planned to enjoy it thoroughly while it lasted. "Good call on the Krabby Patties."

Jack threw her a thumbs up and continued chowing down on his own.

"I've lived plenty of places with beaches," Natalie mused. "Most recently, I was in Colorado. Great mountains, but the lake beaches just don't do it for me."

"I agree. I'm an ocean guy all the way," Jack said.

Natalie studied him for a moment, his strong jaw working as he chewed. "Have you ever wanted to move away from Nantucket?" she asked.

Jack swallowed and shrugged. "Never really thought about it. I've got everything I need here."

"Your brothers left," she pointed out.

"My brothers left because the island couldn't offer them what they needed," he said. "For Fletcher, that was college, and for Beau, it was the police academy. I was a bartender, and there are plenty of bars here."

Jack's bitter tone reminded Natalie that his brothers' success was a point of contention, so she went with a different tactic. "Haven't you ever just wanted a new adventure?"

Jack smiled wryly. "I've kind of got a new adventure going on right here, right now."

Natalie chuckled. "I guess you're right. I've just never been able to stay in one place too long. I get restless."

"Why?" he asked around his burger.

It was her turn to shrug. "I guess it's my artistic nature. If I stay in one place too long, I lose my inspiration. The only way to find it again is to go somewhere new."

"Huh," Jack said thoughtfully. "My mom's been here her whole life, and she still seems pretty inspired."

Natalie thought about his words for a moment. Realistically, she knew that plenty of artists settled in one location. She also knew that her art was only part of the reason she stayed on the move. It was true that travel helped keep her inspired, but deep down, she knew there was a lot more to it than that.

Natalie didn't realize she'd been silent for many moments until Jack asked, "You ok?"

Her gaze snapped up to his. "Yeah, just thinking," she said.

"About what?"

She sighed heavily. "I don't just travel because of my art," she admitted. "I'm also wary of settling down because of what happened with my mom. She wasn't made to settle down, but she tried to, and she ended up leaving and really hurting me and my dad. I can't risk doing that to anyone."

Jack sat back and studied her with an assessing gaze. "What makes you think that you would?"

Natalie took a bite of her sandwich to procrastinate answering that. "Because I'm a lot like her," she eventually said in a soft voice.

"What makes you think *that?*" he repeated.

Natalie took a long sip of her drink, mentally debating whether or not to bring up Griff's latest revelations. In the end, she decided that Jack would be understanding. He dealt with his own issues of parental comparison, so she trusted that he would be empathetic to her situation.

"Remember when you found me crying after that phone call with my dad?"

Jack nodded, silently encouraging her to go on.

"He told me some things that I never knew about my mom."

"Things like what?" he asked.

Natalie took a deep breath and sighed it out. "He told me that my mom left our family to try and become a singer."

She paused, and Jack gently urged her on by asking, "A singer?"

Natalie nodded. "Yeah, apparently she followed this girl group on tour and never came back. She left to pursue her craft, just like I did. My dad's been comparing me to her all these years, and I never quite understood it, but now I do. When I left for art school to pursue a career he deemed unrealistic, it reminded him of my mom leaving to do the same thing."

Jack nodded thoughtfully. "I can see where it would remind him of that, but it's totally different. You were a kid trying to make your way in the world. She was an adult abandoning a family."

Natalie banged her hand on the table, relieved that Jack saw her side. "That's exactly what I said!" she cried then sat back slowly, thinking of the many years Griff had judged her based on something her mother had done. "The problem is, now I'm realizing that I'm even more like her than I ever thought."

Jack gave her a sympathetic, closed-mouth smile. "That doesn't mean you *have* to be like her. You always have a choice, Natalie."

She looked up at him. "Do I? I share her DNA. She wasn't made to settle down, and neither was I."

Jack ran a finger over his chin. "You'll never know if you never try."

Natalie finished off her last bite before replying, "No, but I can be pretty sure."

Jack watched her for a moment, having finished his burger

long before her. "Ready to head home? Or do you want to stay for the sunset?" he finally asked.

"Oh, Jack, let's stay!" Sunset was Natalie's favorite time of day and always brought her a warm sense of comfort.

"Come on." He took her hand and led her down the dune to the beach. They made their way to the empty lifeguard chair and sat on the base of it, resting their backs against the chair's legs.

Jack let go of her hand when they sat down, but he draped one arm lightly over her shoulders in a casual display of affection. They watched silently as the sun began to sink below the horizon and beautiful shades of red, yellow, orange, and pink overtook the sky.

Natalie squinted as she took in the stunning vista. "I always forget how bright it still gets at sunset," she muttered.

"Here," Jack said, removing his hat and placing it atop her head. "It's a perfect fit."

"Thanks," she replied, adjusting the bill with one hand. He was right—the fit was perfect.

"You must have a big head," he added with a playful grin.

Affronted, Natalie swatted at his chest. "I do not!"

Jack chuckled and shrugged. "Guys' heads are bigger than girls'—everyone knows that—so if my hat fits you, that means you have a big head."

"I just have more hair," she argued.

He reached out to finger a strand of her blonde hair. "That must be it."

Natalie resisted the urge to tousle his hair in reply. "Shut up and watch the sunset."

Jack snickered and threw his arm back around her. Without thinking, she tucked herself into his side, melting into his now familiar touch. Like a magnet drawn to metal, her head lowered to his shoulder until each breath he took lifted her cheek, and she could swear she felt his heartbeat speed up.

Realizing she'd probably overstepped, Natalie began to

shift, but Jack's arm anchored her against him. She couldn't tell if he'd sensed her pulling away and tightened his grasp, or if it had always been so strong, but either way, she decided to remain against him. She enjoyed his hold for a few moments as they watched the bright ball of the sun sink lower.

"Hey, I met someone you know recently," Natalie said eventually.

"Hmm?" Jack murmured, the sound making his chest vibrate beneath her cheek.

"I ran into this woman named Dana last week on the beach."

Natalie could hear the frown in Jack's voice when he asked, "Dana Myers?"

"She didn't give me her last name, but she said she knew you from high school," Natalie said.

"Yeah, that's Dana Myers. What did she say about me?"

Natalie tugged her body out of Jack's hold and turned so she could see his face. "Jack McNally, are you actually nervous right now? What did you think she would tell me?"

"I don't know." He mussed up his hair with a big hand. "I wasn't the nicest guy back when she knew me."

"She told me," Natalie said. When Jack's eyes widened in fear, she added softly, "She also told me that you've changed a lot and really turned your life around."

Jack's shoulders visibly relaxed. "I was an asshole in high school," he admitted. "I picked fights. I slept with other people's girlfriends. I failed classes. It wasn't pretty."

"You're not like that anymore," Natalie asserted.

"No," he agreed.

"And you're not a screw-up," she added.

Jack smirked. "Well, not as much as I used to be."

He glanced out over the ocean, and Natalie followed his gaze. The sun had just sunk below the horizon, and the colors were quickly fading to black.

"Let's get home before it's too dark to see where we're

going." Taking her hand, Jack led Natalie up the beach, where they hopped into his Jeep and headed back to the apartment. He stayed quiet, lost in thought, and she hoped he wasn't worrying about what Dana might have said, because really, it was nothing bad.

She vacillated between watching Jack drive out of the corner of her eye, his big hands perched on the steering wheel, biceps just peeking out from under his shirt sleeves, and watching out the window as day drifted into night. One view was definitely more interesting than the other.

When they reached the driveway, Jack parked and hopped out quickly to open Natalie's door for her.

"I can do that myself, you know," she argued.

"I know, but I was raised to never let a lady open her own door," he replied with a charismatic smile.

Rolling her eyes, Natalie followed him up the stairs to the apartment. "Thanks for tonight," she said when they reached the top. "My Krabby Patty was delicious, and the sunset was lovely."

"I enjoyed it too," Jack said. "And God, I love Carter, but it's nice to have a night off."

Natalie giggled at his relieved sigh. "Agreed. It's nice to know I won't have to wake up in the wee hours of the morning tomorrow, too."

"For sure," Jack said. They had reached the hallway and were standing outside their respective bedroom doors. "Well, I guess it's time to turn in for the night."

"Yep." Natalie nodded. She couldn't help but feel like they were at the end of a first date and Jack was dropping her off at her door. If it were a date, he'd be deciding whether or not to kiss her, but Natalie knew that couldn't happen now, no matter how much she may want it to.

"Goodnight," she said, placing her hand on the doorknob to keep herself from placing it on Jack.

"Night," he replied, offering up one of his sexy smiles

before turning and entering his room. Silently blowing out a relieved breath, Natalie did the same, and it wasn't until she passed by her full-length mirror that she realized she was still wearing Jack's hat.

Her mouth curved into a smile as she gazed at her reflection, remembering his gentle teasing followed by the sturdy sensation of his arms around her. With a contented sigh, she tugged off the hat, placed it on the bedside table, then busied herself with changing into pajamas—an old *I Heart NY* tank top and some athletic shorts. When she finally slid under the covers, her thoughts returned to Jack, and she stared at the hat until she fell asleep.

10

The next morning, Natalie finally found time to work on her painting again. Scrunching her nose in concentration, she fleshed out the rock jetty and added more movement to the waves in the ocean, then added in the lifeguard's chair. The large red cross on its weathered white side provided an eye-catching point of contrast to the blues that made up the ocean and sky.

Though still not quite good enough, the painting was coming along. Natalie was analyzing the scene to look for areas of improvement when Jack wandered into the room, once again gawking at her work. He took a step toward the easel and lifted a finger as if to touch it.

"Ah ah!" Natalie shouted. "No touching."

Jack's eyebrows shot up as he tore his hand back. "Sorry, my bad."

She shook her head and brushed past him, accidentally bumping his hip as she did, and scooted the easel back to safety. "Geez, I wouldn't be surprised to have to yell at Carter for that, but you should know better. Or is your skull too thick to comprehend the idea of wet paint?"

Jack flopped onto her bed with a chuckle. "I'm not the one with the big head, remember?"

Natalie balanced herself on the edge of the bed a few feet away and smirked. "Maybe it's just because I have a bigger brain."

Jack's eyes sparkled playfully as he replied, "Or maybe all of your ego just couldn't fit in a smaller skull."

She opened her mouth wide in disbelief and punched him lightly on the arm. "I do *not* have a big ego."

"But you do have a big head."

Natalie placed a hand on her hip and cocked her head to the side. "Did you come in here to make fun of my head size again, or did you need something?"

Jack laced his fingers behind his neck and lounged back against the headboard. "Actually, I came to see if you wanted to pick up Carter from my mom's with me this afternoon. You could see her shop while we're at it."

"That would be great," Natalie said. "I'd love to see your mom's work. I'm going to prime the exterior walls of Danny's this morning to prep them for the new color, but I'll make sure to be cleaned up and ready to go by Carter's nap time."

"Cool." Jack cracked his knuckles and glanced around the room before turning back to her. "So, do you have any color choices for me yet?"

"Yes!" Natalie clapped her hands together and reached into the drawer of her bedside table to retrieve the paint samples she'd collected. Fanning them out in her hands, she held them in front of Jack.

"This one is pretty safe," she said, pointing to a bluish silver that was the closest to Jack's beloved Nantucket gray. "And this one is a little bolder." She moved her finger to a turquoise that had caught her eye because it reminded her so much of the jewel tones in the ocean. "But this one's my favorite." Her finger landed on the muted, minty shade of seafoam green she'd fallen in love with.

Jack silently studied the colors laid out before him.

"What do you think?" Natalie prompted.

He scratched the back of his head. "They're all nice."

"Do you have a favorite?"

"Uh, I guess I like the green one too."

"Try not to sound so enthusiastic," she deadpanned.

Jack scrubbed a hand over his face. "I'm sorry. It's a nice color, but what if it's too bright or too... unique? I like it in this little square"—he pointed to the sample—"but what if a whole building of it is too much?"

"If you hate it when it's done, I'll paint it again," Natalie promised, "but I really think you should give it a try."

Jack caught his bottom lip between his teeth, and she couldn't help but watch as he tugged at it in deliberation. "It's just so different from what's there now," he said.

"I think a new, striking color will really help the aesthetic of the building," she pressed.

Jack released a weary sigh. "If you think so..."

"So, the seafoam green is a go?" she asked, crossing both sets of fingers where he could see them.

Jack shook his head good-naturedly. "Let's give it a try."

Natalie unwound her fingers and pumped the air with her fists. "Yes! Thank you. You won't regret it."

Jack watched her one-woman celebration with an amused grin. "You're kind of invested for someone who's 'just here to paint,'" he said, throwing her own words back at her.

Natalie rolled her eyes. "I didn't say I was *just* here to paint. I'm *mainly* here to paint, but I'm really enjoying this project of fixing up Danny's. Once we get the walls done, we just have to fill the garden with some gorgeous plants, slap a new sign on the building, and the outside will be finished!"

Jack combed his fingers through his mussed hair. "The inside needs a decent amount of work too."

"I don't think we need to change much inside," Natalie reassured him. "It's mostly small jobs and touch-ups—spray paint the tables, reupholster the cushions on the chairs and barstools, and add a few accents. Maybe some large indoor plants and art on the walls? I already measured everything."

Jack nodded thoughtfully at each suggestion but perked up at the last one. "We should put some of your paintings up in the café! That beach scene would fit our vibe perfectly," he said, nodding toward her current work in progress.

"Oh, I don't know about that," Natalie said. While incredibly flattered that Jack wanted to display her work, she was supposed to be making paintings for Ned's show. It had taken her two weeks just to make this one—which wasn't even finished—and she still had nine to go.

But Jack was staring at her painting like it was the *Mona Lisa*, with such adoration in his eyes that she couldn't bear to deny him. "I would be proud to have my work displayed in Danny's," she said, "but only if you promise you're not doing it just because of who the artist is."

Jack looked at her straight on, his face serious but his eyes alight with mischief. "You think I'm biased because you've basically come in here and single-handedly gotten my life together?"

She chuckled because she hardly had her own life together, let alone the ability to help someone else with theirs. "I don't want you to do me any favors. Only put my work up if you really like it."

"I *really* like it," Jack insisted, his sincere appreciation filling her with pride.

"Then, as soon as it's done, I'll hang it up down there," Natalie said.

"Right above the bar," he instructed. "Where everyone can see it."

She raised her hand to her forehead in a salute. "Ay ay, captain."

Jack saluted her back. "I'll see you at 1400 hours."

Natalie narrowed her eyes as she attempted to decipher military time.

He chuckled at her. "I'll see you at two o'clock."

"Got it."

As soon as Jack left the room, her gaze returned to her painting, and her smile faded. It was still lacking something. She had finished all the main elements—the sky, the ocean, the sand, the rocks, and the lifeguard's chair—but something about it felt… lifeless. Jack's desire to hang it up in Danny's added pressure to make it perfect.

Tearing her eyes away from the painting, Natalie collected her used brushes to soak, gently encased her palette in plastic wrap to keep the paint moist, then headed downstairs to get started priming the outside walls. It wasn't quite as fun as the painting she'd been doing that morning, but it was nice to be out in the fresh air.

With all of the weeds removed from the garden, she found she could easily access the lower half of the walls, and Jack had supplied her with a tall ladder to help her reach the upper half. She was up at the top of that ladder, finishing up the last few strokes of primer, when Jack emerged from Danny's.

"How's the weather up there?" he asked, craning his neck back to gaze up at her.

"Ha ha," Natalie shot down at him. "Coming in hot with the dad jokes, I see."

"Just practicing for when Carter is old enough to be embarrassed by me."

Natalie chuckled and began slowly descending the ladder, balancing the bucket of primer and brush in one hand while she held on to the ladder with the other. She had almost made it to the bottom when the ladder wobbled, throwing her off balance. In a split second, her hand flew off the ladder to grab the paint, and she was left completely unstable.

Her whole body began tilting to the side, and she let out a blood-curdling shriek. Jack grabbed her right before she would have fallen, one arm snaking deftly around her waist while the other clutched her shoulder.

"I've got you," he murmured, his deep voice right next to her ear as he lowered her feet to the ground, arms still tight around her.

Natalie blinked a few times and swallowed as it suddenly registered that her free hand had found its way to Jack's back and was fisted in his shirt in a desperate attempt to stay steady. On a deep breath, she gradually unfurled her fingers and disentangled herself from his hold. His hands remained on her body a beat longer than they needed to, then they dropped to his sides.

"You good?" he asked, ducking his face toward her until unruly curls spilled over his forehead.

Natalie swallowed again, her throat dry and scratchy as sandpaper. "I'm good," she croaked. Standing as close as she was, she could make out every inch of detail on Jack's face, from the long eyelashes that framed his smoldering gaze to his strong, square jaw clenched in concern.

A spark of awareness buzzed between their faces, and once again, Natalie felt that magnetic pull, hopelessly attracting her to him. That familiar fire shot through her veins and stirred her insides, just as it had every time Jack had touched her.

Her breathing sped up as she peered into his eyes, now hooded with anticipation. His face moved an inch closer, and she could almost feel what his lips would taste like—but no, this wasn't right. She couldn't kiss her boss... partner... friend... whatever he was. She'd been over and over this in her head. Jack was off limits.

Pulling back abruptly, Natalie flattened her hand on his chest to keep him at arm's length. That decision, however, only brought her into contact with him again. Her hands fell to her sides as if they'd been singed, and she managed to utter,

"Thanks for catching me," before bending down awkwardly to fasten the top onto the paint can.

"No problem," Jack's voice came from behind her.

Clumsily hammering the top of the paint can into place, Natalie took a moment to cool down and regain her bearings. She must have been taking too long, though, because Jack began tapping his foot rhythmically against the ground.

"Need any help down there?" he asked impatiently.

"No!" she said a little too loudly, afraid that if he came close to her again, she wouldn't be able to refrain from kissing him.

When she stood, he was swinging his car keys around his index finger. "We should go get Carter."

"Yes," Natalie said. "Let's go."

They headed for the Jeep, and Jack reached the passenger side before she did, opening up her door and motioning for her to get inside.

"I can open my own door," she argued again, her surliness amped up by the adrenaline rush of the almost-kiss.

"And I can open it just as easily," Jack retorted, revealing his own irritation.

Grumbling under her breath, Natalie hopped into the Jeep and allowed Jack to shut the door behind her. They didn't speak much on the ride over to June's shop, and Natalie sensed the tension that rode along with them, thick enough to slice with a knife. Was Jack upset that she'd pulled away from him? Or was he relieved they hadn't kissed?

Either way, he remained silent as he drove. With no stop-lights and no speed limits over forty miles per hour, driving on Nantucket was typically a pretty relaxing experience. This car ride was an exception.

Natalie fiddled with the hair tie on her wrist and tried to think of something to say. "I'm excited to see your mom's work," was what she finally landed on.

Jack's shoulders relaxed a bit, and a faint smile graced his lips at the mention of his mother. "It's really great. You know, she's been making pottery my whole life, but I didn't really appreciate it until I was an adult."

"It's easy to take for granted when you don't know how much work goes into each piece."

"Definitely. Like with that painting you're working on, it's cool to see the process as you go. I would never realize how many steps it took to create it."

"It's definitely a process," she agreed. "I've really honed my techniques over the years."

"Where'd you learn to paint like that?" he asked, finally glancing over at her after keeping his eyes locked on the road for so long.

She shrugged. "Art school."

"Nah." Jack shook his head. "What I saw in that painting was more than just school. You can't learn to paint with that type of soul from a textbook."

Thinking of all the paintings she'd made over the years, Natalie acknowledged that they contained a good deal of emotion and passion. "I guess my emotions kind of spill out into my art," she said. "I've always used painting as an outlet."

"When did you first start?" he asked.

"I've been painting for as long as I can remember. My dad was always working when I was a kid, and since he was a single father, I had to go to after school activities until he got home from work. Every year when it came time to pick, I chose the arts-and-crafts ones. I tried drawing, collage, puppet-making…" Natalie laughed, remembering all the ridiculous clubs she'd been in as a kid. "But my favorite was always painting. The way it feels to glide a brush across a canvas… there's just nothing like it."

Jack watched her from the driver's seat. "So, you always knew you wanted to be an artist?"

She nodded. "When I was little and going to those after school art classes, I just liked experimenting with the different colors. It was fun. Then, my art got me through some really tough times—being a teenage girl without a mom isn't exactly a picnic—and it became more sophisticated as I got older. By the time I was looking at colleges, I couldn't imagine studying anything other than art. I had found my passion."

Jack shook his head in amazement. "I wish I had lived my life with such purpose. I was a bartender because you can make great tips on the island and it didn't require going to college. It was a natural choice, but I never felt like I had found my true calling, you know?"

"I think a lot of people feel that way," Natalie said thoughtfully. "It takes most people a while to find what they really want to do. I was lucky to find out so young."

"Yeah," Jack agreed. "It sucks that sometimes people have to waste so much time doing the wrong things before they finally find the right one. I spent so many years slacking off, doing the bare minimum, when I should have been working toward something bigger."

"How do you feel now?" Natalie asked. "Do you think you found your calling in running the café?"

Jack considered that with a tilt of his head. "It feels good to run a business. I feel like I'm finally living like a real adult, but honestly, it might have more to do with being Carter's guardian. I mean, I have no idea what I'm doing half the time, but damn if it isn't fulfilling. Never in a million years would I have thought having kids was my calling, but it just feels right."

Natalie's heart did a little dance in her chest the way it always did when Jack talked about Carter with such adoration.

"Taking care of Carter, being responsible for another human being… it's incredible," he added.

"The way you talk about him… I can just tell you love him so much," she gushed. "Most guys wouldn't have been able to adjust so quickly to having to care for a baby."

Jack flashed her a charming smile. "I guess I'm not like most guys then."

"No, I don't think you are," she agreed.

The chill that had pervaded earlier on in the car ride seemed to have lifted. When they pulled up to June's shop, Natalie allowed Jack to open her door for her without complaint, and they walked side by side up the skinny stone pathway leading to the front door.

"Hello!" June cried as they approached the counter, leaping up to give Jack a kiss on the cheek. She even gave Natalie a big bear hug, to her surprise and delight.

"I didn't know you were coming with Jack today!" June said cheerfully. "What a pleasure to see you."

"You too," Natalie replied. "I'm so excited to see your work."

"Of course, of course," June said as she shuffled them toward the displays. "Carter's still napping, so you two look around all you want. I'll just be behind the counter since there are a few customers milling about."

Natalie thanked June and let Jack guide her toward one of the display cases with a hand at the small of her back. Acutely aware of the casual touch, she felt its loss when they reached the case and he dropped his hand to his side.

"These are some of my favorites," he said, pointing to a row of shallow bowls that had etchings of sand dollars inside. On the next shelf were more shallow bowls shaped like fish, each one ornately detailed with a unique blend of bright colors.

"These are so beautiful," Natalie breathed, picking up one of the sand dollar bowls and running her finger over the etchings. "So much detail."

"If you like that, check out these serving trays." Once again, Jack guided her by bringing his hand to the small of her back. This time, he led her to a long wooden shelf that had serving trays propped up on fancy plate stands. Each one was different but equally striking, from a rectangular tray etched with a tree of life design in every shade of green imaginable to a circular one with a design on it that looked like a doily, with a flower in the center and lacy circles radiating out from it.

"These pieces are unbelievable," Natalie said.

When she glanced up at Jack, he was smiling down at her. "I told you that you would like them. I could tell from your painting this morning that you had an eye for detail. I think the magic of my mom's work is how ornate every piece is."

"I totally agree!" Natalie exclaimed. "Most of the time, people look at a piece and they think it's beautiful, but they can't figure out why. They look at it as a whole piece but don't realize the beauty is in the details! So many little things have to come together perfectly to create pieces like these."

"I agree," Jack said warmly. "The beauty is in the details."

Natalie beamed up at him, loving that she could talk art with Jack and he wouldn't say it was a waste of time. He wasn't just putting up with her babbling to keep her happy. He was actually interested in what she had to say.

He showed her a few more shelves containing everything from mugs and vases to pendants and bracelets, each piece more beautiful than the next. Natalie loved meandering around the shop and taking it all in.

"June, your pieces are breathtaking," she said when the older woman came over to view the jewelry case alongside her. "So much thought goes into each one. You can just tell by the amount of detail."

"Thank you, dear," June responded humbly. "Pottery is my passion. To be able to create something of such beauty from scratch, that can mean so much to someone, is a pleasure."

Natalie grinned at her. "I wholeheartedly agree," she said, thinking of her own paintings. Turning to the line of pendants laid out behind the glass case on the wall, she pointed to her favorite—a circular pendant with the sun etched on one half and the moon on the other, plus stars all around the outer edge. "This one here. It must have taken you hours to get all those little etchings onto it."

"Ah, that's one of my favorite designs," June said fondly. "See, I used to call my husband, Noah, 'my sun, my moon, and my stars' because he was my everything. After he died, I transferred it over to my kids. Three boys: my sun, my moon, and my star," she finished, putting her hand on Jack's shoulder.

"Aw, are you saying I'm the star of the family?" he quipped.

Natalie rolled her eyes at Jack's attempt at humor and whacked him lightly on the chest. "You're two for two on the bad jokes today," she warned him. Turning to June, she said, "That was my favorite piece before, but now that I know the story behind it, I love it even more. It's so unique and meaningful."

"Why don't you try it on?" June pulled a key out of her pocket and slid open the glass case.

"Are you sure?" Natalie asked even as June was clasping the necklace at the back of her neck.

"Here." Jack guided Natalie to a mirror on the wall, and she looked toward it, bringing her fingers up to fondle the pendant.

"It's stunning," she breathed.

"It looks stunning on you," Jack agreed, his eyes lingering on her reflection.

"I'd better put it back before I talk myself into buying it," Natalie said, knowing she had little to no money to her name.

"No." June took her hand to prevent her from unclasping the necklace. "I want you to keep it."

"Oh, I couldn't possibly accept that," Natalie countered. It was far too personal a gift, especially with the meaning behind the pendant. This was the type of gift her sons should give their wives or daughters, not their business partners.

"I insist." June's eyes sparkled with sincerity. "I want you to have it."

Babbling coming from the other room broke up their friendly argument.

"Sounds like somebody's awake." Jack headed for the back room where Carter napped, and Natalie stayed behind to barter with June.

"June, I really appreciate this. It means a lot to me, but I have to repay you in some way," she insisted.

"Perhaps you'll share one of your paintings with me one day," June suggested.

"Of course!" Natalie quickly began cooking up ideas of what she would paint for Jack's mother—after she finished her ten paintings for Ned, of course.

June placed her hand on Natalie's arm and caught her gaze. "And Natalie, you're already giving me the most precious gift by caring for my son and that beautiful baby boy. I was so worried about Jack when Danny died and he had to take over so much responsibility. I love my son, but he was a bit of a lost soul. I didn't know how he was going to handle it, but he's impressed me so much, and I am so thankful that he has you to help him. You and Carter are the best things that have happened to him in quite a while."

Almost choked up by June's words, Natalie didn't know how to respond. June took away that problem by enveloping her in another bear hug. Natalie squeezed her back gently, finally collecting her thoughts. "I'm so grateful that Jack took a chance on me. Not many people would hire someone they just met to live in their home and take care of their new baby."

"I think he knew you were special," June said. "With some people, you can just tell."

Natalie smiled at her kind words. "I think they're pretty special too."

June patted her on the arm and led her to the back room where Jack was just getting Carter out of his crib.

"Hey, cutie," Jack whispered as he lifted Carter up. The baby stuck one chubby thumb into his mouth and leaned into Jack's chest. The man placed a kiss on the baby's head and rocked back and forth slightly. Sometimes it took Carter a few minutes of cuddling before he was ready to face the world.

Natalie stood back and absorbed the sight in front of her. Jack, in all of his tall, tan, toned goodness, cuddled sweet little Carter in his arms so tenderly. Knowing how good it felt to be in those arms, Natalie couldn't blame Carter for having no desire to be put down. Jack's embrace was a heady combination of safety and strength that never failed to leave her feeling comforted.

Yes, the man was special, indeed.

11

———————

The next weekend, Natalie once again found herself staring at her painting and trying to decipher what it was missing. Any other artist may have considered it finished—it contained all the main elements of the beach scene, and they were well done—but a gut feeling that she could do better kept her from calling it quits.

Carter was napping, and Jack had blessedly refrained from asking her to help him with anything, for once. She desperately wanted to take advantage of the time and finish this piece, if only the creative side of her brain would cooperate with the logical one.

Frustrated, she turned her gaze toward the beach out her window and watched as a seagull flew by, coasting over the wind with its wings spread wide. Another gull joined the first, and they both began circling the water before the first one dipped down and scooped something from beneath the surface.

Natalie's gaze remained riveted to their sleek movements as they glided majestically through the air. The bird that had swooped toward the ocean drifted over to the jetty, something small and reddish-brown hanging from its mouth. After landing smoothly on its webbed feet, the gull proceeded to crack open a crab on the rocks. Then, the second seagull dove toward it, and they both began gorging themselves on the crab's meat.

The scene had played out in a matter of seconds, but it sparked something in Natalie. Suddenly, the words that both she and Jack had uttered at June's shop popped into her mind like a flash of lightning. *The beauty is in the details.* Looking back and forth between the feasting birds and her painting, it hit her.

"That's it!" Natalie whispered to herself, her heart rate picking up as a reinvigorating wave of inspiration washed over her.

She had learned that when those flashes of inspiration hit, one had to harness them immediately. Before the moment could pass her by, she grabbed a thin, size-two brush and dipped into the titanium white before beginning to outline the shapes of a few seagulls in the cloudless blue sky. The negative space the sky provided was important, but adding a few small details would break up the emptiness and add more move-ment to the landscape.

She shook her head at her own carelessness. Too focused on perfecting the big picture and making it look realistic, Natalie hadn't bothered to consider that a painting was supposed to be a snapshot in time. At any given moment, there were tons of moving pieces. Nature was an ever-evolving entity, which was why she enjoyed painting it so much, but she'd forgotten the importance of adding in those minuscule details that might get overlooked by an untrained eye but ulti-mately contributed to the magic of a piece.

She spent the rest of Carter's nap time putting the finishing touches on the beach scene. By the time she was done, there were three seagulls sailing through the air, two devouring a crab on the jetty, and one perched on the life-guard's chair, its wings spread as if it were about to take flight. The small details were enough to balance out the bigger aspects of the scene without overpowering them. They added some activity and *life* to the picture. The piece had become something that she would be proud to hang in Danny's Place.

And hopefully, her burst of inspiration would stick around so she could squeeze out ten more paintings. Now that she'd decided to give this piece to Jack, she would be starting back at square one.

Carter's cries echoed from where he lay in his crib. Natalie haphazardly cleared her workspace and emerged just as Jack was returning from his late-afternoon run. They arrived at Carter's door at the same time and both hesitated while reaching for the doorknob.

"Go ahead." Jack pulled his hand back and nodded toward the door.

Natalie twisted the knob, and the door swung open.

"Oh, God," Jack choked out as he entered the room, pinching his nose and taking a step back. Natalie would have laughed at his reaction if hers hadn't been the same. The smell in Carter's room was horrific. The baby occasionally woke up with a soiled diaper, but this one smelled particularly rank.

"What the hell did you feed him, Nat? One of your weird vegetables?"

She crossed her arms, not appreciating Jack's accusatory tone. "Nothing that would cause such a foul smell," she insisted. "It must be something you gave him."

"I haven't given him any of his meals today or yesterday."

"Didn't I see you giving him Juice Bar last night?" Natalie accused. She'd caught Jack eating ice cream from the local scoop shop the night before. Carter loved watching them make their homemade waffle cones through the window, and Jack couldn't resist a scoop of their Crantucket flavor—a vanilla base full of chocolate-covered cranberries. The boys had been pretty receptive to Natalie's healthier dietary changes, but old habits died hard.

"Ah, shit," Jack muttered.

"Yes, literally," Natalie replied, shaking her head. "You know he can't have too much dairy. His stomach can't handle it."

"But it can handle all those wacky health foods," Jack said under his breath.

"What was that?" she asked, arms still crossed tightly over her chest.

"Nothing!" he said.

"Mhmm," Natalie muttered. "Whoever causes the disgusting diaper has to change the disgusting diaper."

Jack rolled his eyes but dutifully grabbed Carter out of his crib. "Fine. I was going to take a shower anyway, so I'll just kill two birds with one stone."

Gliding past her toward the bathroom, Jack held Carter at arm's length in front of him, and Natalie noticed that the entire backside of the baby's outfit was stained. Jack looked a little queasy, and she couldn't help but chuckle. When he glared at her, she simply stuck her tongue out, taunting him. He slammed the bathroom door, and the shower immediately started up.

"Such a wimp," Natalie muttered affectionately as she began cleaning up her brushes and palette. The bathroom door swung back open just as she was zipping her storage case, and there was Carter, trotting into her room, stark naked. Jack was close on his heels, wearing only a towel slung low on his waist.

"Carter! Get back here!" he called.

Natalie giggled as she swept the baby up, blowing a raspberry onto his bare belly and making him giggle too. Her humor subsided when she caught sight of Jack, water dripping from his hair and gliding in shimmering beads down his chest and abdomen. She tracked them as they slid down his torso before getting caught in the towel around his waist. He had it fisted in one hand, just barely keeping himself covered. Natalie traced the lines of his muscles with her eyes and wished she could reach out and do the same with her finger.

"Sorry about that." Jack swept a hand through his sopping wet hair, sending water droplets cascading onto Natalie's bedroom floor, not that she had the capacity to worry about that while he stood half-naked in her doorway.

"No problem," she rasped. "Uh, I can get him dressed if you want."

"That'd be great. I think we should just throw out the clothes he was wearing before. They're beyond saving."

"Agreed." Since Natalie did most of Carter's laundry, she had no problem parting with the filthy clothing. "Thanks for cleaning him up."

Jack nodded and left the room—hopefully to get dressed—while Natalie got Carter into his own clean clothes. When she met back up with Jack in the kitchen, he was fully clothed but still looked sinfully handsome in chinos and a short-sleeved button-down.

Luckily, she didn't have to stick around and resist temptation for too long because Jack asked her to close up the café with Derek while he fed Carter dinner. Perhaps he still didn't trust Natalie and her "weird vegetables," even though they hadn't been the cause of the baby's blowout.

Before heading down to Danny's, Natalie snuck back to her bedroom and grabbed her completed painting. Though it wasn't dry yet, she planned to hang it above the bar at Danny's where no one would be touching it, so it seemed safe enough to put it up. She was excited to surprise Jack with it after dinner.

Knowing where he kept a toolbox in the office of the café, she grabbed it on her way there. Derek was cashing out the register when she arrived.

"How'd we do today?" Natalie asked.

"Pretty good." Derek nodded as he sifted a stack of bills in his hands. "Up five percent from last week."

"Awesome!" She high-fived the young man. "You can stick the money in the back office. I've got to do one thing, and then I'll help you clean."

Propping the painting carefully on the counter, Natalie dragged over a barstool and cautiously stood on it while it wobbled precariously below her. Once she found her balance, she reached down for a hammer and nail, but the sudden movement caused the stool to lurch to the side and sent her over the edge. Natalie began to fall and quickly released the tools from her hands so she could catch herself on the counter. Her body made a loud *thump* as the metal tools clattered to the ground.

"Natalie!" Derek called, jogging out from the back office. "What happened?"

Standing up straight, Natalie wiped her hands over her jeans and assessed her body to make sure everything was fine. Nothing seemed hurt, but she would probably have bruises on her thighs from where they'd hit the counter. Two falls in two weeks was not a good look. Damn her fierce independence.

"Sorry about that. I was trying to hang this painting, and the stool gave out on me."

"Those stools are ancient." Derek shook his head in dismay. "You shouldn't be trying to stand on them. Here, let me help you." He picked the hammer up off the floor.

"Oh, you don't need to do that," Natalie said quickly. "I just need to find something sturdier to stand on."

"Really, I've got this," Derek pressed, deftly mounting the counter. He was able to reach the right height standing just on his knees. "Where did you want the nail?"

Natalie directed him to the correct position, where he hammered the nail into the wall in a few quick strokes before gingerly hanging the painting, heeding her warning not to touch the still-drying painting. Unlike Jack, Derek understood the sanctity of wet paint.

Gazing up at her work, she gave a small clap. "It's perfect!"

"What are you doing on the counter?" Jack's smooth voice demanded. Natalie whirled to find him standing just beyond the bar with Carter in his arms.

"Sorry, boss." Derek hopped down to the floor. "Natalie almost killed herself standing on one of those old barstools, trying to put this up. It seemed safer to use the counter to get up there."

Jack frowned and turned toward Natalie. "Why didn't you ask me for help?"

She shrugged weakly. "I wanted to surprise you by hanging the painting." It was partially true—she had wanted it to be a surprise—but it was more than that. She was used to being self-sufficient and didn't like needing to ask for help. Plus, she'd been trying to avoid any excess contact with Jack. He was just too tempting.

Jack's face softened at her explanation, and he turned his gaze toward the new wall art. "It looks fantastic," he murmured. "Exactly like I pictured it."

Natalie warmed at his appreciation. "I think it's the perfect home for it."

"Thanks for your help, Derek. We can take it from here," Jack said. Derek saluted his boss and left out the back door.

"I just have to wash the tables and windows, and we'll be good," Natalie told Jack.

"I've got the tables." He grabbed three rags. "You can get the windows, and let Carter wash the bottom of the door." The little boy loved "helping."

The three of them got to work and had the café clean in no time. Jack's cell rang just as Natalie was throwing the rags into the washing machine. He walked into the back office to answer it, and she busied the baby with pushing the correct buttons to sanitize the rags.

"Sounds great, Mom. Thanks a lot," Jack was saying as he reentered the room. "Love you too. Bye." He shoved his phone into his back pocket and ran his fingers through his hair. "My mom is going to take Carter for another sleepover tonight so I can go out to dinner with a few of my high school buddies. You've got the night off."

"Oh," Natalie said. "Thanks, but are you sure? I feel bad that you hired me to watch Carter and your mom's taking him two nights this week."

"Of course." Jack sighed. "You deserve it. You've been working so hard, and honestly, my mom requested this. I think she thinks you deserve a night off too."

Natalie grinned at June's consideration. "Well, I'll have to thank her for that. I think I'll call Dana and see if she's around."

"Good." Jack nodded. "But please don't believe everything she says about me. I mean, it's probably all true, but I still don't want you to believe it."

Natalie's eyes rolled heavenward. "I'll be sure to tune out anything that doesn't make you sound like an angel."

Jack winked before turning to go back up to the apartment. Natalie followed, glad for the opportunity to get out of the house for a bit. Her entire life had come to revolve around Jack—living in Jack's house, caring for Jack's baby, working in Jack's café. Some time away would help get her mind off of him and the fact that he was something she couldn't have.

She dialed Dana to see if she wanted to grab a drink, keeping her fingers crossed that Ryan would be willing to watch Justin. Dana was really the only person that Natalie had met on the island, and she seemed like she would be a fun companion. Natalie couldn't help but laugh when Dana informed her that Ryan would watch Justin without even running it by him.

Pulling out all the stops for her first-night-out-on-Nantucket outfit, Natalie chose dark jeans and a black tank top with a plunging neckline and a completely open back. Layered silver necklaces brought even more attention to the deep V that showed off her now tan skin. She mulled over the idea of wearing spiky heels but decided wedges were a better choice since she might want to walk home and save a cab fare.

Just as Natalie was about to leave, Jack emerged from his bedroom, looking luscious in dark jeans and a bluish-gray button-up shirt with the sleeves rolled up. His still bare feet padded across the carpet.

"Hey, Nat. You heading out?" he asked, head down as he searched the living room for his shoes.

"Yep. I called Dana, and we're going to go for a drink. She suggested The Gazebo. I think you pointed it out to me once."

"Oh, yeah, that's where I used to bartend," Jack said, then he muttered, "Finally," upon discovering his shoes in Carter's toy box. Sometimes, the little boy did *too* good a job of cleaning up.

Jack sat on the couch and pulled his shoes on, only then looking up at Natalie. His eyebrows climbed his forehead as his gaze roamed over her body and landed on her breasts. He cleared his throat and managed to choke out, "Wow, uh… you look great."

Pleased with his reaction, Natalie replied, "Thanks. It's my first night out here, so I figured I'd do it up big."

"I hope you enjoy yourself," Jack replied, having pulled himself together. "We won't be out all that late. Maybe I'll see you when you get home?"

"Sounds good." Natalie smiled at the hope in his voice. "I'll see you later."

"Later," Jack said, shooting her his signature sexy smile.

12

As soon as she stepped into the space, Natalie understood why Dana had chosen The Gazebo for their night out. The totally outdoor bar allowed patrons to enjoy the fresh air, while a large wooden structure protected them in case the weather turned for the worse. Pop music pulsed through the outdoor speakers, and an electric energy pervaded the area. The night was young, the people were in paradise, and the party was just getting started.

It was crowded but not so much that Natalie felt claustrophobic. Seated at the far end of the bar, she and Dana had the perfect view of everyone coming and going. They chatted for a few minutes before the bartender finally made his way over to them, and it struck Natalie that just a few months ago, before everything changed, that could have been Jack.

She and Dana each ordered a martini from a long list of exotic flavors, and Natalie clapped when the bartender returned, balancing two luxurious-looking beverages on a tray.

Dana plucked the fresh raspberry off of her raspberry-lime martini and chewed it thoughtfully. "You mean, you just decide what you want to paint next and then hop on a plane there?" she asked, continuing the conversation they'd been having before their drinks arrived.

Natalie nodded as she took a sip of her blueberry martini, sighing with delight as the fruity flavor hit her lips. "Pretty much. Right now, I'm working on fulfilling a commitment of ten paintings to a gallery owner and former professor of mine, Ned Brinkley. He gave me an advanced payment that helped me live in Colorado for a bit then fly back to Boston. I desperately needed inspiration, and Nantucket was the best place I could think of to get it, so I hopped on a ferry, and *voilà*. Here I am."

"Man, would I love to trade places with you," Dana said. "I mean, I love my family and our home on Nantucket, but that sounds amazing."

"It is," Natalie agreed, "but you've got a pretty great life here too. You have an awesome son, and you get to spend all day with him."

"I know, and I do love that, but I also love to write, and that's near impossible now." Dana scowled. "I think I mentioned to you that I used to write a newspaper column before Justin was born. It wasn't necessarily my dream job, but at least it was something. Now I'm not writing at all."

"Why not?" Natalie asked. "You don't have to be working for a newspaper to write articles. Can't you do freelance work?"

"I probably could, but what I really want is to write fictional stories." Dana's face lit up as she continued. "Lately I've been working on some ideas for children's books. I buy all these books for Justin, and half of them look like ones he could have written himself, and he can't even form full sentences yet! I know I could write better ones than that."

"I'm sure you could. That's exactly how I feel when I go into galleries. I see what people are paying for some paintings, and I just don't understand why mine don't sell as well."

"Exactly," Dana agreed. "I can sometimes manage to

squeeze in a few minutes of writing while Justin is asleep, but I don't see any way I'll ever get published. It's taken me so long just to get some rough ideas written out. I haven't even had a chance to think about illustrations yet."

"Is that what's holding you back?" Natalie asked, confident that if all Dana needed was some artistic direction, she could help.

"It's a big part of it," Dana answered. "With children's books, the words are only half the battle. Illustrations are just as important, and I don't have any."

A sly smile worked its way onto Natalie's lips. "I think we can change that. I've never painted illustrations for a book before, but it sounds like a fun project. If you can come up with a final draft of your story, I'll work on the illustrations for it."

Dana's jaw dropped so low Natalie was afraid it would get stuck there. "You would really do that?"

"Of course. I'm always happy to help others chase their dreams. I'm sure if we got the boys together to play, they would keep each other busy long enough for us to get some work done."

"Oh, Natalie that would be amazing!" Dana pulled her into a side hug that was so enthusiastic it almost knocked them right off their barstools. "You don't know how much it would mean to me for you to help me out. If I have illustrations, maybe I can get an agent to actually give me the time of day."

"It's a plan," Natalie said, raising an eyebrow conspiratorially. "But only if you'll do something for me."

"Of course," Dana replied as the bartender set down their second round of martinis.

Natalie bit her lip as she gave hers a stir. "Tell me… What was Jack like in high school? I know you said he was kind of a bad boy. I'm dying to know more."

Dana smiled knowingly. "He was charming. Good with the ladies. And yes, he had quite the bad-boy streak."

"What kinds of things did he do?" Natalie asked, her interest piqued.

"Well, he got into more than his fair share of fights," Dana explained. "It seemed like every week he and some other teenage, testosterone-filled ticking time bomb were facing off in the back parking lot of the school."

Natalie snorted at her description of high school boys.

Dana leaned in closer to divulge more juicy details. "I remember going into my first period history class one morning, and Jack was sitting there with a huge shiner on his eye. He was so cocky about it, like he had no shame. When the teacher asked what happened, he said he'd been fighting over a girl."

Natalie shook her head. "It just seems so unlike him, knowing how he is now. He's so sweet and gentle with Carter. I can't imagine him hitting someone."

"In high school, that boy was hell on wheels, but afterward, he started to slow down," Dana said. "He lost that 'big man on campus' persona. I guess other guys weren't as threatened by the loser who stuck around town and never made anything of himself. *Not* that I'm saying Jack is a loser, just that some people viewed him that way."

"He still views himself that way," Natalie said. "It sucks."

Dana took a long sip of her drink. "Then, there was Danny's accident. He's changed even more since then. I guess having so much responsibility thrown at you all at once will do that to a man."

Natalie nodded sadly. "I just wish he could see that he's not a loser or a screw-up. He's making progress with the business, and he's such a good caretaker for Carter. He's gentle, kind, caring. He's perfect."

Dana raised an eyebrow. "Sounds like someone's got a little crush on Jack."

"No, no," Natalie insisted, a blush rising into her cheeks. "I just mean that he's perfect for Carter."

"Sure." Dana rolled her eyes, her voice dripping with sarcasm. "But you can't deny he'd make a great boyfriend. Easy on the eyes too."

"Mmm," Natalie hummed, her inhibitions lowered just enough that she didn't deny her attraction. "Those big brown eyes with the long lashes, and the stubble, and that runner's body." Natalie sighed, practically salivating at the thought of him.

Dana burst out laughing and showed her approval by clinking glasses with Natalie, then she turned toward the entrance as a loud group of men walked in.

"Speak of the devil." Dana pointed toward the fray, and standing there amongst the rowdy group was Jack, hair messy, cheeks slightly flushed, looking even more handsome now that a button or two on his shirt had come undone. He'd known Natalie was planning to go to The Gazebo. Had he come to see her?

Natalie took a big slug of her martini. "He looks really good," she whispered to Dana.

"And he's coming this way," her friend replied with a mischievous smile.

"Stay cool, Dana. I'm his kid's nanny. He's probably just coming to make sure I'm not too wasted to take care of Carter tomorrow."

Jack reached the women before Dana could reply with one of her usual blunt remarks.

"Hey, ladies." He flashed them a charming smile and put a hand on the raised back of Natalie's barstool, just shy of touching her naked back. "How's your night going?"

"Excellent!" Dana replied.

Natalie was glad her friend took the lead to answer, as she wasn't sure she was able to speak with Jack's fingers so close to her exposed flesh.

"It's been so great to have a night out with an adult other

than my husband for once," Dana said. "And Natalie is the best company."

"She sure is," Jack said fondly, placing his hand on her back for just the slightest of moments. Goosebumps raced down her spine, and she desperately hoped he hadn't noticed.

"How's your night, Jack?" Natalie asked, trying to keep her voice even.

"Awesome," he replied. "It's not often the guys and I can all find a time to get together, so it's been fun. I'd better get back to them, but you ladies enjoy yourselves." He motioned to the bartender who seemed to recognize him right away and greeted him with a, "Hey, dude."

"Hey, man," Jack said, giving him a fist bump. He pointed to Natalie and Dana. "Next round for these two is on me. Whatever they want. And let's get a round of beers for me and my buddies."

"Sure thing," the bartender replied. Jack waved goodbye and walked back over to his friends.

"He's totally into you!" Dana exclaimed as soon as Jack was out of earshot.

"No, he's not," Natalie argued. "He was just being friendly."

"Uh-huh. Sure. And I bet you think he totally wasn't checking out your boobs either."

"Dana!" Natalie cried. "He was not. You're awful."

Dana just laughed and finished off her martini. "Think what you want. But that man is into you."

Natalie rolled her eyes as Dana checked the time on her phone and sighed. "I should really get going," she said. "You know, baby and all. I'm sure I'll be woken up far earlier than I want to be in the morning."

"Thank God June has Carter for the night," Natalie said. "And thanks for this, Dana. We'll have to do it again soon. Maybe we can give that free round a rain check."

"I like the way you think! Do you want to share a cab?" Dana asked.

"No, I think I'll stay here for a while longer. I'm not quite finished with my drink." Natalie smirked. "Besides, I've got the perfect vantage point for spying on Jack."

"Girl, now you're thinking!"

After a quick hug goodbye, Dana breezed out of the bar. She'd only been gone a few minutes when a man came over and claimed the seat she had occupied next to Natalie. Watching him warily out of the corner of her eye, Natalie noticed that he was tall, but not quite as tall as Jack, and definitely not as good looking. He already smelled heavily of booze, though she was pretty sure he had just arrived at the bar.

The man ordered himself a scotch then turned to Natalie and gave her a blatant once-over. *Rude.* She focused her gaze behind the bar, ignoring the man altogether, but it didn't deter him.

"Can I buy ya a drink?" he slurred.

Natalie politely declined, telling him that the martini she was finishing was her last drink of the night.

"Aw, come on, sugar. You can have just one more," he said, his words a bit garbled but clear enough that she perceived him as a threat. Angling herself away from him did nothing to diminish the stench of his breath, and she kept scooting back as he leaned in closer. When there was nowhere else to go, she picked up her bag to leave.

"No," Natalie said. "I really have to be getting home." She began to rise from the barstool, but the man grabbed her arm, thwarting her escape attempt.

"The night is young! Stay for one more drink with me." Every word he uttered released more of that rank breath.

"No," she said firmly, shaking off his arm as she managed to stand. But as soon as she was on her feet, he was too.

Standing far too close for comfort, he put his grubby hands on her slender hips.

"Come on, baby, give me a chance," he whined before leaning in and kissing Natalie so quickly she didn't have time to pull away. The smell and taste of strong liquor filled her nostrils, and his slimy lips slid against hers, his tongue roving for an entrance like a burrowing worm.

Natalie tried to push against his chest, but his large frame didn't budge. Panicking, she tried to remember a self-defense move—*any* self-defense move—and was just about to knee the man in the groin when his lips were suddenly wrenched from hers. His hands flew from her hips, and he stumbled backward, holding a hand over the side of his face.

Turning to look for what had sent him flying, she was stunned to see Jack standing there, nostrils flared, eyes flashing, cradling his fist as if it were in pain. Just as Natalie registered that he must have hit the bastard, the man retaliated, charging forward and, though he was unsteady on his feet, packing quite a punch to Jack's face.

"Jack!" Natalie screamed, but he ignored her cry as he pushed the other man backward with such force that, between Jack's strength and the man's intoxication, he fell on his ass on the disgusting bar floor. A bouncer intervened then, coming up to Jack and blocking him from getting to the man on the floor.

"Hey, man," he said, "I'm sorry, but I'm gonna have to ask you to leave."

"No problem, Jerry." Jack shook out his surely throbbing hand. "I was just about to get out of here anyway." Turning to Natalie, he rubbed a comforting hand up and down her arm. The hand she'd planted firmly over her mouth shook as she lowered it.

"Hey, you ok?" Jack asked gently.

"I'm fine," Natalie managed to mumble. "Are *you* ok?"

"Yeah, just fine. Let's go." He took her trembling hand in

his, and she nodded numbly, still reeling, as she grabbed her purse from where it had fallen on the floor. The bartender tossed Jack a bag of frozen peas from a mini fridge behind the bar.

"Here, man. Take care of that eye. You'll have a nasty bruise in the morning."

"Thanks, man," Jack said, tucking the peas under his arm as he led Natalie out of the bar. One of his friends, who'd been the designated driver for the night, drove them home.

The drive felt endless, and silence reigned until the initial shock of the altercation wore off, and Natalie realized just how overdramatic the whole thing had been. As grateful as she was that Jack had successfully gotten the creep to leave her alone, she was kind of pissed that he hadn't given her a chance to do it herself. Given a few more moments, she could have gotten him off her and sicced security on him.

As a young woman who often traveled alone, she'd made sure to learn self-defense. She had been just about to knee the man in the groin when Jack turned up. Realistically, Natalie knew she'd let her guard down too much at the bar. Multiple drinks with Dana mixed with her preoccupation with spying on Jack had left her vulnerable. She didn't know whether she was angrier at herself for putting herself in that position, or at Jack for avenging her in such an uncivilized way.

Ignoring the fact that the driver could hear their conversation, she turned to Jack and frowned. "Why did you have to hit that guy?" she demanded.

Jack's eyes widened, though she could only see one of them. The other was hidden behind the bag of frozen peas. "Are you kidding me?" he asked, his free hand raking roughly through his hair. "He assaulted you."

"I could have gotten him away from me," Natalie insisted.

"It didn't look like you were making all that much progress," Jack grumbled.

She crossed her arms. "I didn't even know you were going to be there tonight. I didn't ask you to save me."

"It's hard to ask someone to save you when some drunk asshole has your lips locked. I assumed by the way you were pushing him away that you'd be grateful if someone got him off of you."

"Well, you know what they say about those who assume," Natalie muttered under her breath.

"I'm not the one being an ass here," Jack snarled.

Natalie's skin prickled at the implication that she was in the wrong. "I was about to kick him in the nuts. If you'd given me two more seconds, I would have, and then maybe he would have been kicked out of the bar instead of you. But no, you had to go full-on macho mode."

Jack opened his mouth to argue then closed it again, his lips forming a thin line as he took a breath. His voice was low and rough when he finally said, "That man had his hands on you. He kissed you. *Forced* himself on you." Jack's hands fisted at his sides as he spoke. "*No one* is allowed to do that. Do you hear me? No one."

Natalie's eyes widened at the vehemence in his tone. Ironically, Jack seemed more shaken up from the altercation than she was. "I can protect myself," she said, though her voice wasn't quite as confident as she'd intended it to be.

"Natalie," Jack murmured, tipping her chin up until she met his gaze. She found a softness in his eyes that made her melt. "I'm sure you can, but you shouldn't have to."

Natalie chewed on her lip as she considered that.

Jack sighed. "I'm sorry if I jumped in too soon and didn't let you defend yourself. Maybe I was a little… hasty… in my actions. Adrenaline can do that to you."

Returning to her usual feisty self, Natalie snorted. "More like testosterone."

Jack's eyebrows quirked up, and he flinched when the movement affected the injured area of his face.

"Sorry," she said quickly. "Sorry. Maybe I *am* the one being an ass."

Jack chuckled softly. "Nah, you're not. You want to take care of yourself. That's fine. But I don't regret helping you. I'd get chewed out by you a million times if it meant keeping you from getting hurt."

Natalie softened at that. "Thank you for helping me," she bit out. The words weren't the easiest for her to say, and Jack's knowing smile said he understood that.

"You're welcome." He cracked the knuckles on the hand he'd used to punch the guy at the bar. "Anyway, it felt kind of good to hit somebody again. Haven't done that in a while."

Natalie rolled her eyes. "You're a neanderthal."

☼ ☼ ☼

They arrived back at the apartment, and Natalie led Jack upstairs to the couch, ordering him to sit. He winced and cursed as she removed the bag of peas from his eye.

"Sorry," she whispered, moving the peas to his hand. "That's going to hurt in the morning too," she said gently. "I'm going to grab some first aid stuff, and I'll be right back."

Jack nodded and held the bag of peas on his knuckles.

Natalie headed to the bathroom. Before doing anything else, she *had* to brush her teeth. Had to get the taste of that disgusting man out of her mouth. *Scotch. Bleh.* She scrubbed her teeth vigorously, spitting over and over.

Eventually, she put the toothbrush down and wiped the back of her hand over her mouth, the malty taste still burning the insides of her cheeks. Pushing back, she leaned her forehead against the cool tile counter and sighed. Though still aggravated at her inability to protect herself, she had to admit that what Jack had done was pretty heroic—putting himself in the face of danger to shield her. And then she'd argued with him and essentially called him an ass for helping her.

Metaphorically tucking her tail between her legs, Natalie grabbed the first aid kit from the medicine cabinet and made her way back out to the couch, where she found Jack tipping his head back, a tissue held tightly beneath his nose.

"Oh, Jack." She rushed to sit beside him.

"It's nothing, really," he said. "Just a little blood."

"Let me see." Natalie took over the tissue he'd been holding and found a steady, but light, trickle of blood leaking from his nose. Replacing the tissue with a clean one, she instructed Jack to hold it there while she tended to a cut by his eyebrow, gently dabbing away the blood as she prepared to clean it. He hissed when the antiseptic wipe hit the split skin.

"Sorry," she whispered, quickly finishing and sealing the cut with some butterfly closures from the first aid kit. Very gently, she pressed the closures to his skin and examined her work. "That's all set," she said. "How's the nose?"

Jack tipped his head forward and removed the bloody tissue. Luckily, no new blood was trickling out.

"Looks good to me." She dabbed at the last of the blood under his nose then tossed the dirty tissues and wipes into a trash can by the couch. "You're all patched up."

Jack smiled sheepishly. "Thanks, Nat."

Natalie shrugged off his gratitude. "It's no problem. It was my fault you got hurt in the first place."

Jack's smile fell into a frown. "No, it wasn't. Don't blame yourself. You did nothing to provoke that guy. You were just sitting there, minding your own business, when he got all up in your space."

Natalie's eyebrows drew together. "Were you watching me?"

Jack rubbed the back of his neck, his elbow bumping her arm in the process. It was then that she noticed how close they were sitting, angled toward each other so their knees almost touched. She'd sworn to herself she wouldn't get this close to

Jack again, but how else was she supposed to patch up his face?

"Well, yeah," he admitted. "After I saw Dana leave, I was keeping an eye on you. As soon as I saw that guy sit down, I got worried. I know his type. A beautiful woman like you alone in a bar is a sitting duck for creeps like that. I'm just glad I was there. Like I said, I don't regret hitting that guy. You can be mad at me, but I'd do it again."

"I'm not mad," Natalie replied quietly, taking Jack's hand and giving it a small squeeze. "I appreciate you helping me, even if my stubborn pride doesn't."

Jack placed his other hand over hers so he was cradling it. "Are you sure you're ok?"

"Yeah, I'm fine, really," she said then licked her lips, which were dry from the excessive brushing. "I just wish I could get that asshole's taste out of my mouth."

Jack watched her lips as she spoke, and his brown eyes seemed to grow even darker when her tongue darted over them. "Maybe this will help," he murmured. Leaning in until his face was just inches from hers, he paused, as if giving her permission to back away. His breath teased over her lips, taunting her. He was so close, and yet, not quite there. On a moan, Natalie closed the small gap between them, molding her lips to his.

Jack's big hand came to her cheek, holding her in place as he guided her lips in a delicate dance. One thumb trailed down her cheek to her chin, tipping it upward to get a better angle. The kiss was tender, sweet—not sloppy like the one from the asshole at the bar.

Natalie pulled away just far enough to mumble, "Yeah, this helps." She felt Jack's answering smile against her mouth.

Weaving her fingers into his loose curls, Natalie relished the chance to muss Jack's hair the way he always did. She was pleased to find it was as soft as she'd imagined it would be. Softer, even. Fisting a hand in his hair, she tugged lightly, eliciting a moan from Jack as he sealed his mouth over hers. His tongue parted her lips, and she sighed into his mouth. Desperate to get even closer, she placed her other hand on his cheek, completely forgetting about his injury until he winced away from her touch.

Instantly, Natalie pulled away. "Oh my God, Jack, I'm so sorry! I totally forgot," she said, covering her mouth with both hands.

"It's ok, really," Jack said, though he brought one hand up to his injury as if to ensure it hadn't started bleeding again. Determining that he was fine, he pulled her hands into his again. "Are you feeling any better?"

"I'm good." She smiled, thinking of his brilliant way of making her feel better. "Are *you* feeling any better?"

"Yeah, that helped me a lot, too," he admitted, his heated brown eyes locked on her icy-blue ones. "I was so pissed when that asshole kissed you."

Natalie sighed. "Me too. He was really drunk. He probably won't even remember it tomorrow."

"Well, he'll have a bunch of bruises to remind him what went down," Jack said just a little too arrogantly for a man that would be sporting his own black eye.

"As will you," Natalie shot back, pointing to his face. "That's gonna look pretty bad come morning."

Jack shrugged. "I've had worse."

"I'll just bet you have." She shook her head, recalling Dana's account of his escapades back in high school.

Jack brushed a lock of hair behind her ear. "We've both had an exciting night. We should probably get to bed."

"Of course," Natalie agreed, standing up from the couch. "Thanks again."

Jack smirked. "For punching that guy or kissing you?"

Natalie smiled smugly back at him. "Both."

Floating through her bedtime routine, she felt as if she was on cloud nine. She found herself touching her mouth as she washed her face and brushed her hair, recalling the delicious pressure of Jack's lips against hers. The kiss had been pure bliss.

On the edge of that bliss, though, laid fear. What had she gotten herself into? She couldn't offer Jack any type of relationship. He was a Nantucket townie with a baby. She was a transient who'd sworn never to have kids. What kind of couple could they ever be?

Not to mention that he was completely in control of her access to food and shelter on the island. If she did something to screw up their relationship, she worried he could fire her or kick her out of the apartment. Then, she'd have nothing.

Natalie sighed as she climbed into bed. It was just one kiss. One exquisite, heart-pounding, knee-weakening kiss. It didn't have to be anything serious. It didn't mean she had to marry Jack or become Carter's mother or some other ridiculous thing. She was getting way ahead of herself.

Those things would never happen because she would eventually leave Nantucket—and Jack and Carter with it. She was as sure about that as she was that the sun would set each evening. Natalie couldn't risk staying somewhere too long that she would hurt people when she left. *Never stop moving. Never settle. Never do what she did.* Her mother had been out of her life for twenty-something years, and yet she still managed to make it difficult.

Pulling the covers up to her chest, Natalie resolved to talk to Jack in the morning and make sure they were on the same page. She would be a fool not to enjoy his company while she was on the island—you shouldn't waste chemistry that good— but she refused to get herself into something she'd regret.

13

Sitting alone at the kitchen table the next morning, Natalie ran her finger over the rim of her mug as her worries from the night before continued to plague her. She wanted Jack. That much she knew. Everything else got murky. He was her boss—or, as he preferred to think of it— her partner. They lived together. He had a child. She would be leaving at some point in the not-so-distant future.

It wasn't like Natalie to overthink things this way. She'd been with lots of men before, and summer flings were somewhat of a specialty of hers, but this one felt different. Jack had told her he felt like he was finally living like a real adult. He was building a life for himself, complete with a business and a baby. A summer fling didn't exactly fit into that picture. Surely he wanted something more serious than she could give.

Taking a sip of her coffee, Natalie let the caffeine massage her brain as she attempted to prepare for Jack's eventual entrance. Being the first one out to the kitchen gave her some kind of home-court advantage, right?

The sound of his footsteps announced his arrival before Jack appeared in the kitchen, his gray sweatpants and sleep-rumpled t-shirt giving him a charmingly cute look. Natalie groaned internally. How was she supposed to remain objective when he looked positively edible?

"Good morning," Jack said cheerfully, heading for the coffeemaker. As the liquid dripped into his mug, he stretched his arms up overhead and let out a satisfied grunt. Natalie's gaze snagged on the swath of skin that had become visible between his t-shirt and pants, featuring a happy trail that began at his belly button and spread wider as it dipped into his boxers.

She swallowed, wishing she could clear her throat without drawing his attention. "Morning," she replied as neutrally as possible.

Jack lowered his arms and removed his mug from the coffee machine, moving over to the fridge to add milk and creamer. Finally able to look away from his midsection, Natalie gasped when she caught sight of the monstrous black eye marring his face. The bruising had darkened a lot overnight.

"Oh, Jack." She jumped out of her seat to get a closer look at his injury.

He looked down and patted his chest, feigning confusion. "What, is there something on me?"

"Not funny." Natalie ran gentle fingertips over his bruised cheek. "Does it hurt very much?"

"It's not too bad, but I do know something that would make it feel better." Jack waggled his eyebrows playfully.

Natalie ducked her face, determined to talk to him before doing anything that might lead him on, including kissing him again. Pivoting toward the stove, she grabbed a pan and placed it on a burner. "How about some breakfast?"

Jack's grin deflated slightly. "Yeah… yeah, sure."

Natalie kept her gaze down at the pan, unable to bear looking at either Jack's puzzled face or his delectable body, and occupied herself with setting the burner to just the right temperature. "I'll make the eggs. Maybe you could make some bacon?"

"Uh… yeah, sure," Jack said again.

The fridge door opened and shut before he appeared beside Natalie with a carton of eggs and a package of bacon. She cracked a few of the eggs into her pan and scraped them back and forth while he worked on his own task.

Painfully aware of Jack standing beside her, Natalie wished the stove's burners didn't have to be quite so close together. His elbow brushed hers every so often, and despite her attempts to ignore the casual touches, each time his skin brushed hers, she grew more and more aware of the fact that he was *right there*, with his big hands, and his bare feet, and his biceps, and—

"Uh, Nat, I think those are just about done," he said, interrupting her line of thought. She looked down at the dry, overdone eggs she'd been shoveling around the pan. Smoke was radiating off the stove in waves, matching the tension in the room.

"Oh, right," she muttered, removing the pan from the heat and mechanically doling out the eggs onto two plates. Jack slid a few pieces of bacon onto each as well, and they sat across from each other at the table to eat.

"Are you ok?" he finally asked.

"Yeah, fine," Natalie replied absentmindedly.

"Really?" he pressed. "Because last night I kissed you, and I'm pretty sure you liked it, and now you're acting like I don't even exist."

Shit. She dropped her head into her hands and groaned. The last thing she wanted was to hurt Jack's feelings with her actions. The whole point of her avoiding him was so she *wouldn't* end up hurting him.

Finally, she looked up into his big brown eyes brimming with confusion.

"I did like it," she said. "A lot. Too much."

"Ok." Jack raked his fingers through his messy mop of hair. "I'm confused."

Natalie sighed. Of course he was. She was sending mixed signals, and she knew it. "I really like you," she confessed, "and I really liked that kiss. Please don't get me wrong. I just don't know if we should let it happen again."

A frown settled onto his face. "Why?"

"Because we work together, and we live together, and I just think it might make things too complicated."

Jack shook his head. "I don't think so. Like you said, we work together, and we live together, and they're both going pretty well, if you ask me. We already know we're compatible."

"Yes, but…" Natalie chewed on her lip, trying to figure out how to nicely tell him that all she could offer was a summer fling.

"But what?" he pressed.

"But I can't be what you need," she blurted out.

Jack's eyebrows flew up in surprise. He seemed to process her outburst for a moment before intertwining his hands behind his head and leaning back in his chair. "And what is it you think I need?"

Natalie looked around helplessly, wishing she'd just told him she wasn't interested and moved on. "You need someone who fits in with this life you're living now. You need someone serious, who can commit to you. I don't do serious relationships."

Jack released his hands and pushed a couple of errant curls away from his forehead. "God, Natalie. I'm not looking for anything serious. I've had way too much serious shit go down these past few months. What I need is some fun, and I've had more fun since you came into my life than I've had in quite some time."

Natalie smiled sadly. "I'm having a lot of fun with you, too, but like I told you… I wasn't built to settle down. I move a lot, and I don't want to hurt anyone when I do. You need someone you can have a future with, someone who has the potential to be your wife and a mother to Carter."

Jack balked at her, his eyes practically bugging out of his head. "I'm not looking for a wife, Nat. I'm sure as hell not ready to settle down. Up until a few months ago, I had never even entertained the idea of owning a home or having a kid or any of it. I have way too much shit to figure out to even think about marriage."

He reached across the table and grasped her hand. "I just want you, Natalie, exactly as you are. You've made my life so much better these past few weeks, and I've loved hanging out with you. I just want to keep doing that."

Natalie looked down at their intertwined fingers. Jack had made her life a lot better, too, and she would love nothing more than to be with him while she stayed on Nantucket. He just needed to know that it wasn't permanent.

"You don't mind that I'll be leaving at some point?" she asked.

Jack's eyes tightened. "The only thing I need to know is that you won't go kissing any other guys while you're here. It nearly killed me when that son of a bitch attacked you last night."

A smile tugged at Natalie's lips. It was kind of sweet that it tore him up so much, even if she resented his barbarianism at the bar the night before.

Jack squeezed her hand. "Listen, Nat. My best friend just died, and other than Carter, you're the only good thing that's happened to me since. I'm not looking for a serious relationship. We can just keep hanging out, like we have been, except I'll be kissing you a lot more."

Natalie couldn't help but smile at that. "That sounds nice."

"I'm glad you think so," Jack said, swiftly rising from his seat and occupying the one next to her. "Because I plan to start right now." Placing both hands on Natalie's face, he gazed into her eyes for a moment. She drank in the sight of those molten pools of chocolate as he used one long finger to brush a stray lock of hair behind her ear.

Finally lowering his lips to hers, the cool taste of minty fresh toothpaste infiltrated her mouth, awakening her senses as much as Jack's expert kissing did. Careful not to touch his bruised face, she wound one hand into his hair and wrapped the other around his back as his lips continued softly caressing hers.

Pulling back, he nuzzled her nose. With his lips so close to hers, he murmured, "Go out with me next Friday night."

Natalie crinkled her nose. "On a date?"

"Yes," Jack said. "A real date, where I don't have to punch anyone to get your attention."

Natalie bit her lip to contain a smile. "Oh, but you looked so hot doing it last night."

His wicked grin told her he liked that answer.

"Yes," she breathed, and Jack's lips covered hers once more, his tongue parting them and licking into her in long, leisurely strokes.

She let out a small groan when he eventually pulled away.

"Our breakfast is getting cold." He smirked.

"I won't complain."

☼ ☼ ☼

They were washing the dishes when June arrived to drop Carter off. She let herself into the apartment and climbed the stairs, placing Carter on the floor when she reached the top. Jack walked out to greet them while Natalie finished up, though she was at a good vantage point to see and hear everything that went on.

"What's up, little man?" Jack picked Carter up and gave

him a squeeze. "Hey, Mom," he greeted June with a peck on the cheek.

His mother gasped and fussed over his bruised face. "Oh, Jack. What happened?"

"It's nothing, Mom," he said, rolling his eyes and turning away from her scrutiny to place Carter down on the floor. The baby immediately toddled over to Natalie, and she swept him up in her arms, smooching him on the cheek.

"A black eye is not nothing," June insisted. "Did someone hit you?"

"No, actually, I just tripped while I was out last night, and what would you know? I landed right on this dude's fist."

Natalie bit back a laugh at Jack's remark.

"I don't like your sarcasm, young man," June chided, pointing an accusatory finger at her son's chest. "You can't be getting into fights like you're a teenager again. You have responsibilities now."

"I know, Mom." Frustration edged into Jack's tone. "It's not what you think."

"Well, I don't know exactly what to think, Jack. I take care of your baby for one night, and you manage to go out and get a black eye. It's obvious you were in a fight."

Jack's voice took on a pleading edge. "Well, yes, I was, but that's not the whole story. Trust me, it's not like it was in high school."

"Then how was it, Jack? Why don't you enlighten me, because right now it looks pretty damn bad."

Jack began to explain his side of the story. "I was at The Gazebo last night, and—"

"A bar fight, Jack, really? You are a thirty-year-old man. You are the legal guardian of a baby boy."

"I know!" Jack's hand raked through his hair so harshly Natalie worried he would start pulling it out. "Mom, I'm not some foolish kid anymore. Please, let me explain."

June exhaled sharply but remained silent. Feeling bad that

Jack had to defend himself for something he'd done to help her, Natalie put Carter down and walked into the living room to back him up.

"Last night, I was at The Gazebo, and Natalie was there too," Jack began to explain, his demeanor calmer now that June had silently promised to hear him out. "Some jackass was all over her, and he wasn't going away without a fight. He kissed her, and she clearly didn't want it. When I pulled him off of her, he hit me."

That… wasn't exactly what had happened. Natalie was ninety-nine percent sure Jack had thrown the first punch in his rage, and the man had retaliated, perhaps even in self-defense, by punching Jack. But June's face softened at Jack's version of the story, so Natalie didn't correct him.

June turned to her for confirmation. "Natalie, is this true?"

"Yes," she answered quickly. "Jack didn't go looking for a fight. He was just protecting me." That much, at least, was true.

June nodded her understanding and ran two fingers gingerly over her son's blackened brow. "Well, in that case, good work, son."

Jack's relief was evident in the brilliant smile he gave his mom. She held up her finger again in censure. "But please, no more bar fights. Coming home with black eyes is not a good influence for Carter."

"It won't happen again," Jack promised.

"It'd better not," June warned, but there was no malice left in her tone. In fact, her eyes sparkled with what looked a lot like pride.

"I'd better be off. I have a full day planned at my pottery wheel. The summer folks are starting to arrive, and my business will only pick up from here. I've got to keep up with the demand."

"Sounds good. Thanks for taking Carter last night," Jack said.

"It was my pleasure," June replied.

Jack engulfed his mother's smaller frame in a hug, and Natalie just barely heard what she said to him as she hugged him back. "I'm glad you did it, son. Natalie's a keeper."

Turning around, Natalie quietly made her way back to the kitchen where Carter was banging on a pot he'd found in the cabinet. She smiled down at him and ruffled his baby-fine hair until Jack joined them in the kitchen.

"Thank you for sticking up for me even though I know you were mad about what I did," he said.

Natalie sighed. "Of course I stuck up for you, Jack. Yeah, I was pissed that you got into a fistfight over me, but I understand that you were doing what you thought was right. I would never want your mom to be mad at you for something you did because of me."

"Well, I appreciate it." Jack shivered dramatically. "God, I hate when she yells at me like that. Makes me feel like a teenager again."

"I'll bet she really put you through the wringer in high school."

"Absolutely. That was nothing compared to when I was a teenager. She would just yell and yell every time I came home like that, and it happened a lot. Of course, I never had a good reason like I do now. God, I was a terrible kid. But now I realize she was more scared than mad. I mean, I look at Carter, and I think about him coming home with a black eye, and I can't even imagine how it would feel." Jack frowned at the baby, who was still sitting on the floor.

"We should take him down to the beach today," Natalie suggested. "We'll be busy all weekend painting."

"Let's do it." Jack scooped the baby up, planted a chaste kiss on her lips, and led the small group toward the beach for a day of fun in the sun.

14

———

The sun beat down on Natalie's back as she rolled the seafoam green paint onto the shingles of Danny's Place. She and Jack had made good headway on Saturday, and there was only a second coat to do once Sunday rolled around. Natalie loved the way the color looked so far, but Jack said he'd wait until the second coat was up to form an opinion. She wondered if he disliked the color or was just being stubborn because she'd been right.

Carter busied himself with toys in the yard but began growing restless as boredom set in on Sunday morning. Luckily, Natalie had mentioned to Dana on the phone that morning that he might need a change of pace, so she'd swooped in like a knight in shining armor—actually, more like a mom in yesterday's outfit and hair full of dry shampoo, which was arguably more impressive—and taken him to the beach with Justin.

Of course, Dana hadn't initially called to set up a playdate but rather to grill Natalie about the altercation at The Gazebo. Apparently, word had gotten around that a fight had broken out, and Dana was upset she'd missed it. She hadn't even realized Jack had been involved and was downright giddy to receive that information.

"A man punching someone over you?" she'd said. "That's hot!" Dana had been even more excited to hear about the kiss, telling Natalie that she should really "tap that" and "get some." Natalie had rolled her eyes so hard she wouldn't have been surprised if they fell right out of her head.

When Dana arrived to pick Carter up the next day, her not-so-subtle looks and wiggling eyebrows had Natalie holding back laughter. Jack just shook his head and muttered, "I'm not even gonna ask."

With Carter occupied for the morning, they were able to work alongside each other undisturbed, and when peak sunlight hours hit, they laid their brushes down and stepped back to survey their handiwork.

"It looks pretty great, if I do say so myself," Natalie said, holding a hand above her brow to block out the sun.

"Mhmm," Jack mumbled, wiping a bead of sweat from his forehead with the back of his hand. "Damn, it's hot out here."

"If you want to take your shirt off to cool down, I don't mind," Natalie suggested with a coy bat of her eyelashes.

Jack's predatory gaze turned on her. "I'll bet you wouldn't," he said, striding toward her. "But I think that might distract you from your work."

Natalie smirked up at him. "Oh, trust me, I'm already distracted."

His mouth curved up in a sly smile. "Is that so?" Looming over her, Jack backed her up into the wall, trapping her with a big hand on either side of her head.

"The paint's still wet!" Natalie cried, trying to wiggle out of his hold.

"Screw the paint," Jack growled, stilling her with a hand on her shoulder and catching her lips with his. Struggling only for a moment, Natalie promptly surrendered to his expert kiss.

Under his spell, the threat of ruining the wall or getting paint on her clothing vanished in an instant.

Jack inched closer until every inch of his hard body pressed her into the wall. She gasped, and he took advantage, sweeping his hot tongue through her open lips and taking his time to probe her mouth leisurely, his tongue licking into her again and again.

Grabbing his biceps, slick with a sheen of sweat, Natalie pulled Jack infinitesimally closer. Heat radiated off his body as the sun continued to beat down on them, mirroring the fire growing in her belly. She kissed him back with abandon, enjoying the sensations of his lush lips against hers and the rough scrape of his stubble against her cheeks.

Though mostly hidden from prying eyes where they stood behind Danny's, Dana still managed to intrude on the moment.

"Woah-oh, babies in the vicinity!" her shrill voice called out. "Babies in the vicinity!"

Natalie giggled into Jack's mouth before he managed to pull away. Clearing his throat, his cheeks turned just slightly pink, which just made her laugh even harder.

"Hi, Dana." Jack removed his hands from the wall, freeing Natalie. She peeled herself away and craned her neck to see if she'd gotten paint on her back, but her cursory glance didn't detect any.

"Hey, kids." Dana smirked. "Working hard or hardly working?"

Natalie crossed her arms defensively. "We actually got a lot done."

"I can tell," Dana said dryly, inspecting the area of the wall that Jack had pressed Natalie up against. Though her shirt hadn't removed any of the paint, the fabric had left a textured imprint on it. "Looks like you may need one more coat."

Jack scratched his head and turned to Natalie. "Maybe I should have listened to you."

She rolled her eyes and gave him a light smack on the chest. "Duh. You really have no respect for wet paint, do you?" Turning to the boys, she picked up a sleepy, slow-moving Carter and surveyed Justin as he sucked a sand-covered thumb. "Looks like they tired themselves out," Natalie noted.

"Yeah," Dana said. "I have to get Justin home for his nap, or he'll be cranky all day. Are you two going to be able to leave your 'work' for long enough to watch your kid?"

Jack rolled his eyes as the adorable pink blush seeped from his skin. "We've got him, Dana. Thanks for helping us out this morning."

"Glad I could help." Dana winked mischievously, scooping up Justin and heading for home.

Natalie hugged Carter to her chest and took another look at the newly painted walls. "So, what do you think of the color?" she asked, hoping she'd only have to fix the area they had damaged and not redo all the walls with a new color.

Jack studied the paint for a moment. "It's... a little bright."

Natalie cocked her head to the side. "Is bright a bad thing?"

"Er, no," he replied. "It's just different."

Natalie patted his arm. "You'll get used to it."

"I guess anything is better than what was there before," Jack admitted.

"Well, that's a glowing review," she teased. "It'll take some time to get used to, as most things do."

She watched Jack's profile as he took one last look at the wall then dropped his head and sighed. "Yeah."

Silently, Natalie waited for him to say more about how he felt, about how it was hard for him to move on and make changes to Danny's, but all he said was, "We should probably get Carter inside for a nap."

Natalie looked down at the baby, who was fighting to keep his eyes open. "Good call."

She rocked Carter to sleep while Jack worked, and once the baby was down, she decided to start a new painting. Since her epiphany about adding in more precise details, painting had come much easier, and she'd already completed two more beach scenes and sent them over to Ned.

Looking for something a little different to paint this time, Natalie scrolled through the camera roll on her phone with quick flicks of her finger. Past the snapshots of boats in the harbor and the close-ups of various flowers, she came across the photo she'd taken of Jack and Carter in the ocean. Jack's swim trunks hung low on his hips, his shoulders and biceps bulging with the effort of tossing Carter up in the air.

That's the one, Natalie thought as she blew up the photo with her fingers. Though she normally preferred landscapes, she couldn't resist that particular picture. Carter wore a huge, heart-melting grin that revealed just how much he loved the man with him. If she kept the facial details to a minimum and focused her efforts on the figures and the ocean, the painting would appeal to a wide audience. Anyone who had fond memories of playing in the ocean with a parent would enjoy having the piece as a reminder of simpler times.

Getting herself into the zone, Natalie turned on her favorite mellow playlist and squeezed out a few colors of paint. The ocean came together quickly, as she was used to landscapes and had gotten the colors down pat on her previous paintings. Jack's and Carter's figures would be more difficult.

Wanting so badly to do Jack's delicious body justice, Natalie bit her lip in concentration as she created the shape of his torso rising out of the waves. Using thin brushes, she carefully carved each individual muscle into his back and shoulder blades. The musculature continued up his arms, from the bulge of his biceps to the veins that popped out in his forearms. She took her time mixing the slightly varying skin tones to create the shadows and dips that formed his athletic figure.

Sitting back to look at her work, Natalie sighed—not because it looked bad, but because she'd nailed it. All that was on the canvas so far was the ocean and Jack's back and arms, but those in themselves made up a masterpiece. Tracing the planes of his painted body with her gaze, she caught a chill that made her shiver and sent goosebumps racing down her bare arms.

What did the rest of him look like? Now that they'd set the parameters of their relationship, and Jack knew that Natalie was only staying temporarily, she could enjoy him guilt-free. And she planned to enjoy him, indeed.

☼ ☼ ☼

"Wow, you've been busy," Natalie murmured as she took in the array of pages scattered across Dana's table the next day. Carter and Justin were playing while the women went over the rough draft of Dana's book. She had a very cute concept of a farm where the animals fight over which one is the superior species, only to find out that each possesses its own unique talent that helps them work together to solve various problems. It was the quintessential children's story. Kids would love the talking farm animals, and parents would love the message it sent about teamwork and individuality.

"Sure have!" Dana said, nudging Natalie with her elbow. "Some of us don't have budding romances to occupy our time."

Natalie grinned at the thought of Jack, trying her best not to look like the heart-eyed emoji. It was difficult with how incredibly wonderful he made her feel.

"How are things going with him?" Dana asked.

"Great." Natalie sighed dreamily. "He's sweet, charming, a perfect gentleman. And an excellent kisser."

"Perfect gentleman, my ass!" Dana hooted. "You've got to get that man in bed. I'll bet he's wild under the covers."

Natalie shook her head but grinned at the thought of getting Jack in bed. "A girl can only hope."

"So you're still hoping? You haven't slept with him yet?" Dana pried.

Natalie rolled her eyes at the intrusive question. "Not that it's any of your business, but no, I haven't. We're trying to take things slow because we work together, and he has Carter, and we need to make sure we don't rush into anything."

Dana tapped her chin. "That makes sense. But don't take things too slow. I'm dying here, and I need some juicy details to keep me entertained."

Natalie turned to the messy table. "Why don't we keep you entertained with work?" she suggested. "I have lots of ideas for the illustrations."

Dana deflated into her chair but said, "Let me have 'em."

Natalie sat down and put her hands on the table. "I'm thinking blurred watercolor backgrounds with more detailed foregrounds. So, the sky and grass and everything will sort of blend together, and then the animals will be in sharp focus." She'd been experimenting with the ratio of detail to negative space in her own paintings and concluded that it would be the perfect balance for the book as well. "The story is all about celebrating individual differences. Putting the detailed animals against a softer background will highlight their unique looks."

Dana nodded her head approvingly. "I like it."

"Why don't we go through the pages you have here and come up with rough drafts of what we'd like on each one." Natalie gestured to the sea of paper scattered across the table.

"Let's do it." Dana held up her hand for a high five, which Natalie enthusiastically gave.

A few hours later, after being interrupted by plenty of diaper changes, snack breaks, and switching of toys to keep the babies interested, Natalie was finally finished drawing out rough sketches of each picture. The story was short, so it didn't have many illustrations, but it took a few sketches of each to satisfy Dana. Natalie didn't mind doing them over a few times. She actually appreciated that Dana cared enough about her work to want everything to be perfect.

Once finished, Natalie gathered up all her sketches and put them in a folder to bring home. She would paint the images over the next few weeks then meet with Dana again to put everything together. When they got the final product in their hands, they'd start sending it out to agents.

The babies were both zonked by the time they'd finally wrapped up their brainstorming, so the women got them down for naps and returned to the kitchen to relax for a bit. Opening up her bag, Natalie removed two small, white boxes.

"I figured we would want to celebrate," she said, opening one of the boxes to reveal a chocolate cupcake loaded with frosting. "I stole two cupcakes from Danny's for us."

"Girl, you sure know how to celebrate!" Dana cried. "I mean, normally I'd suggest wine, but it is the middle of the day and all. And those don't look half bad." Dana eyed the mountain of fluffy vanilla frosting balanced precariously on the small cupcake. Peeling back the wrapper, she sunk her teeth into it.

"Mmmmmm," she groaned. "I think I just had an orgasm."

Natalie slapped Dana's arm, giggling at her crude remark.

"So, when are you gonna get one?" Dana asked, her mouth full. She'd finished off her cupcake on the third bite.

"One what?" Natalie asked, biting into her own dessert.

"An orgasm."

Natalie almost spit out the mouthful of cake. "Dana!" she cried. "Not this again."

"Oh, come on, don't be such a prude." Dana sliced her hand through the air. "I need some details! I've known Ryan since I was sixteen. When you've been with someone as long as I have, things get a little boring. I love him and all, but we're old news. You and Jack are fresh and exciting. I'm living vicariously through you, girl, so you'd better spill."

"Fine." Natalie sighed. "He's a great kisser. We've had some pretty intense moments. You intruded on one of those." She glared at Dana, making her friend's mischievous smile grow even wider. "But I worry about getting in too deep with him."

"What do you mean by that?" Dana asked, putting down her cupcake wrapper and wiping her sticky hands with a napkin. Natalie was grateful Dana had turned serious along with her instead of using the opportunity to make some wisecrack about "getting in deep."

"Jack's different from the guys I've been with in the past," Natalie explained. "He has more responsibility with Carter and Danny's. He can't just have some summer fling. He says he's ok with not knowing how long I'll be here, but I have a hard time believing that."

"Is that what you want?" Dana asked. "A fling?"

Natalie shrugged. "I don't know. It doesn't really feel like a fling. We live together. I care for his kid. I've met his mom. It feels kind of serious."

"Serious isn't a bad thing," Dana said gently.

"It's a scary thing," Natalie admitted.

"It doesn't have to be," Dana said, her tone soft, comforting, and distinctly un-Dana-like.

"I don't even know how long I'm planning to stay," Natalie argued. "I can't give him any commitment beyond the fact that I'll probably stay until summer's over and the weather takes a turn for the worse. I will have finished all my paintings for Ned's gallery by then, so I may be ready to move on."

Dana cocked her head to the side. "Did Jack ask you for a commitment?"

"Well… no," Natalie said. "He said he just wants to have fun."

Dana smacked her hand on the table, back to her usual over-the-top self. "Then have some freakin' fun, Natalie! Don't you want to enjoy Jack while you're here, no matter how long that is?"

Natalie could come up with no answer other than a mumbled, "Yes."

"Then enjoy it. Humans are meant to build relationships. We're hard-wired for it. Don't fight the instinct."

"You don't think it's a bad idea?" Natalie asked, uncertainty edging into her voice.

"Not at all," Dana assured her. "You and Jack are great together."

A soft smile grew on Natalie's lips at that statement. They *were* pretty great together.

Across the table, Dana sighed wistfully. "Ah, young love."

Natalie glanced dubiously at her. "I'm only two years younger than you, Dana. And Jack is older than you are."

"I know." Dana chuckled in reply. "But you two are like lovesick teenagers. I mean, playing tonsil hockey behind the café is *so* high school."

A blush rose into her cheeks as Natalie recalled the kiss Dana had intruded upon. I guess," she said. "But it sure is fun."

Dana scooted to the edge of her chair. "So, when is the fun going to continue? When are you two wild kids going on a date?"

"Friday," Natalie said. "And I've been meaning to ask… would you mind taking Carter for the evening? June will have him during the day, but she has a dinner to go to, so she can't watch him."

"Of course," Dana said. "Why don't I just go ahead and take him for the whole night?"

"Would you mind?" Natalie asked, already picturing how lovely it would be to have an uninterrupted night with Jack.

"Not at all." Dana winked. "It might be a late night, after all."

Natalie shook her head. "Ok, we are so done with this conversation, but thank you for watching him."

Dana smirked. "Anytime."

When the boys awoke, Natalie packed up and drove home. Jack was busy working at the café, so she took Carter up to the apartment, changed him into his swimsuit, and brought him down to the beach, where she spread out a large, colorful blanket to lounge on while the baby ran wildly around the sand.

Removing her cover-up, Natalie revealed her new white bikini. She'd found herself going to the beach so often that she had splurged on some new swimsuits. This one was a bit skimpy, making it ideal for sun tanning. She hoped to get a nice golden glow before her date, so she lay back on her forearms to bask in the hot sun. Closing her eyes for a long moment, she drank in the warmth of the sunlight on her bare skin.

Natalie's eyes popped open when sand began pelting her feet. Looking down her nose, she found Carter kneeling in the sand and dumping handfuls of it right onto both her and the blanket. "Oh, buddy, hang on." She quickly scooted up farther so her feet were off the edge of the blanket. "Ok, now you can bury my feet!"

She'd taught Carter that trick the last time they had been at the beach, and he found it quite hilarious. He continued dropping sand onto Natalie's feet, and she showed him how to pat it down to really make it look like her feet had disappeared.

"Ok, your turn now!" she said when her feet were sufficiently buried. Carter sat down next to her, and she began burying his feet as well. He squealed every time a grain of sand hit his skin, which made her laugh. Once they were both buried, Natalie prepared for Carter's favorite part of the game.

"Ready?" she asked.

"Yeah!" Carter shouted.

"One, two… three!" Natalie cried, and both of them kicked their feet into the air, dislodging the sand so it flew everywhere. Natalie accompanied it with an explosion noise, making Carter shriek until they both erupted into laughter.

"Again!" he cheered.

"Ok," Natalie obliged, knowing that if Carter found something fun, she would have to do it at least fifteen times before he got bored.

They were nearing that fifteenth time when Natalie spotted Jack walking down to the beach, wearing only his swimming trunks. She gazed longingly at his body, taking in his long, muscled legs, flat abdomen, and broad shoulders. While her painting of him was looking rather impressive, nothing could top the real thing.

Jack reached the blanket and sat down, dropping a tube of sunscreen beside him. "Hey, guys." He kissed the top of Natalie's head and mussed Carter's hair with his hand. "What are you two up to?"

"We've been burying each other's feet."

"Ah," Jack said. "That's always fun. Is this munchkin wearing sunscreen?" He tugged on Carter's t-shirt to keep the boy from running off.

"Yep," Natalie replied. "I should probably put some on, though. I was tanning, but I wouldn't want to burn."

"Good idea." Jack handed Natalie the tube, and she squeezed a glob into her hand, rubbing it slowly down her arms and legs, extra careful not to miss any spots. The only thing worse than über-pale skin was splotchy skin.

Jack's gaze remained hot on her as her fingers trailed over every inch of exposed skin. Refusing to meet his gaze, Natalie instead let him enjoy the show. When she was finished with all the skin she could reach, she turned to him and held out the tube of sunscreen with big, innocent eyes and an expectant smile. "Could you do my back?"

Jack blinked and cleared his throat. "Ah, sure," he replied in a gravelly tone, taking the tube she handed him and squirting some sunscreen onto his palm. Natalie held her long, blonde ponytail out of the way so he would have better access to her back.

Kneeling behind her, Jack hesitated for a moment before placing his hands gingerly on her skin and applying the sunscreen. His big hands rubbed small, gentle circles on her lower back, eventually drifting upward, swiping underneath the strap of her bikini, and finally reaching her upper back. His touch became more confident as he went on, his strong hands kneading her shoulder blades until they softened ever so slightly down her back. Natalie closed her eyes and hummed out a sigh, her neck lolling to the side in her relaxed state.

Jack's lips came down on the sensitive skin of her exposed throat. "All done," he whispered in her ear, nipping her earlobe lightly.

A shiver raced down Natalie's spine. "Thanks." Blinking her eyes open, she remained slightly dazed, having almost forgotten that she was sitting on a beach with other people around.

"Hey, Carter, wanna bury my feet now?" Jack asked casually, as if he hadn't felt the intense heat between them just a moment ago. She had put on a sexy show of applying sunscreen to her arms and legs, yet Jack had managed to turn the tables and make *her* blush.

Damn, he was good. And she was more excited than ever for their date.

15

———————

Natalie awoke earlier than usual on Friday, giddy with excitement about her plans. She was headed to Bartlett Farm to pick out new plants for the garden at Danny's, then she would get as many of them in the ground as possible before her date with Jack. Her heart quivered at the thought.

Bounding to the shower, she fit in a quick rinse before Carter awoke, planning for a more extravagant one when she finished her gardening. There was no use in getting all cleaned up if she was going to end up sweaty.

June arrived at nine a.m., right on time to pick up the baby. "Good morning, Natalie," the older woman greeted her cheerfully. "And good morning to you too, little mister," she added, plucking Carter up off the ground and tickling his belly as he screeched with delight.

Natalie got up to give Jack's mom a quick hug. "Hey, June."

June raised an eyebrow. "I hear you and my son are going on a date tonight."

"Yes, we are," Natalie said cautiously, unsure what Jack

had said about it. She wasn't used to sharing any details of her personal life with a parent.

To her relief, June responded, "I'm glad to hear it. You're good for him, you know. He's happier now than I've seen him in quite a while."

"Oh," Natalie said. "I'm glad. He makes me really happy too."

"Good." June's broad smile tightened. "He hides it well, but Jack took Danny's death quite hard."

Natalie nodded. "He doesn't talk about it much, and he changes the subject whenever I try to bring it up, but I can tell he's still struggling."

"Jack and Danny were thick as thieves as kids," June explained. "I was always so thankful their friendship continued into adulthood. My other sons moved off the island after high school, and I was glad Jack still had someone who was like a brother to him here. Of course, Danny had his stint in the Navy, so he was gone for a bit, but that was before my youngest, Beau, graduated. This is the first time Jack hasn't had one of his brothers or Danny around, and unfortunately, it's the time when he probably needs them the most. He won't talk to me. I think he's afraid to dredge up any old memories of my husband's death. I keep telling him I'm here to listen, but he's so stubborn. That's why I'm glad you two have been getting close. He needs someone he can just be honest with."

Natalie's chest tightened at the thought of Jack holding all that inside, but she was honored that June saw her as someone to confide in. "I hope I've been able to help him deal with it, even in some small way. I wish he *did* have his brothers around to talk to. Maybe he'd be more willing to open up to one of them?"

June cocked her head to the side. "Actually, I think you might be exactly what he needs right now. Jack has always feared showing weakness around his brothers. I've tried to tell him that everyone goes through periods of grief—there's no shame in that—but maybe what he needs right now is a softer touch to make him comfortable."

Natalie sighed, hoping June was right. She would love to be the person Jack opened up to.

June bent over to pick up Carter then turned back to Natalie. "I'm going to let you get to work, but I hope you two have fun tonight. I really am happy you're together."

A contented smile worked its way onto Natalie's face as she thanked June with a quick hug and said goodbye to Carter. Bolstered by June's approval, she headed down the stairs and practically skipped into the café. The bell on the door tinkled softly as she entered, and her joyful mood heightened even more when she saw that many of the tables and seats at the bar were occupied.

"Good morning," Jack called to Natalie from his spot behind the counter.

"Morning!" She grinned widely as she headed toward him. "This place is hopping today, huh?"

Jack nodded eagerly. "Business has been great lately."

"Maybe it's the new paint color," she suggested.

A customer at the bar paused between bites of his bacon, egg, and cheese sandwich. "The color looks great!" he said. "I noticed it as soon as you put it up. Really gives the place a fresh look."

Natalie shot Jack a triumphant grin, which he rolled his eyes at but was polite enough to thank the customer for the compliment. She winked and pecked him on the cheek. "Keys, please."

Jack leaned over the counter so he could reach her. "I'm gonna need more than that to fork over my keys to you, missy," he said, bringing their lips together for a healthier kiss.

Natalie laughed as she pulled away, aware they were in their place of business. "I've really got to get going. I have a date with this super-hot guy tonight, and I can't risk running late."

Jack fished the car keys out of his pocket and placed them in Natalie's open palm, closing her fingers around them to form a fist.

"Have fun with the garden," he said, still holding her fist, "but make sure you're done by six. That way you have time to get ready for dinner. We'll leave at seven."

"Got it," Natalie replied. "Where are we going?"

"It's a surprise," Jack answered with a playful smile.

"Oh, I like surprises. But how will I know what to wear?"

Jack craned his neck down to kiss her temple and whisper in her ear. "Wear something short that shows off your legs."

Heat blossomed in Natalie's belly, and she grinned. "Will do."

Jack released her hand so she could leave.

"Any specific plant requests?" she asked.

Jack shrugged. "Hydrangeas are really popular around here. I think some of those would be nice."

"Hydrangeas. Got it. Anything else?"

"Nah, just keep it simple."

Natalie nodded. "Ok. I'll see you in a bit."

"Be done by six," he reminded her.

She saluted him and gave him a quick kiss on the lips. "Ay ay, captain."

Walking out of Danny's, Natalie twirled Jack's keys around her pointer finger then spent the ride over to Bartlett Farm planning the outfit she would wear on their date. She had the perfect thing to show off her legs—a short but tasteful black dress she'd gotten at a boutique in L.A. The harsh color was softened by a smattering of brightly colored flowers, not unlike the ones she planned to buy moments from now. Its zipper went all the way from her shoulder blades to her lower back. She practically cackled to herself as she imagined what Jack's reaction to it would be.

Bouncing through the aisles at the farm, Natalie surveyed the various plants she could choose from. She wanted to get all perennials so they would come back every year, which would make it easy for whoever kept up the maintenance of the garden after she left.

Quickly locating the hydrangeas Jack had requested, she put a handful of them onto her rolling cart. Just beyond that display was another full of gorgeous black-eyed susans, so Natalie claimed a few of those as well. Turning a corner, she discovered some daisies. Simple and classic, their yellow centers made them the perfect counterpart to the black-eyed susans. She added some to her cart.

Around the corner, she spied coneflowers, also known as Echinacea—something she had learned about from a Minnesotan farmer in her travels. The Lakota Sioux had been using it for hundreds of years to cure a variety of ailments. She didn't expect Jack to be harvesting it for medicinal use, but she also knew it tended to attract butterflies, which was something Carter would surely enjoy. Add to cart.

Walking a little farther and pushing her increasingly heavy load, Natalie gasped when she came across an array of nearly full-grown sunflower plants. They had to be at least six feet tall, and each flower dwarfed her head. It brought her back to a sunflower festival she'd attended in New Hampshire, where they had the biggest field of blooming sunflowers she'd ever laid eyes on. She couldn't very well build a sunflower field at Danny's, but she could add a touch of their magic to the garden. After a short struggle with the massive plants, she hefted a few onto her cart.

Natalie was almost to the outdoor checkout counter when a small display of cacti caught her eye. Picking up one of the pots, she inspected the tag for the prickly pear cactus. Though surprised to see that the species could grow in the Northeast, she read on the tag that the hardy plant thrived in sandy soil, like that on Nantucket. The prickly paddles even sprouted little flowers that reminded her of the saguaros she'd painted in Arizona. She grabbed a few to line the walkway to Danny's.

Though no one else may ever realize it, the garden would be like a little ode to all of her travels.

A kind worker helped Natalie load up the Jeep. Thankfully, the car's open roof accommodated the tall sunflower plants. Once she got everything home, she quickly got to work tilling the soil to prepare it for its new tenants.

Getting the plants in the ground proved to be a bigger task than Natalie had originally expected. When Jack had told her to be done by six, she'd scoffed, thinking she'd finish far before then. But, alas, six o'clock rolled around, and she was hurrying to finish. She had just packed the soil around the last prickly pear cactus when Jack sauntered out into the yard.

Natalie stood and wiped her hands over her shorts, watching for his reaction. His eyebrows hiked up as he examined the array of flowers she'd planted. Running his fingers through his hair, Jack muttered a disheartening, "Wow, that's… something."

Natalie's heart dropped into her stomach. "You don't like it?" She had worked so hard picking out the plants and getting them into the ground and had been so proud of herself at how everything had turned out. Jack's lack of enthusiasm knocked her spirit down quite a few pegs.

"No, it's not that," he said quickly, shoving a few curls away from his eyes. "It's just… a lot."

"I know you wanted simple," Natalie said, "but this isn't too over the top, is it? I kept a pretty consistent color theme— mostly yellows and whites with the pops of pink from the coneflowers and hydrangeas. I picked a few different flower heights to really fill in the space. But like I said with the paint, if you hate it, I'll redo it."

"No, no, don't do that." Jack leaned against the building and shoved his hands into his pockets as if his hair couldn't take any more abuse from them. He silently studied the garden for a few moments before looking back up at her. "You really thought this through, didn't you?"

"Well, yeah," Natalie said with a shrug. "I figured that planning a garden is kind of like planning a painting. You pick a color scheme and a few key elements and balance them all out with some negative space." She pointed to the pockets of dirt where nothing grew.

Jack followed her finger and nodded. "That makes sense."

"I know you only asked for hydrangeas, and that's very classic Nantucket, but remember that we're trying to be unique. We need things that set us apart."

Jack lifted a hand toward his head but stopped at his cheek, rubbing it over the stubble that had grown out a bit on his jaw. "Between the paint color and the garden, it looks like a different place," he said quietly.

"It may look different—and if I dare say so myself, better —but it's still Danny's," Natalie reminded him softly. "It's still the product of his dreams and his hard work, just with our touches on it."

Jack bit his lip as he considered that. Natalie watched him work it between his teeth and imagined what it would feel like to have those teeth tugging at her own lip—-or at other things…

"I love the new plants!" a woman walking by with her dog shouted, flicking her thumb up in approval. "The place is really looking nice."

Breaking out of her fantasy, Natalie pursed her lips as she waited for Jack's reaction to the woman's comment. He sighed heavily but called out a polite, "Thank you!" Turning back to Natalie, he said, "You're right. It's really hard for me to see this place changing, but it does look good. It's just different than what I expected. I'm sorry if I hurt your feelings by not being excited. I appreciate your hard work, and it's obviously helping bring customers in." He smiled sheepishly. "So, thank you."

Natalie leaned up on her tiptoes to kiss his cheek. "You're forgiven, and you're welcome. *I* know it looks fabulous, so don't feel pressured to placate me. I just want you to be happy with the changes we're making because they're so good and they're helping so much."

"I'm adjusting." Jack smirked. "It helps that you get so adorably excited over each one."

Natalie grinned up at him. "It makes up for your adorable grumpiness."

He kissed the tip of her nose before moving lower to try and catch her lips, but she put her hands up and backed away. "If I recall correctly, some bossy guy told me I had to go get ready for my date by six, so I'd better get inside before he comes after me."

Jack's eyes took on a predatory glint. "You'd better. Who knows what he'll do if he catches you?"

He took a long step toward Natalie, and she whirled around, shrieking. "See you in an hour!" she called as she dashed toward the apartment door.

16

———————

After a long, hot shower with a deep-cleansing hair wash and multiple rounds of meticulous shaving, Natalie spritzed on a bit of her favorite perfume, slipped into her sexiest, laciest bra and panties, and donned the floral black dress. A quick glance at the mirror confirmed that it did indeed show off her legs to a compelling degree.

Heading for the closet, she rifled through the jumble of shoes scattered over the floor. Her collection had grown immensely since she'd arrived on Nantucket, but who could blame her? The stores along Main Street had the most fashionable pieces, and Natalie hadn't been able to resist treating herself to a few. Toward the back of the closet, underneath a multitude of flip-flops, she discovered a pair of sandals she'd forgotten she had. Their lack straps and block heels made them sexy as sin but still casual enough to wear to dinner.

Slipping them onto her feet, Natalie returned to the mirror and did a quick twirl, landing back in front of her reflection. Her necklace swished around her throat as she halted. Reaching up, she fingered the celestial pendant she'd worn every moment since June gave it to her. It looked rather perfect with her outfit, and the thought had her lips curving up in a small smile.

Taking a deep breath, she headed for the kitchen, her heels clicking against the hardwood. Jack was putting away the dishes but paused midway to the cabinet as she came into view, the plate in his hand suspended in midair. "Wow," he said. "You look gorgeous."

"Thanks," she replied, smoothing out her dress with her hands. "I hope I look alright for wherever we're going."

"You look more than alright," Jack assured her, finally placing the plate into the cabinet. "You look sensational."

Natalie's cheeks heated as his gaze roamed up and down her legs repeatedly, and she took the opportunity to study him too. His white button-up shirt and black jeans made him look hot as hell, but the black Converse sneakers he wore added a bit of boyish charm. The combination was the exact embodiment of Jack.

"Ready to go?" he asked, drying his hand on a dish towel and reaching for hers.

"Absolutely," Natalie answered, taking his hand as he led her to the car. As a gift on this day of their first date, she didn't complain when he opened her door.

After a short drive, they pulled up to a charming brick building with flower boxes on each window and a sign above the door that read *Bella's* in red neon letters.

"This place looks cute," Natalie commented as she gazed at the restaurant.

"Great food too," Jack said, hopping out of the Jeep. Coming around to her door, he swung it open and held out his hand. "Shall we?"

Natalie took it with a smile and allowed herself to be led into the restaurant. The interior immediately captivated her with its exposed brick walls, wrought-iron wall sconces, and portraits of the Italian countryside. The low lighting was very romantic, as were the roses set on each table atop lacy white tablecloths.

"It's beautiful," she breathed as they glided through the dining room.

"Wait until you see where we're sitting," Jack said, his grin buzzing with excitement. Curiosity sparked, Natalie raised her eyebrows in question, but Jack just winked and squeezed her hand as he continued leading her through the sea of tables. They came to a stop toward the back of the restaurant where there was a hostess waiting.

"Hi, we've got a reservation for McNally," Jack said.

The hostess checked her binder and verified their reservation. "Right this way," she said, leading them toward a door at the very back of the room. Feeling like a VIP at some kind of exclusive club, Natalie tried to imagine what kind of surprise the back door may have been hiding. Assuming it would be some kind of intimate dining room, she was pleasantly surprised when it turned out to be a gorgeous outdoor patio.

Dining tables were separated by old-fashioned room dividers in a variety of colors and patterns, making each table seem like it was in its own private room. Around the outer edge of the patio, separating it from the outdoors, were rows of waist-high flower boxes bursting with vibrant blooms. Overhead, strands of twinkling white lights criss-crossed over each other, creating a luminescent canopy over the whole patio. They set a nice ambiance for the area and continued the romantic motif set inside.

"Oh, Jack," Natalie whispered as she took in her surroundings, understanding immediately why he had been so excited for her to see it.

"The beauty is in the details, right?" Jack smiled down at her, and she shook her head incredulously, unsure how the man knew her so well already.

"Here you are," the hostess said as they arrived at a table

bordered by brilliantly colored dahlias. "Your server will be right over."

"Thanks," Jack said, flashing her his sexy smile and making her do a double take. Natalie fought the urge to roll her eyes at the reaction, knowing that hers would have been the same if she'd been seeing Jack's smile for the first time.

Sitting delicately on a chair and tugging her dress down slightly to cover her thighs, Natalie gazed up at the canopy of twinkling lights. "I've never seen anything like this," she murmured.

"I'm glad you like it," Jack said, his smile satisfied as he watched her soak in the atmosphere. "I had a feeling you would."

A waitress came by and took their drink orders—white wine for both of them—and they perused the menu full of classic dishes with unique twists. Jack ordered cocoa-and-coffee-rubbed steak, while Natalie chose shrimp-and-crab ravioli. The waitress returned with their wine, pouring it into their respective glasses with a sophisticated flourish.

"So," Jack said after taking his first sip. "You've been here a few weeks now. What do you think so far?"

Natalie arched a brow. "Of Nantucket, or you?"

Jack's lips broke out in a wide grin. "Both."

She sipped her wine to hide a smile. "Well, Nantucket is fabulous, as I'm sure you well know. As for you...well, I suppose tonight is the true test, isn't it?"

"How am I doing so far?" Jack asked, a hint of vulnerability looming in his voice.

Natalie glanced around the enchanting patio area, smiling as she returned her gaze to his. "I'd say you're pretty much killing it so far."

Jack silently fist pumped the air, coaxing a giggle from her. "I figured The Shack wasn't fancy enough," he said, "and after what happened at The Gazebo, that wasn't an option."

Natalie shook her head. "Jack, I don't care about any of

that stuff. It doesn't matter to me where we go, just that we get to have time alone together."

He rewarded her with a satisfied smile just as the waitress headed over with their food.

"Oh, hey, Jack," the waitress said as she placed his meal down in front of him. "I haven't seen you around here in a while. Not since…" She trailed off, realization dawning on her at the same time it did Natalie. *Not since Danny died.*

"Yeah, I've been pretty busy," Jack said, his hand finding its way into his hair. He raked it through once then seemed to catch himself and picked up his wine, twirling the glass between his fingers.

"I'm so sorry," the waitress said softly. "He was a good man."

"Yes," Jack said brusquely, lifting his glass to his lips for an exaggerated slug of wine. The waitress' eyes widened momentarily before she spun and scurried away. There was nothing but silence for a few long moments as Jack and Natalie each took awkward bites of their meals. He chewed stiffly, and she wondered if he even tasted the delicious food.

"So, you and Danny used to come here?" she eventually asked in a soft voice.

When Jack's eyes met hers, they looked far away but quickly snapped into focus. Clearing his throat, he replied, "Yeah, we used to come to the bar here sometimes." He cast a glance toward the inner part of the restaurant.

Natalie took one of his hands over the table and rubbed gentle circles over his skin. "Tell me more about him."

Jack dragged his other hand through his hair and shrugged. "He was my best friend. Ever since we were kids, we were like brothers." He paused, as if deciding whether or not to go on. Then, after a deep breath, a small grin graced his lips, and he continued. "Danny always did the right thing. I mean, even when we were kids, we would come back from playing outside or whatever, and I would be covered in mud, and he would be spotless. My mother would always ask, 'Why can't you be more like Danny?'" He mimicked his mom's tone with a wry grin.

"She compared me to Fletcher and Beau, sure, but man, did she compare me to Danny. It must've been because we were the same age. She couldn't understand why I was never as mature as him." Jack shook his head. "I wish I'd listened to her. I wish I *had* been more like him. Danny got married at the right time. Had kids at the right time. He owned his own business. He ran 5Ks for charity, for Christ's sake. He did stuff right. I had no family. I was a bartender. No one was counting on me for anything. I'll never understand why he died and I didn't." Jack's eyes clouded over with regret, and his free hand fisted over the table.

Natalie squeezed the other one. "Oh, Jack," she whispered, heartbroken that his thoughts had taken such a dark turn. To miss someone was one thing. To feel like you should be in their place was another. Her chest squeezed as she interlaced her fingers with his. "You can't think of it that way. Death doesn't choose people based on their character. It's a cruel and random animal that picks its victims arbitrarily."

"I know," Jack said. "Logically, I know. It's just hard to wrap my head around it sometimes. How does a man like me get to stay on this earth when a man like him has to leave it?"

"Your life is worth just as much as his was, Jack. No matter what you did before Danny died, you've always been a good man. Just because you made different choices doesn't mean they were wrong. Maybe it took you longer than some others to find yourself and your calling, but that's not a bad thing. Danny would be so proud of how well you're doing." She stroked Jack's hand with her thumb, hoping to bring him some measure of comfort.

"That's why I took Carter, you know," he replied with a sad smile. "I didn't want him at first. When the lawyers told me Danny had appointed me as Carter's legal guardian, I tried to pawn him off. I didn't want a baby."

Natalie's eyebrows rose in surprise. "What changed your mind?"

"Well, I thought about Danny, and I realized it's what he would have done. And if Danny was gone, then I had to try and be more like him, because how could the world exist without a guy like Danny? So, I did what he would have done and took Carter in."

Natalie's heart swelled. "What you've done for Carter is unbelievable," she said. "And the fact that you're so dedicated to keeping Danny's business alive is admirable. Just remember that you're your own man, and your desires matter. You still have a life to live."

Jack nodded. "I know. I just want to make him proud."

"You are," Natalie said. "And I know your mother is proud of you too."

"You think so?"

"I *know* so."

Jack's boyish smile almost did her in. "I just hope I can raise Carter half as well as Danny could have."

"I know you can," Natalie said. "You're a great guardian."

"I'm adopting him," Jack blurted then scraped his hand over his jaw. "Shit, I haven't told anyone that yet."

Natalie leaned back and clapped her hands together. "Jack, that's amazing! You're going to be Carter's dad!"

"Yeah, I guess I will." His grin widened slowly. "It'll take a few months, but yeah, I'll be his dad."

She lifted her wine glass toward him. "Cheers to that!"

They clinked glasses and continued on through dinner, the weight of their earlier conversation vanishing as they segued to lighter topics. Deciding that they were both too full for dessert, they headed home once the meal was over. Natalie peeked at Jack's profile as he drove, her eyes wandering from his mop of curly hair to his sculpted, stubbled jawline.

He grinned when he looked over and caught her staring. "What are you up to over there?"

"Just watching you," she replied, the fuzzy bliss of two glasses of good wine mixing with the relief that Jack had opened up to her and the sheer joy of being together in the moment. "You're very handsome, you know."

Jack grabbed her hand and lifted it up to his mouth for a kiss, then he held it in his for the rest of the quiet ride. It wasn't that they had nothing more to say to each other, but rather that the silence was comfortable. There was something so intimate about finding pleasure in just being with someone else, without talking or doing anything special. Just being.

When they returned to the apartment, Natalie immediately kicked her heels off on the living room floor, sighing in relief as she did.

"Feel better?" Jack asked, his eyebrows quirking up in amusement.

"Much," she replied. "I love those shoes, but they are killers."

"I like them too," he said, dropping his keys on the kitchen counter with a *clink*. Moving into the living room, Jack gestured for her to sit on the couch. Natalie happily obliged, grateful to be off her feet. Jack sat on the other end and startled her by grabbing her ankles and pulling her feet into his lap.

"What are you doing?" she demanded.

"I'm rubbing your feet," he said, as if it were obvious.

Natalie tried to tug her feet away, but he held on tight. "Why?" she asked.

Jack looked at her as if she had three heads. "Because they're sore," he said, speaking as if it were the only natural course of action.

Though Natalie wasn't entirely sure how she felt about the tender act, it did feel awfully good, so she allowed him to continue. Jack assessed her quietly as his fingers dug into her insteps. Her tense body quickly relaxed under his touch, and she moaned softly as his thumbs dug into her arches. Leaning back into the couch, she allowed her eyes to close.

"You're not used to people taking care of you," Jack observed.

Natalie's eyes popped open, and she stiffened again, instantly regretting the involuntary reflex. Jack raised his eyebrows, but his thumbs only dug into her feet harder. Forcing herself to loosen up her muscles once more, she shrugged with as much nonchalance as she could muster. "I guess not."

Jack frowned but continued his lavish treatment. "Why is that, Natalie?"

She didn't answer right away. Then, after a moment, she quietly admitted, "I don't like to have to rely on anyone but myself."

Jack continued to knead her feet with skillful fingers. "But isn't it nice, sometimes, to be able to lean on someone else? To let them shoulder some of your burdens?"

Natalie's eyebrows came together as she considered that. She'd never really had anyone do those things for her. "I guess," she answered uncertainly.

It sounded like it would be nice, in theory, to let someone shoulder some of her load, but it also required a level of closeness that she rarely, if ever, allowed herself to have with anyone. She hadn't been able to count on her parents, and she had learned at a young age that if you want things, you'd better be able to do or get them yourself. It was the same in her career. No one was going to attain notoriety for you or get your work noticed. That was up to you. She supposed she had been taking care of herself for so long that she'd forgotten how to let someone else do it for even a moment.

Jack continued to massage her feet while Natalie sat lost in thought, chewing her lip and rubbing her forehead absent-mindedly.

"You can rely on me, you know," he said quietly.

Natalie looked up to find that Jack had been watching her. Awestruck by the sincerity in his gaze, she did nothing but stare back, aware that his statement was about much more than a simple foot rub. He was imploring her to trust him, to let go of some of her tightly reined control and let him in. And the kicker of it all was that she wanted to.

You can rely on me. Those words, while so simple, meant more to Natalie than he may ever know. After a lifetime of unreliable loved ones, she had resigned herself to self-sufficiency. In all of her travels, she'd remained fiercely independent, never allowing herself to let her guard down.

But here, now, with Jack, she could feel her guard slipping.

"I know," she whispered.

17

Jack grinned at her admission and dug deeper into her feet, his fingers working their magic and relaxing her to her core.

Sighing blissfully, Natalie wiggled her toes to get Jack's attention and asked, "Would you… do you think you could get my shoulders too? They're sore from all the gardening."

A broad grin spread over his face as he set her feet down on the floor. "Sure. Here," he said as he made a home for her between his legs. Natalie scooted to the floor and inserted herself between them with her back to the couch.

Jack's big hands grasped her shoulders, and his thumbs began rubbing slow circles. Natalie groaned when he hit the exact spot that was bothering her, her head lolling to the side as she let out a breathy, "*Yes.*" She could just make out his quiet chuckle. As he kneaded her aching muscles, Natalie decided that Jack was very good with his hands.

And then, suddenly, it wasn't just his hands on her but his lips too. A hot kiss scorched the back of her neck before Jack made his way up to her ear, pressing kisses to all the sensitive skin along the way. He licked over the shell of her ear then nipped her earlobe gently before speaking in a low voice in her ear. "Feeling better?"

"Yes," Natalie said again, her voice a mere whisper. Jack's mouth traveled back down to the side of her neck, licking and sucking and driving her wild. When she couldn't take it anymore, she craned her neck around, searching for his lips, and he obliged, bringing his mouth down to cover hers. She rose up slowly, not wanting to break the kiss, and climbed onto the couch to straddle him.

Tonight, there was no baby in the house to interrupt them. Nothing could get in the way of their desire, and there was plenty of desire flooding the room as Natalie wrapped one arm around Jack's shoulders and brought her other hand to the back of his head, tugging at his hair to bring his mouth to the perfect angle. Grabbing her shoulders, he licked into her mouth, coaxing a small moan from deep in her throat. She mimicked his motions, and their tongues began dueling for dominance.

Jack's hands roamed over her back and then lower to grab her ass, pulling her in closer so she could feel how hard he was beneath her. Natalie ground against him, undulating her hips and working them both into a frenzy.

Releasing her hands, she felt blindly around for the buttons of Jack's shirt and began undoing them one by one. When she got to the last, she broke the kiss so he could untuck his shirt and shrug it off his shoulders. Tossing it over the back of the couch, Jack breathed heavily while she gazed hungrily at his tan chest and abdomen. She ran her fingers over the hard, sinewy muscles, and he shivered when she grazed a fingertip over his happy trail.

"Bedroom?" he breathed out.

Natalie nodded eagerly. "Yes." Standing abruptly, she sped to Jack's bedroom with him hot on her heels. She began to work the top of her zipper on her dress, but it was difficult to reach.

"Turn around," Jack ordered. When Natalie was slow to comply, he took her by the shoulders and gently spun her to face away from him, tucking her hair over one shoulder and kissing the part of her neck he'd exposed. Taking the zipper in one hand, he slowly tugged it down, placing searing kisses along her spine each time he revealed a few more inches of skin.

Natalie squirmed impatiently. When the zipper was finally all the way down, she let her dress drop to the floor. Jack let out a soft grunt when he laid eyes on her backside, barely covered by a lacy black thong. One big palm came to cover each cheek, and he squeezed lightly.

"You are so damn sexy," he growled. Taking her shoulders again, Jack turned her around to face him. His gaze zeroed in on the lacy bra that left little to the imagination and fingered the thin material between his fingers. "This is nice."

"I like it too," Natalie said, cocking her head to the side. "I'd like it better if you'd take it off of me."

Jack gave her a wolfish grin. "Impatient, are we?"

"Just eager," she answered with an innocent bat of her eyelashes.

"Well, I'm only too happy to oblige," he said, reaching around and undoing the clasp to her bra. Natalie brought her arms out in front of her so it slipped right off, baring her breasts to his gaze.

Groaning at the skin he'd revealed, Jack ran a single finger over the top swell of her breasts before brushing his thumb over one nipple. It hardened instantly beneath his touch. With a pleased smile, he did the same on the other side.

Natalie moaned in frustration when Jack removed his hand. She wanted him *now*. He raised a brow and peered down at her, as if challenging her to continue whining about his pace.

"We're going to take this slow," he informed her, moving closer until she was backed up against the bed.

"Why?" she wondered, aware that her voice was tinged with annoyance.

"I want to savor you," he answered, and the simple phrase stopped Natalie in her tracks. Had she ever been savored before? Pleasured, sure. Satisfied, definitely. But savored? No, she didn't think so.

Before she could respond, Jack was pushing at her shoulders, urging her to sit on the edge of the bed. When she did, he knelt before her and bent his head to her breasts, feathering each one with kisses. Natalie moaned as he fluttered his tongue along the soft skin, grabbing at his head to reel him in closer. Jack zeroed in on her already hardened nipples, swirling his tongue around one before taking it between his lips and sucking it in long, slow pulls.

Natalie groaned and arched her back, pushing her chest into his face until he tugged gently on her nipple with his teeth then repeated the process on the other side. There was a reverence in the way that he touched her. A slow, careful deliberateness that revealed the depth of his affection. He wasn't just out to get his. He was truly savoring her.

Though she was immensely enjoying having Jack's mouth on her, Natalie quickly grew impatient with his unhurried actions. Her nipples were impossibly hard, and she craved more, needed more. She needed hard, fast friction, Jack's body over hers, in hers, *something* more.

Pulling back from his torturous tongue, Natalie tried to urge him lower, but he rose from the floor and stood tall above her. "Lie down," he directed, and she slid back eagerly, stretching herself out long, ready to get to the good stuff. Jack began to climb up too, but she reached her foot out to stop him, bumping it against his chest. He raised an eyebrow in question.

"Pants off," she commanded. "It's only fair," she added, shooting a glance down toward her bare legs. Jack followed her gaze, and his nostrils flared at the sight of her legs stretched long in front of him. Sliding off the bed, he fumbled with his belt buckle before shucking off his jeans, leaving him in tight, navy-blue boxer briefs that housed an unmistakable bulge. Natalie pushed herself up on her elbows to watch him disrobe and licked her lips as he kicked his jeans to the side.

Jack's dark gaze met hers as he toyed with the elastic of his boxers. "These too?"

"Mhmm," she mumbled, biting her lip and watching as he tucked his thumbs under the elastic and pulled, the boxers falling into a pile with his jeans. Sitting up straight, she admired his erection, pleased to find that she wasn't the only one excited to the point of torment. Jack was hard as stone, his skin stretched taut around his thick shaft. It bobbed up toward his belly as he slid out of his boxers.

Scooting back to the edge of the bed, Natalie reached out and took him in her hand. He throbbed in her grasp, and she looked up at him as she held him. "This is nice," she said, mimicking his earlier words.

Jack's eyes flashed with heat. "I'm so glad you think so."

Natalie smiled, enjoying the banter, and pumped her hand up and down once, twice, three times before Jack covered her hand with his to stop her.

"You're supposed to be lying down," he reminded her.

She gazed up at him through long eyelashes. "Oh, but this seemed like so much more fun."

"Fun's over," he grunted, climbing up on the bed and dragging her back into a supine position. Looming above her on all fours, he looked like a lion about to catch his prey.

Natalie reached down for his erection again, but Jack pulled back. "Nice try." He grinned devilishly. "But we're not even yet. You're still wearing your panties."

She immediately reached down to pull them off, and he stopped her.

"That's my job," he said.

"Then do it!" Natalie cried, done with talking.

Jack shook his head slowly and lowered down to place hot, wet kisses on her lips, her jaw, her neck, her sensitized breasts, and all the way down her midline until he reached the hem of her panties. Natalie was writhing beneath him, urging him to go faster, but Jack continued taking his sweet time. He placed a quick kiss on the triangle of lace that covered her most intimate parts.

"Is this what you're waiting for?" he asked, taking the hem of her panties between his teeth and tugging them down just enough to expose her.

"Yes!" she urged, bucking her hips toward his face.

Jack grinned up at her, well aware that he was torturing her, and used one hand to draw her panties down her legs at an excruciatingly slow pace while the other rubbed soft circles on her inner thighs. The motion of his fingers would do wonders just a few inches over. She tried to shift so his touch would hit her sweet spot, but he just chuckled and removed his hand.

"Jack!" Natalie cried. Both naked now, he lay atop her and finally brought his big hand down to cup her sex.

"I've got you," he murmured. She bucked up into his hand, searching blindly for the friction that would get her off.

"Settle down," he whispered, his lips close to her ear. "Let me take care of you." Gently, he slid one finger inside of her and hummed his pleasure at the slickness that greeted him.

"You're wet for me," he said, stating the obvious. Natalie responded by arching into his touch, showing him just how wet she was. He slid a second long finger in and worked them both in and out before finding the bundle of nerves just above with his thumb.

Natalie gasped when he exerted just the slightest pressure. "Jack, please," she begged, grinding herself against his thumb, seeking more pressure. "I want you inside me."

He leaned down to kiss her long, slow, and deep before granting her request. Slowly, he slid his fingers out of her and shocked her by bringing them up to his lips and sucking them clean. Wide-eyed, Natalie watched Jack reach over into the bedside table drawer to get a condom. He rolled it over his hard length and finally, *finally*, moved over her and guided himself inside of her.

She accepted him greedily, bucking her hips up to take all of him rather than cede to his casual pace. He groaned and rocked into her, kissing her hard as he did. Natalie wrapped her arms around Jack's back and felt the sheen of sweat that veiled his skin as well as her own. The slick feel of it and the carnal smell that filled her nostrils had her feeling wild and uninhibited.

Thinking that Jack had finally surrendered to his lust, Natalie wrapped her legs around him and tried to speed up. "Faster, Jack, please," she pleaded, and he sped up for a moment, driving into her at the speed she desired. She cried out as she felt herself tighten, but before she knew it, he was slowing down again.

"More! Please, Jack." She couldn't stop her body from squirming as she sought the ultimate pleasure.

"Shhh," he murmured, running his hand down to her breast and toying with her nipple. "I'll get you there," he promised. "Just relax."

Natalie grunted her displeasure and continued rocking her hips up in an effort to urge him on. Jack moved only slightly faster, frustrating her to no end. She reached down between them to touch herself, but Jack thwarted her by grabbing her hand, lacing his fingers with hers, and pinning her hand up by her head.

"Uh uh," he chastised as he did the same with her other hand.

With both hands restrained and unable to get Jack to speed up, Natalie threw her head back in frustration. "Jack, please! I need you. I need more. *Please*."

He grinned down at her fondly and kissed her once on the lips. "Just let go, Natalie," he insisted. "I'll take care of you."

Heaving a sigh, she closed her eyes and resigned herself to Jack's torturously lazy pace. He kissed her once more then moved his mouth to her neck, sucking at her sensitive skin as he continued to slide in and out of her.

Eventually, he let one of her hands go and brought his own fingers down low, slowly circling her clit, finally giving her the friction she hungered for. Natalie moaned at his firm touch as he pressed into her pleasure center, and her climax began to build again, oh so slowly. Lifting her hips into his touch, she sighed into his mouth when his lips found hers. He continued driving into her, his thumb applying sweet pressure and his lips leading hers in a sensual dance. She climbed higher and higher until ecstasy felt only a heartbeat away.

"That's it," Jack urged her in a low tone, his silken voice sending a shiver of pleasure down her spine. "Come for me, Natalie."

His carnal command was the final straw. Pleasure overtook her senses, heat exploding in her belly as she tightened around him. Crying out, Natalie threw her head back and called out Jack's name. Her legs remained locked tight around him as she rode out her orgasm, bucking against him again and again, wringing out every inch of her pleasure.

When the pulsing and throbbing ceased, she opened her eyes to find Jack gazing down at her. Awed by the depth of emotion in his eyes, she understood exactly how he was feeling. Never in her life had a man treated her with such care or paid such attention to her needs. Jack was savoring her, and it was heady stuff.

He'd come to a standstill inside of her as he relished the spasms her climax produced. Leaning down, he locked her lips in a passionate kiss as he began driving into her once again, finally taking care of himself. He moved slowly at first and then faster until he found his own release, shuddering and collapsing on her with a low moan.

Natalie lay with her arms and legs entwined with his, gently stroking the back of his head and neck as they caught their breath. She wasn't sure she'd ever come so hard. In her mind, Jack had drawn out her orgasm agonizingly slowly, though she supposed she was only ever used to hard and fast. If she'd known she could have been having orgasms like that this whole time, perhaps she would have considered following his unhurried lead. Though, it could be more about the man than the speed.

Jack rolled out of her grasp to rid himself of the condom, bending over the side of the bed to deposit it in the trash bin.

When he slid back into place beside her, Natalie placed a hand on his chest. "You're torturous," she accused him.

Jack winked and kissed her on the forehead. "Good things come to those who wait."

Natalie ran her foot up and down his calf, enjoying his closeness. "That was a very good thing."

Wrapping an arm around her waist, Jack pulled her in close. "You're a very good thing."

Natalie smiled against his chest.

"Sleep in here tonight," he requested.

"Yes," she sighed.

The last thing she remembered before falling soundly asleep was Jack's fingertips running gently up and down her body and his lips in her hair.

18

Natalie blinked her eyes open and yawned as she took a big morning stretch, pleased to find herself sore in all the right places. A quick glance to her side revealed that Jack had already awoken and gotten out of bed. Though she'd expected to sleep soundly, Natalie was surprised his exit hadn't awoken her.

Eager to see him, she hopped out of bed to search for some clothes. The black thong she'd worn the night before was slung over the bedpost, so she pulled it on along with the white button-up shirt Jack had discarded on the floor. It fell mid-thigh, revealing just enough skin to tease him. Winding up her hair in a messy bun, she left a few tendrils hanging loose around her face.

An appetizing smell wafted into the bedroom, and Natalie's stomach rumbled as she identified the scent of bacon. Strolling out to the kitchen, she found Jack standing at the stove, wearing only a pair of gray sweatpants, his bare torso on display. She watched for a moment as he flipped French toast in a large pan and bacon in a smaller one. She'd been in the doorway almost a full minute when he finally noticed her.

"Good morning," Jack said, breaking out in a huge, shit-eating grin. His eyes roamed from her face down her body, heating as they took in her scantily clad state.

"Morning," Natalie answered with a smile of her own as she skipped to his side.

"You look much better in that shirt than I do," Jack said, dropping his spatula to pull her in for a kiss.

"I beg to differ," she said, her lips hovering by his. "You looked pretty damn hot last night."

He grinned down at her and wrapped a strong arm around her waist, reaching the other down to squeeze one of her mostly bare cheeks while he ravaged her lips. "God, I love your ass," he muttered between kisses.

Natalie pressed her body into his and felt his hard bulge against her stomach. Pushing him away with her hands on his chest, she took on a stern tone. "We can't! I have to go pick up Carter soon. Dana can't watch him all day."

Jack threw his head back and sighed dramatically.

"Plus, look at this yummy breakfast you made. We wouldn't want it to go to waste. I'm starving," Natalie added.

"Me too." Jack raised an eyebrow, and she pointed a finger at his chest.

"No!" she insisted.

"Fine." He pouted. "Then sit down and let me feed you."

Sitting down brought the hem of Natalie's shirt even higher, and Jack glanced appreciatively at her legs under the table. She raised a stern eyebrow, and he quickly turned to the stove. Filling up two plates with French toast, bacon, and strawberries, he served them both before sitting down across the table from her.

"Mmm," Natalie hummed. "This looks amazing. Thank you."

"My pleasure," Jack said, digging into his meal.

After a few moments of silent chewing, she added, "Thanks for last night."

He grinned wolfishly. "That was also my pleasure."

"Mine too." She smiled as she recalled his slow seduction.

Jack took a slow sip of his coffee, watching her for a moment before he responded, "You were impatient. You know, you can sit back and let people take care of you sometimes. You don't always have to rush ahead or take matters into your own hands."

Natalie pressed her lips together as she recalled trying to do that exact thing. "I'm learning."

A slow, lazy smile spread over Jack's face. "I'm ever so happy to teach you. Especially when you beg me like you did last night."

She rolled her eyes. "I did not beg."

Jack stared her down until she relented.

"Ok, maybe I begged a little."

His eyes softened. "You've been taking care of me ever since you got here. Let me return the favor." He reached over and grabbed her hand, threading his fingers through hers the same way he had to restrain her the night before. "Rely on me, Nat."

Looking down at their interwoven fingers, Natalie saw that they fit together perfectly. Their hands. Their bodies. Their personalities. They gave to each other and took what the other offered. She knew she could trust him and believed he was learning to trust her too.

She leaned over and kissed him. "I will," she promised before they returned to their breakfasts, eating in companionable silence. It was unusual for her to not have anything to say, but once again, the silence didn't feel uncomfortable. Just easy and pleasant.

"I think I'm going to take Carter to the park today. Want to come?" Jack asked after polishing off the last of his plate.

"That sounds fun, but I have a ton of paintings I'm supposed to work on for Dana's book, and I've barely even started. Plus, I have to run to the post office to send my latest piece to Ned. You and Carter should spend some time just the two of you," Natalie suggested.

"Ok, if you insist. But I was thinking about getting Juice Bar with him. Are you sure you want to miss out on that?" Jack's attempt at persuasion fell flat.

"After his blowout last time you gave him ice cream? I'll take my chances," she said.

Jack rolled his eyes. "I won't give him as much this time, obviously."

"I wish I could come, really, but Dana will kill me if I don't finish the illustrations soon. She's dying to start sending the book out to agents."

"When do you think you'll be ready for that step?" he asked.

"Honestly, as soon as I finish the illustrations, we have a pretty solid book. Dana's a really good writer, and she knows exactly what kids like. Anyone would be foolish to overlook her book."

"And with your illustrations, how *could* they overlook it?" Jack added. "It's got the best of everything."

"Well, thanks, babe. Hopefully the agents and publishers see it that way. It would be a huge boost to Dana's confidence to be published again, and it wouldn't hurt to get my name out there as an artist."

"That's a good point. Ok, fine. I guess it's worth missing out on ice cream if it'll lead to you becoming a famous artist."

"It's a small sacrifice," Natalie agreed with a laugh. After finishing her own breakfast, she hopped in the shower for a quick cleaning. If she showed up to Dana's house smelling like sex, her friend would give her hell. As it was, Natalie was sure she'd try playing twenty questions about the date.

She wasn't surprised when Dana answered the door as soon as she knocked, as if she'd been watching for her. Dana ushered her inside and already had coffee waiting at the kitchen table. Natalie stopped short in the doorway to the kitchen, realizing she'd been ambushed.

"Where's Carter?"

Dana brushed her off. "Oh, Ryan's upstairs with the boys." She encouraged Natalie to sit down at the table with a theatrical wave of her hand. "Tell me about your night! I want to know all the details."

Natalie chuckled and shook her head, sitting down in an empty chair. "We had a great night," she said, sipping her coffee as she observed Dana over the rim of the mug.

"And…" Dana waved her hands dramatically around in the air.

"And what?"

"Did you do it?" Dana practically shouted with excitement but caught herself, glancing up toward the second floor where the babies were.

"Not that it's any of your business," Natalie said after another revitalizing sip of coffee, "but, yes, we did in fact 'do it.'"

Dana let out an exaggerated gasp and clapped her hands together. "Was it amazing? Was he incredible? Was it the best of your life?"

Natalie couldn't help but chuckle. "It was, and he is," she admitted, "but it's more than just the sex. Did you know that Jack's going to officially adopt Carter?"

"No way!" Dana seemed as excited as she was about the prospect. "That's awesome. Good for him."

"I know," Natalie said. "I'm so proud of him. He'll make a great father."

"He will," Dana agreed. She silently studied Natalie for a moment. "You'd be a great mother too, you know."

Natalie's eyebrows shot up in surprise. "I don't know about that…"

"You would," Dana insisted. "You're a natural with Carter."

"I guess, but… that's different."

"How so?"

Natalie shrugged. "Because I'm just his nanny. I take care of him, yes, but I don't have to make any decisions about his life. I'm not planning for his future or saving for his college fund or anything like that."

"But can't you see yourself doing those things?" Dana asked. "They're not exactly out of the realm of possibility."

"I guess… I don't know, Dana. I've never even considered kids for myself. My lifestyle isn't exactly conducive to having them."

"Do you ever think about changing your lifestyle?" Dana asked.

Natalie's eyebrows drew into a line. "I guess I always assumed I would eventually settle down somewhere, maybe once my art was selling consistently and I didn't feel the need to chase inspiration so much, but I'm definitely not there yet. Maybe once I'm old and stale like you," she joked.

Dana grinned at the taunt, but her expression grew more serious as she placed a hand over Natalie's arm. "There's absolutely no pressure to have kids—to each woman her own. I just think you'd be a really amazing mom if you ever want to be."

Natalie appreciated Dana's vote of confidence, but her self-confidence was lacking. "What kind of mom could I possibly be?" she asked quietly. She had shared her whole sordid story with Dana, and yet her friend still believed she had what it took to be a parent?

"Nat." Dana squeezed her arm. "I know it must be hard to imagine being a mother when you had no role model to show you what it means to be one. But I see how you are with Carter. So warm, caring, and loving. You are all of those things, even though you had no one to teach you. It just comes naturally to you. Like I said, I'm not pressuring you to do anything more than think about it. Just consider if it's something you really don't want, or if you just *think* you don't want it because it scares you."

Natalie nodded and patted her friend's hand. "I will. I've thought about it more than ever since taking care of Carter. I always assumed motherhood wasn't in the cards for me—in fact, I had pledged to myself that it wasn't—but I'll admit I've had fleeting thoughts of it lately. Caring for Carter has helped me realize that I might actually enjoy having a child. I'm not nearly ready yet, but it's a big step for me just to be considering the possibility."

Dana smiled. "Good. That's all I want from you, Nat. I just want you to be happy."

"I am happy."

"I can tell. And I want you to stay that way. Think about what you really want your future to look like. What will really fulfill you?"

"You know what will fulfill me? When we publish a book together," Natalie said, veering toward safer ground. "I'm working on the illustrations this afternoon. Jack's taking Carter out for a bit so I can give them my full attention."

"Awesome!" Dana lit up at talk of her book. Natalie should have thought to bring it up sooner so as to avoid the unusually deep conversation so early in the morning. "I've already talked to a few agents that said they would love to see the draft once the illustrations are done."

"That's great!" Natalie clapped her hands, which turned into an enthusiastic high-ten with Dana. "I promise I'll have the illustrations ready as soon as I can."

They made a plan to get together once everything was ready and send it out to agents, then Natalie went and got Carter, who was quite enjoying a game of peek-a-boo with Justin and Ryan. She joined them for a few rounds, then Dana walked them to the front door.

Turning to Natalie, she gave her a serious look. "Keep me updated."

"On the illustrations?" Natalie asked. "Of course I will."

"No." Dana smacked her forehead. "On your relationship! I want to know the next time you do it."

"Dana, I am so not going to spill to you every time we have"—Natalie looked down at the baby in her arms and lowered her voice—"every time we do it."

"You say that now, but I know you're gonna be dying to tell someone," Dana chanted.

"Ok." Natalie rolled her eyes. "Whatever you say."

"And think about what we talked about," Dana added.

"I will," Natalie assured her.

Returning to the café, she entered with Carter in tow and was pleased to find that Danny's was buzzing with happy customers. Business had been getting busier and busier lately, ever since the façade of the building had improved. Though she wouldn't throw it in Jack's face, Natalie knew she'd made the right decisions with the aesthetic improvements. It might even be time to hire another barista.

Standing behind the counter with a rag thrown over his shoulder, Jack looked very much like the captain of the ship. He broke out into a broad smile as Natalie approached, holding up Carter's hand in a salute.

"Hi, baby!" Jack took the boy from her arms and tossed him up into the air before tucking him safely into his side. He turned to Natalie. "And hi, baby," he said in a much lower, more seductive voice. She laughed and got on her tiptoes to press a kiss to his lips then settled into his single-armed embrace as he continued to hold Carter.

An older woman eating at the bar piped up with, "What a beautiful family."

"Oh, we're not—" Natalie began, but Jack interrupted her.

"Thanks." He flashed the nice lady a smile. Natalie pulled back and shot him a questioning look, but Jack just kept talking to the woman, who wanted to know all about Carter—his age, his favorite things, what he liked to do.

Though she was surprised Jack would lead the woman to believe they were a family, Natalie figured his answer was easier than getting into the truth, which was a much longer story. She couldn't blame the woman for assuming a young couple with a baby was a family—especially not when Carter had such similar coloring to her.

However, the comment coming right on the heels of her conversation with Dana only set Natalie more on edge. She had told her friend that she'd begun to consider the possibility of having a child someday—a family—but if there was one thing Natalie had learned from her parents, it was that those you love the most also have the power to hurt you the most. What if she made it all the way to having a family, only to screw up and hurt them? She would never forgive herself.

Those familiar words floated through her mind. *Never stop moving. Never settle. Never do what she did.* Natalie recited them in her head like a mantra. A reminder that no matter how tempting it was to consider the possibility of creating little humans as cute as Carter, or how shockingly lovely it felt for some stranger to call them a "beautiful family," that reality may never be in the cards for her.

19

"Why is it green?" Jack asked as he inspected the cookie Jenny handed him. It was the next morning, and he stood in the back room of Danny's with Jenny and Natalie. Natalie was exhausted from staying up late to work on Dana's illustrations, but Carter was as energetic as ever, wandering around the kitchen, touching anything he could reach.

"It's made with matcha," Jenny explained. "It's a Japanese delicacy, and it's very trendy right now."

Jack sniffed the dessert and grimaced.

"Just take a bite, you big baby," Natalie told him. He glared at her but took a small, tentative bite.

"Well, what do you think?" Jenny's voice was hopeful. Natalie watched with raised eyebrows as Jack chewed and swallowed, his Adam's apple bobbing. He puckered his lips and tilted his head. Natalie pinched him on the arm until he released a smile.

"It's actually really good."

"Yes!" Jenny fist pumped the air, as excited as she always was when Jack approved one of her new creations.

"Let me try one." Natalie reached toward the tray, but Jack grabbed her arm to stop her.

"Hey, save some for the customers."

She rolled her eyes. "Take it out of my paycheck."

Jack released her arm with a wink.

"Mmm," Natalie hummed with pleasure as she bit into the soft, warm cookie. "Jenny, you've outdone yourself once again."

The young woman beamed. "I'm working on compiling my own original recipes into a cookbook as part of my culinary school application."

Jack frowned as he swallowed the last of his cookie. "Isn't that still a few years away?"

"Well," Jenny said, tenting her fingers together in front of her. "I'm working with the high school to hopefully graduate a semester early, and I want to start culinary school right away. Some of the people at the Culinary Center have connections they're going to put me in touch with. I might be able to start as early as next winter."

Jack ran a hand through his bedhead. "Damn. I was hoping I'd have you for at least another summer."

"I don't know if I'll be on the island next summer. I'll probably get an internship through whatever culinary school I go to, if I can."

Jack nodded. "That makes sense. I'm happy for you, Jenny. You're going to be great. God knows your talent has helped keep this place running these past few months."

Jenny grinned and wiped her hands over her apron, smearing bright-green matcha goo over it. "It's been an amazing opportunity for me. Most café owners aren't willing to put their entire bakery in the hands of a sixteen-year-old."

"Danny trusted you, so I trust you," Jack said simply. "And you haven't let me down."

Jenny's grin broadened. "Thanks."

Derek's voice boomed from the front room of the café. "A little help out here, please."

Jack looked down at his watch. It was just about time for the morning rush. "Coming!" he shouted.

Natalie scooped Carter up and followed Jack out to the front, where a line of customers waited. He quickly began preparing drinks from the tickets on the machine while Natalie stood to the side with Carter.

"All the more reason to hire a new barista and get them all trained," she said. "With the increase in customers we've been seeing the past few weeks, there must be room in the budget."

"There's just about enough to hire another full-time employee," Jack said as he dumped a scoop of ground coffee in a portafilter. The veins in his forearms popped as he tamped it down, and Natalie watched appreciatively as he snapped the portafilter into the machine.

"Great! Want me to put up a 'help wanted' sign?" she asked, eager to get the process started.

Jack watched the espresso slowly drip into a tiny cup. "I guess we might as well."

Natalie narrowed her eyes, sensing his hesitation. "Why don't you want to hire someone?"

Jack sighed and slid the espresso shot across the counter to the customer with a fake smile, then he turned back toward Natalie. "This will be the first employee I've hired myself. Danny hired Derek and Jenny before he died. I don't know how to vet an employee. What if I hire a dud?"

Natalie's eyes softened. "Jack," she said, shifting Carter to her other hip. "I'll help you. We won't hire a dud, but if we do, then we'll try again. Everyone makes mistakes."

Jack grabbed another ticket off the machine and began preparing another shot of espresso. "I can't afford to make mistakes with this place."

Natalie placed a gentle hand on his back, and he paused his drink preparation, hanging his head until curls spilled over his eyes. "I know every step further away from Danny's original decisions is tough, but you have to trust that you're doing what's right for his legacy," she said. When he lifted his gaze to hers, she gestured toward the multitude of occupied seats in the café. "Look how many happy customers are in here today."

Jack glanced around and brushed his hair away from his face. There were tons of people around, chatting and smiling as they began their perfect summer day with a cup of coffee from Danny's. There were familiar faces that Natalie recognized as regulars as well as tourists toting oversized beach bags, and every single person looked thrilled to be there.

Natalie rubbed up and down his back. "Jack, when I first came here last month, there was only one other customer in the whole place. You've worked so hard, and you've made some changes that I know have been really difficult for you, but you have to see the progress we've made."

Jack nodded once and turned back to the drink he was making. "I know you're right. I just wish Danny was here to see it."

She rubbed his back once more then stepped away and bumped Carter up on her hip. "I do too, but just think… Carter gets to see it—Danny's other legacy."

As Jack waited for the coffee to drip out, he gave the boy a long look, and his mouth softened into a small smile. "Yeah. All of this is for him, really. One day, this place will be his."

"Exactly," Natalie said. "So you have to keep making improvements and doing what you have to do to keep it in tip-top shape for him."

Jack's smile solidified on his face. "You're right."

Natalie raised her eyebrows in mock surprise. "Say that one more time."

Jack chuckled and snapped the lid onto the drink he was making. "Once was more than enough."

☼ ☼ ☼

The afternoon flew by, and after dinner, Jack and Natalie put the baby to bed together and took turns reading him bedtime stories—or, more accurately, took turns reading him the same bedtime story. Carter only wanted to hear *Goodnight Moon,* and if you tried to read anything else, he shoved the book away like it was a hot pile of garbage.

As had become customary, once Carter was asleep, Jack got out a couple of beers, and he and Natalie drank them together while chatting in the living room. She settled in on one side of the couch while Jack grabbed two bottles from the fridge.

"So, I heard from my brother Fletcher today," he said as he cracked open their drinks.

"Oh yeah? How's he doing?" Natalie asked.

"Oh, great as usual," Jack said sourly, handing her a beer and sitting on the couch beside her. "He wants to come visit toward the end of the summer. He'll probably invite Beau too. I'm sure they just want to take advantage of a free place to stay on Nantucket."

"It might be nice to see your brothers," Natalie ventured.

"Yeah, maybe." Though far from enthusiastic, Jack's answer wasn't all that surprising. He took a large swig of his beer and kicked his feet over the arm of the couch, swiveling until his head rested in Natalie's lap. "I'm afraid they'll spend the whole time judging me. They'll see how dilapidated Danny's is, and I'm sure they'll point out all my parenting flaws."

Natalie ran her fingers soothingly through Jack's soft curls. "Well, for starters, you have as many parenting flaws as any normal parent, and if neither of them has kids, then they definitely have no right to judge you. As for Danny's, like I told you earlier, it's doing great. You're doing better than you think."

"Thanks, Nat." Jack smiled up at her. "I want them to see that I'm turning my life around. Things aren't perfect here yet, but they're a hell of a lot better than how they started."

"They'll see that," Natalie assured him. "And I'm sure once they meet your hot girlfriend, they won't even care how well you're doing."

Jack chuckled, his big brown eyes growing soft as he gazed up at her. "I like that you called yourself my girlfriend," he said softly.

His shy smile tugged at Natalie's heartstrings, and since she couldn't bend over far enough to kiss his lips, she settled for raising one of his hands up to her lips. "Isn't that what I am?"

Though she wasn't all that used to relationship stuff, it seemed like if they were dating, sleeping together, and living together, then she was his girlfriend. The thought was equally heartwarming and terrifying. The word *girlfriend* just sounded so permanent, and yet it had slipped so readily from her lips.

"Yes," Jack said firmly, "and that's how you should introduce yourself to my brothers. No matter what you say, Beau will try to hit on you, but maybe if you declare that you're taken early on, he'll back off a little. I think my brothers still see me as that high school rebel who picks fights everywhere he goes. At least it gives me a leg up in situations like this."

"You'd better not fight with either of your brothers over me," Natalie warned, tugging at one of his curls until it uncoiled. "You have nothing to worry about. I'm not interested in any McNally men other than you."

"You'd better not be," Jack said gruffly, no longer sweet and shy as he'd been moments before.

Knowing it would provoke him, Natalie added, "I mean, unless he's way hotter than you."

Jack sat up swiftly, his large figure looming above her. "He's not," he grumbled. "Even if he was, would you let him do this?" He pressed a single, searing kiss to Natalie's mouth.

"No," she mumbled beneath his lips.

"What about this?" he asked, sweeping his tongue in and kissing her deeply for one lingering moment.

"Not that either," Natalie whispered breathlessly.

"Not even this?" Jack asked, his urgent kiss accompanied by a hand snaking beneath her shirt to grasp one of her breasts. He fondled it for a moment before reaching beneath her bra to pinch her nipple between two long fingers. It hardened immediately under his expert touch.

"Definitely not that," she said, her voice high and desperate. Grasping the hem of her shirt, Jack pulled it over her head. Natalie did the same for his and skimmed her fingertips over the taut muscles she revealed. "I only want you," she vowed to him.

"Good girl," he murmured against her lips.

"And I want you right now." Natalie pushed Jack back onto the couch, where he sat a bit stunned, and climbed on top of him, wanting to take control and show him just how much he didn't need to worry. Luckily, he seemed to be in the mood to let her.

After a moment's pause, Jack grinned and wrapped his arms around her, kissing her hungrily. Her breasts rubbed against his rigid chest as they kissed, her hard nipples dragging over the light dusting of hair there.

Breathless, Natalie pulled away and grinned devilishly down at Jack as she reached for his belt, making quick work of unfastening the buckle then the fly of his pants. Lifting his hips, Jack helped her slide his pants and boxers down to the floor.

Natalie licked her lips and knelt in front of him, cushioning her knees with a throw pillow from the couch. Jack moaned as he realized what was coming.

"I wouldn't do this to anyone else either," she whispered, bracing her elbows on his thighs. Taking Jack's length into her hands, she ran her fist up and down a few times before bending to lick a long stroke from bottom to top.

"Jesus Christ." He groaned, throwing his head back.

"Not even him," Natalie joked, taking Jack smoothly into her mouth and swirling her tongue around his head a few times, pausing in between each time to say, "You. Have. Nothing. To. Worry. About."

Jack moaned in response, and she looked up through her eyelashes into his heavy-lidded gaze. "I'm yours."

The words seemed to provoke him, and his hand grasped the back of Natalie's head as she sucked, taking him into her mouth over and over as deep as she could. His fingers wove through her hair, and though he didn't hold her there forcefully, the simple act of possession sent a shiver down her spine.

Jack pumped his hips in small strokes, always mindful of her comfort. Wanting to drive him a little wild, Natalie reached between his legs to cup his balls, drawn tight with pleasure. One roll of them in her hand and he lost it, arching into her mouth and pushing himself deeper. She made a small whimpering sound, and he growled.

"Come here," he ordered, lifting her up by her arms and plopping her down on the couch. He took control, pulling her shorts and panties off in one swift movement. Natalie didn't mind, her trust in Jack to take care of her pleasure solidified after their first time together.

"You're mine," he said as he arranged her on the couch with one leg slung over the back and the other over the side, her foot hovering over the ground.

"Yes," she said, knowing he needed that reassurance.

Jack's answering smile was scorching, one side of his mouth curling up as he ran a long finger through her damp folds. They groaned together. Natalie was wet and ready, and satisfaction at that was evident on Jack's face as he leaned down to return the favor.

She gasped when his lips met her most intimate parts,

kissing her as he nuzzled his nose into the dark curls at the apex of her thighs. Reaching a hand down, she wove it into his hair, holding him to her as he had held her to him. A small tug of his curls had Jack moaning against her skin, and his lips vibrated tantalizingly against her.

"Ah!" Natalie cried as his tongue followed the same path his finger had, then found her clit, where it flicked out like a snake striking its prey. She arched into his wicked mouth, and he sucked on the sensitive nub, setting her nerve endings on fire.

"That's it," Jack muttered, looping his hands around her thighs and holding her wide open, completely at his mercy. He licked her, long and slow, lapping up her wetness. When Natalie began to whimper and writhe beneath his mouth, desperately seeking release, Jack's lips came back down over her clit. He sucked it between his lips at the same moment he slid a single finger inside of her.

Natalie felt Jack's gasp against her skin as she clenched around his finger, the intake of air followed by another round of suction as he worked his finger in and out then added another.

"Come on, baby," he murmured. Her orgasm churned and built, spurred on by Jack's low voice and the whisper of his breath over her skin as she worked herself faster over his fingers.

"Please," she breathed.

With his mouth on her and two fingers inside of her, Jack reached his free hand up to cup Natalie's breast, rolling her nipple between his fingers as he continued his other pursuits. The exquisite sensations across her body collided, and she shot off, crying out and bathing his fingers in moisture.

Release rolled through her, and she lay there, panting, while Jack worked her down with light kisses on her inner thighs, nuzzling into her once again. Moaning as he slowly dragged his fingers out of her, Natalie was pleased when they were soon replaced by something even better.

She only caught a quick glimpse of Jack's rock-hard erection as he sheathed himself with a condom before plunging inside of her. Sliding in easily, he grunted when his balls hit her ass. He held still there for a moment, filling her completely before retreating almost all the way, leaving just his tip inside, then pushing forward and filling her again.

"Holy shit, you feel so good," he growled.

Natalie's body welcomed him, still limber from her orgasm. She pushed her heels into his ass to urge him on, knowing from the hard clench of his jaw that Jack's self-control was strained.

"Let go, Jack," she said, giving him the same advice he'd once given her.

Jack caught her gaze with his own, as if checking to make sure she was game. The intense hunger and desire in her eyes must have done the trick because he began pumping into her, hard and fast. She bucked up and met him thrust for thrust, the sound of slapping skin filling her ears as he consumed her.

"Ah!" Natalie cried out as Jack drove into her at a punishing clip. When he faltered, she tacked on a, "Don't stop!"

Jack continued taking her the way she craved, and it was only made better by the fact that she was heading toward a second orgasm. She reached down to touch herself, and Jack mercifully allowed it this time. His intense gaze followed her fingers as she rubbed in clockwise circles, his nostrils flaring as he let out a feral grunt.

Knowing he was close, Natalie rubbed harder, faster, and crested into her second orgasm as Jack reached his first, cursing loudly as he came buried deep inside of her. He stayed there for a long moment, likely relishing every convulsion of her sex around him while their panting breaths filled the silence.

Eventually, he pulled out and tucked Natalie into his front so they were spooning. Still on the couch, there was little space, so they were mashed together, though neither seemed to mind the close proximity. Both sated and limp with pleasure, neither spoke for a few moments.

Relishing the skin-on-skin contact, Natalie reached back to stroke Jack's thigh while he lazily ran his fingers up and down her side. His lips brushed her shoulder blade, her neck, her temple, and she sighed, totally content.

Thinking back to their conversation from just before, she broke the silence. "I'm excited to meet your brothers."

Jack's fingers stilled. "You are *not* thinking about my brothers after we just had sex," he said in disbelief.

Natalie grinned and had to bite her lip to keep from chuckling. "I wasn't thinking about them *during*. I'm just thinking about them now, and I'm looking forward to meeting them."

His fingers began roaming over her side again. "Why?"

"Siblings are a big part of a person's life," she said with an awkward shrug, her other shoulder buried in the couch cushions.

"Do you wish you had siblings?" Jack asked, his fingers running absentmindedly through her hair.

Natalie paused for a moment then answered, "I think it would have been nice to have siblings, but I wouldn't want another person to have had the parents or childhood I had."

"I understand." Jack kissed her hair. "Siblings aren't all they're cracked up to be anyway."

She frowned. "You say that, but you really love them. I know you do, Jack."

He sounded defeated when he sighed and said, "Yeah, I do, but I'm nervous as hell."

Natalie reached for his hand and held it by her hip. "You have nothing to be nervous about. They're going to be so impressed."

Jack placed a kiss on her shoulder and sighed again. "We should get to bed."

She stretched out her legs and groaned. "I don't think I can move."

"No need." Jack maneuvered himself off the couch and scooped Natalie up easily in his arms. "I've got you, baby."

Gazing up at him as he carried her to his bedroom, Natalie realized that she was getting used to letting Jack help her with things, though it still didn't come naturally to her. Mostly, she was just indulging him because she knew it made him happy to care for her. But an ever-growing part of her also selfishly enjoyed it.

20

The weeks slipped by like sand through Natalie's fingers, and before she knew it, another month had passed. After finishing the painting of Jack and Carter, she'd completed five more pieces: a couple of macro portraits of beach roses; a snapshot of Main Street, including the façade of Danny's Place; and a landscape showcasing Easy Street Harbor and the iconic red "sunken ship" boat anchored there. Added to the two beach scenes she'd already submitted, that brought her to a grand total of eight paintings. Just two more to go.

So far, Natalie had only managed to average a painting a week. If she was being honest with herself, she knew that she should have been finished with her commitment to Ned already. Between working at the café, caring for Carter, her relationship with Jack, and illustrating Dana's book, she'd gotten sidetracked, and time had just gotten away from her. But the book was almost ready to send to agents, and Jack had finally hired a new barista, so she was confident she could knock out the rest of the paintings before her impending September deadline.

It was unbelievable how smoothly things were going, but

even more amazing was how naturally Natalie continued to fall into routines that should have felt disturbingly domestic. She and Jack split Carter's care, took turns cooking meals, and divided household chores between the two of them. Her days had become about housework, play dates, and changing diapers, but it was bearable because her nights were filled with fire, desire, and more passion than she ever could have imagined.

The early morning moments were equally enjoyable in their intimacy. What they lacked in lust, they made up for in sweetness. This August morning, the hot sun beat through the open window and onto Natalie's bare back as she lay curled into Jack's side. The dog days of summer had arrived and brought with them a heat that rose early and dissipated late, if at all. Nantucket remained a solid ten degrees cooler than mainland Cape Cod at any given time, but even so, the windows remained open wide to let in a cooling sea breeze.

Adding to her current warmth was Jack's body, tangled up with hers. One of his long legs pinned her to the mattress as his arm laid slung over her waist in a lazy yet possessive claim. They'd made love for half the night, unable to get their fill of each other.

Feeling so content and deliciously sated, it was a chore for Natalie to open her eyes. Once she finally did, though, she was greeted with the now familiar sight of Jack's slumbering face, his long eyelashes fanned out above his cheeks and his lips slightly parted. She couldn't help but lean in for a quick peck on those lips, and Jack groaned a small sound of contentment but didn't fully awaken.

Smiling, Natalie leaned in to press a kiss to his jaw, loving the feel of his rough stubble scraping her smooth skin. Her lips grazed his chin then moved down to his chest, where the hair was softer and downier. When she darted her tongue over one of his nipples, Jack's hand, which had been laying limply on her back as he slept, grasped her bottom and squeezed.

Sucking in a breath, Natalie looked up to find him gazing at her intently. She kissed his lips once more in greeting. "Good morning, handsome."

This time, Jack reciprocated, his lips molding to hers as he kneaded her bottom. "Morning, beautiful," he mumbled before his lips met hers again, his tongue exploring from the corners of her lips to the curve of her cupid's bow.

"That was quite the wake-up call," Natalie panted breathlessly when he pulled away.

"If I recall correctly, you were the one who did the waking. I was just an innocent bystander."

"Oh yeah, you're innocent alright," she said, rolling her eyes.

Jack looked affronted. "What are you implying?"

"Some of those moves you pulled last night were far from innocent," she said. "I don't even want to know where you learned those."

Jack raised an eyebrow and pushed himself suggestively against her stomach. "You like?"

"Yes, I like very much, but not now!" Natalie cried as Jack rubbed himself against her. "The baby will be awake any second if he isn't already."

"I won't take long," Jack promised, dipping his head down and grazing the swell of her breast with his tongue.

"Jack…" Natalie trailed off, knowing they had little to no time, but his lips just did things to her… things that made her forget her reservations.

"Natalie," he whispered, sucking on her now hard nipple. She moaned and let him continue his escapade without complaint. His fingers were just trailing down her stomach when they both heard the telltale sound of Carter banging against the side of his crib.

Jack hung his head. "He's awake," he groaned, defeated, but he still took the opportunity to nuzzle his face between her breasts.

"I told you he'd be up any minute." Natalie laced her fingers into his hair and tugged.

"Ugh," Jack grumbled, and the way the sound vibrated off her chest made her feel all tingly inside.

"Let's go," she commanded, pulling his head back. "Up and at 'em."

"Jeez, woman, you're demanding," Jack complained but obeyed, rising from the bed as Natalie watched. Walking naked to the dresser, his powerful thighs and glutes were on full display, and she paid close attention as he bent over to open up the bottom drawer.

Mmm, she murmured to herself. Or maybe it hadn't been as quiet as she'd thought, because Jack grabbed a pair of boxers for himself and threw another across the room, hitting her square in the face.

"You're gawking at me," he said dryly.

"I happen to like gawking at you." Natalie pulled on the boxers and searched for a t-shirt. "And if anyone's demanding here, it's not me."

Once again, Jack feigned disbelief. "Surely you don't mean me?"

"'Lie here, Natalie, like this. Good, now open your legs wide. Wider, Natalie,'" she said, doing her best to imitate Jack's tone and the words he'd used the night before.

"Are you saying you didn't like what I did last night?" he purred, stalking over to Natalie and pinning her against the bedroom door.

She looked up at him through long eyelashes. "No, actually, quite the contrary. I liked it very much. I'm just saying you can get a little bossy."

"Ok, I'll admit that's true. But you're not exactly shy yourself. 'Harder, Jack. Yes, rub it like that. A little harder. Faster. Faster, Jack!'" He imitated her in the most ridiculous high-pitched voice. Natalie laughed and punched him in the chest, but he didn't budge.

"You can be quite a bossy little thing yourself," Jack said, dipping his head until messy curls tickled her forehead.

Natalie reached up and tugged on a particularly springy one. "You love it."

"Yes, I do," he admitted, his eyes shining with affection. His lips found hers and began their signature slow seduction, but Carter interrupted them after just a few moments, yelling from the other room.

"Ack! Nalee!" came his tiny voice.

Jack pulled away so Natalie could slip out from under his arms. "I'll get him," she offered. "You go start a batch of those blueberry pancakes like the ones you made last week."

"Mmm, good call." Jack pressed a quick kiss to her cheek then strode off to the kitchen in nothing but his boxers. She watched until he disappeared around the corner.

His brothers were set to arrive in a few days, and Jack really wanted to make sure everything was in place when they did. That meant that the apartment, as well as the café, needed to look perfect. He'd instructed Derek to wash all the windows, inside and out, and even wash the walls inside Danny's.

Natalie was to weed the garden and place fresh bouquets on every table. Jack had also asked her to repaint the sign for the café, and she was hoping he would let her have some artistic freedom on that one. The old sign was nice, but she thought if she added some more color to it and made it a little more whimsical, it might attract the interest of more customers.

Carter called out again, so Natalie went to his room and let him out of his crib. "Hey, little buddy," she said, picking him up and holding him to her chest. "How'd ya sleep?" He stuck one chubby thumb in his mouth in response.

Natalie changed Carter's diaper quickly and carried him out to the kitchen, where the blueberry pancakes were well under way. She placed him on the floor, and he toddled over to where Jack was cooking and hugged his leg.

Natalie grinned at the sight. "Are you going to have him call you Dad?" she wondered aloud.

Jack frowned as he flipped a pancake. "I hadn't really thought about it."

She walked deeper into the room until she could place a supportive hand on his shoulder. "Because, I mean, technically, you will be his dad."

Jack's frown deepened. "I guess. But no, I think I'll still have him call me Jack. Danny's his dad, and I want to make sure Carter knows about him as he grows up. I want to tell him stories about Danny. Show him pictures. I want Carter to know who he was."

"I think that's nice," Natalie said.

"And if I ever get married, then Carter would call his stepmother by her name, not Mom. Isn't that how it usually works?" Jack asked.

"I suppose that's true too," she said.

He braced his hands on the edges of the stove and hunched his shoulders. "Do you think he'll miss out on that? Not having anyone to call Mom or Dad? Will that screw up his childhood?"

Wrapping her arms around Jack's waist, Natalie pressed her cheek into his still bare back. "It won't screw up his childhood, Jack. It doesn't matter what he calls you. What matters is how you treat him. I called my parents Mom and Dad, and look at where that got me—completely estranged from one and barely talking to the other. The titles you use are insignificant. It's how you act that matters."

Jack squeezed her hand where it laid on his chest. "You're right. You always know what to say to make me feel better." He tugged her around to give her a quick kiss.

"Are these ready?" Natalie gestured to the plate of pancakes.

"Yeah," he said. "Let's dig in."

Natalie prepared a plate of pancakes for herself and a smaller one for Carter, then she pulled his highchair over to the kitchen island so he could eat alongside her and Jack.

"Have you spoken to your dad again?" Jack asked as they ate.

"Nope," Natalie said, popping the *p* for emphasis. "And I have no plans to."

Jack nodded understandingly. "I know your last conversation with him really sucked."

She shrugged and pushed a piece of pancake across her plate. "They all do."

Jack nodded and took another bite, silently inviting her to go on.

Natalie sighed. "I can't stop thinking about what he told me about my mom. I remember… I remember her singing to me, Jack. I thought I had no memories of her, but I can remember her voice now. She used to sing 'You Are My Sunshine' to me, and I thought it was the prettiest thing."

Jack reached out and placed a supportive hand on her arm. "That's nice, Nat."

"I guess." She turned to the side on her chair to face him. "It's strange, though, and now I wonder what else I'm forgetting. Like, did she used to tuck me into bed? Take me shopping? Did we dance around the kitchen together? Did she ever love me?"

Natalie's eyes began filling with tears, and Jack tipped her chin up until her gaze found his. "Hey," he said softly. "She was your mom, and I'm sure she loved you, but she made a selfish choice. She didn't deserve you."

Natalie bit her lip, trying to hold back tears. "I just wish I knew if she had ever cared about me. I always assumed she left and never looked back, but now that I know she left to pursue a singing career, I just wonder if there's anything else I'm missing."

"It sucks that your dad hid stuff from you," Jack sympathized, rubbing soothing circles over her arms with his thumb. "That wasn't fair. I'm sorry he kept the truth from you."

Natalie took a deep, cleansing breath. "Thank you. It just sucks that things have always been strained with my dad, and now I feel like I can't trust him at all."

"Maybe it would help to talk to him," Jack said.

She sighed wearily. "I will at some point, but it still feels too raw right now. I feel like I've been lied to my entire life."

"Maybe once my brothers leave, we can invite him here," Jack suggested. "You can talk to him in person."

Natalie cocked her head to the side as she thought about the idea. Maybe being on Nantucket with her again would warm Griff up. On the other hand, maybe it would just anger him to see her unusual lifestyle at play. She couldn't bear the thought of Griff judging the life she'd built with Jack and Carter, and she selfishly wanted to keep it as hidden from him as possible, so she shrugged noncommittally.

"Maybe."

☼ ☼ ☼

The next few days were a frenzy of cleaning and preparation for Jack's brothers' arrival, during which no painting occurred. Natalie's confidence that she would meet her deadline was waning, but there simply wasn't time to worry about that while preparing to host guests.

Every inch of the apartment and the café had been scrubbed clean. The garden was weeded. Natalie had finally repainted the sign for the café using fun, bright colors like yellow, coral, and blue. She'd incorporated lots of swirls and given it a distinctly bohemian vibe. Jack's initial reaction had been an unsurprising mixture of shock and dismay that quickly softened into acceptance. His reactions were gradually growing less and less dramatic, which she took as a sign that he was finally trusting her decisions.

The morning before Jack's brothers were set to arrive, Natalie finally decided to take a break. Slipping into her swimsuit, she headed down to the beach to sunbathe. After spreading out an oversized beach towel, she lay at the center of it and released a hefty sigh. The late summer sun caressed her bare skin, and her body melted into the towel as the minutes ticked by.

Jack's rapid footsteps barreling down the apartment stairs interrupted her serenity. "Guess what!" he exclaimed, plopping himself down beside her on the beach towel. It was nice to see him so excited after worrying so much the past few days about seeing his brothers.

Natalie pushed herself up on her forearms and lifted her sunglasses. "What?"

"My buddy Jerry is going away for the weekend, and he asked me to boat-sit for him."

She cocked a brow. "Boat-sit? Jerry? Isn't he the bouncer from The Gazebo that broke up that fight you were in?"

"Yeah," Jack said with shrug, "but we're old pals. He's seen way worse. Anyway, he wants me to boat-sit."

Natalie swung her leg around to sit cross-legged. "And what exactly does boat-sitting entail?"

"Well, really he just needs me to go to the marina and check that everything's ok with the boat," Jack explained. "But he also said I could take it out whenever I want to, and I was thinking we could do it today and maybe have lunch out on the water."

Natalie bit back a sigh, knowing she should be starting—and ideally finishing—a new painting that day, not gallivanting around Nantucket Sound in Jerry's boat. "Don't you want to wait until your brothers get here? It could be a fun thing to do with them," she suggested.

"Nah." Jack waved off the idea. "We wouldn't all fit. It's a small boat. And anyway, I want to spend some alone time with you and Carter before my brothers barge in here."

Unable to risk erasing the hopeful smile stretched across Jack's lips by declining, Natalie replied, "Ok. Well then, sure, I'd love to spend the day on a boat. You know how to drive it?"

Jack scoffed. "Of course. I grew up on Nantucket. I got my boating license before my driver's license."

"Wow, a man who can drive a boat. That's hot," she teased, wiggling her eyebrows suggestively.

"You like that?" he purred, pulling her into his arms to steal a kiss.

"Hey, captain," Natalie said as she pried herself away. "We'd better get going if we're doing this boat thing. We have to pack lunches and all of Carter's stuff. Babies come with a lot of baggage."

"I know." Jack groaned. "Let's get started then."

She saluted him, and they headed upstairs together. Natalie whipped up the perfect picnic lunch, slicing fruit to make a fruit salad and mixing together leftover chicken from dinner the night before with celery and mayonnaise to make chicken salad sandwiches. Carter would be happy enough with a peanut butter and jelly and some goldfish crackers, so she packed both of those as well.

When everything was ready, Jack drove them over to the marina, and they transferred everything onto Jerry's boat. Though the watercraft was fairly small, there was plenty of room for the three of them. Natalie took a seat on the built-in bench and placed Carter in her lap, where Jack wrestled him into a tiny life vest that made him look like he belonged on *Baby Baywatch*.

Taking his place at the helm, Jack tugged on the bill of his baseball cap. "Here we go!" he shouted as he turned the key, and the boat roared to life. Carter squealed at the loud noise, and Natalie bounced him in her lap.

She couldn't keep her eyes off Jack as he navigated the boat, looking like a complete natural behind the wheel. He skillfully maneuvered them away from the dock and steered them out into the open water. The curls that fell below his hat blew in the ocean breeze as he picked up speed. Putting two fingers in her mouth, Natalie let out a loud whistle.

Jack flashed her a mischievous smile. "Want to see what this baby's got?" he shouted, raising a brow.

"Do it!" she shouted back. Pulling one of the levers by the steering wheel, Jack accelerated the boat faster and faster until the front of the vessel practically floated above the waves.

"Woohoo!" Natalie shrieked, and Carter mimicked her excitement, throwing his hands up into the air as they sliced through the water. A cool spray wicked up from the ocean and misted over their bodies until Jack slowed the boat back to a normal pace, driving them around a bit more before stopping in the middle of the open water. Enveloped by ocean, with no land in sight, it felt like they were on their own little planet, though Natalie knew they could be back to civilization in no time at all if they needed to be.

"This," Jack said, turning off the boat, "is the perfect spot for a picnic."

"It's so beautiful out here," Natalie breathed. The clear-blue, cloudless sky met the cerulean waves in a sharp contrast on the horizon. The hot sun beat down, but before it had a chance to bother them, Jack pulled out an awning that covered the entire front of the boat.

Natalie put Carter down on the floor. The sides of the boat were high enough that there was no way he could escape. "Carter, want some fishies?" she asked, reaching into the cooler to grab the snack she'd packed for him. He waddled over and grabbed the container, more than happy to have his favorite snack.

"And for us," Natalie said to Jack as she procured the sandwiches and fruit salad.

"This looks awesome, Nat." He grabbed a sandwich, and they sat cross-legged on the boat's floor as they dug into their picnic.

"It feels great to get out on the water again," Jack said between bites.

"Mmm," Natalie agreed. "How long has it been since you've been able to get out on a boat?"

"Quite a while." He sighed and pointed to Carter, who was munching away on his snack. "This one makes it a little difficult, so it helps to have an extra set of hands and an extra pair of eyes to watch him."

"Oh, so that's what I am," Natalie drawled. "A set of hands and eyes."

"You," Jack assured her, "are much, much more than that."

"Oh, is that so?"

"Oh yes." He scooted closer until their legs were pressed together. "You've got lots of other wonderful… assets."

"Tell me more," Natalie said, egging him on.

"Well," he said, running gentle hands up and down both arms. "You've got the softest skin I've ever felt—other than the skin on the baby's butt, of course."

Natalie laughed and glanced over at Carter, who was totally oblivious to Jack talking about his naked bottom.

Jack's hands stroked down her legs. "And these legs," he went on. "I love when you show them off. So long and sexy. I want them wrapped around my neck."

Her brows hiked up at Jack's dirty talk, but he just kept coasting his hands along her skin. They drifted back up her arms, one stopping to rest on her shoulder while the other continued up to her face. One finger ran ever so lightly over her bottom lip. "And you've got these lips that taste so good. They drive me crazy."

Natalie darted her tongue out to lick his finger. He smiled and stuck the tip of it into her mouth. Playing along, she sucked on the pad of his finger before taking it deeper into her mouth. He shifted in his seat, and she playfully nipped his finger.

"Keep it in your pants, captain. We've got a baby on board."

"I wanted to get back to this amazing lunch anyway," Jack fibbed, turning back toward the food. Smirking, Natalie unwrapped the fruit salad. Jack picked up a grape that rested on the top.

"Open up," he ordered, holding up the grape as if he intended to feed it to her. Instead, he leaned in and swept her lips into a kiss. Her mouth was already open, giving his tongue easy access, and he explored her for a few moments before leaning away and popping the grape into her mouth.

Natalie chewed and swallowed it. "You don't play fair," she complained.

"Never said I did." Jack flashed her a sexy smile.

"Carter, come over here," Natalie called. "You need to shield me from this beast."

Carter toddled over, and Natalie sat him in her lap.

Jack raised an eyebrow. "Oh, so I'm a beast now?"

"Oh yes. A very… horned one," she said, attempting to keep the language PG enough for Carter. Not that he would understand what the word *horny* meant, but she wouldn't risk saying anything inappropriate that he could possibly repeat.

Jack burst out laughing. "I guess I can't disagree with you there."

Still sitting in Natalie's lap, Carter started to reach one sticky hand into the fruit salad. She quickly thwarted his efforts before he could ruin the appeal of the food for the adults, instead finding some smaller pieces and handing them to him one at a time.

Once all the food was gone, Carter hopped out of Natalie's lap and sprawled himself out on the floor of the boat with a waterproof bath book. Without the baby in her lap,

Natalie was free to sit back against the side of the boat and lounge.

"I've always liked boats," she mused. "I actually always thought it would be cool to live on a houseboat, you know? You could travel all up and down the coast and never worry about finding a place to stay."

"Hmm." Jack seemed unenthused. "I guess it would be pretty cool for a while, but I think I'd get tired of it."

"Really? You would never get bored, and if you did, you could just drive your boat to a new spot to explore."

"Yeah, but then you would never make any friends because you'd be moving around so much," he pointed out.

Natalie shrugged. "You could call people to stay in touch." She'd been doing it for years. "And there's nothing stopping you from visiting that same place again, even if you don't stay there."

"I guess," Jack said noncommittally. "I just don't think that's a life I'd enjoy."

Natalie nodded quietly, thinking about just how different they were. She was a transient artist who never stopped moving, and he was a Nantucket townie, raising a baby and building a business. They both knew the chasm existed, and yet it had become so easy to ignore.

Jack studied Natalie for a moment as she looked out over the water. "You know, you scare me sometimes," he admitted. "I feel like you're this ethereal creature, like a unicorn or something, and someday you're just going to slip right through my fingers or disappear in a puff of smoke."

"Is this another crack about my big head?" Natalie teased, holding a hand to her forehead to simulate a unicorn's horn.

Jack scowled. "I'm being serious."

Natalie sidled up closer to him and wrapped a hand around his arm. "Jack, I'm right here. I'm not going to disappear."

"I know." He placed a hand over hers, anchoring her to him. "But how long will that last?"

She looked up at him and frowned. "What do you mean?"

"I mean, how long before you set off for a new place?"

Natalie blinked. "I haven't really thought about it. The weather will be nice here for a few more months, right?"

Jack tensed beneath her touch. "Is that how you'll decide when you'll leave? Based on the weather?"

Not liking his tone, Natalie tried to tug her hand away, but he held on to her tighter.

"Jack…" she trailed off.

"Natalie," he retorted.

Sighing, she squeezed his arm, relishing the feel of those solid muscles. "Of course it's not just about the weather. I don't know what I'm doing next. I haven't made any plans yet."

"I don't want to lose you," Jack said softly, and Natalie leaned into his hold to comfort him.

"I don't want to lose you either," she assured him, though she knew it would eventually be inevitable. "I'm here right now, and I'm so happy with you, Jack. Let that be enough," she pleaded.

Hoping to end the conversation, Natalie craned her neck up to reach Jack's lips. He accepted her kiss but pulled her in closer to deepen it. She gasped as their bodies pressed together, and he used the opportunity to snake his tongue between her open lips and claim her mouth with a hungry kiss.

Cognizant of the fact that Carter was still on board and couldn't be left unattended, Natalie reluctantly pulled away. Both breathless, she and Jack locked eyes.

Natalie spoke first, choosing her words carefully. "I won't make you promises I can't keep. I don't have plans yet for what's next. I have to finish my paintings for Ned and then figure out what I'm doing."

Pressing his forehead against hers, Jack's breath danced over her face. "Is there any chance that involves staying here with me?"

Natalie chewed on her bottom lip. "It just… depends."

"On what?"

On a long sigh, she shook her head, her forehead sliding over Jack's. "On whether or not the paintings sell. On whether or not my inspiration sticks. It's… it's not just about us, Jack. If I have any hope of making this my career, I have to put my painting first. I've been trying to make this work for *five years*. I'm not ready to give it up just yet."

"I don't want you to give it up," Jack said quietly, his thumb stroking over her cheek. "I just want you to make it work here, with me. I know you're used to traveling all around, but there's a great art community on the island. My mom's included in that, and she's found great success here. Just… please don't give up on Nantucket before you've really given it a chance. Don't give up on me."

Natalie pressed a hand into his chest. "I'll never give up on you, Jack. But I won't give up on my art either, and I'll do whatever it takes to make this career work."

Jack's breath tickled her face as he silently inhaled and exhaled.

Natalie squeezed his arm, hoping to offer him a bit of the reassurance that her words could not. "I don't want this to be on your mind while you're already nervous about your brothers' visit. Let's talk about it again once they're gone."

Jack groaned against her cheek. "If we even make it through this visit."

Natalie leaned back and rolled her eyes, desperate to get back to their usual playful banter. "Oh, don't be such a baby. I don't know if I can handle another one," she added as Carter crawled into her lap, a large yawn escaping his little mouth.

Jack smiled fondly at the tired baby. "What do you say we wrap this up? I think this little dude could use a nap."

"Agreed." Natalie cuddled Carter into her chest so he could rest there on their journey home. Jack kissed her forehead and the baby's head then stood to reclaim his place at the helm.

Once again, Natalie was able to watch him steer the boat and was struck by just how sexy a sight it was. Not only that, but also how solid Jack looked behind the wheel. He was so steady and maneuvered the boat effortlessly, unfazed by any errant waves that came their way. He looked solid as a rock.

So, then what did that make her? Perhaps something more like a piece of seaweed, floating around aimlessly.

Natalie let out a breath, relieved that particular course of conversation with Jack was over. She knew it would come up again—probably sooner than she'd like. Her intentions to move on weren't changing, and Jack's intentions to stay on the island to run Danny's Place and raise Carter seemed pretty set in stone.

All she could hope was that his futile desire for her to be part of that life wouldn't end their relationship before they'd gotten to fully savor it.

21

On the morning of Jack's brothers' arrival, Natalie awoke in his arms and shifted to face him. His eyes were soft with sleep, his breaths long and drawn out. Smiling at his slumbering figure, she ran gentle fingertips over his sideburn and stubble-adorned jawline. A content sound emerged from deep in his throat as his eyes fluttered open.

"Good morning," he said, a lazy, sexy smile spreading across his face.

"Morning." Natalie was unable to contain a smile of her own. "I hate to break it to you, but we have to get up if you want to be on time to pick up Fletcher and Beau."

Jack groaned and glanced over at the clock on the bedside table. "Do I have to?" he whined.

"Yes." Natalie leaned in to give him a quick peck on the lips then sat up beside him "They'll be arriving in just a few hours," she reminded him. "We have to have breakfast, and you wanted to do a few last-minute things before they come, right?"

"Right." Jack reluctantly slid off his side of the bed and reached his arms up in the air, stretching his gloriously naked body. Natalie watched longingly, knowing there was no time to fool around. He pulled on a pair of boxers from his dresser and grabbed another pair plus a t-shirt for her.

"Here ya go." He tossed them onto the bed.

"Thanks, babe." Natalie pulled them on and was pleased to see that Jack had forgone a t-shirt for himself, leaving most of his gorgeous body on display. They went to Carter's room and plucked him out of his crib, where he'd been quietly playing with his stuffed animals.

"Are you excited to see Uncle Beau and Uncle Fletcher today?" Jack asked him.

Jack had told Natalie that his brothers hadn't seen Carter since Danny's funeral, when Jack had still been under the initial shock of becoming Carter's guardian. Although he wasn't exactly eager to see his brothers, he did seem glad that Carter would be able to spend some time with them.

"Come here, big guy." Natalie took Carter into her arms for a hug then carried him out to the kitchen where she and Jack prepared frozen waffles. Between bites, they discussed all the things they had to do before his brothers arrived. She agreed to do the last-minute cleaning and keep an eye on Carter while Jack swung by the grocery store then picked up his brothers from the ferry.

Natalie finished her jobs quickly, especially with Carter helping to put some of his toys away. He had learned that she gave him cookies when he helped with chores like that. Though the summer had started off strong with her healthy habits, she'd broken down after realizing that one of the best ways to bribe Carter—and Jack, for that matter—was junk food.

Since Jack wasn't due back for a while, Natalie decided to take Carter down to the beach, figuring they might as well take advantage of the sunny morning. She exchanged Jack's clothes for one of her many bikinis and wrestled Carter into his swim trunks before heading down. Natalie lounged in the sand while Carter dug holes all around her.

After about an hour of the sunlight beating down on them, her skin was boiling, so she took Carter down to the ocean to cool off. Wading into the water until it reached her waist and just skimmed Carter's toes, she indulged him in a few rounds of his favorite game—the one that Jack always played with him in the ocean and that Natalie had even captured in a painting. She dipped his feet in the water then threw him up in the air before catching him. Dipping him a little further then tossing him again, she continued the cycle until he was dunked up to his chest. Carter howled with laughter as they played.

Natalie had already done several rounds when she spotted Jack walking down to the beach, flanked by two other men. The one to his left was a smidge shorter but stockier and more built. He clearly lifted weights, as his biceps bulged out and his calf muscles were quite defined. That one must have been Beau, the police officer. His hair was a similar chocolatey brown to Jack's, though cut much shorter.

The other man, who she assumed was Fletcher, was built more leanly like Jack. Thin, wire glasses sat atop his nose and gave him a mature appearance but did nothing to take away from his good looks. His blond hair set him apart from his brothers, but the loose curls in it mirrored Jack's.

As they approached, Natalie carried Carter out to the sand. Jack watched as her bikini-clad body emerged from the water, and she noticed the other men staring too.

"Hey, babe." Jack leaned in to give her a deep, healthy, and totally inappropriate kiss, considering his brothers were standing right there. When he was done staking his claim, he draped one arm over Natalie's shoulders and leaned in to whisper in her ear. "Did you have to wear such a sexy bikini?" His hissed question was quiet enough that only she could hear.

Rolling her eyes and ignoring him, she introduced herself. "Hi, guys. I'm Natalie, Jack's girlfriend."

Fletcher and Beau introduced themselves, and she found she'd been correct about which brother was which. When Beau, Jack's notoriously flirtatious brother, introduced himself, he took her hand and raised it to his mouth for a kiss. Jack growled, and Natalie shot him a look.

"It's a pleasure to meet you," Beau said smoothly.

Natalie kept her voice even and casual as she replied, "Nice to meet you too."

"I've heard great things about you," Beau went on, a provocative tone in his voice.

"Same goes for you," Natalie said politely. That was a bit of a lie, but what else was she supposed to say?

"There's the little guy!" Fletcher knelt down to ruffle the little boy's hair, putting Jack out of his misery over Beau's flirtation. "Hi, Carter!"

Natalie was relieved to realize that Fletcher was more interested in the baby than her, and she would only have to worry about fending off one brother.

"Carter, that's your Uncle Fletcher," Jack said. "Can you say Uncle Fletcher?"

"Unca Fetch!" Carter said.

"Very good!" Natalie encouraged.

"And this is Uncle Beau." Jack pointed to his younger brother.

"Unca Beau," Carter said.

"Good!" Jack said. Turning to Beau, he added, "Yours is the only name he can actually say."

Beau chuckled and swung the baby up into his arms. "That's cause I'm his favorite. Right, buddy?" he asked, jiggling the baby up and down. Carter giggled and squirmed until Beau put him back on the ground.

"Why don't you guys come inside?" Jack said. "We can get

you settled. Unfortunately, we only have one bed available. One of you will have to sleep on the couch."

"I'll take the couch," Beau jumped in, clearly trying to be the valiant brother and take one for the team.

"Great. Then, Fletcher, you can sleep in Natalie's bed," Jack said. Fletcher nodded at the arrangement, but Beau raised his eyebrows.

"Can I take back my offer?" He glanced at Natalie, giving her a once-over.

Jack pulled her closer into his side. "No," he spat. "And before you get any ideas, Natalie will be sleeping in my bed. With me."

Beau put his hands up in surrender. Fletcher just snickered.

"Let's get inside," Natalie suggested.

"Let's," Jack snapped.

He picked Carter up and took one of Natalie's hands in his to lead them up to the apartment. If he was that tense already from a little of Beau's harmless flirting, it was going to be a long few days.

☼ ☼ ☼

For dinner, Jack grilled steaks, and Natalie prepared a pasta salad to go on the side. The group sat around the kitchen table to eat, including June, who was beyond thrilled to have all her sons in one place.

Carter was present too, feasting on a hearty helping of macaroni and cheese to please his youthful palate. He'd insisted on sitting in Fletcher's lap to eat, the two having bonded quickly. Beau seemed to think Carter was cute and all, but Fletcher really indulged him, picking him up when he wanted to be held, playing with him when he got bored, and even letting him dump bucketfuls of water on his head down at the beach. It impressed Natalie that a man his age, without kids of his own, was so good with children.

"You really love kids, huh?" she asked, taking a sip of her summer ale.

"Oh yeah. I've always loved kids. Ever since I had to babysit these rugrats every day." Fletcher shot a pointed look at Jack and Beau, who both flashed devilish smiles. "You'd think they would have turned me off kids forever."

"They were hellions," June agreed, "but Fletcher was such a huge help with them." She glanced fondly at her eldest son. "He's going to make an amazing father one day."

Fletcher cleared his throat. "I always thought I'd have a few of my own by now."

"What does Christa think about that?" Beau asked, and Natalie remembered Jack mentioning Fletcher's long-time girlfriend.

Fletcher let out a sigh. "I don't know. We've talked about marriage, but I don't know that she's necessarily a kid person. Sometimes we'll see a baby out at a restaurant or something, and I'll mention how cute it is, and she'll say something like, 'Yeah, until it poops or throws up.'"

Beau snickered. "Typical."

"What's that supposed to mean?" Fletcher demanded.

"Boys," June warned.

"Christa's a priss," Beau said. "Never a hair out of place, always done up like she is. You know what I'm saying, bro. I could *not* picture her changing a diaper."

"People can surprise you," Fletcher responded defensively, though what Beau had said was obviously true, whether or not he wanted to admit it.

"Ok, fellas," Jack broke in. "Let's not start a fight. And Fletcher, take it from me. Kids can show up in your life in the most unexpected ways, whether you plan for them or not."

Everyone chuckled and looked over at Carter, still content in Fletcher's lap and eating macaroni and cheese by the fistful.

Fletcher ruffled the little boy's hair and turned toward Jack. "How are you doing with all the changes?"

"Great," Jack replied, pushing his hair back from his forehead. "I think I've pretty much gotten the hang of the whole parenting thing. Things got off to a pretty rocky start, but I've finally found my groove—mostly thanks to Natalie here." He gazed fondly over at her.

She smiled and leaned in to give him a quick kiss. "You always had it in you. I just helped you discover it."

Beau let out a long groan. "Get a room!" he hooted, though their kiss had been far from racy. Natalie stuck her tongue out playfully as Jack whacked his younger brother on the side of the head.

"Just because you can't find a woman to put up with you, doesn't mean you can begrudge me for getting a little action," Jack taunted.

"Oh, I get plenty of action," Beau said, cracking his knuckles in front of his chest. "In fact, the amount of action I get in a week—both by chasing bad guys at my job and with the ladies, if you know what I mean—would blow your mind. Neither of you bozos could ever handle *all that*."

June covered her ears, humming loudly to drown out Beau's words.

Jack rolled his eyes at his brother. "I get just as much action as you. Only, I get it with the same sexy, wonderful woman instead of a bunch of poor girls whose names go in one ear and out the other."

"Boys," Fletcher chided, pulling the pseudo-father card. "That's enough."

Jack and Beau both sat back in their seats, grimacing.

Ever the practical brother, Fletcher turned the conversation back to neutral territory. Turning to Jack, he asked, "So, you like running the café?"

Jack shrugged. "Yeah, it's not bad. I get a hell of a lot

more respect behind the counter in there than I ever did behind a bar. It makes me feel like an actual adult."

"I'm impressed," Fletcher said. "Running a business and raising a baby. You seem like an actual adult to me too."

"Thanks," Jack said, his eyebrows raised as if he was surprised by his brother's comment, though his smile indicated that he was pleased by his approval. "Speaking of raising a baby… I've gotta get this guy to bed if I'm going to keep my title as a responsible parent." He stood and removed Carter from Fletcher's lap. "Say goodnight, buddy."

Jack placed Carter on the ground, and he walked around to everyone, blowing kisses and saying, "G'night!" When he arrived at Natalie's place, she picked him up for a hug.

"Goodnight, sweet boy." She gave him a smooch on the head. "I love you."

"Wuv ooh," Carter replied. Natalie grinned and handed him over to Jack, who looked over the baby's head at her and imitated him, saying, "Wuv ooh."

She giggled, and Jack flashed her a smile before taking Carter up to his room. It took a moment for her to process that he'd basically just said *I love you*, albeit in Carter's baby language. She was left wondering if he was just imitating the cute phrase, or if he'd actually meant it.

"So, Natalie, I hear you're an artist," Fletcher said, breaking her away from her thoughts.

"A very good one," June said.

Natalie tossed June a look of gratitude and replied, "Yes, I paint."

Beau laced his hands together behind his head in a casual, cocky pose. "You ever paint nudes?" he asked. "I've always wanted to get into some modeling. I think I'd be a great candidate."

"Shut up." Fletcher thumped his brother on the chest.

"It's ok," Natalie replied, unfazed. "I did paint a few nude models in art school. But models are more fun to paint when they're, you know, well endowed," she continued, keeping a totally straight face. "I don't know if you'd be that great of a candidate after all."

Fletcher burst out laughing, Beau grimaced, and June just shook her head.

"I like you." Fletcher clinked his beer against Natalie's.

"I'll have you know all the women I've been with have left very satisfied," Beau grumbled.

"Of course," Natalie assured him. "I'm sure leaving was very satisfying for them."

Beau smirked. "Not the leaving so much as the com—"

"So," Fletcher said loudly, cutting off Beau's lewd retort, "it seems like you and my brother are pretty serious."

Beau lounged back in his chair while Fletcher observed Natalie with sharp eyes. June sent her an encouraging smile.

"We are," Natalie said. "I really like him. He's an amazing guy."

"That he is," Fletcher agreed. "I just want to make sure he won't get hurt again anytime soon. Danny's death crushed him. I wouldn't want him to have any more heartbreak for a while."

"I don't ever want to hurt him," Natalie said. "I know he's been through a lot in the past few months. I'm glad I've been able to bring some happiness into his life again. I wouldn't do anything to jeopardize that."

Fletcher gave her a nod of approval. She completely understood his concern and hoped he realized that hurting Jack—or Carter, for that matter—was the very last thing she wanted to do.

"I'm glad he found you," Fletcher said just as Jack walked back into the kitchen.

"Carter was pooped," he said. "He went down easy."

"Good." Natalie stood up from her seat and smoothed out her cotton sundress. "I'm going to give you guys some family time. I'll be out back for a bit."

Jack caught her arm as she walked by. "You don't have to go."

"It's ok," she replied with a warm smile. "You guys haven't had any time alone together since your brothers got here. And your mom hasn't seen them in a while. You should all catch up."

"Ok." Jack tugged Natalie in for a kiss before she retreated down the stairwell.

22

The beach was completely empty, the tranquil blanket of night having fallen hours ago. Natalie sat with her back against Danny's, the sand and ocean spread out before her and the crashing waves as the only noise to fill the silence. Moonlight glinted off the shimmering water, and stars shone bright overhead.

She sat there for a long while, soaking in the magic as she thought about the day she'd had. Jack's easy, playful banter with his brothers was entertaining, though it was clear they loved and respected one another. Hopefully, Carter would get to experience the bond of siblings one day. He would never get blood-related brothers or sisters, but Natalie could definitely see Jack having more kids with someone.

An image of herself with a big bump popped into her mind. What would it be like to grow a life? The thought was intriguing. Placing a hand on her flat belly, Natalie imagined what it would feel like to have a baby kicking in there, then she shook her head. Dana's words must have been getting to her. *"You'd be a great mother too, you know."*

Jack's footsteps padded down the stairs, interrupting her thoughts, and Natalie stood to greet him.

"Hi," Jack said, his voice husky as he wrapped his arms around her waist and pulled her in for a kiss.

"Mmm," Natalie hummed. "What was that for?"

Jack nipped at her earlobe. "Because you're mine, and my brothers love you—Beau maybe a little too much. He's been flirting with you since the minute he got here."

Natalie pulled back an inch and looked up at Jack sternly. "Yes, but I haven't been flirting back. Did they tell you how I put Beau in his place while you were getting Carter to sleep?"

Jack chuckled and tapped the tip of her nose. "Yeah, they did mention that. Thank you. My mom thought it was pretty great. She told me before she left."

Natalie stood up on her tiptoes to press a kiss to his lips. "It was my pleasure."

"Yes…your pleasure," he repeated. "Let's take care of that."

Natalie didn't get a chance to respond before she was pushed back up against the wall, Jack's hands caging her in on either side of her head. With a wicked gleam in his eye, he leaned in for a deep, longing kiss that had her melting into the hard wall at her back and his hard body at her front. They'd been here before, but this time, the cover of night offered a level of privacy they had previously lacked.

Jack's lips descended to Natalie's neck, and she tipped her head to the side, giving him better access. Stubbly scruff tickled the sensitive skin of her neck as he sucked on it, lingering in one spot and sucking until it was tender then darting his tongue out to soothe it. Natalie moaned as Jack's hot tongue swiped over her cool skin.

Returning his lips to hers, he snuck one hand below her shirt to grasp her breast. Her nipple hardened beneath his touch, and he hardened against her belly. Natalie gasped and freed her lips from his.

"Jack, we can't," she breathed.

"Why not?" He kissed the corner of her mouth and

squeezed her breast at the same time. She gasped and arched into his touch before remembering herself.

"Your brothers are right inside," she whispered.

Jack's gaze darkened. "Then don't be loud."

Desire, hot and heavy, unfurled in Natalie's belly.

Claiming her lips once more, Jack kissed her hard, his tongue's exploration ruthless and unrelenting. Unable to fight him and knowing he needed this, the ultimate possession, she gave in and wrapped one leg around his waist to keep her balance.

His lips found her neck again, this time accompanied by a hand beneath her dress. His fingertips brushed ever so lightly over her panties, then he pushed them aside and ran his index finger through her slickness, eliciting a moan from deep in her throat.

"You like that, baby?" Jack asked in a low voice. "You're so nice and wet for me."

Unable to form a coherent answer, Natalie mumbled, "Mhmm."

Jack rubbed once more as he sucked on that tender spot on her neck, then his lips caught hers again, and his tongue invaded just as he plunged one finger inside of her. Natalie drew in a sharp breath at the invasion, driven by equal parts surprise and pleasure. He dragged his finger out and gently eased two back in. Acclimating to the sensation, she began grinding on his fingers as he plunged them in and out, moving faster as she did. The tortuous sensation had her groaning and begging for more.

"Jack," she breathed.

"Shh, I know. I've got you," he promised, sliding his fingers out to draw her panties down her legs. They fell to the ground and were quickly forgotten by both parties.

Standing tall, Jack unzipped his fly to reveal his hard, pulsing length. Natalie gazed at it appreciatively as even more liquid pooled between her thighs. His pants and boxers remained on his hips. Only his erection was visible above the fabric. The sight was so erotic, so primal, that her heart actually skipped a beat. His brothers could come down at any moment, or someone taking a nighttime walk on the beach could pass them by, and they had to be ready to disengage at a moment's notice. Something about that knowledge made Natalie absolutely feral with desire.

Jack pulled a condom out of his back pocket and rolled it over himself with shaking hands. Grabbing Natalie beneath her bare ass, he hoisted her up and positioned her over himself.

"You ready, baby?" he murmured, his voice strained with need.

All it took was a quick nod of her head, and Natalie was being eased down onto his hard length. Moaning, she wrapped her legs around his waist, and he let out a heavy breath as he impaled her.

"Yesss," Jack hissed, dipping his head down to suck on her neck again. Overcome with the onslaught of sensations and feeling so completely full as he slid in and out of her, Natalie did nothing but hold on for dear life. With their bodies veiled by a sheen of sweat, the act felt vaguely like diving onto a Slip 'N Slide—treacherous and possibly downright dangerous, but so, so satisfying.

She clung to Jack, relying on his hands planted firmly on her bottom to support her. He started to pick up the pace, driving up into her hard and fast as her hips worked tirelessly to keep up. A groan escaped her mouth as Jack's teeth grazed the sensitive skin on her jugular. Molding his lips to hers, he effectively silenced her by jabbing his tongue against hers.

As she rode him, or—more accurately—was driven into by him, Natalie couldn't help but feel like Jack was marking his territory. His frenzied movements could be due to the threat of getting caught or sheer lust, but she sensed the desperation in his actions—that primal urge to claim and mark ownership. It might have bothered her, but she hardly had time to dwell on it as he continued pounding into her, hitting that sweet spot every time.

Growing closer to orgasm, Natalie groaned and threw her head back, knocking it against the wall but barely registering the pain as the bottom edge of a shingle dug into her scalp.

"Careful," Jack grunted, adjusting his grip and lowering her down a smidge so her head rested on the flat part of the shingle. The action, however, also brought him that much deeper inside of her.

"Jack!" she cried as she spasmed around him, her orgasm perilously close.

"Shh," he whispered in warning, and Natalie bit into her lip to contain her groans. Lowering his mouth to her breasts, he sucked on her nipples one at a time until they became like hard little diamonds, then he bared his teeth and tugged slightly, finally setting her off. Pleasure washed through her in waves, ebbing and flowing throughout her entire body, and she had to sink her teeth into Jack's collarbone to keep from crying out.

He grunted but took it, squeezing her cheeks hard as she rode through her peak. Finally, limp with pleasure, she sagged into him, her bite softening into a kiss on his salty skin. Licking up his neck and toward his mouth, she remained fully aware of him still achingly hard inside of her. Finding his lips with hers, she parted them with her tongue, which he seemed to take as permission to find his own satisfaction. Ravaging her mouth as he drove into her, Jack's hips began pumping relentlessly until he found his own release. He squeezed Natalie's ass as he poured himself into the condom.

Both breathing heavily, they stayed connected like that, her entire body wrapped around his, until she lost her balance and her feet fell to the ground. Jack grabbed her upper arms to steady her and pressed a soft kiss to the slightly sore spot on her neck that he'd been sucking.

"Careful, baby," he murmured. Natalie smiled shyly up at him, unsure she could even walk while her legs felt so flimsy. "Are you gonna be able to make it upstairs?" Jack asked as he zipped up his fly, his lips curling into a wry, satisfied smile.

"I'm not sure," she muttered. How unfair that he could walk away looking as if nothing had happened, while her dress was completely wrinkled, and her hair looked like a rat's nest.

"Come over here." Jack knelt and gestured for her to get on his back. Climbing onto him, Natalie wrapped her arms and legs around his body, not unlike what she'd just done, though, this time, she was on his back instead of his front.

"Ready?" he asked.

"Ready."

Natalie shrieked when Jack hopped up with her piggybacking him. She giggled at her outburst the whole way up the stairs, and they were both laughing when they reached the landing, and she remembered that Beau was staying in the living room.

Beau sat up on the edge of the couch and cocked an eyebrow as he took in the sight of Natalie perched on his brother's back. "Hey, bro."

"Hey." Jack was breathless from laughter and the exertion of carrying Natalie. She simply could not stop giggling and buried her face in his neck to muffle the sound.

"'Night, man," Jack said as he dashed to his bedroom. Kicking the door shut behind him, he dropped Natalie on the bed and helped her pull off her dress then her bra.

Placing a soft kiss on her forehead, he pulled back the sheets and gestured beneath them. "Come on, get under the covers."

Natalie crawled in and watched as Jack undressed then slid into bed beside her. Kissing her temple as he got settled in, he whispered a quiet, "Thank you."

"For what?" she asked, rubbing his chest. "The amazing sex?"

"No! Well, yes," he chuckled, "but I meant just for being you. My brothers love you. They've never approved of any girlfriend I've introduced them to."

"And they approve of me?"

Jack rolled her into his front so they were spooning. "Very much so."

Sighing with pleasure, she snuggled into him, somewhat proud that Jack's brothers liked her. She'd never gained the approval of a significant other's family before, though she supposed she hadn't actually met many of their families either. That was a far too serious sign of commitment.

Everything about her relationship with Jack felt different from any she'd had before. He was kind and caring in a way she'd never experienced with a man so virile. He was mature and took his responsibilities seriously, including his vow to savor her. Natalie didn't think she'd ever been treated so well in bed or out of it.

The one thing that felt the same as it always had was the knowledge that she would eventually have to say goodbye. Each day that passed showed her even more just how special Jack was, and she couldn't risk sticking around long enough to do something that might really hurt him.

The troubling thought reminded her of his earlier admission.

"Jack?" she whispered.

"Hmm," he grumbled, placing a lazy kiss in her hair.

"About what you said earlier…"

"What did I say?" he asked sleepily.

Natalie took a deep breath to calm her nerves before explaining. "Well, when Carter was going to bed, he came over to me and said, 'Wuv you.' Then, you repeated it. But I didn't know… were you really saying it? Or just repeating it because it was cute that Carter had said it?"

Jack was silent for a few moments, and she was glad she was facing away from him so he couldn't see the unease on her face.

"I wouldn't have said it if I didn't mean it," he finally said, coaxing her to roll over with a hand at her waist. Natalie waited a moment before raising her gaze to his. His eyes were soft and warm with… *love?*

"I love you, Natalie Walker," Jack declared, his eyes trained on hers. "I love your smile, and your laugh, and the way you make love. I love how kind and gentle you are with Carter. I love how you're not afraid to dream and follow your heart. I love everything about you."

Tears sprang into Natalie's eyes as he said the sweetest words anyone had ever said to her.

"Hey." Jack wiped away a stray tear with his thumb. "It's ok. I don't expect you to say it back. I just didn't want any more time to go by without you knowing how I truly feel."

Natalie shook her head in disbelief, awestruck that Jack actually *loved* her. No one had said those words to her in a long, long time. Her head felt fuzzy, like it was filled with television static, and her heart leapt and pounded, threatening to jump right out of her ribcage.

The next few tears that leaked from her eyes were a mixture of awe at this man's affection and the harrowing realization that she couldn't return his sentiment. Regardless of what she may feel for him, Natalie refused to lead him on or give him the wrong idea. Love implied commitment, and commitment implied staying.

"You're the best man I've ever known," she said, giving him the only reassurance she was ready to give. Though she couldn't declare undying love, she needed Jack to know that he meant something to her—something real and true and so, so rare. Even if that something wasn't enough to make her stay forever.

Leaning in, she pressed a soft, tender symbol of her feelings on his lips, hoping it conveyed what she felt in her heart in a way that words never could. Jack returned her gentle kiss, pulling her close into the cocoon of his hold. Being in his arms never failed to make her feel safe in a way she longed to hold on to forever, but she had to keep reminding herself that this wasn't forever. It couldn't be. *Never stop moving. Never settle. Never do what she did.*

It would be more important than ever that they had that talk after his brothers left.

23

Natalie awoke with Jack's arms wound around her like vines. Yawning, she rolled onto her back to take a big morning stretch. Beside her, Jack's eyes opened slowly, still weighed down by the heavy burden of slumber.

"Morning, baby," he said, a lazy, sexy smile spreading across his face.

"Good morning," she replied, taking in his sleepy eyes, mussed hair, and raspy morning voice. Leaning in, she aimed to give him a quick peck, but Jack grabbed the back of her neck and held her face to his, kissing her slowly and thoroughly instead.

When she finally came up for air, Natalie glanced over at the clock on the bedside table and frowned. "We slept late."

"We exerted ourselves last night," Jack reminded her with a sly smile.

Giving him one more quick kiss, she said, "We have to get up."

"I'll check on Carter," he volunteered, rolling out of bed so she got a prime view of his delectable backside. Disappointment dawned when he quickly pulled on a pair of boxers.

Wanting to make sure she looked decent before she went

out and saw Jack's brothers, Natalie got up too. "I'm gonna get ready quickly." Her usual morning outfit of Jack's boxers and t-shirt wouldn't be acceptable today, so she slid into a pair of athletic shorts and a ribbed tank top instead.

Padding her way to the bathroom, Natalie stretched her arms overhead and strode toward the vanity. Before she could get to washing her face, something caught her eye in the mirror. There, smack dab in the middle of her neck, was a giant, angry, impossible-to-hide *hickey*.

"No," she gasped, brushing her fingers over the tender spot. A memory of Jack kissing her there flashed through her mind. She recalled him sucking on the tender skin, driving her wild with lust. Little did she know, he'd been marking her.

"Jack!" Natalie shouted as she stared at her reflection.

He poked his head into the bathroom with Carter in his arms and asked, "What's up?" in an annoyingly innocent tone.

"What the hell is this?" Natalie pointed angrily to her neck.

"Woah, language!" Jack covered Carter's ears and smugly added, "I do believe that's a hickey."

"Yeah, I got that," she spat. "Wanna tell me why it's there?"

"Well, you see, sometimes when two people are really in love…" he began, his charming, happy-go-lucky attitude angering Natalie to no end. Jack wisely closed his mouth when she let out a sharp breath.

"Seriously, Jack. This thing is huge, and I can't hide it. What are your brothers going to think?"

"They're going to think that you're taken," he ground out, his eyes narrowing.

"I'm pretty sure they already know. But you still had to visibly stake your claim, didn't you? Why do you need to act like such a caveman?"

Jack pursed his lips as if he was trying to hold back a smile. "Caveman?"

Natalie's eyes widened, and she reached out to thump him on the chest. "I'm serious!"

Jack grabbed her hand and encased it in his own. "I can tell," he said gently. "But I need you to explain what you mean by me acting like a caveman."

"You know. You, Natalie. Me, Jack. You, my little woman," she said, doing her best impression of a primitive human. Jack continued to try and fail at hiding his amusement, but he had the good sense to look remorseful before opening his mouth again.

"You're right. I'm sorry." He ran his fingers harshly through his hair. "I guess I got carried away. I don't ever want anyone to look at you and get any ideas. I want everyone to know you're mine, because I love you."

Sighing heavily, Natalie shook her head. Pulling out the *L* word wasn't going to soften Jack's actions. If anything, it put her back up more. "It's not ok to physically mark me just so others back off," she said. "You're not a dog pissing on a fire hydrant."

Jack shifted Carter uncomfortably in his arms. "I know."

"People will know I'm yours, because if they try to hit on me, I'll tell them. Don't you trust me?"

He held her gaze for a long moment then nodded slowly and said, "I do. I do trust you, but like I told you yesterday, you scare me sometimes. You have all these places you want to go and all these people that want you—my damned brother included—and it makes me... nervous."

Natalie shook her head and blew out a pent-up breath. "I'm sorry that you're feeling nervous, but I don't think it's about your brother, because I don't think you really believe I would do anything with him. I think it's about our conversation yesterday, which I know we need to continue, but we agreed to hold off until your brothers are gone."

Jack nodded slowly. "Right. We need to talk about when you might be leaving me."

"Jack!" Natalie cried, unsure whether she was more upset by his bluntness or by the fact that he'd hit the nail on the head. "We are so not doing this right now." She glanced toward the kitchen, where someone could be heard moving about. "Can we please just go have a nice breakfast with your brothers?"

Jack exhaled forcefully and raked a hand through his hair but said, "Yes. Let's do that."

Natalie's shoulders sagged with relief. There was a conversation to be had—one that was sure to be uncomfortable and difficult, which was why she'd been avoiding it for so long—but it was not a conversation she wanted to have with others present.

"Good," she said, shooing the boys off as she inspected her hickey in the mirror. "Let me finish getting ready. This thing is going to be a bitch to cover with make-up."

☼ ☼ ☼

Jack, Fletcher, and Carter were all sitting out at the kitchen table when Natalie entered the room. Well, Carter was standing on a kitchen chair and banging on the kitchen table under Fletcher's watchful gaze.

"Good morning," she greeted them brightly, successfully hiding the fact that Jack had royally pissed her off just a few minutes before.

"Morning," Fletcher replied, his eyes never leaving Carter.

"Where's Beau?" she asked, realizing the kitchen was missing his larger-than-life presence.

"I think he went out for a run," Fletcher replied. "He should be back soon."

"Oh, ok. Should I start breakfast now or wait for him to come back?"

"Just start it," Jack said. "He'll probably be back before it's ready."

"Ok," Natalie said. "Omelets sound good?"

"Perfect," Fletcher answered, finally looking over at her to give her a thumbs up.

"I'll help you," Jack said—a peace offering, if she'd ever heard one. And though she was still annoyed with him, Natalie wouldn't turn down the help.

"Here you go," he said, handing her a cutting board from the cabinet and placing another on the counter beside hers. They stood side by side, chopping vegetables for the omelets, while Natalie chatted with Fletcher, carefully avoiding looking at or talking to Jack.

He was just putting the vegetables into the pans when Beau trotted up the stairs, wearing only a pair of long shorts, his bare torso dripping with sweat. Natalie blinked at his razor-sharp abs before her gaze roamed over the tattoos on his broad chest and right bicep.

"Hey, bro," Fletcher greeted him.

"Morning." Beau grabbed a bottled water from the fridge and chugged half of it in one big gulp then poured the rest over his head. The excess water flooded to the floor, creating a puddle in the middle of the kitchen.

"Really, man?" Jack gestured to the water pooling at his feet.

"Relax, Mr. Mom," Beau retorted. "I'll wipe it up." Snatching a hand towel off the oven door, he mopped up the water he'd spilled then tossed it in the laundry room. When he returned to the kitchen, he was toying with a different piece of fabric in his hands.

"So, I found something interesting on my run..." Beau turned toward Jack and Natalie, a mischievous expression on his face. "It looks like someone was having a little fun out back last night. You two wouldn't know anything about that, would you?"

Natalie's eyes flared as she recognized the skimpy pair of panties dangling from his finger as her own. "Oh, come on," she groaned.

Beau shrugged. "I could do a little investigating to figure out who they belong to… unless you already know." He snickered as Natalie snagged the panties and shoved them into her pocket. She shot a glare at Jack, who kept his gaze downcast.

Pointing to his neck, Beau added, "Hey, Nat, you've got a little something on your neck. You might want to get that checked out."

"Shut up!" she cried, reaching out to slap Beau's bicep. He danced back out of her reach. "Oh, she's a feisty one!"

"Beau," Jack warned.

Beau snickered and put his hands up. "I know, I know. I'll stop." He turned to the table and sat at an empty chair next to Fletcher, ruffling Carter's hair in the process. "How's this little man this morning?"

"He's great!" Fletcher placed the baby on the floor so he could run over to the living room where all his toys were.

"We going to see Mom today?" Beau asked, kicking his feet up on a vacant chair.

"Yeah," Jack replied. "I was thinking we could all go over for lunch and maybe go to the beach together?"

"Sounds good to me," Beau said. "I'm dying for some fun in the sun."

"Me too," Fletcher added. "You coming with, Natalie?"

"Oh, no, I wouldn't want to impose on your family time."

"You wouldn't be imposing"—Jack's dark gaze met hers—"on our *family* time."

Natalie swallowed, remembering the day at the café when he'd led a customer to believe they were a family. "No, no," she pressed. "I'm going to stop by Dana's today. We're picking out which agents to pitch the book to."

Jack watched her closely but seemed to come around. "Ok, but you're welcome to change your mind."

Natalie nodded in thanks and served the finished omelets to everyone.

"Jack mentioned you were working on the illustrations for a children's book," Fletcher said before taking a big bite of his breakfast.

"Yes, I am. My friend Dana wrote it and asked me to illustrate," Natalie explained.

"Very cool," Fletcher replied. "When it's published, I'll have to buy some copies for my classroom."

Natalie smiled at his thoughtfulness. "That would be awesome."

Fletcher tapped the end of his fork against his chin. "I remember Dana. Her last name's LePage, right?"

"It's Myers now," Jack said around bites of his omelet.

"No kidding? She and Ryan Myers got married?" Fletcher asked.

"Sure did," Jack confirmed.

Beau whistled. "Man. Am I the only one from this godforsaken island that hasn't settled down yet? Dana and Ryan are married. Fletcher's been dating Christa forever. Jack, you have a damn kid."

"If you look at it like that, I guess so," Jack said, slapping his brother's back. "We're growing up, man."

"Not me." Beau stretched his arms above his head. "I'm going to stay young a while longer, thank you. I'm in no rush to be tied down."

"You say that now, but when you least expect it, you'll change your tune." Jack glanced over at Natalie and sent her a soft smile. For the sake of everyone's comfort, she forced a smile back, but it felt wrong and unfamiliar as she pasted it on her face. Being compared to a married couple and a couple that had been dating for years confirmed that Jack was in a totally different headspace than her.

"All right," Jack said, completely unaware of her thoughts.

"I'm going to get Carter ready to go, and then we'll head out?"

His brothers nodded and stood. Fletcher headed to Natalie's room to get ready, and Beau headed for the bathroom. Jack grabbed Carter and paused in front of her.

"You *sure* you don't want to come today? I know my mom would love to see you again."

"I'm sure. I have a lot of work to do, and I want you and your brothers to be able to visit with your mom without me intruding."

He studied her for a moment before leaning down to give her a kiss goodbye.

☼ ☼ ☼

"Jack and I had a fight today," Natalie announced as Dana typed out yet another email to an agent. They were sitting at Dana's kitchen table with a physical copy of the completed draft between them. It had also been scanned in, and a digital copy was attached to the email Dana was composing.

Her fingers paused on the keyboard. "What did you fight about?"

Natalie scowled. "He gave me a hickey."

Dana burst out laughing. "I told you that you two were like a couple of teenagers!" she hooted.

Natalie shook her head. "This wasn't cute, passionate, heat-of-the-moment affection. It was an intentional marking of territory."

Dana frowned. "Who was he marking his territory against?"

"Beau."

"You and Beau?" Dana snorted.

"I know. It's silly. I said that to Jack, but any time a guy even looks at me the wrong way, he jumps all over it. He seems to have this irrational fear of losing me."

Dana's eyes softened. "Do you think maybe he has good reason to feel that way?"

Natalie chewed on her lip. "Like what?"

"Like, do you think maybe he senses that you have one foot out the door?"

"I don't have one foot out the door," Natalie insisted. "I've been very clear with Jack that I'm here for the summer to stay inspired and complete my commitment to Ned. After that, I have to reassess, and I don't know what my next steps will be. Jack knows where I stand."

Dana folded her hands on the table in front of her. "It sounds to me like you don't even know where you stand."

Natalie bit her lip then released it for fear of biting off a chunk with her ruthless chewing. "I guess I don't, really. I have two more paintings I need to send to Ned—God knows when I'll manage to get to them—and then I need to wait and see how they sell at the show next month. Then I can figure out my next steps."

"I think you're going to have to figure out those next steps sooner than later," Dana said. "Jack sounds like he's only getting more serious."

"He told me he loved me last night," Natalie blurted.

Dana's eyes lit up. "He did? How did that feel?"

"It felt… scary? I mean, it was nice to hear those words, I guess, but it's big, and I'm afraid he's getting too invested."

Dana nodded. "It is big, but you two have been together for a couple of months now. It's a little fast, but your whole relationship has been fast. You were already living together when you started dating."

"Exactly," Natalie said. "Everything moved too quickly. I've never gotten to this point with a man before."

Dana smiled sympathetically. "New is always scary. Isn't it a good thing, though, to have gotten to this point?"

"It feels good, but it's even more nerve-wracking. The closer I get to him, the more I could hurt him."

"Why do you think that way?" Dana asked, shaking her head.

"Because I learned the hard way that loving someone can end in major heartache," Natalie snapped.

"Nat," Dana said, grabbing her hand and gently squeezing it. "I say this as your friend and someone who cares about Jack too. You need to make up your mind about whether or not you're going to stay and try to make this thing work with him, or if you're going to leave when the summer ends. Keep in mind that Jack just lost his best friend, and he's terrified of losing you too. If you keep stringing him along, you're only going to hurt him more."

"Fuck," was all Natalie could think to say. On a groan, she dropped her head into her hands, rubbing her eyes until she saw stars. She knew she'd gotten in too deep, but having Dana spell it out like that was just a little too real. "Jack and I agreed to have a talk when his brothers are gone. I need to figure out what I'm going to say."

"You've got to go with your gut, kid," Dana said. "I think you'll eventually come to a moment of clarity. I just hope it's soon."

"Me too," Natalie huffed.

They got back to work and ended up getting emails out to ten different agents, but Natalie's mind kept returning to their conversation. She longed for the clarity Dana spoke of. Everything had gotten too jumbled. She liked Jack too much to break up with him, but she cared about her art too much to commit to Nantucket forever and risk losing her inspiration again. So where did that leave her?

They could try a long-distance relationship. She could continue traveling and visit Nantucket between stops. Natalie could see herself spending summers there too. Maybe Jack would even want to take Carter on some travels with her.

Except, that wasn't the life Jack envisioned, and she knew it. He wanted the perfect, happy little family that lived together all year round and had all they needed in each other. He wanted to give Carter what he was supposed to have with Danny and Carrie. And Natalie didn't have that particular gift to give.

24

———

The brothers seemed to have enjoyed the beach day with their mother, but Carter was pooped when they returned, so Jack brought him straight up to bed. Fletcher decided to turn in early too, but Jack and Beau were still looking for trouble—a course of action that Natalie deduced was quite natural for the three brothers.

Jack suggested they set up a campfire on the beach and toast s'mores for dessert. He and Beau grabbed firewood from a stash at the bottom of the staircase while Natalie toted a box of graham crackers, a bag of marshmallows, and two bars of chocolate down to the beach.

While the boys got the fire started, she hunted around for some sticks for roasting the marshmallows. After finding three that were suitable, she returned to find a pitiful excuse for a fire. Jack and Beau brothers had dumped a bunch of the logs into a hole in the sand and were simply throwing matches at it.

"Step aside, boys." Natalie waltzed up to where the brothers were epically failing to build the campfire. They eyed her skeptically but obeyed. "I've done this once or twice before," she said, deftly arranging the logs into a tent-like shape. Pointing to the sticks she'd collected, she said, "Go grab me some more small sticks like those ones."

Jack waggled his eyebrows. "Bossy little thing."

Natalie pointed a finger at him playfully. "Do as you're told, or no s'mores for you!"

He saluted her and began his hunt. Beau narrowed his eyes at Natalie but dutifully followed his brother. After a quick search, Beau came striding back with two handfuls of sticks and Jack right on his heels. "These good?" he asked.

"Perfect." Natalie added them to her array. "Now we're ready to light it." She struck a match against the box and tossed it in the center of the pit. The smaller kindling immediately caught fire, and flames licked up toward the heftier logs in a hypnotizing display of color and light.

"Take a seat and watch the magic happen," she said, sitting close beside Jack and laying her head on his shoulder. His arm snaked around her waist as he pressed a kiss to her hair, and they watched the fire grow into a large blaze.

"How did you learn to build a fire like that?" Beau asked, mesmerized by the flames.

Natalie shrugged. "I've done some camping in Arizona and Nevada. You learn really quickly how to make fires to keep warm." On this late August night, there was no need for excess warmth, but the fire did provide a cozy ambiance and, of course, the ability to make s'mores.

"Wow, I didn't know you were so well traveled," Beau said, savagely spearing a marshmallow on a stick.

"I've lived all over the country," Natalie explained as she did the same.

"How did Nantucket make it onto your list?"

"I used to come here every summer as a kid and always loved it. It's such a beautiful island."

"Agreed," Beau said. "So where haven't you been? What's the next destination on your list?"

Jack's whole body stiffened beside her. His arm squeezed

tighter around her waist, as if trying to keep her from escaping. Natalie did her best not to react, instead positioning her own marshmallow over the now flourishing fire.

Instead of blowing off Beau's question, she decided to answer honestly. Jack needed to hear the truth, even if it might upset him to hear about the places she still longed to go.

"I've always thought it would be fun to paint in the middle of New York City. You know, set up an easel right there in Times Square and capture that busy, chaotic atmosphere. Or if I could save enough money, I think Hawaii would be really sweet. I just love beaches."

"Nothing better than a good beach," Beau agreed.

"There's a beach right here," Jack broke in, his voice low, "and it's not five thousand miles away."

Natalie felt his gaze hot on her profile but couldn't bring herself to turn to him.

"Yeah, bro," Beau said, "but Nantucket doesn't have the palm trees or volcanoes or any of that other cool shit that Hawaii does. I bet Natalie wants to see that stuff. There's only so many places around here she can paint before they all start looking the same."

"Butt out, Beau," Jack snarled, and Natalie winced at the fury in his tone.

"I'm just saying, man, eventually she'll get bored here. She's used to traveling around and doing all kinds of cool things."

Natalie opened her mouth to speak but closed it again because Beau was exactly right. What if she got bored of Nantucket? She'd lose her inspiration, and her art career would spiral the rest of the way down the drain.

"This has nothing to do with you, Beau," Jack barked. "Back. Off."

Beau glared at him. "Just because you chose never to leave this godforsaken rock, doesn't mean everyone else who comes here wants to stay forever."

In the blink of an eye, Jack was on his feet, and Beau quickly followed. It was another course of action that had obviously played out before, and Natalie watched in horror as they each raised their fists.

"You want to fight, bro?" Beau taunted. "Bring it."

Jack took a step toward him. Natalie eyed Beau's impressively large biceps and suddenly feared for Jack's life.

"Guys!" she shouted, and they both turned to her. "Put your damn fists down," she snarled. Beau obeyed quickly, dropping his arms to his sides. Jack was slower to comply and ran a hand through his hair as he did.

Beau cleared his throat. "I'm gonna grab myself another beer."

Natalie watched him walk away and waited until the door slammed behind him to approach Jack. "What. The fuck. Was that?" she demanded.

"You're asking me?" he roared. "I could ask you the same question."

Her brow furrowed. "What are you talking about?"

"My brother basically just asked you when you're leaving me, and you actually *answered* him!" Jack cried, tension rolling off him in waves. The fire roared and crackled—a mirror of his rage.

"Woah, woah, woah." Natalie put her hands up. "We were having a friendly conversation, and I answered his question. What else was I supposed to do?'

Jack raked his fingers roughly through his hair. "So, when do you think you'll leave? Next week? Next month? Next year? How long will you string me along before deciding it's time for you to move on?"

He used those same words Dana had—*string along*. Is that really what Natalie had been doing? Simply by being here and being with him? They were having fun, enjoying each other's company. He had always known she planned to leave.

With her back up now, Natalie replied, "This shouldn't

come as a surprise to you. I told you the very first day we met that I move around a lot."

Jack ran a hand through his hair again, slightly less violently. "A lot has changed since then." Though she was grateful he was no longer yelling, the disappointment and weakness in Jack's voice threatened to break Natalie's heart.

"A lot *has* changed," she agreed softly. "I found my inspiration. I'm almost done with my paintings for Ned. Danny's is doing so much better. You've hired another barista. You don't need me here, Jack."

"I may not *need* you, but I *want* you, Natalie. I want you to stay. I want us to try and make this thing work."

"I can't commit to staying here forever," she said. "You know that."

Jack's voice rose again. "So what, I'm just supposed to keep doing this thing with you until you decide it's time to leave and then just be ok with that?"

"You don't have to do anything you don't want to do, Jack. You're a big boy. You can make your own decisions about whether you stay with me or not, but you can't blame me for planning for my own future."

"I kind of thought I might be part of your future," he said softly.

Tears threatened at the sadness Natalie heard in his voice. "I wish you could be," she whispered, "but our lives don't fit together."

"Why not?" he asked, his tone a mix of hope and desperation. "You said you're happy here. You've got a job. You've made friends. Carter loves you, and you're so good for him. And… me. I love you, Natalie."

She dropped her head into her hands. "Stop," she groaned.

"Stop what?"

"Stop fighting people over me, and giving me hickeys, and telling me you love me!" she wailed. Every time he said those words was another nail in the coffin. It was too much—his declarations of love, his acts of possessiveness, the fighting, the hickey, the implications that she was part of the family. It was too much. Invisible walls began closing in around her, though they were out on an empty beach, and she felt the urge to run blast through her stronger than ever.

Jack's voice floated softly over her ears. "But I do love you, Natalie."

Risking a look up at his handsome, broken face, she said in a low voice, "How long do you think that'll last, Jack? How long until I screw up or you get sick of me? I'm not built for this kind of life. I'm bound to wreck it."

"You're not going to screw up, and I'm not going to get sick of you. You're not going to wreck anything," he insisted.

Natalie snorted, a harsh and bitter sound. "That's sweet, but you can't predict the future."

"Neither can you!" Jack yelled.

Taking a deep breath to refrain from shouting back, she said, "Maybe not, but I know myself, and I know that I can't commit to this. To you. I've been through this enough to know that I'll eventually have to move on, whether for my art or for my sanity. And if I can't, I'll resent everything that's keeping me here."

"Why can't you just try?" he asked desperately.

"I *have* tried. I *am* trying. It's too much, Jack. I can't do this."

"Can't do what?"

"I can't be with you," she snapped. "I can't do this anymore if you can't accept that I'll eventually leave. I always leave."

"I don't give a shit what you always do. Things don't feel different to you now? *This*"— he waved his hand back and forth between them—"doesn't feel different to you?"

Natalie forced herself to hold Jack's gaze as his eyes grew dull and flat. "Jack, I… I don't know what to say. I've told you the truth from the beginning. I'm not staying forever. If that's what you need… then this isn't going to work."

He looked away, and Natalie was terrified that when he turned back, he'd have tears in his eyes. Unable to bear seeing him cry, she was oddly relieved that when Jack turned back toward her, his expression wasn't sad. It was furious.

"Maybe you're right," he said, his tone detached, as if he'd closed himself off. "It's not going to work. I wasn't going to show you this until after my brothers left, but maybe it's worth showing you now because I'll probably never get another chance."

Pulling something out of his shorts pocket, he dropped it unceremoniously on the sand in front of Natalie. Her eyes widened as she stared at the small, black velvet box that could only possibly hold one thing. Her head spun as she fumbled for her words. "Jack…"

"Don't worry," he snarled. "I'm not asking you. I wouldn't want to tie you down or anything."

Natalie's eyes filled with tears at the ire in his voice. "You don't have to be mean." Feeling incredibly small, her mind flashed back to the day Jack had found her sleeping on the beach. She'd woken to him looking down upon her, a frown stretched across his face that was nothing compared to the ferocious one he wore now.

"I'm not saying anything you haven't been thinking," he said. "You don't want to be tied down. So why don't you just go, Natalie? Why prolong the inevitable? I don't want you getting any closer to Carter if you're just going to abandon him at some point. He doesn't deserve that, and neither do I."

Jack was right. Neither of them deserved it, but Natalie had convinced herself that this was better than the alternative —trying to stay, getting in deeper, and eventually hurting them even worse.

"I'll go, if that's what you want," she whispered, a few tears escaping down her cheeks. A flash of agony tore across

Jack's face, but it quickly settled into contempt. His anger and hurt tugged at her heartstrings, threatening to rip it right out.

If she'd ever had any doubts, Natalie knew in that moment that she'd gotten in too deep. She'd stuck around too long, gotten too close to Jack and Carter. She'd meant to get out before something like this could happen, but she had let herself get too comfortable in a life she'd sworn never to let herself have.

"I'm so sorry, Jack," she choked out, a few more tears sliding down her cheeks as she stood up and ran toward the house, heading straight for her room. She groaned when she saw the closed door and remembered that Fletcher was staying in there.

Tentatively, she knocked on the door. Fletcher answered after a few moments, his eyebrows shooting up as he took in her tear-stained face. She wiped at her eyes in an attempt to look presentable but knew the effort was futile.

"I… I'm sorry, I just need to grab some stuff." Sliding past him, Natalie headed for the closet. She couldn't bring herself to care that she'd totally disrupted Fletcher's night, but she did note the open book sitting on the bed and was grateful that at least she hadn't woken him up from sleep.

Snatching her duffel bag and wheeled suitcase, she began attempting to fit all her possessions into them. When she'd arrived on Nantucket, they had held everything she owned. Now, as she tried to pack them, she realized there was no way she could fit everything she'd accumulated. The tears flowed steadily as she attempted to shove more and more of her possessions into the duffel, only to come to the harrowing realization that she simply had too much.

Natalie had broken every rule in her book. She was supposed to be able to fit her whole life in those bags. She wasn't supposed to let herself get too attached to anyone. And she was supposed to cut and run far earlier if she accidentally did.

Fletcher stood to the side, watching Natalie haphazardly toss things into the bag. Unable to placate him or explain why she was acting so erratic, she just shoved as much as she could into her luggage. She grabbed the lone framed photograph off her bedside table and tossed it atop the mountain of things in her duffel before trying to zip up the bag to no avail. A sob escaped her mouth. *How did I let this happen?*

Fletcher finally spoke, asking her in a gentle voice, "Do you need any help?"

Natalie sniffled and managed to choke out, "No, thank you."

In the end, she decided to leave everything she couldn't fit in her bag in the bedroom closet. Jack would just have to deal with it.

Glancing at the painting supplies and empty canvases that she'd planned to fill with more picturesque Nantucket scenes, she realized that there was no way any of that would fit in her bag. She would have to abandon it all, along with the half-finished painting that sat on the easel, depicting the farm in Dana's book. The work in progress was yet another distraction that had kept her from completing her paintings for Ned. Natalie had meant it to be a gift for Dana when they eventually got published.

Dana. Natalie was about to leave without even letting her know. Obviously, she would call her friend but not before hopping on the first ferry off the island. She hoped to hell that Dana would understand her leaving. They could still be friends, keep in touch, and publish the book together. Natalie just couldn't stay any longer, knowing each moment would break Jack's heart—and hers—even more.

A completed canvas sitting against the wall caught her eye, kicking off a new round of tears. It was the painting of Jack and Carter in the ocean, both looking so happy and carefree. She hadn't shipped it over to Ned yet, and now it just seemed wrong to. The picture belonged on Nantucket. Lifting the painting onto the easel, she scribbled a note to stick to the front of it:

"Jack, I can't tell you how sorry I am. I never wanted this to happen. I will always cherish this summer I got to spend on Nantucket, especially my time with you and Carter. You are going to make an amazing father. Love, Natalie."

Wiping the tears from under her eyes, she hoisted her duffel bag onto her shoulder and dragged the suitcase behind her. Turning toward Fletcher, who'd remained immobile, she said, "I… Goodbye."

Finally emerging from her room, Natalie found Jack and Beau sitting on the couch, Jack's head buried in his hands. Beau gave her a dirty look.

"Goodbye," she said quickly, barely stopping before hurling herself down the stairs and out of the apartment. A huge breath of relief turned into a sob as she opened up the door and found herself on the beach, that familiar white sand creeping in between her toes.

Memories flooded her mind. Making sandcastles with Carter. Watching Jack toss him into the air amongst the waves. Jack rubbing sunscreen onto her back and giving her the best massage of her life. The picnic on the boat. All those times she spent with Jack and Carter, falling in love with them both.

Then, she noticed the little black box still resting on the sand, and her heart, which had been cracking all night, broke into a million pieces. Dropping her duffel onto the sand, Natalie sank to her knees and covered her face with her hands as she sobbed.

She cried for the life she knew she could have had. If she'd been any other woman, she would have stayed on Nantucket. If she wasn't her mother's daughter, she could have done as Jack wanted and tried to make things work. She could have married Jack and raised Carter with him. But Natalie simply wasn't built for that life, and she never should have let herself pretend that she was.

She cried for Carter, whom she desperately hoped would get to have a mom someday. Everyone deserved to have what she hadn't, and Natalie wished so much that she could be that for him. But she didn't believe that she could.

She cried for Jack—the kindest, most caring man she had ever been with. The only man who had ever truly savored her. Natalie hoped that he would allow himself to fall in love again. If she had ruined love for him, she would never forgive herself. Already, she wouldn't forgive herself for hurting him this way.

At that thought, Natalie cried even harder for herself. For the little girl whose mother had walked out without an explanation. For the teenager who'd had to navigate the murky waters of adolescence alone. And for the woman who was now breaking her own heart because, despite her attempts to avoid becoming like her mother, she had inadvertently done just that.

The sound of a slamming door startled her from her thoughts. Two large feet appeared in front of her, and Natalie looked up into the furious face of Jack's little brother.

"You've gotta go," Beau said icily, crossing his arms over his chest.

"I know." She sniffled pathetically. "I'm sorry."

Beau sighed and uncrossed his arms. Thawing just a bit, he held out his hand to help her up. "I booked you a ticket back to the mainland. It's the first ferry out in the morning. It leaves in four hours. I'll drive you over there."

"You don't have to do that," Natalie argued. "Jack needs you here…"

"Jack needs you gone. Hearing you bawling isn't exactly helping him deal with you walking out on him."

"I'm sorry," Natalie said again, feeling even worse because she knew he was right. "Thank you for the ticket."

The ride to the ferry with Beau was, hands down, the most awkward car ride of her life. They barely spoke, and when he dropped her off in front of the terminal, all she could say was, "Tell Jack I'm sorry."

So once again, Natalie found herself alone, in a terminal, without anyone to see her off. Only this time, she knew she didn't deserve anyone.

25

———————

The ferry crawled past Brant Point, and Natalie watched miserably as several other passengers threw pennies off the side of the ship. Children cheered as the coins plunked into the water below. She and her father used to partake in the tradition every summer. Throwing a penny overboard was supposed to bring good luck that one would return to Nantucket again. This time, though, Natalie didn't see any chance of that happening, so she stayed glued to her seat, not even bothering to reach for her wallet.

The ride to the mainland took twice as long as the one there. In his haste to get her off the island, Beau had booked her on the slow boat. It served her right, giving her more time to think about the mess she'd made.

After spending the first hour crying quietly, Natalie tortured herself by going through all the photos of Jack and Carter on her phone. Already missing them terribly, it took everything she had not to call them. She hadn't gotten a chance to say goodbye to Carter and desperately wanted to at least let him hear her voice one more time. But she couldn't hurt Jack any more, so she closed the camera roll and leaned back in her seat, letting the tears drip down her cheeks.

The sun was just peeking over the horizon as Natalie exited the terminal and hailed a cab. She hesitated when the driver asked where to take her, the painful realization that she had nowhere to go crashing over her like a wave. Too lost in her grief to think clearly, she said the first address that came to mind: her father's. Though she hadn't been there in many years, her childhood address was permanently etched into her mind.

A knot grew tight in Natalie's stomach as the cabbie drove through the familiar maze of streets toward Griff's. Her father was unpleasant on a good day, but showing up unannounced was sure to agitate him further. After years of Griff telling her that she was unrealistic and her dream wouldn't work out, Natalie dreaded admitting to him that he'd been right all along.

Working for Jack in exchange for room and board hadn't allowed her to save up any money, and she'd spent what she made from tips at Danny's on new clothes and shoes from trendy Nantucket stores, fancy cocktails with Dana, and all the other things that had made her stay so enjoyable. She had no money, no job, no home. She was right back where she had started, and she hadn't even finished the minimum number of paintings she'd needed to.

As the cab pulled up to her childhood home, the knot in Natalie's stomach twisted like a knife. Trying to brace herself for what was to come, she took three deep breaths and rubbed her eyes, hoping they weren't as puffy as they felt.

When she got to the apartment door, she stood outside for a moment, focusing on keeping her breaths deep and her heartbeat even. Raising her fist, she knocked twice. When the door swung open, Natalie was greeted by a familiar and strangely comforting sight.

Griff still had his signature salt-and-pepper hair—though now it looked to be more salt than pepper—and matching beard. The wrinkles running across his forehead showed his age, and his crow's feet were more prominent than she remembered. The one thing that most definitely hadn't changed were his clear-blue eyes that perfectly matched her own. Anyone who saw them together would make no mistake that they were related.

Sometimes, it seemed like those blue eyes were the only thing they had in common. On this particular day, those eyes had even more in common than usual—they were both filled to the brim with tears.

Speechless, Natalie watched as a single teardrop trailed down Griff's cheek. She couldn't recall ever seeing her father cry before. What had him so distressed? She hadn't even stepped in the door, so it couldn't have been her presence that was upsetting him.

Griff spoke first. "They called you too?" he asked sadly.

"What?" Natalie asked, flying through the doorway and dropping her bags on the floor. "Who called? Dad, what's wrong?"

Griff shut the door quietly and turned to her. "The police… Natalie, they found your mother early this morning. She's dead."

Natalie gasped. "Oh, Dad," she breathed as she pulled him in and, without hesitation, embraced her father for the first time in years. Griff froze for a moment then wrapped his arms tentatively around her. As his hot tears hit her shoulder, Natalie's own began flowing again.

This gruff man, who had given her hell for so many years, was now literally crying on her shoulder. The only thing that could have affected him this much was the death of his wife, who Natalie knew he'd never stopped loving, even after she had abandoned him. Griff may have grieved the loss of her back then, but the process couldn't be completed until now. Leaving the Earth completely had an air of finality that leaving their home never had.

The timing of Natalie's return was uncanny. It seemed

that at possibly the same moment she'd been breaking Jack's heart, her mother's had stopped beating. There had to be some cosmic logic for why the universe had coincided those two incidents.

Natalie pulled away and was relieved to find Griff had stopped crying. "Come, sit down." She motioned to his couch. "I'll make us some tea."

Mechanically boiling a pot of water, Natalie set teabags into two mugs as she mulled over this shocking revelation. Of course she hadn't expected to hear the news, but in all honesty, she had wondered more than a few times over the years if her mother was even still alive. She had no way of knowing, and Griff had never been forthcoming with information about his wife.

"Here," Natalie said, handing her father a mug of piping hot tea with one ice cube—just how he liked it.

"Thank you, Natalie." Griff rubbed one red, puffy eye.

"So, what happened?" she asked as she sat beside him on the couch, taking a sip of her own chamomile tea.

"I got a call a while before you got here. It was a police officer in Florida. They found her this morning, in her trailer… I guess she's living in a trailer now… and she had passed out in her bed. There were pills all around. They tried CPR, but she'd been gone too long."

"Oh God, Dad, I'm so sorry." Natalie cringed at the nasty picture that conjured up.

"They want me to go identify the body," Griff said, running a hand wearily over his face.

"What?" Natalie asked. "Why? Can't one of her friends down there do it? You haven't seen her in years. Who's to say she even looks the same?"

"I don't know." Griff's voice was weak, defeated. "They have some kind of rule. Since we're still technically married, I have to be the one to do it."

Without thinking, Natalie said, "Then I'll come with you."

She had never seen her father so broken up over anything, and she couldn't let him do this alone. He may have let her down in a million ways over the course of her life, but he was still her father, and it was still her mother who had passed.

"You don't have to…" Griff trailed off, too proud to admit he didn't want to go alone.

"I'm coming," Natalie said firmly. "Have you booked a flight yet?"

"No," Griff replied numbly.

"I'll get us tickets for the soonest flight." Taking charge of the situation, Natalie immediately went online and booked two tickets to Florida—a direct flight leaving at noon. It was still quite early, so they'd have plenty of time to prepare. Returning to the living room, she found Griff still sitting on the couch, looking exhausted and barely having sipped his tea.

"I'll make us some breakfast. You pack a bag for yourself, and we'll leave for the airport in a couple hours, ok?" Natalie said gently.

"Ok. Thanks, Nat," Griff said with a weak smile, surprising her with the use of her nickname. He hadn't called her that in years. In fact, no one had called her that in a long time—not until Jack. Natalie supposed she'd never let anyone close enough to her to call her by a nickname. Not until him.

She shook her head and headed to the kitchen to make breakfast. Realizing that she had no idea what her father usually ate nowadays, she went with the safe option of bacon, eggs, and toast.

As she cooked, Natalie's thoughts drifted back to Nantucket, where she and Jack had cooked breakfast together so many times. She pictured his big, strong hands chopping vegetables for omelets. Saw his bare feet padding across the kitchen tile as he wore nothing but boxers hanging low on his slender hips. Remembered the feeling of his arms snaking around her waist as she stood facing the stove. He was always—

"Smells great," came Griff's raspy voice, and all thoughts of Jack vanished.

"It's ready." Natalie split the food between two plates, and she and her father sat across from each other at the dining room table—the same one they had shared family dinner at all throughout Natalie's years in school. Just the two of them.

It dawned on her that Griff was her only family now. Though she had let it feel like Jack and Carter were her family for a little while, that had all been a fantasy, a dream she allowed herself to indulge in for far too long. This was her reality: a miserable father who would never accept her; a deceased, absentee mother; and two measly bags of belongings.

Unsure what to discuss, Natalie pivoted to the matter at hand. "Did they say anything else about her? Like, did she have a job? Was she still singing?"

"They didn't say much. We'll meet with the police when we're down there. Maybe they can give us a clue as to what she was up to."

"I hope her life down there was worth it," Natalie said bitterly.

Griff sighed. "I know it's been hard for you, living without a mother all these years. I did the best I could to make up for it. It's hard to be a mother and a father at the same time."

"I didn't need you to be two people at once," Natalie argued softly. "I only needed one person, but I needed a supportive one. I needed you to encourage me to chase my dreams, not to give up on them."

"You didn't need me to do that," Griff argued. "You had enough of your mother's spirit in you already. Unrealistic, impractical, silly girls." Natalie watched his expression morph from sad to angry—an emotion she was sure he was far more comfortable with.

"You still think I'm just like her, don't you?" she cried, unable to rein in her feelings. The past twelve hours had been all too emotional. Natalie had, in fact, realized that she was more similar to her mother than she liked, but she wouldn't give her father the satisfaction of being right on that count too. "Well, guess what, I'm nothing like her. In Nantucket, I fell in love with a guy, Dad. Jack. And he had a son. Carter. And I was so good to them. I was there for them. I supported them. Carter was a baby, but I told him he could do anything he wanted. Be anything he wanted."

"Then why are you here?" Griff asked, a sad smile tugging at his lips. "You ran away. Just like she did."

The blow hit Natalie hard. "We got in a fight!" she exclaimed. "Jack got pissed. He wanted me gone. He *told* me to go."

"I'm sure he didn't really want you to leave," Griff challenged. "He wanted you to change, but you wouldn't even consider it. Natalie, you've been running all your life."

"I've been running from you!" she screamed, the outburst oddly cathartic. "And people like you. People who don't support my dreams. I never let myself fall in love with any of the guys I dated, because I knew they would want me to stay. Just like you did. And I can't. I won't. I won't risk hurting someone the way Mom hurt you and me."

"What is your dream then, Natalie?" Griff asked. "Is it really to keep running all the time?"

"No! You know what it is, Dad. You've made fun of it enough. My dream is to be a successful artist."

"And why can't you be that *and* let yourself fall in love?"

"Because…" Natalie said, unable to answer right away. She spoke quietly now, no longer yelling. "I have never let myself fall in love because I knew this would happen. You've always said that I'm just like Mom. And when you told me that she left us to become a singer and pursue her artistic dream, it only cemented that even more. I've been so afraid that I would fall in love and then hurt someone, just like she did. I never wanted anyone to feel how she made me feel by abandoning us. So I tried to avoid love at all costs. But then I let my guard down, and I let things go too far with Jack. And now, exactly what I didn't want to happen *did* happen."

Griff stared at her for a moment, his eyes filling with tears once again.

Natalie quickly joined him. "Oh, Dad, I'm so sorry. I've been yelling at you, and you're still upset over Mom."

"No, it's not that." He wiped his eyes roughly with the back of his hand. "I just… I think this is all my fault."

Natalie blinked hard. "What?"

"I think it's my fault you left Nantucket."

She shook her head. "How could that be your fault? I told you, Jack and I had a fight. He wanted me to say I was going to stay on the island with him, and I couldn't promise that, so he *told* me to go. He didn't want me to stay any longer if I was just going to leave anyway. So I left."

Griff shook his head. "But it's like you said. I've been telling you for years that you're just like your mother. I planted that seed in your head. But you're right, Natalie. You're nothing like her."

"How can you say that?" Natalie cried. "I just did exactly the same thing she did."

"That's not true," Griff argued. "Do you see how upset you are over leaving Jack and Carter? Your mother was never upset over leaving you and me. She never called, never wrote. I only spoke to her one time after she left. She called to ask me to send her money. I asked her how she was, and she said, 'Great.' She was never anywhere near this broken up about leaving. She made that choice gladly. You are not your mother, Natalie."

That statement hit Natalie like a slap in the face, hurtling her back into reality. She realized she had been waiting her whole life for Griff to say something like that, and she let his words soak in as silent, cleansing tears fell down her cheeks.

"Sweetheart," he said, wiping away a tear with his

calloused thumb. "The fact that you're sitting here crying because you're so broken up over leaving proves that you're nothing like her."

Natalie nodded her understanding, though it would take a bit for that reality to really sink in.

"I compared you to her for so many years," Griff continued. "And in so many ways, you are like her. You look just like her—so beautiful. And my God, you've got her talent. But Natalie, you are so much warmer. So much more loving. You care so deeply about the people around you. You are not your mother. You are your own person. And that person is a kind, beautiful, wonderful woman."

"Oh, Dad," Natalie sobbed, getting up to give her father another hug. After a long moment, she pulled away, and Griff was smiling at her in a way she'd never seen before. He actually looked *proud*.

"Listen." He rubbed her back in a soothing, fatherly way. "Did you book the flight one way or round trip?"

"One way," Natalie said, rubbing at her now tender eyes. "It was the only way to get a flight that quickly."

"Good," Griff said. "Let's stay in Florida for a few days. We haven't been on a vacation together in years, and it might take a bit to get everything sorted out down there."

"Really?" Natalie asked, a broad smile spreading across her face for the first time in what seemed like forever, though it had only been twelve hours since she'd left Jack. "I would love that."

"It's settled, then. After we get this business dealt with, we can drive wherever you want—Orlando, Miami, Jacksonville, Tampa. Just say the word."

"I don't care where we go," Natalie replied honestly. "I'm just happy we're going there together."

26

Just like in all the television shows Natalie had ever watched, the morgue at the hospital in Florida was located in the basement. She tugged her cardigan a little tighter as they neared the entrance, shielding herself from the chill that pervaded the space. The door marked *Morgue* came into view, and she took Griff's large hand in hers, giving it a reassuring squeeze. He responded with a tight smile. *Here we go.*

The medical examiner opened the door and gestured to where Griff and Natalie should stand. Their eyes remained glued to the table, silently appraising the distinctly human-shaped figure beneath the draped sheet.

The medical examiner took his place at the head of the table and bowed his head solemnly. "Ready?"

Griff gave a stiff nod, and the medical examiner pulled back the sheet to reveal Natalie's mother's face and shoulders. Natalie let a small gasp slip out. It was most definitely her mother, but her face had taken on a grotesque gray pallor. Her sharp, angular cheekbones rose up above the deep hollows of her face. Her once beautiful blonde hair was graying and chopped into a hideous, uneven bob.

"That's her," Griff whispered. Natalie gave his hand another light squeeze.

"Thank you, Mr. Walker," the medical examiner said. "I'm very sorry for your loss."

"Thanks," Griff said roughly, choking back tears. The medical examiner pulled the sheet back up and asked if they wanted another minute. Natalie deferred to Griff, who said he was all set, so they walked in silence back to the car.

Once comfortably seated, Natalie blew out a big breath. "Well, that's over. I guess it wasn't all a dream," she said in a lighthearted tone.

Griff let out a small laugh, so she allowed herself a short chuckle. Then, he laughed a little harder, and she did too—from the sheer joy she felt at seeing her father laugh. He continued until his laughter turned into tears, and like something out of a movie, Natalie began crying too.

And so, sitting there, in that boiling-hot car, in the parking lot of the hospital that housed her dead mother and his dead wife, Natalie and Griff embraced over the center console and cried in each other's arms. It was a wonder that Natalie had any tears left after the past twenty-four hours, but somehow, her body managed to continue producing them.

Eventually, Griff pulled back to wipe his face and sat up straight behind the steering wheel. "Glad that's over," he grumbled, exhaling sharply. "Where are we headed to next?"

Natalie watched as he zipped up his emotions and could tell he was as eager as she was to put death and morgues out of his mind.

"How about Miami Beach?"

"It's a deal." He plugged the location into the GPS of their rental car as Natalie plugged her phone into the radio and set one of her favorite playlists to stream.

"You like Guns N' Roses?" Griff asked as "Sweet Child O' Mine" began blasting through the speakers.

Natalie grinned. "You used to listen to them all the time when I was a kid. How could I not grow up to love them?"

Griff's answering smile was warmer than any she could remember. "I had no idea. You always used to complain about my music back then."

"Of course I did." Natalie rolled her eyes. "Back then, I was only interested in Britney Spears and boy bands—which I still love, by the way—but these are the classics."

She queued up her favorites from AC/DC, Aerosmith, The Rolling Stones, and Queen—all songs she knew Griff would appreciate. To her surprise and delight, he began singing along with her. They rolled their windows down and turned the music up loud enough to drown out their horrible singing voices, dissolving into laughter after a particularly ear-splitting rendition of "Bohemian Rhapsody."

Natalie lowered the volume as their laughter subsided. "I'm really glad we're doing this, Dad," she said, strangely excited to spend time with him.

Griff reached over and squeezed her knee. "Me too, hon."

☼ ☼ ☼

They spent the night in a posh hotel that Natalie wouldn't have been able to afford without Griff's assistance. In the morning, they rented jet skis and explored Biscayne Bay, a place that had been on her bucket list for years. Afterward, they returned to the hotel and sat side by side in matching lounge chairs, sipping exotic beverages and chatting with an easy rapport.

Griff surprised Natalie by asking, "So, how's the painting going?"

She raised her eyebrows and sipped her drink. "You really want to know?"

He shrugged. "Sure."

Natalie looked out over the hotel's sprawling pool. The

marine-blue tile made the water look darker than it really was —almost as dark as the Atlantic. Of course, there were no waves, but if she squinted hard enough, it almost looked like one of Nantucket's north shore beaches.

"It *was* going pretty well. It took me a bit to find my groove again, but once I did, I made a bunch of nice pieces. Do you remember my old professor, Ned Brinkley?"

Griff shook his head, his bushy eyebrows scrunched together. Of course he didn't remember Ned. Griff had never been interested in anything about her life during art school. But in the spirit of letting bygones be bygones, Natalie decided not to comment on that.

"Well," she said, "he gave me an advance for ten paintings that he wants by next week. I managed to get eight done on Nantucket and sent them over to him, but I'll never finish two more. Now I owe him a thousand dollars." She rubbed her hands over her face. "I should have easily been able to finish all ten in the time frame, but I let myself get so distracted."

"By that man and his son?" Griff asked.

"Yes, Dad," Natalie said, watching out of the corner of her eye as a young father splashed in the shallow end with his baby. "Their names are Jack and Carter."

"Tell me more about them."

Natalie sighed. She'd been doing her best to put them out of her mind, especially since Jack hadn't reached out since she fled. But Griff *was* actually showing interest in her life, so she decided to answer his question.

"Jack's an amazing man. Kind, caring, thoughtful. His best friend, Danny, died earlier in the year, and Jack got custody of his son, Carter. Jack took over Danny's café too, and he's been doing an amazing job with both."

"That's… honorable," Griff replied. "What did you do for him? You said you were working for him and dating him?"

"And living with him," Natalie said with a sigh. Looking back, the whole situation had been one big red flag. She should have known better. "I did pretty much whatever Jack needed: fixed up the café, worked at the counter, or watched Carter. We went to the library, the playground, and the beach. He was an active little guy."

Griff smiled fondly at her, and Natalie wondered if he ever dreamed of having grandchildren. She was his only child and therefore his only hope of getting any. Would he treat them the way he'd treated her? Or go easy on them the way so many grandparents did?

"He sounds cute."

"He's adorable," Natalie agreed, unable to hide her affection for the baby, "and so mischievous. He was always getting into things—digging in the dirt, finding any snacks we left out, making huge messes. But he's so cute that you could never be mad at him for it."

Griff chuckled. "It sounds like you miss him."

"I do. But I can't exactly go to see him without seeing Jack."

"And you don't want to see Jack?" Griff asked.

"I mean, I do. I'm just not sure he wants to see me. He was pretty mad when I left."

"What exactly happened, if you don't mind my asking?"

Natalie picked at her nail. "Jack and I got into an argument. I was telling his brother some of the places I might want to visit in the future, and Jack freaked out. He couldn't stand the thought of me leaving, even though I'd told him I would be from the beginning! He practically threw an engagement ring at me and told me not to worry—that he wasn't going to propose to me because he knew I'd say no."

"And would you have said no?" Griff asked.

"Under those circumstances? Definitely." Natalie shook her head. "I think... I think I do love Jack, but I wasn't ready to settle down for the rest of my life, and that was the only way he was willing to stay together. Plus, he got so overbearing. He was always protective, but it got to the point where he really pissed me off."

Griff scratched his chin. "I don't know that I blame him."

Natalie's gaze whirled to him. "What?"

"I was the same way with your mother. When she started hinting that she might want to pursue her singing, I got… controlling. I begged her to stop going to open-mic nights and started giving her random, unnecessary chores to keep her busy. I think I saw what was coming. I saw her pulling away from us, and I was desperate to stop the inevitable, but all I did was drive her away." Griff's gaze was out over the pool, but his eyes were far away. "It sounds to me like Jack was trying to prevent the inevitable, too."

Natalie slumped back in her chair. "What else was I supposed to do? I shouldn't have stayed so long, but wasn't it better to leave before getting in even deeper and hurting them even more?"

"Who's to say you would have ended up hurting them?"

"It's inevitable, isn't it?" Natalie's tone was bitter.

Griff put his drink on the table and turned toward her. "You don't think it may have been worth staying to find out?"

"I've been traveling nonstop for years. I don't know if I *can* stop," she admitted.

Griff treated her to an uncharacteristic wink. "You'll never know if you don't try."

"Live in one place for the rest of my life?" Natalie asked skeptically.

Griff placed a hand over hers on the arm of her lounge chair. "Sweetie, it's not that scary. Most people live in one place for their whole life. It doesn't mean they suffocate there. There are plenty of opportunities to get away. Heck, pretty soon you'll probably be doing international art shows or going on a book tour. Maybe we could get back into our yearly vacation tradition. Settling in a home base is nothing to be afraid of."

"I didn't think I would be doing it so soon. I didn't see my life going this way."

Griff gestured toward himself. "You think I ever saw my life going this way? No way in hell. But hey, I haven't got it so bad. I've got a solid job and a wonderful daughter. It might've taken me a while to appreciate those, but I got there in the end. Honey, sometimes you have to abandon how you think things should be and just accept them as they are."

Natalie nodded. "Thanks, Dad."

Griff patted her hand awkwardly, as if uncomfortable with her gratitude. "And listen," he said, "I'm happy to lend you the thousand dollars you owe that Ned guy."

"No." Natalie shook her head quickly. "I don't need you to bail me out of this. I got myself into this mess."

"Honey." Griff squeezed her shoulder. "It's not because I don't think you're capable of coming up with it. You're so resourceful. Just look at how you've supported yourself all these years. It's not because I don't think you can but because I don't want you to have to."

Natalie blinked up at him. "You really think I'm resourceful?"

"I *know* you are," Griff replied. "Look at you. You've become this incredible, savvy woman—certainly with no help from me. You've found creative ways to support yourself for years now, but you've been looking out for yourself for too long. You deserve some support, and it's high time I give it to you."

Natalie let out a heavy sigh. She'd craved her father's support for years, but accepting it now felt like failure. It felt like admitting that everything she'd done to make her career as an artist work wasn't enough. That *she* wasn't enough. She had found the type of support Griff spoke of in Jack, and she'd blown it. What she'd been able to offer him wasn't enough, either.

"I'll think about it," Natalie replied. "I've still got a few more days to get things together. I'd rather spend the rest of this trip hanging out with you, not worrying about my mess of a career."

Griff grinned over at her, a rare, full-toothed smile. "You've got it, kiddo."

☼ ☼ ☼

Natalie spent the next few days reveling in her father's undivided attention as they toured the coastal city. There was no shortage of parks, museums, and beaches to explore. They knocked several destinations off her travel bucket list, like Little Havana and Coral Castle.

On the sixth day of their stay, Natalie and Griff sat in the hotel's restaurant, enjoying an extravagant brunch of shakshuka, sourdough toast, and the most ornate fruit bowl they'd ever laid eyes on. Griff had been unusually pleasant, asking her more about her art and her time on Nantucket. In return, Natalie got the scoop on his job and tried to coax him into telling her about his love life.

"It's none of your business," Griff said, his cheeks reddening.

"Oh, come on, Dad. I told you all about my sordid love affairs. You've got to give me something."

"I don't have time for women," he answered gruffly.

"Seriously? What do you do on the weekends?" Natalie asked.

Griff ticked up a finger for each activity. "Fishing. Golfing. Poker."

"Wouldn't you rather be hanging out with some hot M.I.L.F.?"

"Some hot what?"

Natalie burst out laughing, slapping a hand over her mouth as she let out a particularly unsophisticated guffaw. When she calmed down enough, she explained the meaning of the acronym *M.I.L.F.* to Griff, and he ended up laughing almost as hard as she had.

They were still catching their breath when Natalie's phone began buzzing. Her heart skipped a beat as she glanced down at the screen but quieted when Ned Brinkley's name flashed across the screen. It wasn't the man she hoped would be calling.

"Shit," she muttered, swallowing her disappointment. "Hang on a sec, Dad. I've got to take this." Walking out onto the patio, Natalie answered with a tentative, "Hello?"

"Hey, Nat," came Ned's familiar throaty voice. They hadn't talked all that much over the years, but his rasp always brought Natalie right back to those long days at the studio, learning how to mix colors and choose which size brush to use to achieve different effects. In many ways, Ned had been a father figure to Natalie after Griff had written her off for choosing to go to art school.

"How are you?" Ned asked.

"I'm… fine," Natalie answered, sweat beginning to bead on her brow as she mentally pictured her calendar. She did still have a few days before the deadline, right?

"Good to hear," Ned replied. "I just wanted to let you know that I received the final two paintings you sent, and they're fantastic."

The final two paintings? The ones she hadn't even started yet?

"Uh…" Natalie mumbled. Was Ned getting senile? She didn't think he was any older than her father, and Griff was still quite mentally sharp.

"The one of the man and the boy in the ocean is especially moving," Ned went on. "I know you don't usually do portraits, but you conveyed so much emotion about a father's love for his son. The beach scene with the seagulls in flight is excellent too. You just keep getting better, kid!"

Natalie's jaw dropped. Ned was describing the two paintings she'd left on Nantucket—her parting gift to Jack and the beach scene that had been hanging in Danny's for weeks now. Had Jack sent them to Ned? And what did it mean if he had?

Had Jack tried to help her out by sending the paintings, or did he want to erase any trace of her from his life?

"Thanks, Ned," Natalie managed. "I, um… found a lot of inspiration on Nantucket. I'm glad you like the pieces."

"I love them. I'll definitely be calling you before my next show. I'm sure I can sell all ten pieces I have now, and people will be writing down your name to watch for future works. Mark my words, Natalie."

Her stomach fluttered with excitement at the prospect. Here was a gallery owner actually seeking out her work, confident that people would love it. It was what she had always wanted. So why did she still feel so sad?

The butterflies solidified into a pit in her stomach. "That means a lot, Ned. I'd be thrilled to work with you again." Despite her anguish, her words were very true.

"Gotta go, Nat, but I'll call you after the show to let you know how your collection does."

"Thanks, Ned," Natalie said. "And thanks for calling today." If he hadn't, she would still be worried about accepting the money from Griff.

"Sure thing," Ned replied. "Talk to you later."

As soon as the call ended, her phone lit up with another. This time, Dana's name appeared. Though Natalie's mind was still reeling with confusion over the call with Ned and what it meant about Jack, she accepted the call and held the phone to her ear.

"NATALIE!" Dana shrieked.

Natalie pulled the phone a few inches away from her ear. "Hello to you, too," she said dryly.

"You will NEVER guess who just called me!" Dana squealed.

"Who?" Natalie asked, thinking Dana's call couldn't have been anywhere near as surprising as Ned's.

"One of the agents we sent the book to! They loved it, and they want to represent it!"

"No way!" Natalie cried, finally matching her friend's volume. "This fast?"

"Yes! They thought your illustrations were absolutely perfect. They're interested in meeting with me in New York next week!"

"Dana, that's amazing! You really deserve this. I'm so proud of you."

"I couldn't have done it without you, Nat," Dana said. "Both your encouragement and your illustrations were invaluable. Now, get your butt over here! I'm opening a bottle of champagne as we speak, so you'd better get here fast, or I'll drink it all on my own."

Natalie bit her lip. "Er, that might be a little tough. I'm actually in Florida."

"What?" Dana asked. "Why didn't you tell me? I am so jealous!"

"Don't be. My mother died, and I came with my father to identify the body."

Dana's voice dropped a few octaves. "Oh geez, Nat, I'm so sorry."

Natalie shrugged then realized Dana couldn't see her through the phone. "It's ok. It had to happen sometime."

"It still sucks," Dana said. "Jack didn't come with you, did he?"

Natalie looked down at her feet. "No."

"Oh, well, I'm sure he'll be doing everything he can to make you feel better once you get back here," Dana said. "I can only imagine the kinds of things…"

Natalie grinned briefly at her suggestive tone, but it quickly turned into a grimace. "I don't think so… Jack and I broke up."

"WHAT?" Dana shrieked.

Natalie rubbed her temple. "Dana, if you yell like that one more time, I'm hanging up. My eardrums can't take this."

"I'm sorry," Dana quickly apologized. "But why? What the hell happened?"

Natalie sighed. "We had that moment of clarity you thought we needed." She went on to explain the whole debacle, and Dana listened quietly for once.

"Wow," she said when Natalie was finally done. "I'm sorry, Nat. You've had a pretty sucky few days."

"Yes," Natalie agreed. "It's like some kind of cosmic joke. But your good news made today much better!"

"We really do have to celebrate," Dana said. "I know you're with your dad, but would you consider coming back here just for a weekend or something? We could have drinks, and maybe you could get more of those delicious cupcakes you brought to my house that time?"

"Those were from Danny's…" Natalie trailed off, but Dana heard her unspoken words. *And I'm not going back there.*

"Oh, then we'll just have to find something else. No biggie."

"This sucks," Natalie huffed. "I loved Danny's Place, and now I can't even think about going in there."

"Afraid you'll see Jack?"

"Of course! I think he hates me now. Did you know he sent the two paintings I left him over to Ned? It's great that I don't have to worry about them now, but I'm afraid it means Jack is done with me and doesn't want any reminders sticking around."

"I doubt that he hates you or that he's done with you," Dana said gently. "From what I could tell, that man loved you more than anything he has in a long time—besides Carter. Are you sure it's definitely over?"

Natalie threw herself down into a lounge chair on the

patio. "Well, considering he chucked an engagement ring at me then told me to go, I'd say yes."

Dana was uncharacteristically silent for a moment then quietly asked, "Do you want it to be over?"

Conflicting feelings darted through Natalie's mind. Of course she wanted to be with Jack again, but being with him would mean making a serious commitment that could lead to more hurt… but it would also lead to more precious time with him.

"No… yes… no. I don't know," she muttered.

Dana's voice remained atypically calm and gentle. "How are things going with your dad?"

"Actually, really good," Natalie answered. "We've been talking. Shocking, right? And he has me thinking that maybe I'm not so much like my mother after all. He said she never felt any remorse or regrets about leaving, but I'm full of them."

"It must have felt nice for him to differentiate you two that way," Dana said.

"It did. He's been very validating. He's convinced that I could have the life that Jack wanted us to, if I want it too."

"You can," Dana agreed. "You should come back here and give it a try."

Natalie shook her head to herself. "I don't even know if Jack still wants that. I'm leaning toward not. You didn't see the look on his face when he told me to leave, Dana. What if I broke his heart and he never wants to see me again? He hasn't even tried to contact me. What if he's totally over me?"

"Only one way to find out," Dana said.

Natalie sighed. "I guess you're right."

"So you'll come back?" Dana's voice was hopeful.

"I'll come back to celebrate getting an agent," Natalie clarified. "I'm not brave enough to face Jack quite yet."

"You're welcome to stay with me as long as you want," Dana said. "We have a lot of celebrating to do, after all."

Natalie couldn't help but smile at that reminder. "We definitely do. I would love to stay with you, though I might spend all my time holed up at your place to avoid Jack."

"That's fine," Dana assured her. "But do you want to see him, if he's willing?"

"Oh, I'm dying to see him," Natalie said, "but I want to wait until I'm certain he wants to see me too."

"I could stop by Danny's and do some snooping…"

"Dana," Natalie warned. "Give it some time, ok? It's only been a week."

"But you *will* see him as soon as he's ready?" Dana asked.

"Sure," Natalie said to shut her friend up.

She could hear Dana's clap through the phone. "Great!"

Glancing back toward where Griff sat in the restaurant, Natalie began wrapping up the call. "Let me check when my dad is planning on leaving, and I'll text you once I have my plane ticket."

"Can't wait!" Dana said. "I love you, you know.

"Oh, Dana, I love you too," Natalie said. "I can't wait to see you."

"Ditto."

"Talk to you soon." Natalie hung up the phone, hope surging through her veins for the first time since she'd left Nantucket. Seeing Dana would be a balm to her aching heart, and she couldn't wait to celebrate taking the next step in their journey toward publication. As nervous as it made her to enter Jack's proximity again, it also gave her a rush of excitement. Perhaps she would work up the courage to go see him, and perhaps he would be open to trying things again with her.

When Natalie rejoined her father, he was staring intently down at his phone, hastily trying to navigate the touch screen with his thick thumbs. He looked up as she approached the table. "I found a flight to Boston tomorrow at 6:30 a.m."

"Oh," she said. "Are you that eager to get back home?"

"Not particularly," Griff answered, "but you're eager to get back to Nantucket, right?"

Natalie reared her head back. "How did you know that?"

Griff answered with a knowing smile. "Honey, it's written all over your face. I can tell you miss your life there. Plus, you left the door open, and I overheard your entire conversation."

"Dad!" Natalie slapped him playfully on the shoulder.

He put his hands up in surrender. "Sorry! But for the record, I think you should go see Jack. I know you don't want to hurt him any more, and you want to make sure he's ready, but I'd be willing to bet a lot on the fact that he misses you as much as you miss him, and I'm not a betting man."

"You think so? You don't think he's pissed at me?"

"I think he's probably more pissed at himself for scaring you away. I know that's how I felt."

Natalie pursed her lips. "I guess it's worth a try. We have a lot to talk through. Even if it's over, I'd at least like to get some closure."

Griff nodded and looked back down at his phone, ceremoniously tapping a button with his thumb. "There. We've got two tickets to Boston, one with a second leg to Nantucket. We leave in the morning."

Natalie let out a breath she hadn't realized she'd been holding. "Thanks, Dad. And thank you for this trip. It really meant a lot to me."

"To me, too," Griff said, his usually gruff voice suspiciously soft. "I'm really proud of you."

"Oh, Dad." Natalie wrapped her father in an embrace, giving him a squeeze for each year they'd been distant from each other. It was unfortunate that it had taken her mother dying for them to reconcile, but at least that was one thing Natalie could be grateful to the woman for.

"I'm proud of you too," she whispered in his ear.

27

Natalie's second arrival on Nantucket was laced with just as much hope, excitement, and nervousness as the first, albeit for totally different reasons. The island felt even more like home after living there for the summer, but she still wondered if she'd be welcomed by the one person that meant the most.

Her stomach dipped as the plane touched down on the tarmac—a reaction to being back on the island as much as to the landing of the aircraft. She planned to get her bags, grab a taxi, and go straight to Dana's house. There would be no stopping for coffee or groceries or a walk on the beach. Natalie couldn't risk seeing Jack too early.

Her jitters had her rushing through the terminal. She collected her two bags and hurried for the exit, doing her best to ignore the loved ones reuniting all about. Though it was a different venue from her initial arrival on the ferry, it still dredged up that same sense of loneliness.

As Natalie dashed through the airport, a spark of awareness settled heavily on her chest, stopping her short. Goosebumps raced down her arms, and the soft hair there stood at attention. She frowned and glanced around for the source.

There were people everywhere, rushing in every direction, and her head whipped around as she sought whatever had put her gut on high alert.

A mop of brown curly hair poked up above the crowd walking toward her, and Natalie froze. Blinking hard, she dropped the duffel from her hand, and it fell to the floor with a thud. She could have spotted Jack from a mile away. As the crowd thinned, his tall, lean figure came into view, wheeling a suitcase behind him as he hurried toward his terminal.

Natalie stood stock still, watching him approach and brimming with confusion. Where could he possibly be going? And without Carter? Had she hurt Jack so badly that he was running away from his family? No, he would never do that. And now Natalie knew that she wouldn't either.

The moment Jack laid eyes on her, he froze, halting so abruptly that someone bumped into him from behind. He appeared to apologize to the man before turning back toward Natalie and pinning her with his gaze. Brown eyes met blue and burned into them as Jack began walking toward her again.

Licking her bone-dry lips, Natalie gave him a weak wave. "Hi," she said when they were finally face to face. It came out as quiet as a whisper, so she cleared her throat to try again. "Hi," she repeated more confidently.

Jack ran a hand through his already messy hair, revealing his own uncertainty. "Hi."

There was a pause as they appraised each other. He looked tired, with dark circles rimming his eyes and his hair sticking up at odd angles. His shirt was wrinkled, and Natalie wondered if this wasn't the first day he'd worn it this week. Jack looked much like he had when she'd first met him.

"What are you doing here?" he finally asked.

"I was going to ask you the same question."

"I, uh… well… I was headed to Boston," he said.

"Oh." Natalie failed to keep the disappointment from her

voice. Whatever Jack was up to, it meant he wouldn't be on the island, and they wouldn't get to talk. "What's in Boston?" she asked.

"You," he replied, a heartbreakingly sad smile forming on his perfect lips.

"Oh," she breathed. Maybe she hadn't blown it after all. "You were coming to find me?"

"Yes," he answered, and that one simple word sent a surge of hope through her.

"What were you planning to do when you found me?"

"Well," Jack said slowly. "First, I was going to apologize for all the terrible things I said that night."

"I'm sorry too," Natalie interjected. "I shouldn't have discussed those things with Beau without talking to you about them first."

"It's ok." Jack waved it off. "You were just sharing your truth. There's nothing wrong with that." Natalie opened her mouth to speak, but he cut her off. "Then, I was going to apologize for stifling you with my possessiveness. You were right. I acted like a caveman, and I see now why that drove you away. I have no excuses for acting like that, and I'm sorry."

She began to speak again, but Jack held a finger up in front of her face. The proximity of his skin to her lips had her snapping her mouth shut to keep from kissing his finger.

"And finally, I wanted to tell you that I still love you and that I will do anything to make this work. I know we'll have to figure out the logistics of you traveling, but I hope you'll always return here, to me. You will always have a home above Danny's Place, with me and Carter. I don't want to hold you back from your dreams, Nat, but you're *my* dream. I can't lose you."

Tears began burning Natalie's eyes. "Oh, Jack." That he would offer such an arrangement when she knew how much he really wanted her to stay permanently showed just how desperately in love with her he truly was. It broke Natalie's heart that he was willing to compromise so much to have her, but she was determined not to make him do that.

"Jack, I was wrong when I told you I couldn't stay on Nantucket. I've never committed to one thing in my entire life because I didn't think I could. I've always thought that I was just like my mother—the good and the bad parts of her. I was always terrified of getting too close to someone and hurting them, and when things got serious, I got scared. You sensed it —I know you did—and I see now that that's why you were overbearing sometimes. I don't blame you, and I accept your apologies."

Jack gawked at her, and Natalie stopped to take a breath. "I've been talking to my dad," she continued, "and he's helped me see that I'm not like my mom after all. She never gave a damn about leaving us, but I've been miserable since leaving you. It feels like a piece of my heart got ripped out that night on the beach and I left it here. I can't live without you, Jack."

He continued to watch her, wide-eyed, as she poured her heart out to him.

"I thought I needed to keep moving and finding new inspiration for my art, but nothing has ever inspired me as much as your love. I did some of my best work on Nantucket, and I don't think it was just because of the scenery. I think it was because you made me happier than I've been in years. Ned was so thrilled with the paintings I sent him that he's going to ask me for more for his next show. He especially loved the one I did of you and Carter, which I can only imagine you sent him."

Jack nodded sheepishly. "I hated to let it go, but I realized that you were two paintings short, and I didn't want you worrying about that when you were already so upset."

"So you weren't trying to erase any memory of me?"

"No!" Jack said with a sharp shake of his head. "Of course not. In fact, I sent those two paintings to Ned with a note that I'd like to buy them both back from him. They'll hang at the show so everyone can see your amazing work, and then they'll be on their way back here."

A tear slipped down Natalie's cheek. Not only had Jack *not* been trying to forget about her, he had saved her ass—for the second time, now—and he'd done it in the sweetest way possible.

"I'm so in love with you, Jack. I'm so ridiculously in love with you, and I can't believe how incredibly foolish I was to give up on us. I want to come back, and I want to commit to you, to this, to *us*. Please give me another chance. I love you."

Natalie held her breath as Jack processed what she'd said. After a grueling wait, his lips curved up in a tender smile. "Say that again."

"The whole thing?"

"No," he chuckled. "Just the part about you loving me."

Her eyes softened. "I love you, Jack. I love you so much it scares me to death, but I'd rather be scared with you than scared without you."

In the blink of an eye, he swept her up in his arms and spun her around. Natalie smiled at his joy through the tears rolling down her cheeks. When Jack put her back down, her vision was glazed with tears, but as she lifted her gaze to his, his eyes came into sharp focus, and all she could see was the love shining within them, like a lighthouse beckoning her home.

"I was hoping you would say something like that, because I'm desperate for another chance too, Nat. I want you back. I'm willing to make compromises, and we both have shit to work on, but I want to work on it together."

"As a family," Natalie added.

"Yes," Jack breathed, reaching out to grab her hand and lacing their fingers together. "On that note… I have another proposition for you."

Her gaze snapped up to his. "What?"

Keeping hold of her left hand, he knelt down before her. Her jaw dropped as he pulled that same little black box out of his pocket. While it had terrified her just days ago, it was now a welcome sight. She watched with bated breath as Jack's chest rose and fell rapidly.

"Natalie Walker, I am so desperately in love with you," he began. "I can't imagine going the rest of my life without you. I've barely been able to breathe this past week with you gone."

He snapped open the box to reveal a striking silver engagement ring with a sunburst-shaped diamond flanked by two thin crescent-shaped ones. The rest of the band was wrapped with tiny star-shaped diamonds. Natalie reflexively fingered the celestial pendant she still wore, despite everything, which seamlessly matched the ring Jack had picked. It was perfect, just like the man kneeling before her. When her gaze returned to his, both sets of eyes were shining with unshed tears.

"You are my sun, my moon, and my stars. I want you by my side for the rest of my life. I want to marry you and spend the rest of my life adoring you."

Natalie found herself nodding as the tears began to escape her eyes. Though she had cried so much over the past week, these happy tears felt refreshing.

"There's one more thing," Jack said. "Marrying me means being Carter's mom. I haven't signed the official adoption papers yet, and I don't want to until we're married. I want us to be Carter's parents together. Are you up for that?"

Natalie nodded even harder, though he hadn't officially asked the question yet.

"And… I really want Carter to have some siblings some-day. Does that sound good to you too?"

Natalie continued nodding, like a bobblehead that had been pushed too hard.

"Good." Jack's face split into a grin as he finally asked, "Will you marry me?"

"Yes," she uttered. "Yes, of course I will, Jack. Of course I will."

He beamed up at her and slid the ring onto her finger, where it fit perfectly. Leave it to him to get all the details right.

As soon as the ring was in place, Jack stood and pulled Natalie in for a searing kiss. She vaguely registered the applause that enveloped them from all around, too focused on her fiancé to care. *Fiancé*. What a trip.

Midway through the kiss, it dawned on Natalie that she finally had someone to reunite with at the airport. It was a dream she'd never expected to come true, and it felt better than she could have ever imagined.

Pulling away, Natalie tipped her face up to Jack's. "I love you so much," she whispered breathlessly.

"I love you too, future Mrs. McNally," Jack said with a wide grin.

She smiled back. "I like the sound of that."

"Me too," he said. "I can't wait for our wedding… and our wedding night."

Natalie slapped him lightly on the chest. "You are so bad!" She winked. "But neither can I." She gave him another quick peck on the lips, afraid that if she let herself really kiss him again, they would never make it out of the airport.

"Let's go back to your place," she suggested.

"Let's go back to *our* place," Jack corrected her.

"I like the sound of that too."

They headed out to Jack's car, and Natalie let him hoist her bags into the trunk and open up her door without complaint. Compromises, right?

"You know, you left a lot of shit behind," he accused as he began driving away.

"I know." Natalie wrinkled her nose in apology. "Sorry. Maybe I was always meant to come back here."

Jack reached over and squeezed her knee. "I think you're right."

When they pulled up to the apartment, Natalie couldn't help but sigh with pleasure at the familiarity of the place. It felt like home.

Jack grabbed their luggage and led the way up the stairs to the apartment, reminding Natalie of the day he'd first asked her to move in. She never would have guessed that day that she would be staying permanently. When they reached the top of the staircase, Carter ran into her open embrace, and she smooched both of his cheeks repeatedly before noticing Dana sitting quietly in a chair in the corner.

Natalie's jaw dropped. "What are you doing here?" she asked, knowing she was supposed to be on her way to Dana's house right now. Yet, here her friend sat in Jack's living room, like some kind of elaborate prank.

Dana arched a brow. "I was taking care of Carter. Someone had to do it after you left."

"Oh, screw you," Natalie said affectionately. "I assume you also had something to do with me bumping into Jack at the airport?"

Dana feigned confusion. "I have no idea what you're talking about. I simply spoke to Jack and suggested he go to Boston to get you back. And I might have used my knowledge of when your flight was to guide him when he was buying his ticket."

"You're a devil, Dana," Natalie said, shaking her head, "but thank you."

"You're welcome," Dana replied, getting up to embrace Natalie, who still held Carter in her arms. Pulling away, Dana added, "So, let's see the rock!"

A wide grin spread over Natalie's face as she held out her hand, admiring how the light glinted off of the ethereal stones on her ring.

"Oh, that's nice," Dana cooed, stroking the main diamond. "Good work, Jack."

Jack saluted her. "Go big or go home."

Dana nodded her approval. "Is that your way of telling me to screw off?"

When Jack opened his mouth to reply, she chuckled and said, "Just kidding. I really do have to be going, though, so you can enjoy your newly engaged bliss. Shall I take Carter to my house for the night? I wouldn't want him to be kept awake all night on account of all your loud, hot, make-up sex."

"Dana!" Natalie cried, covering Carter's ears. "Don't talk about that stuff in front of the baby. He's repeating more and more words every day. But yes, thank you. It would be great if he could sleepover at your place tonight."

"Absolutely." Dana took Carter from Natalie's arms. "Enjoy your night, you two."

Natalie rolled her eyes but said, "Thanks, Dana."

"We will," Jack added, taking Natalie into his arms as Dana retreated down the staircase.

As soon as the door slammed shut, Jack murmured in her ear, "We will be having loud, hot, make-up sex tonight, right?"

Natalie giggled. "Of course. But I need to talk to you about something first."

Jack released her so they were face to face. "Ok, shoot."

"When I left… I went straight to Boston."

"Mhmm," Jack crooned.

"Well, I went to my dad's house. He was really upset when I got there, and it turned out that my mom passed away earlier this week."

"Oh shit. Nat, I'm so sorry." Jack rubbed a reassuring hand up and down her arm.

"Thanks," she said. "My dad and I went down to Florida together to handle her affairs. It was hard, but then we stayed down there together for a little mini-vacation. And it was so nice, Jack. It was just like those summers we spent on Nantucket. He finally admitted that he's been resenting me all these years because I remind him so much of my mom, but he's realizing that we're not the same person. It was so helpful to finally hear that."

"That's amazing. I'm happy for you, Nat. I know you've waited a long time for him to say those things."

"I really have. I feel like I'm finally free from my mother's reputation. It's like I don't have all of her bad decisions weighing me down and affecting my life anymore."

Jack nodded. "I know you've never had a good relationship with your mom, and she's led to a lot of heartache in your life, but I have to say that I'm grateful to her."

Natalie reared her head back. "For what?"

Tipping her chin up, he explained, "Because, without her, there wouldn't be a you. And a world without a you in it would be a world I wouldn't want to be in."

Natalie beamed up at him. "You're very sweet, you know that?"

"Mmm." Jack leaned in to give her a kiss. "You're awfully sweet yourself."

"Oh yeah?" she mumbled under his lips.

"Mhmm," he hummed, the sound vibrating against her mouth. "Let's go to bed."

Natalie laughed. "It's only noon.

"I know," he said, "but we're gonna need all day for what I have planned."

"Oh, I like the sound of that," Natalie replied. "But wait, I have more news."

"Yeah?" Jack asked between the kisses he was pressing all over her neck.

"Dana found an agent for her book!" Natalie exclaimed. Jack lightly bit her neck, and she pushed him away, laughing.

His forehead settled against hers. "Natalie, that's amazing. You're going to be a published illustrator!" He kissed her sweetly. "That just gives us more to celebrate. We'd better get to the bedroom ASAP."

Before she had a chance to respond, he was sweeping her legs out from under her.

"What are you doing?" she shrieked.

"Carrying you over the threshold," Jack replied.

"Of your bedroom?"

"Yep," he said.

"You're not supposed to do that until we're actually married."

"I know," he said, "but I just can't wait that long."

Natalie resigned herself to holding on tight as Jack carried her to the bedroom. Dropping her gently on the bed, he crawled up until he hovered over her.

Gazing down at her, he said, "I can't wait to be married to you, Natalie Walker. I can't wait to make cute little babies with you and give Carter all kinds of brothers and sisters. I can't wait to grow old with you. I am so damn lucky that I get to spend the rest of my life with you."

"Jack," Natalie sighed, gazing adoringly up at him as she imagined all the things he spoke of. "Is it time for loud, hot, make-up sex yet?"

"Oh yeah," Jack said, tugging off his shirt. "It most definitely is."

EPILOGUE
6 MONTHS LATER

"*H*appy *birthday to you, happy birthday to you, happy birthday dear Carter, happy birthday to you!*"

Carter beamed at the crowd of singing voices. All his favorite people were there—Jack, Natalie, June, Fletcher and his girlfriend, Christa, Beau, Dana, Ryan, Justin, and Griff (who had come to love the little boy as much as everyone else).

Griff had also brought along his new girlfriend, Susan, who Natalie suspected had been in his life for longer than he cared to admit, though he hadn't introduced Natalie to her until a couple of months after her mother's death. Natalie was thrilled for Griff and the happiness he had found.

When the song ended, Jack showed Carter how to blow out the two candles atop his birthday cake, and everyone clapped as they flickered out. Beaming at her two boys, Natalie placed a hand on the growing bump of her belly and fleetingly wondered if this baby would be a boy or a girl. It didn't matter to her, and they were planning to keep it a surprise until the birth. Either way, she couldn't wait to give Carter a sibling. He would always be their first child and would make the best big brother.

Standing on either side of Carter, Jack and Natalie smiled for the camera while Dana snapped a picture of them—a recreation of the one Natalie had with her own parents. The photo represented such a happy time in her life, and she wanted Carter to have a similar reminder of how loved he was, though they would also make sure to show him every single day with their words and actions.

"Ok, time for presents!" Dana said once everyone was sufficiently stuffed full of cake. Jenny had made an elaborate three-layer, chocolate-and-vanilla checkerboard cake covered with blue frosting and decorated to look like the ocean with fondant shells and gummy sharks. The party had to be indoors since it was wintertime, but the cake brought a bit of the beach in to them.

Dana pulled out a flat, wrapped present. "I have something very special for you, Carter."

The boy immediately began tearing off the wrapping paper—a skill he'd perfected over the winter holidays. Holding up the square book, he exclaimed, "Wow!"

Natalie recognized the book immediately and covered her mouth with her hand, but not before a gasp escaped.

"This is the very first copy of my book," Dana explained. "Remember when we had that big dinner to celebrate getting a publisher? They sent me this copy to make sure everything looked good before they printed a whole bunch of them." She pointed to the farm scene on the cover. "And do you know who made all of the pretty pictures in this book? Your Natalie did!"

A stray tear slipped out and rolled down Natalie's face. Dana hadn't told her she'd received the proof copy, much less that she was gifting it to Carter. Wiping her eyes, Natalie knelt down to flip through the book with her son.

"Do you like the animals?" she asked, smiling as he nodded enthusiastically.

"Moo!" he sounded, pointing a chubby finger at a cow.

"That's right!" Natalie laughed. "You're going to love this book." She stood up to face Dana as Carter looked through the rest. "Dana, it's beautiful. You did an amazing job."

"*We* did an amazing job," Dana corrected. "I couldn't have done it without you."

Natalie embraced her friend and business partner, overcome with gratitude for all the good she'd brought into her life —from the opportunity to illustrate a book to the courage to get back together with Jack.

"Oh, and did I forget to mention," Dana said, "that the publisher loved the book so much that they want to make it into a series?"

"What?" Natalie squealed.

"They want sequels about jungle animals and ocean creatures," Dana said. "And, of course, they want to use the same illustrator."

"Seriously?" Natalie screeched. An ongoing book contract would bring in a steady stream of income—something she never thought she'd be able to obtain through her art.

Dana nodded. "Yup. They talked to me the other day, and I told them we'd set up a meeting, but I wanted to be the one to tell you. I also wanted to be the one to give you this," she said, reaching into her pocket and pulling out an envelope. "They gave each of us one of these—an advance bonus to keep us interested, because they want the sequels so badly."

"What?" Natalie asked, ripping the envelope from Dana's hands. "The first book isn't even on the market. How are they already giving us an advance on the next books?"

Dana shrugged. "They're predicting that it'll be a hit. The concept did really well in their focus groups. Plus, they want us to get started right away, so I think it's a bit of a bribe. Open it!"

Natalie tore open the envelope and took out the check, gasping when she read the number written on the line.

Dana grinned. "I figured you and Jack could finally go on that honeymoon you never got around to."

They had gotten married quickly and quietly, right on the beach behind Danny's Place. Natalie wore a white, lacy, vintage wedding dress, and Jack wore a light-gray suit, both sporting bare feet. Carter made the most adorable little ring bearer, toddling up the sandy aisle with the rings. Afterward, the small crowd feasted on Danny's finest cuisine, including an extravagant wedding cake that Natalie considered to be Jenny's finest work.

After the wedding, they stayed home for a couple of reasons. They weren't financially able to take a big honeymoon vacation, but they also wanted to celebrate their new married life with Carter, who had officially become their son on the very same day as the wedding. They'd driven to the courthouse with a "Just Married" banner across the back of the car, tin cans tied to the tailpipe, clinking away as they drove.

This gift from the publisher would allow them to do something even more special to celebrate their matrimony and promise to love each other forever.

Natalie flung her arms around Dana. "This is amazing!" Still embracing, they danced around in celebration for a moment.

"I've already talked to June and we've decided that between the two of us, we can watch Carter for as long as you want to go," Dana said.

"Dana, I can't thank you enough." Natalie smacked a kiss on her friend's cheek then called Jack over, waving the check in her hand.

"Look at this, babe." She handed him the slip of paper.

"Woah!" His eyes bugged out as he read the number.

"I'm thinking Greece? Oh, or maybe Bali?" Natalie mused.

Jack grinned fondly at her. "I'll go anywhere as long as I'm with you."

Natalie rewarded him with a long kiss. His words mirrored the ones she'd said to Griff before their Florida trip, and she couldn't be more thrilled that the two most important men in her life were both back in it for good.

Grinning from ear to ear, she walked over to where her father sat on the floor with Carter. Susan sat nearby, chatting with June. The two women had become fast friends. Griff's rough, callused hands flipped through the book Natalie had illustrated, his rusty voice making animal noises that Carter giggled at.

"Dad, guess what?"

Pride shone in Griff's gaze as he glanced up at Natalie. "What, honey?"

"The publisher wants me to illustrate some more books, and they sent me a big check to entice me. Jack and I are going to use the money to finally go on our honeymoon!"

Griff grinned widely. "That's wonderful, Nat. I am so proud of you."

Leaning down to kiss his forehead, she decided that she would never tire of his praise.

Jack joined them, coming up behind Natalie and snaking his arms around her waist, covering her pregnant belly with his hands.

"I love you, Natalie McNally," he whispered in her ear. He'd taken to using her full name as often as possible, satisfied that it now included his own. Once a caveman, always a caveman.

"I love you, Jack McNally," she returned, leaning back into his strong body until she was enveloped by safety, comfort, and love.

They watched Griff read the rest of the book to Carter, both grinning knowingly when the boy asked him to read it again. Some things never changed.

Natalie covered Jack's hands on her stomach with her own and immediately felt the baby kick. Judging by the way Jack kissed her softly behind her ear, he'd felt it too. Their child. The life they'd made together. A physical symbol of their love for one another.

Her life looked completely different than it had just a year ago, but resting in her husband's arms, surrounded by the low din of beloved friends and family, watching her son play while her unborn child kicked in her womb, Natalie appreciated the beauty in every single detail of her life.

WANT MORE?

Gain access to a bonus honeymoon epilogue when you sign up for my newsletter! Visit my website www.mollymccarthybooks.com for more details.

ACKNOWLEDGMENTS

When they say it takes a village to raise a baby, it turns out they're also talking about a book baby! When I started this journey, I had no idea just how important it would become to create a community I could rely on for help, feedback, and encouragement.

Thank you, Mom, for being the first person I ever trusted to read my words, and for reading multiple drafts of this book. Sorry about all the sex scenes!

Thank you to my beta readers: Alyssa, Hanna, Krista, Laura, and Lisa. Your feedback was absolutely invaluable. You have all helped make me a better writer, and I couldn't be more thankful for that.

Thank you to my copyeditor, Jenn, for fixing my heinous commas and em dashes, and to my cover artist, Wilette, for bringing my characters to life exactly how I envisioned them.

Thank you to all of the indie authors on Instagram. I truly wouldn't be here without you. You all are a constant source of inspiration, motivation, and knowledge.

And finally, thank YOU, reader, for giving this book a chance! If you enjoyed it, I hope you'll recommend it to a friend and consider leaving a review of it on Goodreads, Amazon, Instagram, or another platform. Indie authors rely on reviews and recommendations to get our work out there. Thank you!

ABOUT THE AUTHOR

Molly McCarthy is an avid romance reader and writer living just outside Boston, MA. She can often be found typing away in a café, drinking a latte, and dreaming of happily ever afters. Keep up with Molly on Instagram @mollymccarthybooks.

facebook.com/mollymccarthybooks

twitter.com/mollykmccarthyy

instagram.com/mollymccarthybooks

WHAT'S NEXT

See Beau get his own suspenseful, swoon-worthy happily ever after in A New Beau. Coming in fall of 2022!

9 781737 627685